HIS MARRIAGE DEMAND

YAHRAH ST. JOHN

FROM RICHES TO REDEMPTION

ANDREA LAURENCE

MILLS & BOON

First Published in Great Britain 2019
by Mills & Boon, an imprint of HarperCollinsPublishers,
1 London Bridge Street, London, SE1 9GF

ISBN: 978-0-263-27190-4

0819

MIX
Paper from
responsible sources
FSC™ C007454

This book is produced from independently certified FSC™ paper to ensure responsible forest management.

For more information visit: www.harpercollins.co.uk/green

Printed and bound in Spain
by CPI, Barcelona

HIS MARRIAGE DEMAND

YAHRAH ST. JOHN

To my best friend and sister,
Dimitra Astwood, who passed away
while I wrote this, but will live on in my heart.

Prologue

Fallon's hands trembled with anger as she placed the phone receiver in its cradle. Rising from her chair, she strode across her stylishly appointed corner office and stared out the window overlooking downtown Austin. Although she understood why her older brother, Ayden, wasn't returning her calls, she was still annoyed he'd gone to Jamaica while she was in such a desperate state.

Stewart Technologies was on the brink of bankruptcy. As CEO, Fallon had done her best to keep the company afloat, working sixty-and eighty-hour work weeks, but she was bailing water from a sinking ship. The last few weeks she'd been unsuccessful in her attempts to secure a bank loan.

She'd gone to Ayden, the black sheep in the Stewart family, for assistance nearly a month ago. Ayden had rejected her assertion that he help the "family business." The more Fallon thought about it, why should Ayden rescue the company started by a father who would never claim him as his son? Ayden owed no allegiance to her or any other Stewart for that matter.

Was it any wonder he'd ignored her calls?

Although she'd acquired personal wealth of her own through sound investments, Fallon wasn't in a position to bail out the company. Her baby brother, Dane, certainly wasn't about to, either. He, like Ayden, wanted nothing to do with Stewart Technologies. Dane was happiest in front of a camera being someone else, and it served him well. He was an A-list actor and got paid millions of dollars. Fallon doubted he'd put up his hard-won earnings to save a company he'd never wanted any part of in the first place.

What was she going to do?

"Perhaps you should let it fail," Shana said when they met up for drinks at their favorite martini bar across town an hour later. Shana Wilson was one of Fallon's favorite cousins on her mother's side. Nora hated them spending time together because she tried to disassociate herself from her back-country roots. But Fallon didn't care. Shana was loud and opinionated but down-to-earth.

Fallon stared at Shana incredulously. After all the hard work she'd put into Stewart Technologies, interning in the summer while home from Texas A&M University, learning the business from the ground up and climbing the ladder to finally sit in the CEO chair, she was supposed to give it all up? "Have you lost your mind?"

Shana chuckled. "Don't have a coronary. It was just a suggestion. I hate seeing you stressed out."

An audible sigh escaped Fallon's lips. "I'm sorry, Shana. I know I haven't been a joy to hang with lately."

Shana had come dressed for the evening. She was wearing a glittery sleeveless top, miniskirt, strappy heels and large gold-hoop earrings. Her curly weave hung in ringlets to her shoulders. Shana was on the prowl for more than a martini and usually Fallon didn't mind playing wing woman, but she was in a sour mood.

"No, you haven't been," Shana said, sipping her drink, "but that's why I asked you to come out tonight. All you do is work and go home to that mausoleum. You are too uptight." Shana looked around the room at the host of men milling around. "Maybe if you met a man and got some good loving, you'd loosen up a bit. I bet I know who could loosen you up while supplying you with the cash influx you need."

Fallon sat forward in her seat. Although she loved her cousin, she doubted Shana, who worked as a hair stylist at a trendy salon, knew much about finance. "Oh, yeah? And who might that be?"

"Gage Campbell ring a bell?"

Fallon's heart plummeted at the sound of his name. "G-Gage?"

"Yeah, you remember him? The guy you had the hots for, for over a decade?"

How could Fallon forget? She'd thrown herself at him and inadvertently set in motion a course of events even she, at her tender age of sixteen, couldn't have predicted. "Of course I remember. What about him?"

"Word in the salon is he's back in town," Shana responded. "A couple of clients have come in talking about dating him. He owns a successful mutual fund business and has become quite the catch. Not to mention, he's still as sexy as when we first saw him when we were eight years old."

Fallon would never forget that day. She'd been prancing around on her pony when Gage and his mother Grace toured the estate with Nora. Fallon had been showing off and the pony had become agitated and thrown her. If it hadn't been for Gage's quick reaction and his catching her before she landed, Fallon would surely have broken something. When he'd looked at her with his dazzling brandy-colored eyes, Fallon had fallen head-over-heels in love with the twelve-year-old boy.

Fallon blinked and realized her cousin was still talking. "According to his current lady loves, he knows his way around the bedroom, if you catch my drift."

There was no mistaking Shana's meaning and Fallon blushed.

"Oh, lord." Shana rolled her eyes upward. "We really do need to get you out if a little girl talk makes you blush. Perhaps Gage could help with Stewart Technologies? I hear he's quite the financial wizard."

"That might be so, but Gage would never lift a hand to help me," Fallon replied. Why would he? She'd ruined his life and she only had herself to blame.

One

Two weeks later

"Stewart Technologies is in dire straits," Fallon told her parents over Sunday dinner.

Thinking about the past and what she'd done to Gage Campbell had weighed heavily on her mind ever since she'd had drinks with Shana a couple of weeks ago.

Fallon had never been able to forget the hateful stare Gage had given her moments before her father had closed the cottage door all those years ago. She'd never learned what had happened to Gage and his mother after they'd left Stewart Manor. She hadn't wanted to know because she'd been the cause of his mother losing her livelihood and the guilt had eaten her up. She'd felt so bad that she hadn't balked when her parents had sent her to a finishing school her final year of high school to avoid her spending time with the "wrong crowd."

"Must you be so dramatic?" Nora Stewart said, glancing at her daughter from the opposite end of the table. Even though it was just the three of them at dinner, her mother had insisted on eating in the formal dining room when Fallon would rather be in the kitchen.

Her mother was the epitome of sophistication, wearing cream slacks and a matching cardigan set. Her smooth chestnut-brown hair was stylishly cut in a chin-length bob while her makeup was perfection. Nora was well-preserved thanks to personal trainers and weekly visits to the salon and spa for massages and facials. Since marrying Henry Stewart and becoming pregnant with Fallon, Nora hadn't worked. *Why should she when she was lady of the manor?*

"I'm not being dramatic," Fallon responded. "We're bleeding money and it has to stop."

"And whose fault is that?" Henry inquired. "You've been CEO for two years now."

When she'd turned thirty Fallon thought she'd finally achieved the height of her career only to find out it had been built on quicksand. Stewart Technologies was leveraged to the hilt all because of her father's poor judgment and her mother's notorious spending habits. Every few years she was constantly redecorating Stewart manor to keep up with the latest fads and, as for fashion, there wasn't a bag, shoe or piece of clothing in her mother's closet that didn't have a designer label.

"Not mine," Fallon said hotly. "Stewart Technologies was in trouble well before I became CEO."

"You're the leader now and it's up to you to fix things. It's what you said you wanted, Fallon," her father replied. "It's time you show what you're made of instead of running to me."

Fallon bristled at that. She'd come to level with her parents, but clearly they were beyond reason. They wanted to stick their heads in the sand and refuse to accept the inevitable: that they were running out of funds and wouldn't be able to live in the style to which they were accustomed. "I have shown my commitment to the company over the last decade. But since it's clear I don't have your support, I'll take my leave." She rose from her seat and made for the door.

"Sit down, Fallon." Her father trained his hazel-gray eyes on her, causing Fallon to pause and retrace her steps.

"If you're going to talk business—" Nora used her napkin to lightly tap the sides of her mouth "—I'm going to make myself scarce because it's such a bore."

Fallon sucked in a deep breath and reminded herself to count to ten, which was more than enough time for her mother to depart. She loved Nora, but she found her exhausting.

"Yes, Father?" Fallon turned and, for the first time, truly looked at her father. She saw more salt and pepper in his normally black hair and a few more lines were etched across his features, showing life wasn't as easy as her mother portrayed.

"I'm sorry if I was harsh before," Henry said. "I know you've been doing your best."

"Which isn't good enough," Fallon stated. "Don't you get it? We could lose everything."

"Surely it's not as dire as you predict?" Henry countered.

"It is. I've exhausted all options," Fallon said. "I even asked Ayden for the money."

Her father's eyes widened. "Why on earth would you do such a thing? He isn't a member of this family. How much did you tell him of our circumstances? What did he say?"

Fallon waited for her father to finish peppering her with questions before answering. Did he wonder if Ayden had told her about his infidelity with her mother? "I was desperate. But I didn't get to explain because he told me he isn't interested in bailing out *our* company because he's not a part of this family." She didn't share that Ayden had had a change of heart and had come to her days ago.

Henry sighed. "It's just as well. We don't need him. You can figure this out, Fallon. There's a reason I let you become CEO."

"*Let me?*" Fallon repeated. "I worked hard to get where I am. I don't recall Dane or even Ayden getting in line to step in your shoes."

"Listen here, young lady—" he began.

"Don't bother chastising me, Father," Fallon interrupted. "I'm the only child you have who cares one iota about Stewart Technologies, so I suggest you stop fighting me and get Mother to understand we are just a few steps away from going broke."

Fallon shot to her feet and, without another word, left the room, her stunned father sitting with his mouth open at her insolence. She walked quickly to the door and headed for her cottage. Her haven. Her safe place.

The cool night air hit her immediately when she exited. The leaves that had begun falling a few weeks ago crunched under her heels, signaling fall was in full swing. Once inside the cottage, Fallon turned on the lights and sagged against the door. Why was it she felt safe here? The one place that had once caused such misery to others.

Her mother had long since renovated the cottage after the Campbells left. It now had an open concept with a stainless-steel kitchen, sitting area, master suite with en suite bath as well as guest bedroom and powder room. It was all Fallon needed while allowing her to be close to her horse, Lady.

Kicking off her boots, Fallon plopped onto her plush leather sofa, leaned back and thought about the weekend. Once again, she'd scoured the books looking for ways to make cuts and keep the company afloat, but it was pointless. They were going under. And tonight was a complete bust. Her parents refused to accept their new reality: they were broke. The only bright spot had been on Friday evening when Ayden had shown up at her office. He'd looked drawn and tired, and there were lines under his eyes, but he'd wanted to talk. She'd been hard on him because he'd treated her like the enemy for years. She and Dane had been the chosen ones, the children Henry Stewart claimed while leaving Ayden to languish in poverty with his mother.

Fallon understood she'd had the life denied him: the houses, cars, travel, fancy clothes and schools. He'd listened when she'd explained it hadn't been easy for her, either, with a disinterested, self-absorbed mother and a demanding father who'd pushed her to excel. She was angry that Ayden blamed her when she'd only been a child. However, Ayden had told her he was sorry for ignoring her calls and for turning down her requests for a loan. He wanted to start over, to try to be a family, a brother to her and Dane.

Fallon had been overjoyed. Then Ayden had held her hand and shockingly offered to give *her*—not the company—a personal loan. Fallon knew the sacrifice it had taken for him to make the offer. But, after everything he'd been through, her pride wouldn't allow her to accept his money, knowing how their father treated him. He hadn't supported Ayden as a child. Not to mention she'd had more advantages than Ayden had ever had. She couldn't take his hard-earned money, money he might need one day for his future. He'd nodded and let her keep her pride. And they'd agreed to take baby steps and work on their sibling relationship. Fallon couldn't wait to tell Dane. She hoped he would be as happy as she was to forge a bond with their big brother.

"Welcome back to Austin, old friend," Theo Robinson said to Gage Campbell when they met up for lunch at the country club. They were sitting outside on the terrace by the fire pit, drinking brandy and reminiscing about the good old days.

"It's good to be back," Gage said. And it was. It had been well over a decade since he'd lived in Texas. After finishing college at the University of Texas at Austin, he'd gone on to New York and then overseas to make his fortune. Now that he was a successful man in his own right, he'd come back to his hometown to settle down and take care of his mother. Though he doubted Grace Campbell felt she needed taking care of. Although she'd retired a few years ago, his mother was active and traveled the world with her circle of friends. She deserved it after all the hard work she'd endured to ensure he'd had a future.

"What're your plans now that you're here?" Theo inquired.

Gage sat back in his seat and regarded his friend. "Settle in, find a nice home and a good woman and have some babies."

"Oh, really?" Theo raised an eyebrow. "Since when? I thought you were a die-hard bachelor."

"I was. Hell, I still am," Gage replied. "I'm still indulging until I find Mrs. Campbell."

"Look out, women of Austin!" Theo laughed and drank his brandy.

"There's only one woman who should ever fear me," Gage said, a serious tone to his voice.

"Let me guess. Fallon Stewart? I would think after all this time and your success, you would have forgotten the mistakes made by a young, naïve girl."

"She wasn't so naïve if she had the audacity to show up to my house half naked," Gage responded. He'd never forgotten how stunned he'd been after having a few beers at the bar only to come home to find Fallon in his bed.

"She was sixteen with a crush on you," Theo said. "She

was feeling herself, but then her parents caught her. She got scared and lied about what happened."

"Her lies cost my mother her job. And without references from the Stewarts, Mama couldn't find work. It took her months to recover, especially since the Stewarts were paying her minimum wage to work day and night."

"Well, she recovered and so have you. I mean look at you." Theo motioned to him. "You're the wizard of Wall Street. I'd say you've done well."

"No thanks to the Stewarts."

Theo sighed. "Then you'll probably be glad to hear this. The rumor is that Stewart Technologies is leveraged to the max. No bank will loan them money and they've run out of options."

"Serves Henry right," Gage responded. "Though I have to wonder what happened. I thought he had a good head on his shoulders. I even looked up to him once upon a time, admired him when he took me under his wing."

"Henry Stewart isn't running the show."

A knot formed in Gage's stomach. He didn't need Theo to say his next words; he already knew. "Fallon's in charge."

"She's been looking for a handout from anyone she can and has come up empty."

"Is that so?" Gage rubbed his jaw. Fallon Stewart had been taken down a peg and was essentially on the street begging for scraps. Now, if that wasn't karma, he didn't know what was.

"Could be a good time to go in with a consortium and pick up the pieces," Theo stated. "Think about it."

The two men parted right after lunch, but Gage didn't return home to his penthouse at the Austonian in downtown Austin until late evening. It was a temporary oasis with all the modern conveniences a bachelor required. There was a large television with a surround-sound system, an enormous master suite with a king-size bed and a luxurious master bath with room for more than one occupant in the hot tub and massive steam shower.

He went to the wet bar, opened the snifter of brandy and poured himself a glass. He swirled the alcohol around and took a generous, satisfying sip. Sliding the pocket door to his balcony aside, he opened the living room to the oversize terrace with its panoramic views. Austin's city lights twinkled in the distance, but Gage didn't see them. All he saw was a beautiful teenager, wearing the sexiest teddy he'd ever laid eyes on, in his bed. Gage gritted his teeth and forced himself to remember that night. He hadn't just been angry when he'd found Fallon in his bed. He'd been intrigued.

Fallon had been everything he wasn't. Spoiled. Rich. Entitled. She'd had more money than she'd known what to do with, ponies and cars, while he'd worked two jobs. He hadn't wanted to want her, but he had. He'd seen the coy looks Fallon had given him when she'd thought he wasn't looking, but she'd been sixteen. Jailbait. Gage had been determined to steer clear, but she'd poked the bear and Gage had hauled her against him and kissed her.

If her parents had found them any later, the result might have been him being led off in handcuffs. Instead he and his mother had been shown the door. But now things had changed. He held all the cards and Fallon was on the bottom. He was no longer at the mercy of the Stewarts and whatever scraps they doled out to him. Gage relished how the tables had turned.

Fallon arrived at the Stewart Technologies' offices the next morning feeling out of sorts. She hadn't slept well the night before. She'd been thinking about her lack of a love life. It had been ages since she'd been on a proper date, let alone had a steady boyfriend.

She tried to focus on the day ahead. There were several meetings scheduled, including a negotiation to sell off one of the company's long-held nanotech patents. Fallon didn't want to do it—it was one of her father's significant achievements—but she was running out of options. The cash influx would stave off the bank and ensure thousands of employees kept their jobs.

The morning flew by quickly with Fallon only stopping long enough to eat a quick salad her assistant, Chelsea, had fetched from the deli downstairs.

Fallon was poring over financials when a knock sounded on the door. "Not now, Chelsea, I'm in the middle of something," she said without looking up.

"You don't have time for an old friend?"

Fallon's heart slowed at first and she closed her eyes, leaning back in her leather executive chair. *Surely, it couldn't be.* Perhaps she was imagining things, conjuring up the past. Because she hadn't heard that deep masculine voice in over sixteen years. Inhaling deeply, she snuck a glance at the man standing in the doorway of her office and was bowled over.

It was none other than Gage Campbell.

How? Why was he here at her office? A morass of feelings engulfed her and she tingled from head to toe. The last time she'd seen Gage there had been nothing but hatred in his eyes, not the amused expression he now wore. Fallon reminded herself to breathe in then breathe out.

Calm yourself. Don't let him see he's affected you.

So instead she took the offensive. "What the hell are you doing here?"

Two

"Hello to you, too, Fallon." Gage closed the door behind him and strode toward her desk.

Fallon regarded him from where she sat. Her blood pumped faster as she took in the sight of him. Time had been very good to Gage Campbell. Immaculate and imposingly masculine, he was utterly breathtaking. With his neatly cropped hair, warm caramel-toned skin, thick, juicy lips, bushy eyebrows and those brandy-colored eyes framed by black lashes that always drew her to them, he was impossible to ignore.

He was even sexier than the last time she'd seen him especially with those broodingly intense eyes. He reeked of money and looked as if he was born to wear the bespoke three-piece designer suit, cream shirt with striped tie and polished designer shoes. Fallon knew he hadn't always been this way. The Gage of yesteryear was happier in faded jeans and a wife-beater mucking out stables. The man in front of her was far removed from those days. He stood confident and self-assured.

"I hope I pass the mustard," Gage said after her long perusal.

Fallon blushed at having been caught openly staring and glanced up to find Gage's eyes trained on her. She blinked to refocus. "My apologies. I'm just surprised to see you after all this time."

"I'm sure," Gage responded as he unbuttoned several buttons on his jacket before sitting across from her. Fallon remembered how impossible it had always been to resist those dangerous gleaming eyes of his and today was no different. He looked intriguing, like a total enigma. "It's been what—sixteen years since we last saw each other? You're all grown up." He dropped his gaze and used the opportunity to give her a searing once-over.

Fallon was in her usual work mode. Her naturally wavy hair had been tamed with a flat iron until it lay in straight layers down her back while her makeup was simple: coal eyeliner, mascara, blush and lipstick. Having been blessed with her mother's smooth café-au-lait skin, she required little makeup. And although she was no clothesmonger like Nora, Fallon always managed to be fashionable. She was sporting linen trousers with a sleeveless silk top. She'd abandoned the matching jacket earlier in the day. She wondered what Gage thought of her.

"Oh, yes, you've definitely matured since I last saw you."

Fallon noticed his eyes creased at the corners when he spoke. The sly devil was actually staring right at her breasts and she felt her nipples pucker to attention in her blouse. Immediately she rose. "What can I do for you, Gage? I'm sure you didn't come here for a walk down memory lane."

His eyes narrowed and she could see she'd touched a

nerve. "Now that wouldn't be pleasant for either of us, would it?"

Fallon flushed. She'd never forgiven herself for the horrible action she'd taken that had caused his mother to lose her job. She wanted—no, she *needed* to apologize. "Gage, I'm—"

He interrupted her. "I'm here because Stewart Technologies is in financial trouble and I thought I could help."

Her brow furrowed. "And why would you want to do that?"

Gage laughed without humor. "Is that any way to treat a potential investor? Or don't you need an influx of capital to save your father's company?"

"My company now."

"I stand corrected." He inclined his head. "I thought perhaps we could discuss the matter over dinner. My afternoon is rather full and I barely managed to squeeze in this reunion."

"Dinner?" she choked out as she looked at him in bewilderment. Why would he want to break bread with her after their checkered past?

He tilted his head to one side and watched her, waiting for her to speak. "It's the meal commonly eaten after lunch. Or do you have a problem being seen with the former maid's son?"

Fallon looked him directly in his eyes and replied coolly, "Of course not. I'm not a snob."

"Really?"

"You sound surprised."

"If I recall, back in the day you wouldn't be caught dead with me except in the stables or when we were alone."

"That's not true." She felt the flush rise to her cheeks at the memory. "I didn't want us to be disturbed. If my mother found out, she would have forbidden it because..."

"Because I wasn't good enough for you." Gage finished the sentence.

Fallon lowered her head. He was right. It's what Nora had thought. But never Fallon. She'd been too much in love with Gage to see his class or station in life. Agreeing to dinner would show him he was wrong about her and that they were equals. It would also enlighten her as to his true motives.

Several seconds passed and she glanced up to find he'd leaned closer toward her. "Shall I pick you up?"

Fallon shook her head. "No, that's not necessary. I can meet you wherever you like."

"Still not wanting to be seen with me, eh?" Gage uncoiled his tall length, stood and rebuttoned his jacket. A deep chuckle escaped his lips as he made his way to the door. "I'll meet you at the Driskill Grill at seven."

And then he was gone, leaving Fallon to stare at the door. *What was his real agenda?*

Irritation fueled Gage as he headed for the elevator. He was offering Fallon a lifeline and she refused to even allow him to pick her up for dinner! Her arrogance irked him, but so did her beauty. He'd hoped to find a spoiled, selfish shell of a woman, but instead he'd found a stunning and fierce ice princess. Fallon Stewart wasn't the young teenager he remembered. She was a woman. And it angered him that he still found her so…so damned attractive.

When he'd walked through the door and seen her, blood had stirred in his veins and his belly had clenched instantly. He'd wanted to touch her. To refamiliarize himself with her exquisitely soft skin. To crush those sinfully pink-tinted lips underneath his and lose himself. But Fallon had cast her eyes down and acted as if she was unaffected by him.

But the willful sexy teenager who'd come to his bed in

the middle of the night wearing nothing but a teddy was still there. Gage was certain he'd seen a spark flare when her eyes traveled the length of him. Now they were both grown and consenting adults, and it was time they finished what they'd started sixteen years ago.

Resolve formed deep in the pit of his stomach. A twist of circumstances had turned the tables and the Stewarts were no longer on top and in a position of power. Gage was. Fallon was exposed, vulnerable and his for the taking. Last night he'd come up with a plan for revenge to finally get back at Fallon and the Stewarts for their treatment of him and his mother.

Stewart Technologies needed cash and Gage was the money man. He not only had loads of it himself, he knew how and where to acquire more. He would convince Fallon bygones were bygones and *help* the company with an influx of cash. Meanwhile he'd secretly purchase stocks until eventually he owned the lion's share and could take it away from them. The best part in this entire scenario was the chance to bed Fallon, the overindulged princess.

Today when he'd seen her, something indefinable had happened. It was as if the years had melted away. Gage had been hit in the gut with the incredible need to possess her. He didn't want any other man to have her, at least not until he'd had his fill.

When he exited the building and slid into the Bugatti waiting for him at the curb, a new idea began to form in Gage's mind.

What if he married Fallon! For his *help* in saving the company, he would become a member of the acclaimed Stewart family and finally not only have Fallon in his bed, but have the prestige he'd always wanted. Because, try as he might, no matter how much money he made, there was a certain echelon of society that still saw him as the maid's son. Wouldn't it get their goat to have him rubbing elbows with the lot of them? To show them he wasn't just the underprivileged kid-made-good? It was a brilliant strategy.

Fallon had no idea what was in store for her tonight.

As he started the engine, Gage's cellphone rang. The display read Mom. "Hey, Mama. How are you?"

"I'd be doing a lot better if you came to see me. You've been back for a while and I've yet to see you."

"I'm sorry. I've been a little busy, and you were away on one of your trips. But I'll visit this weekend."

"Good. It's good to have you back in Austin. It's been much too long."

"Yes, it has." He hadn't been home since he'd finished college and they both knew why. The Stewarts. Gage hadn't thought he'd get a fair break in a town where Henry Stewart had so much power. But the tide had changed, providing Gage the opportunity to put a plan in place to give the Stewarts the comeuppance they so richly deserved.

Fallon didn't have time to go home and change if she was going to be on time for dinner with Gage. A departmental meeting ended later than she'd anticipated, leaving her precious little time to shower in the private bathroom in her office and change into one of several dresses she kept on hand for such occasions. She chose a beaded champagne cocktail dress that accentuated her curves. Refreshing her makeup, she added a touch of blush to her cheekbones to go along with the mascara, eyeliner and pale pink lipstick.

Glancing at herself in the mirror, Fallon felt armed and ready for a night in Gage's company. And she felt like she needed every bit of armor for this unexpected invitation.

Throughout the remainder of the afternoon, Fallon had wondered why Gage wanted to help her family. She'd come up with only one reason: comeuppance. After the way he'd been treated by the Stewarts, he wanted to be the one to come in on the white horse and save the day. Him, the man her father had thrown out of the house because he'd dared to touch his daughter. Gage wanted them to *owe* him.

Fallon didn't much blame him.

Gage had every right to be angry over how he and his mother had been treated. But now the shoe was on the other foot. The Stewarts were the laughingstock of the business community, turned down by every bank in town because of her father's poor decisions and financial mismanagement. Fallon hoped seeing how far they'd fallen from grace would be enough to salve Gage's wounds.

She made it to the restaurant at seven o'clock on the nose.

The hostess led her to a secluded corner booth where Gage was already seated, wearing a fine, tailored suit. Had he booked this? Did he intend for it to be as romantic as it looked? A dark, quiet corner with a table for two?

He stood when she approached. "Fallon, you're looking lovely this evening." She was stunned when he kissed her on the cheek before she slid into the booth.

"Uh, thank you," she returned, her pulse thumping erratically from the contact of his lips.

"I took the liberty of ordering wine," Gage said, pinning her with his razor-sharp gaze. "A Montoya Cabernet. I hope that's all right?"

She nodded, somewhat amazed at how at ease he was in a restaurant of such wealth and sophistication. He poured her a glass. She accepted and tipped her glass to his when he held it up for a toast.

"And what are we toasting?" she asked.

"New beginnings."

Fallon sipped her wine. "Sounds intriguing."

He grinned, showing off a pearly white smile, and Fallon's stomach flip-flopped. "I've been away in New York and London the last decade. So, get me up to speed, Fallon. How did you end up as CEO of Stewart Technologies?"

"It's really quite simple. My father needed an heir apparent," Fallon said, "and I was the only one willing to step up to claim the throne."

"You make it sound so medieval," Gage responded, tasting his wine.

She smiled. "It isn't that elaborate, I'm afraid. My brother Dane wanted nothing to do with the family business, much preferring his acting career to being an active member of the Stewart family."

"Was it really so horrible growing up in the lap of luxury?" Gage inquired wryly.

Fallon detected the note of derision in his tone. "You'd have to ask him."

The waiter interrupted them to rattle off the daily specials. They both ordered the soup to start, followed by the spinach salad and fish for their entrée. It was all very civilized and Fallon couldn't understand Gage's agenda. Why was he treating her like an old friend when she knew that was far from the case?

Once the waiter left, Gage prompted Fallon. "Please continue with your story, I'm fascinated."

"After what happened between us all those years ago, my father was very unhappy with me."

"Explain."

She sighed softly but didn't stop. "You have to understand, I was his baby girl."

"Dressed like you were ready to take me to bed?"

Fallon didn't rise to the bait. "Seeing me like that made him realize I was growing up too fast and he didn't like it. And I was desperate to regain his affection."

"Had you lost it?"

Gage was perceptive, picking up on what she hadn't said. She didn't answer. "He sent me to a finishing school to ensure I was exposed to the 'right' crowd."

"And were you?"

Her lips thinned with irritation. "They were the snobbiest, cattiest girls I ever met. The teachers were like prison wardens. The entire experience was unpleasant.

"When I returned home, I started accompanying my father to the office and soon I wanted to learn more. My father put me in the intern program and, much to his surprise, I soaked up everything like a sponge. I was interested in learning what it took to run a multimillion-dollar company, so I majored in business. During breaks, I worked at Stewart Technologies, learning the business from the ground up while earning my MBA. Until, eventually, I proved to all the naysayers I had the chops to run the company.

"And, as it turned out, my father was ready to take a back seat. He's now chairman of the board. Of course, I had no idea of the financial straits he was leaving me to tend to. He'd leveraged the business and owed the banks a substantial amount due to projects he'd started but failed to get across the finish line."

"Very intriguing indeed," Gage replied. "And here we are."

Fallon took a generous sip of her wine. She hadn't planned on revealing so much, but Gage was looking at her so intently, as if hanging on her every word.

"And you? Fill me in on your time abroad."

Gage leaned back against the cushions. "I don't think my story is quite as intriguing as yours."

"But it clearly has a happy ending," she replied. "I mean, look at where we are. The roles have been reversed."

"Yes, they have," Gage said quietly. "But I won't sugarcoat it. After my mother and I were kicked off the Stewart estate, she had a hard time finding work, especially because your parents refused to give her a reference."

"Gage..."

"I was young and resilient, with only a year left of college. I worked two or three jobs to keep us afloat. Once I finished school, I struck out on my own. A friend of mine worked on Wall Street and told me I could make a lot of money. The stock market had never really been my cup of tea but, lo and behold, I had a knack for it. From there I went to London, Hong Kong, making money in stocks and foreign trade. Until I settled on mutual funds and started my own business."

"So why come back here?"

"Simply put, I missed home," Gage replied. "I haven't been back since I graduated other than the odd trip. Mostly, I've sent Mom tickets to meet me at some exotic destination. She deserved it, after all her years of menial labor."

Although she'd never experienced the kind of hardship Gage mentioned, Fallon understood his drive to succeed because she shared it.

Over dinner they continued talking about his trading career, lifestyle and trips abroad before returning to the subject of Fallon. It surprised her how easy it was to talk to Gage, considering all that had transpired between them. It felt like a lifetime ago, but she was sure at some point Gage would be getting to the point of the evening.

"Are you having dessert?" Gage asked after they'd polished off nearly two bottles of wine with their meal.

She shook her head. "I couldn't eat another bite." She wiped her mouth with a napkin. "It's been a lovely evening, Gage, but I'm sure that's not the reason you asked me to dinner."

"What do you think the reason is?"

"Payback. What else?" Fallon asked with a shrug of her shoulders. "And although I'm not destitute and put out of the family home, we are in a bind. Surely this must delight you?"

"Not everyone is like you and your family."

Ouch. Fallon took that one on the chin because, after

all this time, he deserved to speak his mind. "Why am I here, Gage?"

Gage leaned forward, resting his elbows on the table and arresting her with his eyes. "I have a proposition for you."

"And what might that be?"

"Marry me."

Three

Fallon coughed profusely and reached for her water glass. Her hands trembled as she placed the glass to her lips and sipped. With all the wine they'd drunk, she must have taken leave of her faculties because Gage Campbell couldn't possibly have asked her to marry him. *Could he?*

"Are you all right?" Gage asked, his voice etched with concern.

"Y-yes." Fallon sipped her water again and placed the glass back on the table. "Can you repeat what you said?"

Gage's mouth curved in a smile. "You heard me, Fallon. Marry me and, in exchange, I'll give you the money you need to save your family business."

She had heard correctly. But he was dead wrong if he thought for a second she would take him up on his outrageous offer. "Gage! What you're suggesting is insanity! You didn't even give an expiration date for this union. How long would you expect this to last?"

"It's a business deal that will last as long as needed,"

he stated calmly. "You get the money you need to save a dying technology firm, while I get a wife from an upstanding Austin family. Think about it, Fallon. Our marriage would legitimize my social standing while simultaneously letting all those pesky bankers who have been hounding you know the Campbell/Stewart family is as solid as ever."

"That's real vague. Plus there's any number of society debutantes out there waiting to meet a catch like you, Gage. You don't have to marry me."

"But it's you I want," Gage responded. Within seconds he'd slid closer to her in the booth, until they were thigh-to-thigh.

Fallon flushed. "What are you saying?"

"A caveat to the marriage is it will not be in name only."

"Meaning?"

"Do you really need me to spell it out?" His piercing look went straight through her. "We would consummate the marriage and share the same bed. Become lovers."

Fallon sucked in a deep breath. *Sweet Jesus!* She had drunk too much wine because the words coming out of Gage's mouth didn't make any sense. She took another small sip of water.

"I think we would be quite good together," Gage said, picking up her hand and turning it over palm side up.

Immediately she tried to pull it back, but his grip was too strong. "How can you say such a thing? I haven't seen you in sixteen years."

"Yet, you still want me." His hold softened but he didn't let her go. Instead his thumb began circling the inside of her palm, making her pulse race erratically. "I can see all the signs of arousal in you, Fallon—the way your eyes dilate when you look at me, the way your breath hitches when I come near. Even the way your breasts peak with one look from me."

Fallon felt her cheeks flame. Was she so obvious that he

could read her like a book? It was as though he'd put her under some kind of spell, the same as when she'd been sixteen. And why oh why wouldn't he stop circling her palm with his thumb? He was teasing her and she didn't like it. She jerked her hand free. "Stop it, Gage."

"Stop what?" he asked so innocently she would have thought he meant it, but she knew better.

"Whatever game it is you're playing."

"No games. Just facts. I'm willing to give you millions to help Stewart Technologies, even though it's been hemorrhaging money. I'm willing to give my money to help save your company. And in return, I offer you the chance to be my wife. I think it's a fair trade."

"Of course you would." Fallon scooted out of the booth. "But I'm not a stock to be bought and traded. Furthermore, you got your signals wrong. I'm not interested in you in the slightest." She made it as far as the foyer of the restaurant before Gage caught up to her and swung her into a nearby alcove.

"You're not interested in me, eh?" Gage asked, stepping closer into her space. So close, her body was smashed against his. "How about we test that theory, shall we?"

She saw the challenge in his eyes seconds before his head lowered and he sealed his lips to hers. Fallon wanted to refuse him but the thrill of having his lips on hers again was too much to resist. Need unfurled in her, the likes of which she hadn't felt since…since the last time he'd kissed her. No other man had ever come close to making her feel this way.

This hot. This excited.

Gage's arm slid around her waist to the small of her back and he pressed her body even closer to his. Meanwhile his tongue breached her mouth, allowing him to increase the pressure, demand more and compel her to accept him. The kiss was hard yet soft, but also rough enough to thrill her.

Fallon's lips parted of their own accord and his tongue slid in. Teasing, stroking, tasting the soft insides of her mouth.

Fallon whimpered and her stance relaxed as the sheer power of his kiss enflamed her. Sliding her arms around his neck, she held his head to hers, reveling in the deeply carnal kiss. Gage ground his lower half against hers and she felt every inch of his hard body. Her tongue searched his mouth ravenously and he met her stroke for stroke. Her breasts rubbed against his chest and her nipples hardened. Fallon had never felt so desirable and could have gone on kissing him, but Gage pulled away first.

His breathing was ragged but he managed to say, "I've proven you are interested, but I'll give you some time to think about my offer."

Fallon looked up, dazed and confused. "Wait a minute." How could he compose himself after that kiss? "How much time?" she croaked out.

"Forty-eight hours."

She shook her head. "I can't make a decision about the rest of my life in two days."

"Well, that's too damn bad because that's my offer," Gage responded. "You can take it or leave it. It's up to you." He tapped the face of his Rolex watch. Then he reached inside his suit jacket and pulled out his business card. "My personal cell. Call me when you're ready to say yes."

A whirlwind of thoughts swirled around Fallon's mind as she somehow managed to drive herself home from her dinner with Gage. When she got back to the cottage she kicked off her heels, undressed and removed her makeup, and put on her old college T-shirt. Sliding into her king-size platform bed and falling back against the pillows, Fallon recalled the bombshell Gage dropped.

Marry me.

Gage had proposed marriage in exchange for saving

Stewart Technologies, the company her father started forty years ago. Could she let it slip through her fingers without a fight? But Gage wasn't offering a marriage in name only. He wanted them to become lovers.

The thought both excited and terrified her, especially after that hot kiss at the restaurant. Her attempt to appear unaffected had been smashed to smithereens. The chemistry between them was off the charts. He'd smelled and tasted so good. And the way he'd held her close, her heart had fluttered unlike anything she'd ever felt with other men. Had his one life-changing kiss all those years ago ruined her for anyone else? Because there hadn't been many men. Since Gage she'd never succeeded in finding someone who could fulfill an ache. So instead she focused on her career at the expense of her personal life. Work was her baby, so much so she hadn't given much thought to marriage or children.

Would Gage want children?

No, no, no. She shook her head. She wouldn't have children with a man as part of a business arrangement or for money like her mother had. She was no fool. She knew Nora hadn't married her father for love. Instead she'd married him for the life he could give her. Fallon wouldn't want that for herself or for Gage. And why would he want to marry her anyway? She'd lied and cost his family their livelihood. He should hate her but instead he was offering her a way out. It didn't make sense. He could be setting her up for failure so he could give her the comeuppance he thought she deserved.

Was she honestly giving Gage's proposal serious consideration? She couldn't. Shouldn't. He'd been a brute, only giving her forty-eight hours to make a life-changing decision. Marry him or risk losing the company. Marry him and agree to be his wife, *his lover*. He could have been her first if they hadn't been interrupted by her parents. Fallon remembered the passion she'd felt in his arms then and now. Was it fate they would end up in this predicament? Was she always destined to be his?

Unable to sleep, Gage restlessly prowled his penthouse. Wondering. Wishing. Hoping.

Would Fallon say yes?

Would she agree to marry him?

He knew it was wrong to give her an ultimatum but he'd had to. Once she committed, he didn't want her to change her mind. When she agreed to be his and his alone, they would have a quick engagement, a big splashy wedding and a satisfying honeymoon. He wanted the entire community and all of Austin society to know *he*, the maid's son, had bagged Fallon Stewart, heiress to Stewart Technologies. He would rub it in all their faces that the young man they'd bullied because of his humble background had turned into a successful and wealthy entrepreneur.

Fallon *needed* to agree. She wasn't going to get a better offer. She'd exhausted every avenue. No one was going to lend her the amount of money required to turn the company around. A personal gift from him to Fallon would ensure Stewart Technologies stayed viable. In the meantime, since most investors were ditching shares, he would gobble them up until he owned the majority interest. Once he owned enough shares in the company, he would ensure it turned a profit or he'd die trying.

The best part of the deal was that he would finally take Fallon to bed. It was long overdue and very, very necessary. Tonight, when they'd kissed, he'd nearly combusted. She'd tasted exquisite and he remembered how her nipples had turned to stiff peaks against his chest. He'd wanted to break through the icy barrier she'd erected and find the passionate girl who'd stolen into his bedroom. And he had. When she'd opened her mouth to let him in, he'd taken all she'd had to give. He still had a thick, hard erection to prove it. If they hadn't been in a restaurant, Gage would have ravished her where she stood. But he was no animal. He was willing to wait. Hell, he'd waited nearly two decades to *be* with her—another few weeks wouldn't make much difference.

Four

"He did what?" With a look of shock on her face, Shana sat back on the couch in Fallon's cottage the following evening. She'd arrived a half hour ago. After the pleasantries were over, Fallon had uncorked a vintage bottle of Merlot and gotten right down to the matter at hand.

"There's nothing wrong with your hearing, Shana," Fallon replied. "I was just as floored as you were."

"When I mentioned Gage the other day, I was trying to get a rise out of you. I never dreamed he'd ever loan you the money let alone ask you to *marry* him. It's crazy!"

Fallon nodded. "I thought the same thing."

"Thought?" Shana peered at her strangely. "As in past tense?"

"Yes. But after considering it—and trust me, I couldn't sleep a wink last night—it kind of came to me."

Shana's eyes grew wide. "What came to you?"

"It makes an odd sort of sense in a way," Fallon responded. "Gage has always wanted to be part of the *in crowd*, but growing up on the estate, he was always thought of as the help. Marriage to me would be a way for him to even the scales."

"And make you pay on your back."

"Shana!"

"C'mon, doll." Shana scooted closer to Fallon on the sofa. "Don't tell me Gage didn't make a play for you. You're a grown woman now and a beautiful one, I might add. There's no way he's not trying to tap that." She patted Fallon on the behind.

"My God, Shana. Have you no shame?"

"Do you? Because it sounds to me like you're giving Gage's offer some serious thought."

"Wouldn't you?" Fallon asked. "A sexy, gorgeous, *rich* man is offering to solve my financial problem and save my family. How can I let the company fail under my watch?"

"See?" Shana pointed her index finger at her. "That's how he got you. He's tapping into all your fears and insecurities. Let it fail, Fallon. You didn't create this mess, your father did. You inherited it. And now you're supposed to—what? Give up your chance of finding Mr. Right and settle for Mr. Payback? Because that's exactly what this is. Mark my words. Gage wants revenge for how your family wronged him and he's using all the weapons in his arsenal."

"You make it sound like we're at war."

"You are. Think about all the anger, hurt and humiliation he must feel after *you* threw yourself at him and caused him and his mother to be kicked out on the street. The man must despise you, but clearly he wants you in equal measure. It's all kinds of messed up."

"You're not helping me, Shana."

"I have always been a straight shooter, Fallon," Shana replied. "It's what you love about me, so I'm telling you how I see it. I want you to consider what you could be getting yourself into before you make a life-altering decision."

"Aha!" Fallon said. "You've given me an idea."

"Oh, yeah? What's that?"

"If I agree, I can stipulate the marriage is temporary. I think six months is enough time to get Stewart Technologies back on its feet with an influx of cash and cement Gage's place in Austin society. What do you think?"

Shana shook her head. "I don't know, Fallon. You're playing with fire."

"Without risk, there can't be a great reward." Fallon sure hoped she was right because she was banking her future and Stewart Technologies on making the right call.

Gage couldn't wait forty-eight hours for Fallon to make a decision. He had to persuade her. All day in his home office he'd been thinking about her and he knew the only way to stop himself from going crazy was to see her again.

He picked up his cell phone and called her.

"Gage?" Fallon said. "Have you changed your mind? Did you come to the conclusion your arrangement was just as crazy as it sounds?"

"Quite the contrary. I wanted to *see you.*"

"You told me I had forty-eight hours."

"And you do," Gage replied smoothly. "I'm going to do everything in my power to convince you to say yes. Starting with a date tonight."

"Tonight? I can't. I have to work."

"Excuses, excuses, Fallon. You're afraid to be alone with me after what transpired between us last night."

"That's not true." She paused for several beats. "I admit I find you attractive."

"Face facts, Fallon, if we hadn't been in public, the evening might have ended differently."

"You're very sure of yourself."

"I know what I want."

"And…oh, that's right, you want me," Fallon finished. "Well, I'm not that easy, Gage."

"I didn't think you were, but I admit I'd like to know more. Last night was the tip of the iceberg. Let me see you tonight."

"I need time to think, Gage. I don't appreciate the strong-arm tactics."

"I would think if you're going to agree to shackle yourself to me, you would want to get to know the man you'll marry. Or would you rather walk into this as strangers?"

"You seem to think it's a forgone conclusion I'll say yes to your outrageous proposal."

"I'm encouraged because you haven't said no."

"Fine. I'll meet you. Where and when?"

Gage shook his head. Oh, no, he wasn't falling into this trap again. He wanted a proper date. "*I* will pick you up at Stewart Manor. And, Fallon?"

"Yes?"

"Dress to impress. Because I'm taking you to the opera."

Gage ended the call with a smile on his face. That hadn't been as hard as he'd imagined. She was recalcitrant, but he'd convinced her it was in both their best interests to get to know one another. The problem was he didn't have tickets, but he'd heard from Theo that Puccini's *La bohème* was playing at Austin Opera and he knew anyone who was anyone would be there.

Austin society would see the former maid's son out on the town with Fallon Stewart. It was brilliant. He would kill two birds with one stone. Cement his place in society and spend time with the woman who would be his wife. Now he had to convince Fallon there was no way she could walk away from him.

Dress to impress.

Fallon stood in front of her gilded pedestal mirror and

glanced at the double-strapped, off-the-shoulder red gown with a deep side slit. The dress showed a generous amount of leg while the sweetheart neckline revealed a swell of cleavage.

She didn't want to give Gage any ideas that the evening would end differently than it had last night with them each going home *alone.*

After applying some red lipstick and a touch of blush to her cheeks, she was ready for an evening at the opera. *But was she really ready?* The remainder of the afternoon after Gage's call, she'd picked up the phone to cancel a half a dozen times. Yet she'd always stopped herself because maybe deep down she really did want to see him.

Fallon couldn't understand the pull Gage had on her after all these years. He'd awakened something in her and she wasn't sure how to get it back under control.

The doorbell rang and her stomach lurched. There was no turning back. Grabbing her matching red clutch purse and wrap, she made for the front door. When she swung it open, Gage stood there, resplendent in a black tuxedo with satin lapels. He was wearing a red tie that complemented her dress.

Fallon felt his eyes rake her up and down. It made her feel as if she was plugged into an electrical socket because currents were running through her veins. When she looked into those brooding brandy-colored eyes, her insides hummed.

"You look incredible!"

"Thank you," Fallon said coolly and wrapped her shawl around her shoulders.

Gage took her arm and led her outside to the waiting limo. He helped her inside, picking up the hem of her dress as she slid in.

Once he was seated beside her and the chauffeur closed the door, he reached across the short distance to the ice bucket and pulled out a bottle of Dom Pérignon. He uncorked it easily and poured them a glass. He handed her one and dinged his flute against hers. "To an unforgettable evening."

Fallon was sure it was going to be nothing but.

La bohème was everything. Gage had spared no expense. When they arrived, they were shown to box seats near the front of the opera house with a clear view of the stage. The singers were amazing and, by the end of the night, Fallon was on her feet along with the entire theater giving them a standing ovation.

"I didn't realize you were such a fan," Gage said from her side.

"I've come from time to time with my father," Fallon replied. "Mama couldn't be bothered. Said it was much too boring for her, but I loved it. Plus, it was something my father and I could do together."

"Must be nice," Gage said wistfully as he led her out of the theater and away from the throng.

"Did you know your father?" Fallon asked, turning to give him a sideward glance.

Gage's glare told Fallon she'd made a misstep in asking something so personal. Wasn't the point of tonight's exercise for them to get to know each other?

Their limousine was waiting by the curb. Fallon was thankful they didn't have to wait with the crowd lining the streets. Within minutes they were pulling away and Gage asked the chauffeur to raise the privacy screen.

"Where to next?" Fallon inquired. There had been an uncomfortable silence between them since she'd inquired about his father. It was clear Gage didn't wish to speak of him.

"I didn't know him," Gage said finally.

Fallon didn't need to ask what he meant.

"My mother never spoke of him. Only told me that he was an older gentleman who'd taken advantage of her youth and naïveté. Once she was pregnant, he turned his back on her and she never saw him again."

"That's why you pushed me away," Fallon replied softly. "Because you didn't want to be like him."

When Gage turned to her, his eyes were cloudy. "Very insightful of you. But know this, Fallon. If you had been a few years older, I wouldn't have turned you away."

"You wouldn't?"

"No. I would have taken what you offered."

"Why?"

"Because I wanted you. I wanted you *then* and I want you now."

His face was starkly beautiful in the dim light coming from the street and Fallon felt as if she were being hypnotized. Her hand went to her throat. Her mouth felt parched as if she'd walked hours in the desert with no water to hydrate her. She reached for the champagne bottle; a new one had miraculously appeared.

Gage grasped her arm and a tingling went straight to her core. "Does it scare you when I speak so openly?"

"You mean bluntly?"

"I was being honest. You should try it."

Her eyes flashed with anger. "I have been honest. I'm here with you now, aren't I? When every instinct I have tells me I should be running in the other direction, away from danger."

"You think I'm dangerous?"

"Hell, yeah! But I can't..."

"Can't what?"

"Can't seem to stop myself from wanting you, too. How's that for honesty?"

"It's great because I've been craving your sweet mouth all day," he growled. Within seconds he'd slid her along the seat until she was sprawled across his lap. The air around them was heavy and thick with desire. When Gage trailed a finger down one of her cheeks, Fallon felt her pulse beat hectically at her throat. "I know you don't want to want me, Fallon, but your body betrays you." With one arm securely around her waist, the other hand was free to cup her jaw and, with a surprising gentleness, Gage angled his head and his mouth closed over hers in the most persuasive of kisses.

Tender yet insistent, his mouth claimed hers again and again and her lips clung to his, seeking closer contact. Fallon gave herself permission to enjoy the taste and lush depths of his mouth. Gage gathered her to him, his fingers at her jaw, holding her captive as he lazily explored her mouth. His tongue teased and stroked hers, causing heat to pool low in Fallon's belly and spread like wildfire, incinerating everything in its path. Her breasts felt heavy and swollen. Gage sensed her ache and cupped the underside of one breast. His thumb grazed over the nub until it peaked and hardened.

Fallon moaned, loving the delicious yet tormenting strokes of his fingers. She wanted his mouth on her nipple, wanted him to feast on her. She became dimly aware of Gage pushing down the top of her dress and taking the rigid peak in his mouth. His mouth and tongue worked the nipple with licks, flicks, tugs and suction. The ache inside her intensified when Gage transferred his attention to her other nipple.

Hadn't she known they might end up like this? This was no longer about a kiss. It was about need. And now that the desire had been unleashed, she didn't know if it could be bottled up again.

Gage ran his hands down Fallon's body. Touching her in ways he'd imagined for far too long. Of course, now that he had her exactly where he wanted her, his brain had short-circuited. He was hardening underneath her sweet little bottom, and he was completely useless. All he could think about was how he'd love nothing better than to wrap her legs around his hips and take her right there in the limousine.

And her breasts. God, they tasted heavenly. It made him want more. He moved upward so he could slant his mouth over hers again. He loved the hot slide of her tongue in and out of his mouth and the way her hands clutched his tuxedo jacket as if she was seeking something to hold on to. But there was nothing. Nothing but this white-hot arousal between them. His free hand went up and undid her hair, which fell to her shoulders. Gage slid his hands through the tendrils and cupped the back of her head so he could give her another mind-numbing kiss.

But a kiss wasn't all he wanted. His hand moved lower until he came to the slit of her dress. He hiked it up to her waist and moved his hands up her bare legs. She trembled when Gage's finger found her thong and pushed it aside so he could trace the most intimate part of her. She was so wet for him. Her body was betraying her, showing him physical evidence of her arousal. And when he began to circle the top of her clitoris with a feather-light touch, she gasped. When he slid one finger inside her, her body tightened around him.

Gage watched Fallon's face as he worked her with his fingers. Slowly, deliberately, he brought her higher and higher. The sounds of pleasure she was making, and especially the way she writhed against his hand, turned him on. Her sexy bottom was brushing his erection and he was going mad. He added another finger and her eyes became hazy with passion.

"Come for me, Fallon," he commanded. She closed her eyes and he sensed her resistance, but his hands were insistent. He could feel it when she orgasmed and clenched around his fingers. Satisfied, Gage claimed her mouth with his, whispering his approval as aftershocks shuddered through her entire body. He kissed her through them until she eventually quieted.

Fallon's uninhibited response was more than Gage could ever imagine. Now he realized *he* needed her to say yes because they were far from over. In fact, they'd just begun.

Five

Fallon was embarrassed as she came back down to earth and registered what had happened. She'd allowed Gage to make love to her in the back of the limousine. Her breasts were bare, aching and wet from his mouth, while her dress was pulled down to her hips. Did he think she behaved this way with every man? Well, she didn't!

She quickly scrambled out of his lap to pull her dress up over her breasts and push it down her thighs.

"What's wrong?" Gage asked.

"How can you be asking me that? After I— After we—"

"Behaved like two consenting adults?"

Fallon flushed and moved as far away on the seat as humanly possible without falling out of the limo.

"Tonight was inevitable, just as it's inevitable that we'll become lovers. Marriage agreement or not."

The limo stopped and Fallon realized they'd made it to her cottage. She was thankful when the door opened and she was out in the cool evening air, briskly walking to her front door. Unfortunately she was not alone. Gage followed her.

"I'd like to walk you to your door."

Fallon spun around on her heel, "Oh, no, you don't." She held her hand up against his hard chest. "We'll say our good-nights here."

"All right." Gage handed Fallon her wrap. "You might want this."

"Thank you."

"Good night." He started back toward the limo but then turned around. "About tomorrow…"

"I'll call you," Fallon responded.

"Very well, I'll await your answer." He'd slipped inside and the limo took off down the gravel driveway.

Once inside, Fallon grappled with how the situation with Gage had escalated. One minute they were enjoying the opera and the next she was coming apart in the limo. How was it possible they still shared such a passionate connection after their storied past? Whenever he was near, she felt weak, fluttery and out of control. Her feelings for Gage had always been complicated, but adding sex into the equation would make it a hell of a lot harder to walk away from a marriage. Was she honestly considering going through with it and locking herself in unholy matrimony with Gage?

Yes.

The next day Fallon was as jittery as ever. She had a hard time focusing on work as the clock tick-tocked. The forty-eight-hour deadline Gage had given her loomed. And she couldn't get the man out of her mind or the way she'd burned up for him with every kiss and every caress. She was unnerved at how far things had gone. She was thankful it hadn't gone any further. She didn't need full-blown sex clouding the picture when she had such a momentous decision to make.

On the one hand, Gage was offering her a way out. It would save thousands of jobs and allow her employees to keep food on the table. She would show her father and all the naysayers that she had the expertise to run Stewart Technologies. On the other, marrying Gage and agreeing to his nonnegotiable terms would mean consummating the marriage. If she agreed, all the old feelings she'd once had for Gage could come bubbling back up to the surface, making her vulnerable. Because could she really trust him, given their history? And she doubted he trusted her, so what was in it for him?

She was reading through some reports when her baby brother, Dane, swept into her office and swung her out of her seat into his arms. "Fallon! Baby girl, I've missed you."

"I've missed you, too, you big oaf. Now put me down, so I can have a look at you." She hadn't been expecting a visit from him, but then again Dane danced to the beat of his own drum, doing things in his own way and his own time. "What are you doing here? I didn't know you were coming for a visit."

When Dane finally set Fallon on her feet, she peered up at him. Dane had inherited their mother's dark brown eyes instead of their father's hazel-gray ones like her and Ayden. His classical good looks, tawny skin, chiseled cheekbones and smile had won the world over, making him one of America's favorite actors. Today he was dressed casually in Diesel jeans, a black T-shirt and biker boots, and was rocking a serious five-o'clock shadow like he hadn't shaved in days.

"When did you get in?" Fallon inquired, leading him over to her sitting area.

"An hour ago, but I'm not staying long. I decided to lay over here for a couple of hours on my way to Mexico for a movie shoot."

"Dane? You promised me that the next time you came to town, you'd stay for a spell."

"I'm sorry, sis, but we have a tight schedule," Dane responded, flopping down on her sofa and putting his booted foot on her cocktail table.

Fallon came forward and knocked it off. "Have you forgotten your manners out there in LA?"

Dane grinned mischievously. "Not all of them. But I had to come. You sounded down the other week when I called, so I had to see for myself what all the ruckus was about. Everything looks the same."

"That's because I've been keeping the bankers at bay."

Dane frowned. "And now? Are they threatening to take the house? I think Nora would have a fit if she lost her gravy train."

"Must you call our mother by her first name?" Fallon replied.

"C'mon, Fallon," Dane said, "When has that woman ever been a mother to us? She was always pawning us off to a nanny or maid. Well, that was until you ran off the one good maid we had."

Fallon felt her face flush and cast her eyes downward. She wished Dane hadn't brought up Grace Campbell. It was still hard remembering how Fallon's actions had affected not only Gage but his mother, as well.

"Fallon." Dane scooted over on the couch and grabbed her hand. "I'm sorry, okay? I didn't mean to stir up the pot and bring back bad memories. Anyway, I realize I've been out of commission and on the sidelines in this family, but I know money is tight. How much do you need? I can liquidate some assets and get you probably a couple of million in a few days."

"It wouldn't be enough."

Dane's dark brown eyes grew large. "It's that bad? Why

didn't you tell me? I could have been helping instead of frivolously spending on houses, cars and trips."

"It's okay." Fallon patted his hand. "I didn't want to bother you. And, furthermore, it's your money. You earned it."

"But I'm your brother. I want to help."

"Ayden offered to help, as well."

"Ayden? Wow!" Dane shook his head. "I'm still in shock over your call. After all this time, he wants a relationship with us? Do you know why?"

Fallon shrugged. "Does it matter? We're family."

Dane was noncommittal. "Sure. And I can see how important it is to you, so I'll make the effort. All right?" He tipped her chin up to look into her eyes.

Fallon grinned. "Great! I'll plan something soon for the three of us."

"What are you going to do in the meantime about the company?"

"Don't you worry, your big sister always has a plan."

Why wasn't she here yet? Gage paced his penthouse like a panther stalking its prey. Fallon had called him earlier and asked to meet at his place, so he'd given her his address. And waited. But the call had been over an hour ago. Gage wondered if Fallon didn't want to be seen with him. Is that why she was coming to him? Did Fallon want to keep their association a secret from her family? Was she having cold feet?

He went to his subzero refrigerator and pulled out a beer. Unscrewing the top, he took a generous swig and slid open the sliding pocket doors to the balcony.

Gage was certain she would agree to his terms. Why else would she bother coming? If she wasn't interested, she'd have laughed in his face when he'd first made the offer and told him where to go. But she wouldn't. Not after last night. They'd given in to the fiery passion between them. And now she was coming to him. She'd be on his turf. *Did she know the danger she was in?*

Gage found himself wondering what it would be like when they were finally together. When there were no parents standing in their way or terms to discuss. Just a man and woman in the throes of passion. Blood rushed to his head and his groin, making him both dizzy and hard at same time. He still couldn't wrap his mind around why she affected him this way. It mocked everything he'd ever said about what he'd do to Fallon if he ever saw her again. He thought he'd throttle her for her careless behavior, but instead all he wanted to do was to drown himself in her. She was the key, the final piece to achieve all he'd ever wanted.

He already had money and power, but by marrying Fallon he would have the grudging respect and acceptance of society. He would no longer be living in the shadows and envying the Stewarts' charmed life, which had been utterly different from his humble roots. Instead he would be living it with them. But, unlike the Stewarts, he wouldn't take what he had for granted because he knew what it was like to go without.

The sound of his doorbell forced Gage from his thoughts. With a loose-limbed stride, he walked to the door and opened it.

Fallon was wearing a black sheath with a sharp asymmetrical collar. Her hair was pulled up into a high bun and she wore little to no makeup. She looked effortlessly beautiful. Gage yearned to touch her but her features were schooled.

"Come in." He motioned her forward.

"Thank you." She walked inside and paused when she reached his living room. It was large, with sweeping views of the capitol building and the University of Texas tower. "Great view."

"Yeah, I like it," Gage replied. "But I'm sure you didn't come here for the scenery. Have you made a decision?"

Fallon eyed him warily. "Yes, I have. But I have a few stipulations that aren't open for negotiation."

Gage chuckled to himself. *Did she actually think she was in a position of power?* He held all the cards and he was damn well going to play them. But he would humor her. "All right, let's hear them."

"I'll agree to marry you."

His mouth curved into a smile. Of course she would. She was desperate to save her father's legacy. Was that her only reason?

"But only for six months."

"Excuse me?"

"Six months is enough time for you to ingratiate yourself into Austin society and get the full benefit of the Stewart name and all its connections. I see no reason for us to continue the charade a moment longer than necessary. Wouldn't you agree?"

Gage had to admit he was surprised; he hadn't thought of making their arrangement temporary. The only thing on his mind was Fallon in his bed and getting a foothold into Stewart Technologies. "I can live with that. What else? Because I suspect there's more."

Fallon stood straighter and stared at him. "The marriage must be in name only."

Gage laughed. "Do you really think that's possible, Fallon, after the way you were crawling all over me last night?"

"I—I..." She stuttered but then stopped. It appeared as if she was regrouping. "I don't want to muddy the waters and complicate what is essentially a business arrangement. You must see that."

"No, I don't." Gage plopped his beer on the nearby cocktail table, causing some to spill over. "What I see is a woman afraid of taking what she wants. You and I know this isn't just about business, Fallon. It never was."

Her eyes narrowed. "What is it?"

"It's a reckoning. Between you and me. About what we both wanted but didn't get years ago. Don't you think it's time we find out what could have been?"

Fallon turned and walked onto the terrace. She was quiet, contemplative, as if she were battling herself, and Gage feared she would say no to him. It was imperative she agree. It would finally give him the means to avenge his mother while simultaneously getting Fallon in his bed.

Gage touched her shoulders and she jumped. Rather than touch her again, he placed his hands on either side of the railing, closing her in. She was out of options. He heard her sharp intake of breath as he inhaled the sweet fragrant smell of her perfume. "Fallon…"

"All right," she whispered.

Gage sucked in a breath and leaned in closer. "Say it again."

"I said, all right." Fallon turned around to face him and he appreciated how she looked him in the eye. She was no coward. "I'll agree to the stipulation we share a bed."

Victory surged through Gage and a large grin spread across his lips. "Then how about we get a head start." He hauled her to him. He was following his base instincts of taking her here and now. He didn't care. On the couch or his bed, it didn't much matter to him. She was his now. He lowered his head to finally have a taste of her delectable lips, when Fallon placed her hands against his chest.

"No."

"No?" Fallon made him feel a little wild and out of control while she still looked poised. "You said that you were agreeing to my terms."

"And I will." Fallon slid out of his grasp to walk back into the living room. "When we're married."

"You expect me to wait until our honeymoon?"

Fallon chuckled. "As shocking as that sounds, yes, Gage. You've called the shots up to this point, but not on this. I'm agreeing to marry you and to share your bed, but not until then."

Gage gave her an eye roll and sighed. Fallon played hardball and was a shrewd negotiator. He could see now how she'd climbed the ladder to become CEO of Stewart Technologies. "Fine."

"Good." She inclined her head. "I assume you'll have your attorney draw up a prenuptial outlining terms, including your *gift* to your fiancée?"

"Of course. The prenup will state the exact amount of funds I'm giving you to bail out your company. Other matters will be between us—a gentleman's agreement, if you will."

"Excellent."

"And as for the wedding, it needs to be arranged quickly yet lavishly so the entire community can see it."

"Why the rush?"

"You need a reminder of our explosive chemistry? Then let me remind you." He slipped his arm around her nape and covered her mouth in a searing kiss. She was stiff at first, but it didn't take long for her to warm up and to delve into the kiss. He angled his head for better access and reveled in how Fallon tasted like no other woman. Over the next six months he intended to get rid of this craving he'd developed for her.

His hands skimmed down her back to cup her bottom and she groaned. Jesus, if he continued, he would have her flat on her back despite her protests. Gage pulled away and took a shuddering breath. "You should go now while you still can."

"I think that's a good idea." Fallon grabbed her purse and was out the door, leaving only her scent in her wake.

Oh, yes, they needed to have a very short engagement.

Six

"Gage, darling. It's so good to see you." His mother enveloped him in a warm hug. Gage returned her affection, squeezing her small frame.

He pulled back and regarded her. She wore a simple shift-style dress and espadrilles, and looked youthful. The earlier years of hard menial labor couldn't be seen in her smooth caramel complexion. Her dark brown eyes were warm and inviting, reminding him he had been away from home far too long.

"C'mon in." She motioned him inside the five-bedroom palatial home he'd bought her a decade ago when his finances had begun booming. Gage had ensured that his mother could retire from a life where she worked late into the night cleaning other's people houses and looking after their children.

"The place looks great." Gage followed her into the sunroom where she had set a pitcher of sweet tea and her famous oatmeal-raisin cookies in the middle of the cocktail table. Gage snatched one from the platter and began munching away happily as they sat on the sofa.

"The interior decorator you hired had a great eye. Once I told her I wanted modern contemporary, she came up with this." Grace motioned to the sleek white furniture and the room mostly done in creams and light beige with a few colored throw pillows here and there. "Now, let me pour you some sweet tea."

"Good, you deserve it." He accepted the glass when she handed it to him.

"Tell me what's new. You must have something on the horizon. You wouldn't leave your precious London otherwise."

Gage shrugged, not meeting her eyes, and reached for another cookie. "Why don't you tell me about your next trip?"

His mother eyed him suspiciously and Gage squirmed in his seat. "Don't play with me, boy. Your mama can tell when you're not being forthright. So spit it out."

Gage sighed. He would have to tell her about Fallon, but he didn't relish her response. "I ran into an old friend recently and we reconnected."

"Really?" His mother poured herself a glass of tea. "Anyone I know?"

"Fallon Stewart." Gage didn't look up when he spoke. He didn't need to because the silence permeating the room was deafening.

"The Stewart girl who caused me to lose my job of ten years without so much as a reference?" his mother responded. "What in hell's name is going on, Gage? I thought you despised that family as much as I did."

"I do but…"

"But what?" Her fierce gazed rested on his. "Explain yourself."

Gage wasn't sure how much of his plan he wanted to tell

his mother, so he gave her a half-truth. "She's turned into a beautiful young woman."

"She's deceitful. Had Fallon Stewart spoken up years ago, she would have saved us years of struggle."

"She apologized and wants to move on."

"And you've forgiven her?" his mother asked incredulously. "After you vowed vengeance? I can hardly believe that."

"Believe it, because Fallon and I are getting married."

"What?" Her eyes grew wide. "Over my dead body."

"Mama, don't be melodramatic."

"I'm not. That girl is your Achilles' heel, Gage. She always has been. I remember how she used to fawn over you and follow you around like a little puppy dog and you never put her straight. And now you're turning the other cheek? Sounds to me like you're thinking below the belt and not with your head."

Gage reached across the sofa and grasped his mother's hand in his. "I know what I'm doing."

"Do you?" She gazed deep into his brown eyes. "Because I think the Stewarts will do nothing but destroy you. Mark my words. You're playing with fire, Gage."

"Trust me, Mama, I have the situation under control." *Or did he?* Was he blinded by Fallon's charms and headed for a fall?

"I don't think so, but then again you're a grown man and capable of making your own decisions."

"I'm glad you recognize that because I will make them pay dearly for how you were treated. I promise you." He would take sweet revenge on Fallon. In bed.

"Let me get this straight. After I told you the Stewarts' company was in trouble, you thought it would be a good idea to confront Fallon?" Theo asked when he and Gage met up to play pool late Saturday afternoon.

"Yeah," Gage responded. "I had to see for myself if she was still the spoiled, overindulged princess she once was."

"Well, apparently not, because you asked her to *marry* you," Theo said, taking a swallow of his beer. "Have you lost your mind?" He leaned over to feel Gage's forehead.

"No. I haven't," Gage said. "Fallon's not sixteen anymore, Theo." He used the cue stick to get the green ball into the corner pocket. Then he eased the cue into position for the blue ball and aimed for the middle pocket. He missed and it was Theo's turn. "She's a grown woman."

"Then sleep with her," Theo stated. "You don't have to marry her. I mean, I know she's hot and all." He glanced over at Gage and laughed when his best friend gave him a jealous glare from across the pool table. "Hey, I have two eyes, I'm not blind. But since it's clear you're the possessive type, I'll keep my opinions to myself."

"You do that."

"Answer me this. I get why she's doing it. You're offering her a ton of money to save her business and you two have a history, so I understand the attraction. But what do you get out of all this, because a bed partner seems like a flimsy excuse to tie yourself to another human being in holy matrimony."

Gage reached for his beer on a nearby table. After telling his mother, Gage had been shaken. But on his way over to meet Theo, he'd had to remind himself of why he was doing this and his resolve strengthened. "I told you. Fallon will secure my place in society and while she's so busy focused on the wedding, I'll be secretly buying up stock of Stewart Technologies until I own a majority interest."

Theo pointed at him. "I knew you had a trick up your sleeve, but this is pretty underhanded, even for you, Gage."

"Don't you think they deserve it?" Gage countered. "Henry Stewart threw us out on the street with just the clothes on our backs. We weren't even allowed to get our meager belongings. And after working for them for years, they wouldn't even give my mother a reference. All because she stuck up for me." He slammed his hand against his chest. "Do you know how the guilt ate me up at causing my mother harm?"

"I know it wasn't easy."

"It was hell. We had to scrape by with the little savings we had. I blame the Stewarts. And I will feel triumph the day I can ruin them."

"And Fallon. Even though she was a naïve young girl?"

"She was old enough to know better and she's no young ingénue anymore. She's well aware of what she's agreed to."

"She's not the only one," Theo responded. "I worry about you, Gage."

"Don't. I've been on a collision course with the Stewarts for sixteen years and the moment has finally come for me to get vengeance. And after telling my mama, I'm even more convinced I'm doing the right thing."

"You told your mother?"

Gage nodded. "And she pretty much blew a gasket."

"Can you blame her?"

"No. But I'm on track to get everything I ever wanted, including Fallon."

This marriage was one of the best decisions he'd ever made and the unexpected bonus was the sizzling sex awaiting him once he finally made Fallon his. He wasn't going to let up on the gas. Gage had to push forward until he took over the Stewarts' empire. Only then would he feel like he had avenged his mother.

Fallon was happy to receive a lunch invitation from Ayden. She arrived before him on Monday afternoon and had several minutes to settle her nerves. Their meeting would be very different from the tense scenario a couple of months ago. Fallon would get to know Ayden on a personal level. She didn't know why she was nervous at the prospect, but she was. She wanted this so bad and it had meant everything that Ayden extended the olive branch.

She noticed her big brother the moment he arrived. He was over six feet tall, bald with tawny skin, and impressively male in his tailored suit. He was impossible to miss. He waved when he saw her and stalked toward the table. His eyes creased into a smile and she was surprised when he leaned toward her and offered a hug. They were off to a good start.

"Sorry I'm late. A client meeting wrapped up later than I anticipated," Ayden said as he sat across from her. "How are you?"

"I'm good. Thank you for the invite." Fallon glanced over and found herself looking into the hazel-gray eyes they shared with their father.

"You're welcome," Ayden responded, unbuttoning his suit jacket and leaning back to regard her. "When I said I wanted a relationship, I meant it."

Fallon nodded and smiled. "I know. So did I."

"So, in the interest of family, I'd like to know how you're really doing. Any luck on getting a financial bailout with any of the banks I referred you to?"

After he'd told Fallon he wanted to forge a sibling relationship, Ayden had sent her some leads. As owner of Stewart Investments, Ayden's clients were quite wealthy and might be looking for an investment vehicle.

"No, I didn't get any bites," Fallon responded, reaching for her sparkling water.

His gaze bore into her. "What are you going to do then? You're running out of time."

"I've found a private investor."

Ayden frowned. "Who would have that kind of cash?"

"Gage Campbell. You may have heard of him."

"Yeah, I have. They call him the Wizard of Wall Street.

But usually he's making other people money, not investing his own." He peered at her with a strange expression. "What gives?"

"Gage and I have a personal connection," Fallon replied, forcing her eyes to meet her brother's. "And..." She tried to find the right words but it was hard with Ayden staring at her so intently. She could lie. Spin it that they were old acquaintances. But Ayden wouldn't believe it. And she didn't want to start out their newfound relationship that way. She had to tell him the truth. "We're getting married. And in exchange, Gage is giving me the money to bail out Stewart Technologies." Fallon shot Ayden a glance, but his eyes were blazing with fury, which stunned her. She didn't know Ayden cared.

"Marriage?" His eyes widened in concern. "Why would you agree to such a thing? I will *give* you the money. You don't have to marry this man."

She shook her head. "It's all right, Ayden. I've known Gage for years. We grew up together. And..."

"And what does he get out of this arrangement?" His eyes narrowed as he waited for her answer.

Fallon blushed and he caught it. "So you're willing to pros—"

Her eyes flashed a gentle but firm warning. "Don't you say it, Ayden, not unless you want this relationship to end before it's begun."

She heard his sharp intake of breath and his eyes were hooded when he spoke next. "You're my sister, Fallon. A fact I've been trying to hide from a long time but not anymore. I'm responsible for you taking such drastic action. I made you feel like you had no other choice."

Fallon leaned across the table and placed her hand over his large one. "Listen, I appreciated your offer. Ultimately it was my choice, Ayden. Not yours. You're not responsible for my actions."

"And you're not responsible for Henry running the company into the ground, especially after he frivolously spent money on new inventions that never went to market," Ayden responded hotly. "Yet you're willing to sacrifice yourself."

"Please respect my decision," Fallon implored. "I need your support on this."

Ayden sighed and sat back in his chair. "I'm worried for you."

"Don't be. I know Gage. He won't hurt me." Fallon certainly hoped that statement was true because she wasn't only risking her pride. Gage had the power to hurt her more than any other man because of the long-ago buried feelings she had for him. She had to protect herself at all costs. She might be giving her body, but not her heart.

Fallon was exhausted. It had been an emotionally draining day. All she wanted was to go home and soak in a long, luxurious bath. So much had happened in the last couple of days. Dane and Ayden were both so concerned for her well-being she needed to regroup, to make sure she could handle what she'd signed up for.

Seeing Gage again and finding out the passion she'd once had for him hadn't died but blossomed was disconcerting. Over a decade had passed. He should no longer cause her pulse to race, but he did. She was a bundle of tight emotions and lust. Whenever she was in his company she acted completely out of character, starting with the heated kiss at the restaurant then again in the limo after the opera.

Is that why she'd agreed to his marriage proposal? He was a rich and successful man with deep pockets that could help save her company, but was it more than that?

Her phone rang and she answered it from her car. "Fallon?"

"Gage. What can I do for you?"

"I'm here at Stewart Manor and thought you'd like to join me."

"You're at my house? Why?" Panic surged through Fallon. *What was he doing there?* They hadn't even had time to get their story straight. And then it dawned on her: he couldn't wait for the opportunity to rub it in her parents' faces. He was marrying their daughter. It was a *take that* to her father. It would serve him right if she told Gage to go to hell, but then she would still be in the same predicament tomorrow.

She heard his chuckle from the other end. "I thought it would be obvious. I'm here to share the news of our impending marriage with your parents."

Fallon sucked in a sharp breath. "You had no right to do that. *I* was going to tell them."

"*We* are going to talk to them, so meet me here." The call ended and Fallon glared at the display screen. Anger coursed through her and she let out several choice words. Who did he think he was, running roughshod over her? She had been planning to tell her parents in due time. What right did he have to force her hand like this?

Apparently, in his view, every right. He wanted to be able to rub the fact they were getting married in her family's face. The maid's prodigal son had returned and was there to save the day. This was all part of his retribution. She could only imagine what her mother's response would be: sheer and utter embarrassment at having to kowtow to Gage Campbell.

She was wrong.

After parking her red Audi in the circular driveway, Fallon walked into the manor expecting to hear loud voices, but she found Gage and her parents lounging on the sofa as if they were fast friends instead of known enemies.

She caught Gage's compelling stare the moment she entered the room. With his height and broad shoulders, he was beyond handsome. The words that came to mind were *potent*, *vital* and *commanding*. Fallon found herself mesmerized.

"Babe." Gage rose and strode toward her, a barely leashed tension radiating off him. He leaned forward and brushed his lips across her temple before circling his arm around her waist. Fallon allowed herself to be ushered to the sofa where they sat side-by-side, thigh-to-thigh.

"Fallon, darling." Nora was perched in a chair opposite her father while she and Gage sat on the sofa between them. "Why is this the first we're hearing that you've been seeing Grace's son?"

Fallon was vexed. The innocuous question made it seem as if Nora and Gage's mother were old friends rather than boss and employee with a bad history. She didn't get a chance to respond, though, because Gage was quick to answer.

"We were keeping it private, Mrs. Stewart. We reconnected some months ago." He turned to Fallon at his side. His eyes, fringed with long black lashes, held hers for several seconds before he faced her parents again. "We didn't want to let the cat out of the bag, so to speak, until we were sure of where the relationship was heading."

"But Fallon never keeps anything from me." Her father glanced in her direction.

Fallon attempted a half-hearted smile. "I'm sorry, Daddy."

Gage reached for her hand, which she'd kept firmly in her lap, and laced his fingers through hers. "Don't apologize, Fallon. We wanted privacy. Besides, it doesn't matter now. We're in love and we want to get married as soon as possible."

Nora gasped. "Why the rush? You aren't pregnant, Fallon, are you? I mean, what would everyone think?"

The horror in her mother's voice over the idea that *she*

would get knocked up by Gage of all people was clear to everyone and Fallon felt Gage stiffen at her side. She patted his leg and answered. "Of course not, Mother. We see no reason to wait. We're both very eager to tie the knot."

"Perhaps it would be best if you had a long engagement." Henry eyed them both. "It would give us time to get to know Gage again."

Gage looked at her father. "Oh, I'm sure you know me quite well, Mr. Stewart, considering I grew up in this household and you took me under your wing."

Fallon's stomach plummeted and her father bristled.

Her mother spoke first. "That may be so, Mr. Campbell, but—"

"Gage," he interrupted. "I mean, I am going to be your son-in-law, after all."

Fallon watched her mother plaster on a fake smile. "Gage, it's clear you've done quite well for yourself..." she began. Fallon knew her mother had noticed his Tom Ford shoes, Rolex watch and tailored designer suit, but did she have to be so *obvious*? "But we really know nothing about you."

Gage leaned back against the sofa, one arm draped casually behind Fallon. "Well, after my departure from Stewart Manor, I went on to graduate from the University of Texas with a degree in finance and economics."

"You were always a whiz with numbers," her father said.

Gage continued as if he hadn't spoken. "After college, I went to work on Wall Street, then in London and Hong Kong, where I made a number of substantial investments that have put me in the position I'm in today."

"And where is that exactly?" Her mother pursed her lips. "As you can see—" she swept her arms across the room "—Fallon has grown up in a certain lifestyle and we wouldn't want her to do without."

Gage's eyes narrowed as he sat forward. "As my wife,

Fallon would want for nothing. Money is no object for our wedding."

Her mother's finely arched eyebrow rose. "No object, did you say?"

"That's right."

"Well then, Henry." She turned to her husband. "Seems like our daughter has landed quite the whale. Having Gage here—" she inclined her head in his direction "—should most assuredly fix the company's dire straits."

"Mother, please."

"It's all right, Fallon." Gage patted her thigh. "I'm aware of the company's financial problems."

"And will you be assisting in that effort?" Henry responded. "Or is this all a ploy to get back at me? Do you even love my daughter? Because I'm finding it very hard to believe, after all these years, you're willing to let bygones be bygones."

Fallon could tell Gage was seething with rage. He slowly stood. "The time for me justifying myself to you, Mr. Stewart, is long since over. I suspect it's you who should be thanking me for even considering jumping onto this sinking ship." He buttoned his suit jacket. "Fallon?" He glanced down at her. She had no choice but to stand, as well. "If you'll excuse us."

"Wait just a second, Campbell." Her father jumped up. "I'd like to talk to my daughter *alone*."

"So you can talk her out of marrying me?" Gage asked with eagle-eyed precision. "I don't think so. Fallon is coming home with me."

Fallon looked at her father and then back at her fiancé. She could feel the hostility emanating from both men and realized she was caught in the middle *again*. If she went with her father, he would surely ask questions she wouldn't want to provide him the answers to. She had to go with Gage because she needed to lay a few ground rules on how this engagement and marriage were going to work. Gage couldn't have everything his own way. He would have to give.

She nodded her acceptance and Gage placed his hand at the small of her back and ushered her out of the room.

Seven

Gage fumed as he and Fallon strode toward the front door and he didn't say a word as he walked her to his car. He'd known facing the Stewarts after all this time wouldn't be easy. He'd hoped to get some satisfaction at seeing the shocked expression on their faces, but he hadn't expected the rage that had grown deep in his gut with each passing moment. Perhaps he shouldn't have been hotheaded and waited for Fallon. He'd been on edge because his mother had called him earlier and tried to talk him out of the marriage. He'd had to do something big so *he* wouldn't change his mind.

Once they made it to his Bugatti, Gage opened the door for Fallon and she glared at him. "Is this really necessary? I can go home. I'm right here."

"Yes, it is. Get in."

Fallon must have thought better of arguing with him and slid inside the vehicle. He closed the door behind her, came around to the driver's side and started the car. He didn't need to look at his passenger to know she was angry with him.

Once they pulled away from the estate, she turned to him. "There was no reason for you to behave like a caveman back there. My father gets we're together. He didn't need to know you were taking me back to your place."

"I had cause."

"You rose to the bait," Fallon said.

It galled Gage that she was right. He should have acted as if he couldn't care less about their disdain, but instead he'd shown his hand. "Your father needs to know I won't be pushed around, not again."

"Well, neither will I, Gage," Fallon replied, folding her arms across her chest. "I agreed to your terms, but I don't take orders from you or anyone. You got that?"

Gage glanced at her sideways. Fallon had guts and he liked that about her. Not to mention those luscious, ripe lips of hers. He felt himself getting hard.

"The light changed," Fallon commented.

Gage glanced up; indeed it had. He slid the car forward. "I'm sorry if I was a bit *heavy-handed.*"

Fallon eyed him narrowly. "An apology? Wow! I'm surprised you could manage it."

"I can admit when I'm wrong." He heard her mumble something underneath her breath. "What was that?"

"Oh, nothing," she said. "Since we're going to your place, I hope it's your intention to feed me because I'm starved. I was looking forward to a meal and a hot bath."

Envisioning Fallon naked underneath a sea of bubbles was quite the erotic fantasy. "Both of those can be arranged."

"I'll take the meal now. Bath time will be later at my cottage alone."

"Damn." He snapped his fingers. "I was hoping you might want some company."

"Not a chance, Campbell. If you recall, our agreement was to wait until after the wedding."

"C'mon, don't tell me you're not tempted. I give great back rubs."

"I bet you do. Now, drive please."

"With pleasure," he replied.

When they made it to the penthouse, he started for the kitchen. He tossed the jacket he'd been wearing aside and rolled up his sleeves to rustle up some steaks and a salad for dinner. He noticed how Fallon made herself comfortable in his home and he liked it. She busied herself, taking off her jacket, kicking off her heels and following him into the kitchen. He watched her pull two wineglasses from the cupboard and a corkscrew from a drawer. Then she went over to the wine rack nestled in the living room corner and pulled out a bottle of his favorite red wine. Clearly she was as on edge as he was as she quickly set about opening the bottle. He stopped her.

Taking the corkscrew from her hands, he uncorked the bottle and poured them both a glass. Fallon moved over to the sofa and drank in silence while he prepared dinner.

"I'm sorry about my parents," Fallon said after some time had passed.

"Why are you apologizing for them?" Gage asked as he placed the steaks in the microwave to thaw and turned on the broiler.

"Because…"

"Just stop, Fallon." She had no idea what it was like to escape the dead-end world he'd grown up in. To claw his way out, inch by painful inch, to make something of himself. To achieve the heights he hadn't thought he could. And to have her parents look down on him angered Gage. Henry didn't think he was good enough for Fallon. Nora was a different story; as long as Gage kept their bank account flush, she was content to pawn her daughter off. It disgusted him. But Gage reminded himself of his end goal. Bed Fallon. Take away Henry's most prized possessions—his daughter and his business—and leave him with nothing.

He gathered the fixings for a salad from the refrigerator and began cutting up the vegetables.

"You sound as if you're angry at me," she said softly, turning to face him from the sofa. "It was your decision to go off half-cocked. I would have told my parents on my own. In *my own time.*"

"And when might that have been? On our wedding day?" he asked, taking the steaks from the microwave and liberally seasoning them.

She shot him a penetrating glare. "No, but you jumped the gun and now you're mad because you didn't like their reaction. Well, tough! You didn't give me time to set the stage. You went in guns blazing. If you'd given me time for a little diplomacy, I could have smoothed the waters."

"There's no time for diplomacy, Fallon," Gage said, placing the prepared salad in the fridge until the steaks were done. "They were never going to approve of you marrying me. What's done is done. They know. We set a wedding date." He placed the steaks in the broiler.

"Christ! Can you let me catch my breath?" Fallon implored.

No! he wanted to scream. If too much time passed, she could change her mind or his mother would change his. It was imperative the train left the station. He'd already contacted his attorney last night and told him to prepare the paperwork.

"I'm sorry if I'm being pushy here," Gage said, finally answering Fallon's question, "but I see no reason to delay the inevitable. I would think you would welcome a swift engagement and wedding to secure Stewart Technologies."

Fallon flushed. "Of course I want that. I just..." Her voice trailed off and she took a sip of wine.

"Just what?"

"Nothing." She reached for her purse on the cocktail table and pulled out her cell phone. "What date were you thinking of?"

"October first sounds great. A fall wedding would be brilliant."

"That's a month away!"

"I know, but your mother can help," he responded. Nora Stewart loved spending money. Although he wanted a big splashy wedding, he would have to keep Nora on a short leash because she was a notorious spendthrift. Did it really matter anyway? In the end, he'd have his way. Fallon in his bed.

"You still seem worried about the wedding," Gage said a few minutes later when they were seated for dinner.

"I have a lot on my plate right now." Fallon glanced down at the steak and spinach salad with a balsamic vinaigrette Gage had prepared. "No pun intended."

They both laughed. "How'd you learn how to cook anyway?" she inquired. She wasn't much of a cook herself and was surprised at Gage's talent. She told him so as she cut into her perfectly cooked steak.

"From my mom," Gage replied. "She didn't always have time to cook for me if she was at the main house. Some nights I had to fend for myself."

Fallon was quiet. She'd never thought about what happened to Gage when Grace was cooking all their meals. "I'm sorry, Gage."

"For what?"

Tears welled in her eyes and she said, "For everything. For how I treated you back then. For not thinking about you when your mother was at the house catering to mine, to me and Dane. I—I guess I didn't care about anyone else but myself back then. And I'm sorry."

Gage stared back at her, his expression unreadable, but Fallon wasn't stopping. She owed him this and it was long overdue. "I'm sorry I lied about you to my father and accused you of seducing me when we both know it was untrue. I was afraid. I didn't know what my father would do after he caught us. I didn't want to disappoint him and the way he was looking at me frightened me. I was afraid of losing his love."

"I doubt one mistake would have cost you his affection."

Fallon lowered her head. "Maybe. Maybe not. I'm trying to give an explanation for why I did what I did."

Gage stopped eating and watched her warily. "I'm listening."

"All my life I tried to be the son he never had because he and my brother were like oil and water from the day Dane was born. I knew Daddy wanted a son to follow in his footsteps, so I tried to be that person. Then one day I learned Dane wasn't Daddy's only son. He had an older son, Ayden, from his first wife, Lillian."

"I heard rumors Henry had another son. The papers alluded to it when they were covering Ayden Stewart of Stewart Investments, but he would never confirm it."

"Because Ayden hates our father. Wants nothing to do with him. Blames him for the awful childhood he had growing up."

"And you?"

"He knew of me, but I was the one who made contact with Ayden when I was eighteen. I was in college and away from my parents and wanted a relationship with the big brother I never knew existed."

"What happened?"

"Ayden wasn't interested in being a family and I accepted that. But things have changed. He's ready to put the past behind us and be siblings." Fallon didn't share that initially she'd gone to Ayden for help but upon further thought had realized she wasn't being fair to him. She couldn't ask Ayden to save a company he'd been cut out of. She'd agreed to Gage's marriage proposal and that's all that mattered.

"Then I'm glad for you," Gage replied. "I wish I had siblings growing up when I lived on the estate. It would have made it a lot easier to deal with the bullies. We could have double-teamed them. Instead it was just me. But eventually I grew up. Got taller. Stronger. And no one dared to approach me."

"Until the day a sixteen-year-old stole into your cottage and ruined your whole life," Fallon responded.

Gage glanced at her. "Fallon, I thought we agreed to let this go."

Like her father, Fallon had her doubts. She didn't want to be played. "So you've said, but I just poured out my guts to you and yet you haven't said whether you accept my apology."

"I accept. There, are you happy?"

"Only if you mean it. If you truly mean it."

"I can accept, but it doesn't mean I've forgotten. Is that fair enough for you?" Gage inquired.

Fallon nodded because she suspected she wasn't getting any more blood out of that stone. "All right. Now, about this wedding. You realize you told my *mother* you want something lavish."

Gage pursed his lips. "True. I'll meet with my accountant and we'll give her a substantial budget for the wedding. But in general you need to get her spending under control or you'll never stabilize the company."

They continued talking finances until they retired to the living room and killed off a second bottle of wine. At some point Gage swung her legs into his lap. He closed his hands around her heels and began massaging her feet. His long fingers slid from her heels to her toes as he encompassed them in firm, sure caresses. Fallon allowed herself to relax and rest her head back against the sofa. The slide of his hands against her skin felt so unbelievably good. Warm, gentle…and erotic.

"Mmm…that feels good," Fallon moaned as Gage used his thumb and fingers to hit the pressure points.

"My pleasure," Gage murmured. "Can you make that noise again?"

Fallon popped an eye open and caught his sly grin.

"C'mon, you must recognize how sexual that moan was," he said. "And I'm a man, after all." He pressed his fingers against the soles of her feet and Fallon's body arched off the sofa. "A man who's attracted to you."

Fallon straightened and wondered frantically how she'd got herself into this. When she looked up, she found him watching her intently. Desire had been awakened in the dark depths of his eyes; they glittered in a way that unnerved yet excited her, speeding up her pulse. She moved to turn away, but Gage wouldn't let her up. Instead he leaned forward. Her hands pressed into the silk of his shirt. She felt the solid wall of his chest and the rapid thump of his heartbeat.

She tried to push him away but somehow her fingers had a mind of their own and instead slid along his arms, molding his incredibly muscled biceps. Sensation coursed through her and she was transfixed as he lowered his head and kissed her with a thorough slide of his lips against hers. They traded kiss for kiss and Fallon clasped his face in her hands and angled her head for deeper contact. Gage plundered every inch of her mouth and she gave him full access.

How was it they always managed to end up here? Like this?

From her sensual fog, reason emerged. Then caution. If she allowed herself, she'd get caught up in the fervor because when they were together like this, Fallon was certain Gage had forgiven her and the past was long behind him.

But she was afraid to allow herself to believe it. As he'd said, he'd accepted her apology but hadn't forgotten what happened. It would always be between them.

Fallon pressed her hands against his chest and Gage stilled. He must have sensed her pulling back since he stopped and was already on his feet. She saw him rub his head in frustration.

"I think it's best if I leave." Fallon reached for her purse behind her on the console and stood. "We should refrain from spending too much time alone together until the wedding. I'm going to call an Uber."

"Fallon, you don't have to do that. I can drive you home."

She held up her hand. "Please, let me have some time alone, okay?"

"All right, all right. We'll talk soon?"

"Of course." Fallon knew Gage would make sure of that. He'd staked his claim not only on her but on her body. And if she didn't get some distance between them there was no way they would remain celibate until after the wedding.

Eight

"Care to tell me why you're marrying the housekeeper's son? A man who nearly assaulted you years ago?" Henry Stewart stood at Fallon's office door the next morning wearing a dark gray suit and a scowl.

"Daddy, what are you doing here?"

"I'm here to find out what the hell is going on." Her father closed the door and headed straight to her plush sofa.

Fallon released a deep sigh. She'd known this day was coming, but it was here. To move forward, she had to tell the truth about what really happened when she was sixteen.

"You have it all wrong, Daddy." Fallon came from behind her desk.

"What do I have wrong, pumpkin?" He patted the seat next to him.

Fallon sat beside him and looked into his hazel-gray eyes. "When I told you Gage came on to me, I lied. It was the other way around. I came on to him and *he* pushed me away."

"What?" Her father's eyes grew large with concern. "Why on earth would you do such a thing? Grace Campbell was good people and I threw her and Gage out on the street."

Fallon bowed her head and smoothed the pale pink dress she wore. "I know. And I've never forgiven myself for the pain I inflicted on their family. But in that moment I panicked."

"I see. And is this marriage some sort of penance? Because you feel like you owe him? Well, guess what? You can't make up for the past, sweetheart."

"It's not like that." She shook her head. "Gage and I… well, like he told you before, we've reconnected."

"If that's code for you slept together, I don't want to know." Her father bolted to his feet. Then he spun back around quickly. "But if you did, why marry? Although Gage may not be the scoundrel I thought he was, he still has to harbor resentment. There has to be more to the story because this is all too sudden."

Fallon wasn't going to explain the conditions under which she'd agreed to marry Gage. She'd already done enough to disillusion her father for one day. "There is no catch, Daddy. Gage and I are getting married and you'll have to accept it."

"I have to do no such thing. Gage Campbell isn't good enough for you, Fallon. I hope you see that before it's too late."

Gage hadn't seen Fallon in a week. He was anxious. The prenup was ready—his lawyers had couriered it over just this morning—and he wanted her to sign it before she changed her mind.

Although he'd agreed to her request for some space, it had been much harder to honor than he'd anticipated. Far too hard. Business was no longer paramount in his mind even though his attorney told him they were close to acquiring a big round of Stewart Technologies' stock through several different obscure holding companies. It would take someone months to discover that he owned all of them. It should make him feel good that he was achieving his goal to squash the Stewarts, but it didn't. His mother was disappointed he would even consider "marrying the enemy," as she put it. He'd tried to explain that he had a plan, but she would hear none of it.

Today, however, he and Fallon would cement their relationship by meeting for lunch at Capitol City, Austin's most exclusive country club. It was a blatant statement they were together and would certainly start the rumor mills churning. For privacy, he'd reserved the entire terrace for just the two of them. He glanced down at the manila envelope that held the paperwork formalizing the agreement between them. It was all in black-and-white. It laid out the monetary gift that would help her keep Stewart Technologies, some of the terms of their marriage, and the fact they'd each keep their individual assets in the event they divorced. Now all Fallon needed to do was sign.

He glanced at the entrance to the terrace. Fallon walked in wearing a simple navy sheath with a deep V, and desire flared hot in his belly. She smiled at him when she approached and he couldn't stop himself from grinning. She had a tantalizing figure with her long, shapely legs and pert breasts. His pulse quickened. He couldn't wait to find out firsthand how she would come apart when he had her underneath him.

Gage rose and schooled his features as he prepared to finally make Fallon his.

Fallon paused by the terrace doorway. The last week away from him had been good for her equilibrium. She'd been able to get her rampant lust for the man under control by explaining it away. Gage was a skilled lover. He knew how to seduce women and, given her limited dating experience, she'd been pulled into his web.

She wished her explanation to her father had gone equally as well. It hadn't. When she'd finally spoken with him after the night of their announcement, he'd been less than pleased, but Fallon had stood her ground. She'd even gone further and told him she was putting him and her mother on a budget. Stewart Technologies would no longer fund their lifestyle and their expense account would be shut down.

Her father had been furious and told her she had no right to do such a thing, but as CEO she had every right. Although he was chairman of the board and still had shares, Fallon wasn't going to kowtow to him anymore. She had the board on her side. Henry hadn't been pleased, claiming Gage was asserting undue influence over her, which was ludicrous. Fallon was finally doing what she should have done years ago when she'd been appointed CEO and realized the dire situation the company was in.

Meanwhile her mother was in serious spending mode. She'd already recruited Austin's top wedding planner to organize their hasty nuptials. She wanted to sit down with Fallon and go over color swatches, flower selections and cake choices, but Fallon wasn't interested. She'd told her mother whatever she selected was fine. Knowing her mother, it would not only be flashy, but lavish enough to appeal to Gage and ensure he got his money's worth because he wanted everyone in Austin to know he'd landed the golden goose. Her.

When she arrived at the table, Gage helped her into her seat. "Thank you. You're looking well," she commented when he sat across from her.

"And you're looking good enough to eat," he responded, placing his napkin in his lap.

Fallon noticed the amused expression on his face and realized how formal she'd been. Then she noticed the envelope on the table. "I take it that's the prenup."

"Yes."

"Hand it over." She held out her palm.

"In time. Let's have a drink." A waiter came forward and, after taking his wine order, departed. "We need to milk this." He inclined his head toward the window of the club dining room where several sets of eyes were watching them from inside.

She plastered a smile on her face. "Of course. I know how important appearances are."

His eyes narrowed. "Yes, they are. If you recall, that's one of the benefits of marriage *for me*."

She'd offended him, but it was too late to take it back now. "I'm well aware of the *mutual* benefits of this marriage. You don't have to remind me."

"Good."

The waiter returned with the wine and poured them each a glass. They both ordered the seafood entrée and the waiter left, giving them the privacy Gage craved.

Fallon didn't wait for a toast. She quickly took a long sip of her wine. She noticed Gage staring at her. "What?"

"Are you nervous?"

"Why would I be?" she asked tartly. "I'm just agreeing to bind myself to you, a man I hardly know, for the next six months."

"You didn't mind being with me last week." He drank some of his wine.

"How gentlemanly of you to remind me," Fallon answered. "We may not have a problem in that department, but I would have preferred it if we could have kept this strictly business."

"I'm sure you would," Gage responded, "but it's because of our *personal* connection the opportunity to save your company is even possible." He slid the envelope toward her. "You'll find everything is in order as per the changes requested by your attorney."

"You've already signed," Fallon commented as she flipped through the pages.

"I know what I want." The smoldering flame she saw in his eyes shouldn't have startled her, but it did. Fallon swallowed the frog in her throat.

"It appears in order. I should have my attorney review it one more time."

"That's a stalling tactic. Sign it, Fallon."

Her eyes flashed fire. "Don't bully me, Gage."

"We made the changes he requested, you can see for yourself. I want this settled between us." Gage sipped his wine again, watching her over the rim of his glass. "As you know, I don't have the full amount you need sitting in a bank account. I need time to make it happen. The sooner I get started, the better."

"You make it sound so easy. It's not." If she did this, there was no turning back. She would become Mrs. Gage Campbell and all that entailed, in and out of his bed. It was overwhelming. She sucked in a deep breath.

As if sensing her unease, Gage went in for the kill.

"If you don't sign, it's only a matter of time before you go belly-up. Think about all those lost jobs. It's a win-win for both of us, Fallon. Sign the document." Gage pulled a pen from the inside pocket of his suit jacket and handed it to her.

Fallon looked down at the pen in her hand for several beats. He was right. The sooner they got this over with, the better. Lives depended on her decision. She had to get the company back on its feet as soon as possible and Gage wouldn't turn over the money until Fallon walked down the aisle. Then, and only then, would Stewart Technologies be in the black.

Fallon scribbled her signature on several pages, slid the document into the envelope and handed it back to him.

"I imagine you should feel relieved," Gage commented.

"Not in the slightest." Her feelings for Gage were intensifying and now she'd agreed to marry him, to share his bed for six months. She feared for her heart because she could easily fall for him as she had in the past. And would he want her if she did? Gage had agreed to a temporary marriage of convenience. For him, they would be completing their unfinished history because, really, that's what this was. Somehow she would have to maintain her dignity.

"Be relieved," Gage suggested. "We're a team now. No matter how crazy life gets, you'll have me to rely on at least for the next six months."

"You make it sound so easy."

"There's no time for doubt or second-guessing, Fallon. It's done. Don't tell me you're not up for the challenge?"

"Of course I am," Fallon retorted.

Gage surprised her by reaching across the table, threading his fingers through hers and placing a kiss on them. "I promise you. We've got this."

Gage was on his way to the Stewart Technologies' barbecue the next Saturday to make an appearance as Fallon's fiancé. He was in the clear to attend because Henry had long since retired from coming to company functions, allowing Fallon to spearhead them. Now that the paperwork was signed, Gage felt like he was back in the driver's seat because he understood what was at stake. He doubted Fallon did.

She'd taken a calculated risk in accepting his offer without really understanding his motivations. His hatred of her family went deep. Deep enough he would do anything for revenge, including marrying the woman who'd started it all while secretly buying up shares of her company. Her apology for her actions had come a little too late in his opinion. For years all he could see was red and now he had the Stewart family right where he wanted them. Dependent on him.

My oh my, how the tables have turned, Gage thought as he pulled his Bugatti into a parking space at Mayfield Park. Stewart Technologies had rented the park for the company event, which would include food, games and prizes. He wore his favorite pair of faded designer jeans, a T-shirt and sneakers since they were experiencing a sort of Indian summer.

From the large cloud of smoke coming from several enormous grills and smokers, Gage could see the barbecue was already underway. There were large arrays of delicious fixings—including beans, macaroni and cheese, greens, potato salad and coleslaw—covering the large rectangular tables. At least two hundred people were milling around and getting involved in various activities. Men were on the football field while women played cards at a picnic table. Children tossed Frisbees or horseshoes. Quite an event to pull off for such a large group of people.

Gage was impressed by Fallon's managerial skills and her generosity, because Fallon was sponsoring the event from her personal finances. He found the lady of the hour passing out lemonade. It made his mouth water—not the delectable drink, but the outfit Fallon was wearing. She had on a crossover halter top showing off her sleek shoulders and buff arms while her cut-off jeans hugged her behind. Gage wanted to growl in protest because every man here could see what would soon be his.

Fallon turned around at that moment and saw him. She wiped perspiration off her brow. "Can you believe how warm it is today?" she said, smiling. "Would you like some lemonade?"

"I'd love some." He needed something to quench the desire that overtook him at seeing her half naked. She handed him a cup and he damn near guzzled the entire thing.

"Easy," she said, laughing. "You'll want to stay hydrated. Hey, Laura," she yelled to a woman standing nearby, "can you take over for me for a while?"

"Sure thing, boss."

Once Fallon came out from behind the table, he wasted no time circling her with his arm and giving her an open-mouthed kiss right in front of the entire table. When she pulled away she said, "What was that?"

"A proper hello."

She grinned and he allowed her some distance. "So, what do you think?" She motioned around the park. "Pretty awesome, huh?"

"You really know how to put on an event."

"Walk with me a minute." She surprised him by shoving her arm through his and leading him away from the group. Was it for his sake or their audience's? Because several people had watched their kiss. "I know you probably think we don't have the money for this, but morale has been at an all-time low. The employees heard rumors. They think we're going to fold. I want them to know we care."

"You mean *you* care," Gage corrected.

She gave him a sideward glance. "Yes, I do. Some of these people have been with us for years and have been loyal. I can't allow them to lose their livelihood."

"That's admirable."

Fallon snorted. "I know you think because of how I was raised I don't have a grasp on the plight of the everyday man, but I do, Gage."

She was right. He didn't think she understood, at least not entirely, but she was trying. "I can see that."

"Hey, you two lovebirds," a man wearing a T-shirt with

the company logo interrupted. "Would you like to join in? We have a friendly game of tug-of-war going."

Gage turned to Fallon. "You game?"

"Hell, yeah!"

And that's how they spent the afternoon, joined at the hip playing tug-of-war, hunting for treasure and tossing water balloons. The balloons were by far Gage's favorite activity of the day. He hadn't intended it to happen, but when he'd tossed Fallon a balloon, she hadn't caught it. Instead it exploded on her top and revealed her small round breasts to anyone with eyes. He'd immediately grabbed her by the arm and led her to a nearby tent being used as a diaper changing station for small children.

"What's wrong?" Fallon asked when she saw his thunderous expression.

He glanced down at her chest and she followed his eyes to see her nipples protruding through the thin material of her tank top. "Oh!" she exclaimed.

"Yes 'oh,'" he hissed. "Do you have a change of clothes? I can't have you out there looking like that."

She jutted her chin forward and with a smirk asked, "And why not?"

"Those are your employees out there." He pointed behind him. "I don't want the men ogling you."

"You mean, ogling what's yours?"

His eyes narrowed. "That's right, what's mine. Those—" he glanced down at her breasts "—are for my eyes only."

Color washed over her face and neck and Gage could see he'd gotten his point across. "If you were trying to seduce me, you win because," he said, taking a step toward her, "I'm willing to renegotiate our agreement to wait until we're married."

She bit her lip nervously and Gage caught the action. He wanted to soothe her lip with his tongue. But just then she reached inside her pocket and thrust her car keys at him. "I have a bag in the trunk with a change of clothes. Do you mind?"

He shook his head, eager to be out of the fog of desire he was in. "I'll be right back."

Fallon was contemplative after he'd gone. The naked hunger in Gage's eyes frightened her in its intensity because it mirrored her own. They were like two cats in heat, constantly circling one another. They couldn't be alone together. It wasn't a good idea.

Yet she'd enjoyed their day more than she thought she would. Gage was charming and engaging with all her employees. And there was more than one woman who'd given her an envious look throughout the course of the day. Fallon knew how lucky she was. Her eyes had drunk him in when he'd casually strolled to the lemonade stand earlier today. Tall. Good-looking. He looked sexy in his jeans and a T-shirt, with all that leashed testosterone. Fallon had to stop herself from drooling over him.

The games had been a welcome diversion from her riotous emotions and she'd been able to keep her feelings for Gage under wraps. But just now, when his intense dark eyes had landed on her breasts, she'd wanted to rip the damn tank off and beg him to take them in his mouth. That's how much she ached for his touch, for his mouth. Her body still remembered how he'd made her hum in the back seat of the limo.

Heavens. She needed to get a grip. He would be back any moment. He mustn't know the lustful thoughts going through her mind.

Gage returned several minutes later with her bag in tow. "Here you are."

"Thanks." She accepted the bag and rummaged through it, finding the extra tank she'd tossed in. She wanted to put it on, but Gage was staring at her. Awareness was burning in his eyes. "Do you mind turning around so I can put this on?"

"I've already seen it all before," he said, smiling.

"But you still have two more weeks to let the memory sustain you."

His eyes flashed but he spun on his heel, allowing her time to whip the tank over her head. "Damn the two weeks. If you would stop this madness, you and I could do what comes naturally instead of remaining in this constant state of arousal you have me in."

As Fallon adjusted her shirt, Gage's words sank in and she paused. *He was in a constant state of arousal?* It was news to her and she wondered if he'd meant to be so open with his *condition.*

Gage turned around then and caught Fallon in a half state of undress. His gaze met hers and held. Understanding passed between them, as loud and clear as church bells on a Sunday morning. Gage prowled toward her and Fallon sank into his arms. He ran his hands down her body, touching her in all the places she'd been thinking about, dreaming about. He adjusted his stance and shifted her until she was between his thighs and could feel the swell of his arousal at her core. Then he finally gave her what she wanted: his lips on hers.

Their mouths connected. They were hungrily kissing—deeper, harder and longer. Her arms clung tightly around his neck as she held his head in place, their lips meeting in a passion so strong it obliterated everything else. The world ceased to exist and their tongues tangoed and dueled for supremacy. They were both so caught up in the moment they didn't notice they had company until a very loud cough came from behind them.

Startled, they pulled apart and Gage stepped in front of her. It was one of her employees holding a baby in her arms. "I—I'm sorry. I didn't mean to interrupt. I needed to use the tent."

"Of course." Gage spoke up first. "Give us a moment, would you?"

The mother nodded and quickly hurried out.

"That was a close call," Gage said.

"Yeah." Fallon lowered her lashes. "We should go." She started for the exit but Gage stopped her.

"When we're finally together with no interruptions, it's going to be amazing."

And that's what Fallon was afraid of. Because she was starting to fall for Gage Campbell.

Nine

"When are you finally going to get excited about this wedding?" Nora Stewart asked her daughter as the limousine drove them to the bridal gown shop. "You do realize it's only a couple of weeks away? I can't believe you've pushed back getting a dress this long. You're going to have very little time for alterations. Thank God Gage said money was no object because it's going to cost a fortune to turn it around this fast."

"I know, Mother," Fallon said, clenching her teeth. The woman had been on a tirade since the moment they'd gotten in the vehicle, talking about flowers and centerpieces and the like. Fallon didn't care. It didn't mean anything because she wasn't marrying for love. This was an expedient marriage, a marriage of convenience. It wasn't some grand love story.

"Then act like it," her mother responded. "When we go into the bridal shop, you'd better act like the giddy bride. I won't have you embarrassing me with your somber mood."

"Duly noted." Fallon stared out the window. Heaven forbid she embarrass her mother in front of Austin's society ladies. She knew that's why Nora had chosen this particular store. It's where *everyone* went when they wanted a one-of-a-kind, jaw-dropping dress. And she was sure Nora wanted the same for her daughter.

When they arrived, they were immediately greeted by a sophisticated saleswoman. The blonde looked every bit the fashionista in a crepe sheath and Manolo Blahniks. She ushered them to a private area complete with a three-way mirror, pedestal and plush sofa. A bottle of Dom Pérignon was already chilling in a bucket nearby.

As her maid of honor, Shana was already waiting for them on the sofa. "Hey, cuz." She rushed over to give Fallon a hug and then glanced at Nora. "Auntie." Shana's new look consisted of kinky twists that hit her shoulders, a cold-shoulder top and ripped jeans. Fallon was sure her mother was horrified at her niece's appearance.

"Shana." Her mother was not a fan of Fallon's opinionated cousin and had no qualms about showing it. She left them to speak with the staff, allowing Shana to pull Fallon in for a private word.

"How are you doing, cuz?"

"I'm fine."

Shana stared at her. "Are you sure? You're marrying a man you hardly know. And you've allowed your mother to hijack the whole wedding like it's her own."

"It's fine," Fallon replied. "I told Nora she could plan to her heart's content."

"Because the wedding means nothing to you?" Shana asked. "It might not in theory, but it is legal and binding."

"I'm aware of that, Shana."

"I don't know if you are." Shana shook her head. "I think you're in way over your head on this one, Fallon. When I mentioned Gage to you, I thought you'd get a loan from him. Not go off and marry him."

Fallon shrugged. "What can I say? I like to live dangerously."

"Yeah, you must. Because Gage Campbell is dangerous to your well-being."

Fallon sighed. "You realize you sound ridiculous, Shana. Gage would never hurt me."

Shana folded her arms across her chest. "Maybe not physically, but he could emotionally. I know the huge crush you carried for this dude. Remember, I listened to you wax poetic about this man for years. And you're not like me, moving from man to man. Once you guys have sex, it's going to be a game changer."

"I may not have your vast experience, but I am capable of guarding my heart."

"You'd better be."

The saleswoman came over and interrupted their conversation. "Are you ready to find the dress of your dreams?"

Fallon feigned a smile. "Absolutely."

An hour later Fallon stood on the pedestal staring at herself in the three-way mirror. The wedding dress was everything she never thought she wanted. A shimmering tulle bodice accented in intricate beaded patterns trailed into a voluminous glitter tulle ball gown. Then there were the beaded spaghetti straps gliding from the sweetheart neckline to a sexy V-back with its crystal buttons.

The salesperson added another touch—illusion open-shoulder sleeves accented in beaded lace motifs—and the look was complete. Fallon was a princess.

"She's stunning," her mother cried from the sofa. "This is the one."

Nora had had Fallon try on nearly a dozen dresses before the beleaguered saleswoman had brought out this confection. Nora was right. This was *the one*.

"For once, I'm going to have to agree with Auntie," Shana said. "You've found your dress, Fallon. You look beautiful."

Fallon smiled genuinely for the first time all day. The wedding hadn't seemed real until this very moment. Until she was standing in this fairy-tale gown.

"Are you saying yes to the dress?" the saleswoman asked.

Tears sprung to her eyes and all Fallon could do was nod. She was just so overwhelmed and remained that way during the ride home as she tuned out her mother's non-stop chatter about how the dress would look lovely with the flowers she'd chosen. She was getting married. To Gage. Suddenly, Fallon wanted out of the limo as quickly as humanly possible. She was thankful when her mother exited after a quick kiss on her cheek.

Once she made it to her cottage, she went to her bedroom and fell across the bed. It was happening. She was going to be a wife. Gage's wife. His *lover.*

The implications were finally hitting home when her cell rang. It was Gage, as if he had ESP.

"Hello?" she answered.

"Hey, how'd it go today? Did you find a dress?"

"Yes."

He chuckled. "Are you not going to give me any more than that? No hint? Nothing?"

"I'm sorry. You're going to have to wait until the wedding day."

"Thank God that's only two weeks away. This is the longest month of my life. All the anticipation is driving me crazy."

Fallon sat upright. "Really?"

"Isn't it for you? Aren't you tired of waiting? Don't you want to know if we'll live up to the hype?"

"From what I've experienced thus far, I imagine you're

a very good lover," Fallon responded, priding herself on keeping her cool as they discussed their soon-to-be sex life with such casualness.

"I wasn't looking for a compliment," Gage murmured.

"Of course not." Fallon was sure he was very confident in his sexual prowess.

"But I would be lying if I said I wasn't looking forward to the day when you're my wife in every sense of the word."

When they ended the call, Fallon realized she was thinking the exact same thing.

The day of their wedding came much quicker than Fallon would have liked. It seemed as if she'd been trying on dresses with her mother and Shana only yesterday. But the day was finally here and she was a nervous wreck.

She woke up that morning in the Fairmont—where the wedding was being held—with a knot in the pit of her stomach. *Was she doing the right thing?* Logically, she knew that she'd done what she'd had to. Stewart Technologies and its employees depended on her making the right decision. Yet intuitively she knew today would change everything.

"Good morning." Her mother flitted into the room with a tray. "I've come bearing gifts." She approached Fallon and put the tray on the bed. "I have some tea and toast for you. Don't want you to bloat. And some cucumber slices for your eyes." She glanced at Fallon. "You did get some rest last night?"

Fallon nodded but she was lying. It had been hard to sleep. She'd been on pins and needles during the rehearsal dinner, afraid of some sort of outburst. How could she not be? Gage's mother had had to face her parents, the people who'd fired her and run her off the estate. Grace couldn't be happy her son was marrying the daughter of the man she surely despised. It was awkward to say the least.

Nonetheless, Nora acted as if it was water under the bridge and carried on as lady of the manor as she always did on such occasions. And if Fallon had wanted to confide in her cousin, that had been impossible because Shana had kept a steady drink in her hand all night while flirting with Theo, Gage's best man.

As for her fiancé, Gage had been surprisingly stalwart all evening. He'd kept his hands to himself the entire night and only showed signs of affection when he thought someone was watching. He wasn't his usual amorous self and it didn't help her mood. When the night finally ended, Gage had walked her to her suite and placed a quick peck on her forehead before leaving.

Was he regretting asking her to marry him?

Was that why she was having second thoughts this morning?

Fallon attempted to eat the toast, but it tasted dry in her mouth so she sipped on some tea while she slipped into her robe. One of Austin's top hair stylists and makeup artists would be here within the hour to begin working on Shana's, Nora's and Fallon's makeup for the big day. She wouldn't have much time to herself after that.

A knock sounded on the door and Shana walked in wearing sunglasses. "Rough morning?" Fallon asked.

"Yeah, you could say that," Shana murmured, snatching off her glasses. "How are you doing?"

"I'm fine." Fallon turned her back so her cousin couldn't read her true emotions. She busied herself with pulling out the new lingerie she'd purchased for the day. She was sure Gage would appreciate the silky, lacy pieces of fabric when he unbuttoned her.

"Fallon, are you sure?" Shana asked, touching her shoulder. "You don't have to do this. There's still time to change your mind."

"It's normal to have second thoughts," her mother interjected, apparently having overheard their conversation. "I had them when I married your father, but ultimately I knew I was making the right decision. And you are, too, Fallon. You're going to have an amazing life. With a husband as successful as Gage, anything you want will be at your fingertips."

"I thought you didn't like him," Fallon responded evenly.

Her mother chuckled. "I admit he isn't the man I would have chosen for you. But surprisingly he's done quite well for himself, so I have no reservations. Though I doubt Grace agrees. Did you see the evil eye she gave me last night? It was positively wretched."

Of course Nora would take Fallon's wedding day anxiety and make it about her. "Thank you, Mother. Now, if you'll excuse me, I'm going to shower before the dream team arrives."

Fallon quickly rushed off before Shana could say more. Too many thoughts were whirling through her head and she needed some breathing room.

"Are you sure you want to marry her, son?" Grace Campbell asked as she fixed Gage's tie and straightened the lapels of his custom-made tuxedo.

He was surprised she'd come. He thought she'd boycott the ceremony altogether, but she was here supporting him, so he tried to be gentle in his response. "We've already discussed this, Mother. I have my reasons." *Did she notice he hadn't said love?*

She eyed him warily. "I don't know, Gage. I feel like you're not being truthful with me and there's more to this story. I mean, you tell me you're getting married to the woman who caused us so much misery?"

"She was sixteen when it happened, Mama."

"True, but old enough to know right from wrong, Gage.

And she willfully lied about you and cost me my job. Have you honestly forgotten how hard it was for us back then?"

"Of course not."

"Then how can you do this?" She folded her arms across her chest, waiting for his answer.

"Trust me, okay, Mama?" He unfolded her arms and grasped her small hands in his. They weren't as pitiful and worn with cracks and calluses as they'd once been. When he'd made his first million, he'd made sure his mother never had to work another day in her life. "I know what I'm doing."

"I hope you do. Because if this is about revenge, it won't change the past. We have to make our peace with it. And apparently I have to make mine today as I make nice with the Stewarts and watch my only son marry their daughter."

"I don't know if I will ever be at peace after how you and I were both treated, but I've put some measures in place that will settle the score between our families." Theo walked in, breaking up their mother-son moment. "A word, Gage."

Gage nodded. "Be right back, Mama." He left her in the suite and closed the door behind him because he didn't like the look on Theo's face. "What's wrong?"

"I ran into Shana in the corridor."

"And?"

"She mentioned Fallon was having second thoughts."

"Second thoughts?" Anger blazed through him. "On our wedding day? Fallon had weeks to change her mind. Does she honestly think she can humiliate me and leave me standing at the altar? Where is she?"

"Gage." Theo placed a sobering hand on his arm. "Maybe it's best if you take a minute to cool down."

Gage shrugged his hand off. "Like hell I will. I will not be made a fool of again."

"I'm told she's still in her suite."

Gage wasted no time storming toward the elevator bank.

He and Fallon were staying on separate floors to prevent him from seeing her before the ceremony. But he couldn't care less about some stupid superstition. He was acting now. He jabbed the elevator button for the top floor and waited.

His nostrils flared when he thought about Fallon backing out. He simply wouldn't have it. She *would* marry him. He would not have his plans thwarted, not when he was so close.

The elevator arrived and he jumped in. Within minutes, he was knocking on her door. Shana answered and he must have looked thunderous because she immediately backed away. "Where is she?" Gage bellowed.

Shana pointed to the bedroom.

He stalked to the master bedroom and found Fallon seated in front of the mirror with several women surrounding her. She must have heard his voice because she turned and looked behind her. Her face blanched when she saw him.

"It's not good luck for you to see the bride," one of the women objected. But he didn't see them. His focus was on Fallon.

"Leave us," he ordered.

The women glanced at Fallon and she nodded her acquiescence, so they left the room, closing the door behind them.

Damn it. She was stunning with her hair in a mass of pinned-up honey-blond curls. And her face? Well, that was a work of art. Whoever those women were, they knew how to accentuate her best features—her high cheekbones, hazel-gray eyes and pouty lips.

"Are you having second thoughts?" he asked, his eyes never leaving her face. He was afraid to move closer because he feared he'd toss her on the bed and strip her naked and make her agree to be his.

She stared at him for several beats and he wondered if

she was going to be stubborn and not answer him. "Yes," she finally replied.

"Then perhaps this will make you reconsider." He pulled out the check he was giving her to save Stewart Technologies and handed it to her.

Fallon stared down at the figure. "I—I thought you weren't giving this to me until we were married."

"I'm not. I'm showing you I've kept up my end of the bargain. In my hands I have the means to save your company from ruin. Are you honestly going to turn your back on the men and women at the barbecue who depend on you, all because you're afraid to be my wife, my lover? You told me you cared about them and their well-being."

Fire flashed in her eyes. "That's not fair. I do care."

"Then prove it. Marry me."

Fallon turned and faced the mirror. He approached to stand right behind her where he could see her reaction. Her eyes were cloudy and he couldn't read her expression. "Fallon, you have a choice. You've always had a choice. Save your company. Or not. The decision is yours."

He turned on his heel and started for the door but she called out after him. "What are you going to do?"

Gage didn't turn around. "I'm going to walk down that aisle as I expect you to." He glanced at his watch. "In an hour."

Gage left the suite. Once he was outside, he leaned against the wall. He didn't know what he was more afraid of. That Fallon wouldn't walk down the aisle. Or that she would.

Ten

"Are you okay?" Fallon heard Shana's voice from behind her. Her hands were shaking so badly she had to clasp them together. She nodded quickly and then felt her cousin's arms wrap around her shoulders. "What did he say?"

"Nothing I didn't already know." She knew what she had to do, but it didn't make it easy. To survive marrying Gage, she'd have to bury her feelings so deep he wouldn't be able to use them against her. She took a deep breath. "Will you help me get into my dress, please?" She spun around and faced Shana.

The look of pity on Shana's face was nearly her undoing but she kept it together. "Yes, I will. If that's what you want."

"I do." Fallon moved toward the elegant princess dress hanging in the closet and pulled it off the hanger. "It's time."

Fallon didn't remember much else after that. Not removing her robe. Not Shana buttoning her into the delicate beaded fabric of her dress. Not her mother bursting in with the flowers, handing Fallon her bouquet and helping put on her veil. The next thing Fallon knew, she was in the elevator with Shana, her mother and the wedding planner, who held her train.

It was only when she was walking down the corridor and saw her father standing resplendent in a formal white tuxedo that she snapped out of it. He slid his arm through hers and looked down at her. “You’ve never looked lovelier, baby girl. Are you ready to do this?”

She nodded. And slowly the doors to the ballroom opened and they were walking down the aisle.

Fallon saw Gage standing at the end, waiting for her. He looked sinfully handsome, just as he had earlier when he’d walked into her bedroom and taken her breath away. He hadn’t needed to show her the check. Although she’d had doubts earlier, she’d gotten through them and had already planned to marry him. But seeing how upset Gage was that she might back out showed her this marriage meant something to him whether he was willing to admit it or not.

Or at least that’s the lie she fed herself as she made her way up the aisle to him. When she arrived at the altar, her father placed her hand in Gage’s and her breath caught in her throat. He rewarded her with a smile, which she returned.

She could do this. Would do this. Why? Because Gage meant more to her than she was willing to admit.

Gage had never been happier than when he saw Fallon walking down in the aisle in that magnificent dress. He was glad he hadn’t seen her wearing it earlier and they could retain some tradition because, quite literally, she was breathtaking. He found himself having to truly listen to the minister’s words to be able to repeat the traditional vows to love, protect, honor and cherish her.

He sensed Fallon was nervous because her hands were

shaking as he placed the ring on her finger and she did the same to him. But she didn't back out. She honored her commitment to him and when they were pronounced husband and wife, Gage was beyond ecstatic. He slid his arm around her petite waist and pulled her to him. Then he softly kissed her before pulling away. They'd have all the time in the world later in the presidential suite when he would finally make Fallon his.

The reception was a blur. There were handshakes and hugs from friends, acquaintances and employees who were there to celebrate their wedding. There were frowns from Fallon's parents and Ayden, who were both there on sufferance. Ayden had only stayed for the wedding and stood in the shadows while her younger brother, Dane, chose to not attend at all. He only remembered the moments when it was the two of them.

Nora had transformed the ballroom into a winter fairyland. Crystal chandeliers hung from the ceilings, illuminating an explosion of beautiful white flowers. Frosted trees, sparkling crystal garlands and candles were everywhere. Nora had decorated each table in white and silver while their sweetheart table had two thronelike chairs.

For their first dance Gage held Fallon in his arms and she felt so good, but delicate in a way he couldn't quite put his finger on. Then there was the cake cutting. Rather than use a fork, he'd used his fingers to feed Fallon a piece. She'd been shocked at first, but had opened her mouth and accepted it, wiping his fingers clean with her tongue. It had been the most singularly erotic moment of his life.

He was thankful when the night began winding down. He made quite the show of going underneath Fallon's dress to get her garter, which Theo caught while her cousin Shana caught Fallon's bouquet. Gage sure hoped there wasn't a love connection there. He doubted Theo could handle Shana; she was a whole lot of woman.

Finally the night was over and he and Fallon were able to escape the ballroom to head upstairs as they were sent off with bubbles and well-wishes. They were led to an elevator exclusively for their getaway. Gage took her hand but it was a bit cold and clammy.

"Are you all right?"

"Yes."

"You haven't given me much tonight, Fallon," Gage said. "You've been quiet. Reserved, even."

"I kept up my end of the bargain, yes?" She turned away from him and Gage didn't like it.

"About earlier—"

"You made your point," Fallon interrupted, looking straight ahead. "And I heard you, okay? The day was a bit…overwhelming."

He squeezed her hand and she finally glanced in his direction. "It was for me, as well. I'm sorry, too, if I came across a bit…" He searched for the right word. "Rough. I always seem to be that way with you. Can we agree to put it behind us?" He needed things between them to be okay, because he was so ready to start their life together *in bed.*

She gave a hesitant smile. "Yes."

The presidential suite was a honeymooner's paradise complete with chocolate-covered strawberries, a bucket of champagne chilling in the living room and a trail of red rose petals leading to the master bedroom. Dozens of candles gave the room a romantic glow. Fallon stared at the enormous bed, picked up her train and came back into the living room. She wasn't ready to face the night ahead.

Once Fallon entered the room, Gage held up the bottle. "Care for champagne?"

"I'd love some." Fallon needed liquid courage for what was ahead. She didn't know how not to show her true feelings because her heart was involved now. Her whole heart.

Somehow she'd tripped into a state of love without knowing it and she knew with certainty Gage could break her heart. Because for Gage tonight was all about desire. Sexual desire. And she felt it, too. This raw, carnal, all-consuming lust. It was why she was so out of control whenever they were together. Even now her stomach was pulled tight in knots wondering what it would be like to *be* with him.

Gage made Fallon aware of her own body and she knew before the night was over he would become familiar with every inch of it. Of that she was sure. It was in the flare of his eyes as they drifted over her. He handed her a flute of champagne. She accepted and downed the entire glass in one gulp.

"There's no need to be nervous, Fallon," Gage assured her as he sat on the couch. "We have all night. There's no rush. Come here." He patted the seat next to him.

At first Fallon didn't move a muscle but when he gave her an imploring look, she relented and sat. "This feels a little surreal."

Gage reached for her hand and turned it over. When he did, the impressive six-carat diamond ring he'd purchased caught the light. He fingered it with his thumb. "I would disagree. It feels very real."

He cupped her face in one hand. "Is it really so scary to be married to me, Fallon?" His thumb swept across her lips, making her flesh tingle.

"I'm not scared," Fallon responded. "I made a choice and I stand behind it."

Gage straightened. "I'm glad. I would hate for you to regret the time we spend together."

Fallon had her doubts about the marriage but not about the pleasure she would find in Gage's arms. Leaning forward, his lips found hers. It wasn't a tentative kiss, nor was it a kiss meant to entice. The touch of his mouth was soft, yet it shot volts of electricity right through Fallon and she wanted more. When he lowered his head again it wasn't to her closed mouth—she'd already parted her lips. She gave in to his hungry mouth. Her hands moved to his chest and upward to link her arms around his neck to bring him closer, but Gage pulled away.

She didn't understand. "What's wrong?"

"I promised you we'd take this slow…"

Fallon rose and held out her hand. "I don't want it slow."

His dark eyes landed on hers and Fallon's breath caught in her throat. Slowly and seductively his gaze traveled over her face, searching her eyes. For doubt? He wouldn't find any. They were married and it was time. Gage must have seen her acceptance because he was on his feet within seconds and they were walking to the bedroom.

They stopped at the foot of the bed. Fallon felt Gage's hands on the back of her dress as he unbuttoned each crystal button until eventually she felt a cold gust of air against her back. Then Gage's fingers were on her shoulders, easing down the sheer gossamer straps until the dress fell to her waist.

She felt his mouth pressing soft kisses on her shoulder and tried to steady herself, but a dizzying current of attraction raced through her as he wet her neck with his tongue. He used his fingers to caress, tease and stroke her bare breasts. There hadn't been a need for a bra because it came built-in. She was naked and completely open to Gage, her husband. His palms cupped her aching breasts and when he skated his thumbs across her engorged nipples, she let out a low moan.

"You're so sensitive," he rasped and continued brushing his thumbs over her breasts. Fallon closed her eyes, allowing her head to fall back against the wall of his chest. Gage held her to him, pressing her hard against him and leaned down, rewarding her with a deep kiss, which merely increased their mounting desire. She spun around to face him.

"Tell me what you want," Gage rasped.

"I want you." To prove it she stepped out of the flowing dress, letting it pool at her feet until she was standing in nothing but her thong and bejeweled high heels.

"God, you're beautiful!" Before she could react, he sank to his knees in front of her and moved his hands to her hips until he arrived at her inner thighs.

"What are you doing?"

"Tasting you." He slid his finger along the edge of her lace thong and Fallon hissed out a breath. He pushed the fabric aside and his thumb traced along her cleft. Fallon jerked when his fingers delved and began gently exploring her inner folds. He lifted his head to look at her and smiled. "Hot *and* wet."

She was consumed with heat and when he slid one finger inside her, she shuddered. "Oh." But there was more to come, because he slowly withdrew it, only to add another finger. Meanwhile his thumb was working her clitoris. Pleasure was building, taking her to a fever pitch, making her want to whisper his name like some sort of mantra. "Gage, please—"

He wasn't listening, he merely plunged his fingers deeper inside her, filling her. "You like that?"

"Yes," she implored when he repeated the action, "but I—I need more."

"Like what?"

"Your mouth. I need your mouth on me." Fallon was embarrassed to say it out loud. She'd never been so vocal with her desires, but if she couldn't tell her husband, who could she tell?

Gage gripped her hips and within seconds had deposited her on the bed and disposed of her thong. Fallon shamelessly spread her legs and watched as he cupped her bottom and then raked her with his tongue. She arched off the bed, but Gage held her firm. His hands were against her pelvis, spreading her legs wide so his tongue could work her over and over again with such sensuous abandon that Fallon squirmed, begging him to end it.

He merely laughed and continued flicking his tongue over her core, laving her with deliberate yet feather-light movements. He had her wound so tight, she was aching for him to relieve the pressure building inside her. And when he circled her clitoris with his tongue while simultaneously pumping his fingers deep inside her, a scream rang out from deep within her.

"Omigod!" Fallon pressed her hands to her face, but Gage refused to allow her to hide.

Instead he crawled up her body and gave her an open-mouthed kiss. It was heady and erotic because she could taste herself on his lips.

"Don't hide. I want to see your face. I want to know you're enjoying our lovemaking."

Eventually, when her breathing returned, she smiled. "Don't you think you're wearing too many clothes?" She was naked while he was fully clothed save for the jacket and tie he'd discarded when they'd walked in.

"Indeed, I am, Mrs. Campbell. Care to help me with that?"

Gage sat upright and watched Fallon as she excitedly attacked the buttons on his shirt. When they didn't unbutton fast enough, she ripped it open and buttons went flying. He liked that she was as desperate and eager as he was for their union. The anticipation was heightened by the fact they'd waited a month—hell, years—to get here and he supposed that's why it felt so momentous. He was making love to his *wife*.

Fallon was his. There was no escaping it. She'd signed her name on the marriage certificate, sealing her fate. Because tonight he intended to possess her. Over and over again until they were both spent.

As she pulled the shirt down his shoulders and he shrugged it off his arms, Gage felt like a king. He moved off the bed long enough to strip off his pants and boxers and then, naked, he joined her on the bed. He reached for one of her feet that were still encased in her bejeweled shoes. "These are incredible," he said with a grin as he unbuckled the ankle straps.

"And they cost a fortune," Fallon responded as he removed one and then the other. He took the pins out from the elaborate updo and ran his fingers through the mass of honey-blond hair.

Finally he could feast his eyes on her with no barriers. And he certainly looked his fill, from her round breasts to her slim waist to her flat stomach to the curve of her hips, before ending his tour with the patch of dark curls between her thighs. He wanted to reach out and touch her, but Fallon took over. She pushed him back against the pillows and straddled him. Her silky-soft hair slid onto his chest as their mouths fused together, tongues tangling in heated lust. Gage dragged his head back; he wanted to look at her. Her eyes were wide and dilated while her lips were parted and swollen. His need for her grew exponentially and he reached for her again, this time putting his mouth on one of her full, round breasts. His tongue swirled around her nipple, which tightened and puckered. She threw back her head in abandon so he took his time worshipping the bud and then paid homage to its twin with his mouth and tongue.

"Hmm...no fair," she murmured when he finally lifted his head. "I'm on top. I'm supposed to be in charge."

"Oh, but you are," Gage said as his fingers moved between them to slip through her slick folds. He dipped inside and found her as wet as when he'd made her come earlier. It was time. He was throbbing with a need to be inside her and now there was no need for protection. Last week, Fallon had asked whether he'd been tested. It was a fair question given they were becoming lovers and he'd answered honestly that he was clean. She'd shared the same news and they'd agreed she would be on the pill. Gage was happy because there would be no barriers between them. Just two people sharing the most sensuous of acts.

He grasped her hips and lifted her so the wide tip of his erection nudged at the entrance to her hot, damp flesh. She gasped, but he held her firm as she took him deep inside her. He loved the way her tight core clenched around his thick, hard, pulsating length, but he wanted more. He thrust his hips upward in one savage thrust and impaled her.

"Oh, God!" Fallon moaned, resting her palms on his chest. Her eyes were closed and he couldn't read her expression no matter how badly he wanted to.

"Look at me, baby," Gage urged and, when she did, he caught the passion in those hazel-gray depths and knew this was more than sex.

Fallon moved, lifting off him and then coming back down again. Over and over. She eased off and down onto him. Gage was blind with lust, gripping her hips and urging her on, but Fallon was in control, undulating against him, finding her own rhythm. He met her by pumping his hips up as his entire body stirred to life. He reached for her, his tongue raking her lips, demanding entry, and she parted for him. Gage thrust deep inside her mouth, mimicking the movements of their lower bodies. He heard Fallon's breath hitch and could feel her body tensing as if she was poised on the abyss. He wanted them to go over the cliff together so his thrusts became deeper, harder and more animalistic in nature.

Fallon moaned when he cupped her buttocks, so he drove harder until soon her body was clenching around him and pushing them both over the edge as he found his release.

Gage growled as the world righted itself and Fallon quivered over him, slumping against him. He'd suspected but hadn't been prepared for how sexually compatible they were. He was already feeling a resurgence of desire after being completely satisfied moments ago. The voracious hunger he had for her couldn't last, right? Because if it did, it would derail all of his best laid plans.

Eleven

Fallon woke with a start. Sunshine was streaming through the sheer curtains.

She'd succumbed to every illicit sensation Gage evoked throughout the course of the night. She wanted everything he had to offer. Gage understood and matched her in his unparalleled desire. Not once, not twice, but three times last night, their coupling had been wild and erotic. At one point he'd lifted her legs to his shoulders and she'd arched into him as he'd pumped into her, hard and fast, until she'd panted out his name.

Fallon hadn't known sex could be that good, that she could literally burn up with wanting for a man. But it was what Gage brought out in her. And that scared her because although it was thrilling, Fallon knew loving Gage was dangerous. They were in a temporary marriage of convenience, one that allowed them to both get what they wanted, though Fallon still didn't understand what she'd brought to the table. Status? Acceptance into Austin society? She would have given up her status in a heartbeat to have Gage fall in love with her.

Her husband stirred beside her. “Good morning,” he slurred with eyes half open. “What are you doing up? Did I not wear you out last night?” When she didn’t respond right away, he continued. “Then I didn’t fulfill my husbandly duties.”

Gage rolled over, positioning himself above her. “Gage…” she sighed as molten heat formed in her core.

“Hmm…don’t worry. I’ll be gentle.” Slowly he nudged her entrance with his shaft, all the while looking straight at her. There was no hiding behind a façade. Fallon had no choice but to stare into his intense eyes as he thrust deep inside her.

There was a fierce need for possession in his eyes and Fallon was surprised by the depth of emotion she saw there. *Did Gage care for her more than she thought?* Fallon couldn’t say because he gave her no reprieve. Instead he continued his merciless assault, molding her closer, pressing their bodies together so he could go deeper. Take her higher. Urgency expanded within her until Fallon’s entire body erupted and she saw stars.

She struggled not to give away too much with her expression, but Gage surged inside her again and again and the delicious friction of their bodies caused her to come apart. She clutched at his biceps as another orgasm overtook her. Gage groaned in her ear and she tasted his passion as his tongue pressed past her lips to caress and stroke hers.

When he collapsed on top of her, his breathing slowly began to even out. Then he shifted to his side and relieved her of his weight. Fallon stroked his cheek and traced his mouth with her fingers. The uncontrollable lust and hunger for Gage was like nothing she’d ever known. This man was burrowing into her soul.

“Are you all right?” he asked, searching her face.

"Yes."

He touched the bridge of her nose. "But you're pensive. I can see the thoughts whirling around in your brain. Let them go, Fallon, and be present in the moment with me."

"I am."

"You're thinking about later and what comes next. About why it's so good between us. Isn't it enough that it is? Can't we enjoy each other?"

Until it peters out, Fallon wanted to add but didn't. She nodded.

"Good." Gage smiled.

Gage stared at Fallon from his poolside seat at the luxury resort in Punta Cana where they were staying for their honeymoon. He couldn't resist watching her every move as she made her way to him. His wife was a knockout. She wore a halter-style bikini held together by rings in the center of her bust and along the sides of her slim hips. It did wonders for her cleavage. Her round, pert breasts were pushed up and enhanced for the entire world to see. Although she'd wrapped a sarong around her waist, Gage knew men were looking.

The last several days they'd been soaking in the sun and swimming in the private pool of their beachside villa. Fallon had teased him he was keeping her naked and barefoot. They'd hardly left the villa except for a romantic candlelit dinner he'd arranged on the beach upon their arrival and the one day they'd spent sightseeing and snorkeling. Today they'd finally ventured out to the main building and now Gage wished they were in their private world again. He didn't like men wanting what was his. Because Fallon was *his*.

They'd been together in every possible position. He was very imaginative and Fallon had been enthusiastic about all of his ideas, adding a few of her own that had him begging and pleading with her for more. Her soft cries of delight, her hungry moans as their bodies moved faster and came together in mind-blowing release, were overwhelming. When it came to his wife, Gage was insatiable. But it was more than that. He'd thought that once they became intimate, his ache for her would go away. Instead it seemed to have metastasized and he was incapable of controlling himself. He wanted her all the time, but their marriage had an expiration date.

At least that was the verbal agreement they had. At the time, Gage hadn't seen a problem. He assumed he'd be ready to move on when the hunger and passion subsided. Plus, he had a plan in place to take over Stewart Technologies once he had enough stock. He'd already purchased a substantial amount on the open market with his holding companies. Now it was a matter of finding those investors who were eager to sell.

Gage tried not to think about how this would affect Fallon. He couldn't. Business was business. What they shared was something altogether different. Something that was just between them. Special, even.

"I arranged for our massages on the beach," Fallon said as they retreated to the loungers in their private cabana.

"Sounds marvelous." Gage eyed her as she removed the sarong from around her slim waist to reveal the barely there bikini that covered her curvy bottom and the patch of curls between her thighs. Thinking about when he'd been buried there this morning had his penis stiffening in his swim shorts.

Fallon reached for her drink, a fruity concoction inside a pineapple. He'd opted for a beer. "I had to do something. Otherwise, we'd never enjoy any of the resort's luxurious amenities."

"I have all I want right here." His eyes scanned hers. She blushed as she always did when he talked about their lovemaking. Over the course of the last four days, he'd made it his mission in life to help her shed her inhibitions. They'd made love in the shower, pool, hot tub, even on the beach near their villa. That had taken a little more coaxing, but once his hands and mouth had been on her, Fallon had given in and allowed him to have his way with her.

He smiled at the memory.

"What's so funny?" she inquired.

"Just remembering the other night on the beach."

Fallon's face flamed.

"And hoping for a repeat."

"You're terrible, Gage. And that's not going to happen. We could have been caught. If anyone had found us, I would have been so embarrassed."

"Trust me, babe. We weren't the only ones out there," he replied. "This is an adults-only resort, known for honeymooners and anniversaries."

Fallon shrugged, placed her pineapple on the table between the loungers and eased back. "We'll leave them to their shenanigans. I prefer the privacy of our villa."

"And where's the fun in that?"

Their butler, James, came to the cabana, interrupting the moment. "Mr. and Mrs. Campbell, can I get you anything? Another refreshment, perhaps?" He nodded to their drinks on the table. "Or a light snack?"

"I would love some fresh fruit," Fallon said. "And maybe some cheese and crackers?"

"Another beer for me," Gage answered.

Once James departed, Gage turned to Fallon. "I have a very special evening planned for our last night here."

"I can't believe the honeymoon is nearly over. Why did we only give ourselves five days?"

"Because someone—" he glanced in her direction "—is a workaholic and refused to take the entire week. But don't you worry, I will make tonight unforgettable."

* * *

Gage made certain the evening was beyond Fallon's wildest imagination. After their afternoon massages, they'd gone back to the room where her husband had turned showering into an erotic experience. He'd thoroughly soaped and washed her body with his hands before falling to the floor in the oversize super shower and loving her with his mouth. Then he'd hoisted her off her feet and made passionate love to her against the tiled wall while water pounded on his back. Fallon had melted into a sea of lust as she did whenever she was around him. His every touch, kiss and possession caused an inferno of passion to consume her.

Eventually they'd left their villa and ended up on a yacht for a sunset cruise Gage had arranged. It took them around the island while they enjoyed a four-course meal prepared by a private chef in the state-of-the-art kitchen belowdecks. The captain had given them a tour of the yacht's modern amenities when they'd come aboard; it had a kitchen, living area, dining room, two guest bedrooms and a master suite complete with a king-size bed and full-size master bathroom.

Now they were on the deck, lying on the plush recliners and stargazing while drinking Cristal. Fallon had chosen to wear a simple color-blocked maxi dress in deep orange, navy and white, pairing it with low-heeled white sandals. It was nautical and comfortable. Gage had opted for linen trousers and some sort of tunic shirt he'd picked up during their one and only sightseeing trip. But all she could see when she closed her eyes were those broad shoulders, chiseled eight-pack abs and trim waist.

Fallon felt fulfilled in Gage's arms. For the first time in her life, she was beginning to understand the addiction to sex. It hadn't even been a week and she wanted Gage with a pride-destroying hunger. She, who had never *needed* anyone, needed him.

Which was why Fallon was looking forward to flying home tomorrow. Life would go back to normal after the craziness of the wedding and honeymoon. She would dive back into work immediately. She had some thoughts on paring down the staff by retiring some of her father's old friends and bringing in new talent who were forward thinking.

"Penny for your thoughts?" Gage inquired.

"I'm thinking about going home."

Gage frowned. "I didn't realize spending 24/7 with me was such a chore."

Their eyes met.

"Of course not. I've enjoyed our time together."

"But you're ready to get back to work?" Gage finished.

Fallon shrugged. "There's much to be done to get Stewart Technologies back on track. I'll be very busy."

"Is that your subtle way of telling me that you'll be too busy or too tired to fulfill your wifely duties? Because that's not going to fly."

"No… I—" Fallon wasn't able to utter another word because Gage's long body came up and over hers, crushing her against the lounger as his heavy, muscular legs slid on either side of the thin fabric of her dress, caging her in. Her head fell back as Gage gave her a fierce, demanding kiss, plundering her mouth with his invading tongue. He was like a marauder, taking what he wanted.

She felt the weight of one of his palms at her ankles as he slid the maxi dress up her thigh.

"Gage, wait!" Fallon stopped his hand. "What about the staff?"

"They've all retired for the evening, per my instructions." Then he was underneath the hem, his hands searing every inch of her skin. Instinctively, she pressed herself further into his touch. Their bodies shifted and she was able to feel the hardness of his erection against her core. Fallon was needy and hungry—for him and no one else. His body was like a drug. When he touched her, what little was left of her functioning brain gave way to pure lust and all rational thought fled her body.

He lifted his mouth to trail kisses along her face and jaw, murmuring, "I had better get my fill now."

And so had she.

She feverishly tugged at his shirt. He had too many clothes on. Within seconds, he'd pulled it up and over his head. Electricity buzzed when she felt the crisp brush of his chest hair on her fingertips. She lowered her head and pressed her lips against the wall of his chest, tasting and tantalizing him with no restraint.

"Fallon..."

She liked how his voice was rough and raw with emotion, so she continued her ministrations. But Gage stopped her. Clenching his hands in her hair, he pulled her away so he could crush his mouth against hers in a hungry kiss turned sensual dance. She felt his urgent hands at her waist as he levered himself away long enough to remove the maxi dress and leave her naked save for the thong she'd been wearing. She'd taken to going braless the entire honeymoon.

"I want you so bad," he growled and cupped her breasts, teasing them into aroused peaks with swirls and flicks of his tongue and nips of his teeth.

"Me, too." She clenched her hands around the corded muscles of his biceps. The man had a wicked way with his tongue. She arched against his invasion, all the while feeling the hot moisture of need between her thighs that only he could assuage. She began shoving his trousers and his underwear down his legs. He stood long enough to rid himself of the offending garments before they were back together on the lounger.

"This has to go," he said and gave her thong a gentle tug, snapping the fabric asunder.

That was fine with Fallon; she didn't care about restraint. She wanted him right here, right now—regardless of who might find them. This is what he'd done to her: he'd made her a mass of need. His hands slid between them to brush the damp curls between her thighs. She was already wet and he easily slid not one but two fingers inside her. She encouraged him by moving with his hand. She was so desperate to come, but he didn't let her.

"I want to come with you," he murmured, removing his hands. His legs came between hers, nudging them apart. She spread her legs wider, inviting him in, and he surged inside her in one powerful movement.

Fallon let out a sharp, keening cry of delight and her arms went around his neck as she brought his mouth back down to hers. She was on fire. He pushed in again then withdrew. Fallon wanted to cry out in protest but he surged in further, deeper, than he had before. She wrapped her thighs around him and reveled in the way Gage took her higher, again and again, until there was only them, as connected as two people could be. Fallon arched her hips when he angled himself so he could take her harder and faster. The storm built, swirling until there was nowhere else to go but over the edge. Simultaneously they tumbled into ecstasy and cried out their release.

And Fallon knew, as she'd known for days, that somewhere along the line, passion had developed into love.

Twelve

After realizing the depth of her feelings for her husband in Punta Cana, Fallon hoped returning to Austin would give her peace. It didn't. The time they'd spent together during the honeymoon had been a revelation. Her husband wasn't the arrogant, bossy alpha male she'd thought she knew. Instead he'd been relaxed and easygoing, as if a weight had been lifted off his shoulders. And in bed he'd been a passionate yet tender and giving lover.

She was just as crazy about Gage as she'd been before except now, a month after the honeymoon, she knew even more about the man. It frightened her to know she could be in a love with a man who didn't return her feelings and considered her an added bonus to their business arrangement. Once they'd come back to the States, Gage immediately moved her into his penthouse and ensconced her even deeper into his world. Morning, noon and night, he was either in her head with constant calls or texts to check in to see how her day was going or making surprise visits to her office just to take her to lunch. And the nights…oh, the nights were something else entirely.

If Fallon thought she would get some sort of reprieve from their lovemaking, she'd been wrong. Gage was as hungry for her as he'd been on their honeymoon, maybe even more so. He seemed determined to not let her keep her distance. *Did he know that had been her goal?* On the plane ride home, Fallon had decided to limit sex between them, but Gage had seduced her nearly every night since. It was so intense, she'd had to beg off the other night, claiming it was the wrong time of the month. She knew her excuse wouldn't hold much longer, but the last few days had been bliss. She'd finally been able to clear her head of the sexual fog.

As she drove home late Friday evening, Fallon contemplated how she had to face facts. She was hopelessly in love with Gage. She'd been carrying a torch for him ever since she was a young girl. It had only grown when she'd thrown herself at him and he'd kissed her with such fervor. It was a double-edged sword knowing she was Gage's wife and loved him with heart and soul, but at the same time he didn't love her and had only married her for lust and acceptance into society.

How was she going to navigate the next five months feeling this way? It was going to be pure torture, but somehow she would. She had to turn off her emotions, not give herself completely over to Gage as she'd been doing. She had to focus on self-preservation because their marriage of convenience would end in the near term.

She pulled her Audi into the parking space next to Gage's Bugatti and turned off the engine. She inhaled, mentally steeling herself for the evening ahead, and eased out of the car. The ride to Gage's building had seemed like the longest ride of her life. But when she finally entered their living room, the atmosphere was relaxed. Jazz was playing softly in the background, candles were lit and the smells coming from the kitchen caused her stomach to stir. She'd only had a salad for lunch and that had been hours ago.

Gage came padding toward her barefoot, wearing low-slung jeans and a T-shirt, two wineglasses in his hands. "Thought you might need this after a long day of work." He handed her a glass, which she accepted.

"Thank you." Fallon had always imagined having a marriage like this one day, but she'd never dreamed of Gage in the role of caring husband. She followed him into the living room and plonked down on the sofa. She was about to remove her stilettos when Gage joined her and took over the task, removing one shoe and then the other. He helped her remove the suit jacket she'd worn, revealing the thin cami underneath.

When his gaze zeroed in on her breasts, Fallon felt as if she were naked because on cue her nipples pebbled at his searing gaze. She reached for her wineglass and liberally drank.

"Was it that bad at the office?" Gage asked, watching her intently. "I thought things were settling down a bit."

"They are," Fallon said. "I've settled some debts and made payment arrangements with other creditors. As we discussed last week, I want to use some of those funds for development to make Stewart Technologies what it once was."

"Did you meet with the head of R and D yet?"

Fallon was happy they were talking shop. She'd been nervous because he'd given her one of those hungry gazes when she'd come in, which usually ended up with her on her back. Or on top. Or on the side. Or the floor. It didn't much matter.

"Fallon?"

He was speaking to her. "Oh, yes, I did."

Over the delicious dinner a private chef had made for them, they continued discussing the viability of several options the department head had come up with. Gage opened up about some new deals he was working on and she offered advice Gage seemed to find valuable. Fallon relaxed as the evening progressed, especially when they retired to the sofa and streamed some television shows on Hulu. An hour in, Fallon couldn't help but stifle a yawn.

"Tired?" Gage asked.

She nodded.

"C'mon, let me put you to bed." Gage rose and helped her up.

Once they were in the bedroom, Fallon went about her normal routine of preparing for bed, but she felt Gage's eyes on her every movement. She knew she was pushing it when she reached for a sexy nightie. It had spaghetti straps and stopped midthigh, but it was clothing. Since their honeymoon, she'd forgone pajamas because she and Gage were so insatiable for each other.

After washing her face and brushing her teeth, she headed to her side of the bed. Gage was sitting upright with his phone in hand, but appearances were deceiving. Fallon didn't doubt for a second he hadn't noticed her attire. She slid in beside him, turned off the lamp and faced the opposite direction. She heard him move around before the room fell into darkness. Fallon tried to calm her breathing and act as if she were falling asleep, but Gage called her out.

"I know you're not asleep, Fallon."

"Nearly. I'm exhausted."

She felt his arms encircle her as he pulled her firmly to him until her backside was against his very hard shaft. She sucked in a breath.

"Too tired for this?" He planted hot, openmouthed kisses

on her neck until he came to her ear and gently tugged on the lobe with his mouth.

Sweet Jesus! He knew all her erogenous zones. Fallon closed her eyes and willed herself to stay strong. "Not tonight, all right?" Fallon managed to say despite her body's yearnings. "It's been a long day."

"That didn't seem to bother you before. Why now?"

Anger coursed through her and she spun around to face him in the darkness. "Really, Gage, I ask for one night to sleep and suddenly I'm in the wrong? Or am I supposed to be at your beck and call every night? Is that what you expected out of this arrangement? Because if so, you're in for a rude awakening. I'm my own person with my own mind, my own thoughts, my own feelings."

"I recognize that, Fallon. I didn't realize I was pressuring you. I thought the feeling was mutual and you wanted me just as much. Consider me duly warned off." He turned away and this time his back was to her.

Fallon felt terrible. She hadn't meant to hurt him, but she'd needed some breathing room because she was afraid of the tender feelings she'd developed. Afraid he might see them and then where would they be? She had to stay the course. It was best not only for her sanity but her pride.

Gage ran. On Saturday morning, he ran as fast as he could on the treadmill in his building's gym until he'd exhausted himself. He hadn't slept much last night because Fallon had shut him down. Literally. There was no mistaking the off-limits sign she'd been wearing for days, except last night she'd made it very clear she didn't want him. Before she'd been more than happy to sleep nude because they'd been so attuned to each other's needs.

Over the last month they'd awaken during the middle of the night and reach for each other. Sometimes he started it. Sometimes she did. They'd make love into the wee hours of the morning and *now* she was tired. Tired of him? Gage wondered.

He'd seen the way she responded to him. Felt her clench around his shaft when he'd been buried deep inside her. Watched the bliss come over her when she'd climaxed. Why? Because he'd felt it himself. An unexplainable ecstasy had plagued him since they'd become intimate. He'd thought he'd get the hunger for her out of his system, but he hadn't. And he'd tried. Perhaps he'd come on too strong? No. No. No.

He wasn't wrong about how Fallon felt about him. If he was honest, there were times another emotion had been visible in her expression. Something he was afraid to say out loud. She hadn't been able to hide it, but she'd tried to. And now she was acting as if their lovemaking had become burdensome when that was far from the case. She was feeling too much the same as him.

He was on the verge of everything he'd wanted in this marriage. The other day he'd secured another five percent of Stewart Technologies' stock, bringing his total to forty-five percent. He'd been slowly acquiring the stock through several holding companies to ensure it wouldn't be traced back to him. As for his wife, the attraction he'd felt for her had materialized into the most spectacular sex of his life. The problem was, the triumph he'd thought he'd feel as the moment of success got nearer left a bitter taste in his mouth.

Whoever said revenge was a dish best served cold had no idea what it would feel like mixed with white-hot sexual need. The anger he'd felt toward Fallon and her family was the reason he'd chosen to go down this path, but it was getting harder and harder not to want more out of this relationship than either one of them had wanted to give.

Gage stopped running and pressed the stop button on the treadmill.

The marriage was convenient. Fallon got her money and he got Stewart Technologies and Fallon in his bed. However, Gage wasn't satisfied. He wanted both, but deep down he knew there was going to come a time he would have to choose.

Thirteen

"Are you sure you want me to attend this dinner with you two?" Grace asked from the back seat of Gage's car. Gage had invited his mother to come to Thanksgiving at the Stewarts' with Fallon and him, because his wife had adamantly refused to miss it, claiming she always shared the meal with her parents.

"Of course. We want you there." He hazarded a glance at Fallon, but she was staring out the window. When Gage had first invited Grace, he'd been certain she would decline, but he'd been wrong. She claimed she hadn't seen much of him since the wedding and didn't plan on missing out on the holiday.

Gage wasn't looking forward to the hostility that could break out on all sides tonight. He and Fallon hadn't been on good terms in weeks. The night after she'd refused to make love, Gage had felt hurt and so he'd chosen to withhold any affection. The problem was, he was hurting himself in the process because he missed being close to his wife, but he was too proud to admit he was wrong and so their standoff had continued.

"I made one of my famous sweet potato pies," his mother said. "Wonder if Nora will mind."

"I'm sure Mother will welcome the pie."

She didn't.

When they entered Stewart Manor, the matriarch had air-kissed his mother and then handed the pie off to the butler, never to be seen the rest of the evening. From then on, Nora was overly solicitous, which made his mother uncomfortable. The night didn't get any better, especially when Dane called to inform them he'd missed his flight and wouldn't make it. Meanwhile Henry kept giving Gage the evil eye. And why wouldn't he? Fallon was being as warm as a lump of coal. Could her father sense their acrimony?

After dinner they retired to the family room and the night went further downhill.

"So what have you been up to, Grace?" Nora inquired.

"I wasn't cleaning houses, if that's what you're after. I've been retired for years because my son takes great care of me. He even bought me a house in Lost Creek." She winked at her son.

"You really have done well, Gage." Nora smiled. "You take care of your mother while our daughter harps about our spending and has placed us on allowance. Or was that your doing?" She eyed Gage suspiciously.

"No, Mother, it was mine." Fallon perked up after being surly all night. "Perhaps if you learned to curb your spending, I wouldn't be in the position I'm in."

"Married to my son?" Grace inquired. "You would do well to remember he forgave you your past transgressions, my dear."

"Leave my daughter out of this, Grace. Your beef is with me," Fallon's father interjected.

Grace glared at him. "Do you blame me, Henry?" She

used his given name, which she never would have years ago. "I'm still waiting on an apology."

"Mama..." Gage didn't need his mother to defend him.

"Don't *Mama* me." Grace stood. "You ask me to make *nice* with these people when they've yet to acknowledge the harm they caused both of us. And now..." Her eyes bore into Fallon, but one look at Gage made her not finish her sentence. "Please take me home."

"That might be best," Nora responded.

"Don't patronize me, Nora Stewart, when you can't be bothered to clean your own house or make your own meals. You would do well to learn a little humility as fortunes change." His mother walked to the exit and Gage made to follow her but looked at Fallon. "Are you coming?"

Fallon shook her head. "I'll stay here, if you don't mind. I'll get a taxi home."

Gage clenched his jaw. He didn't want to get into a fight in front of the Stewarts. "Fine. I'll see you at home."

On the way back to her house, his mother made it clear that, going forward, she wanted limited contact with the Stewarts. For his part, Gage was just glad they'd made it through the evening, though his thoughts kept circling back to the sullen look on Fallon's face and whether the chill between them would ever thaw.

"Can you help me with this?" Fallon asked Gage the following Saturday evening. It had been a tense few days since Thanksgiving and Fallon was hoping the ice would thaw between them. They were getting ready for a hospital fund-raiser where the crème de la crème would be in attendance. She would have to shine tonight. The Givenchy gown she'd chosen had sequins from top to bottom along with dramatic layers of silver and gunmetal fringe. It would certainly help draw attention to her and Gage. It fit perfectly with the nights' Roaring Twenties theme and, with her hair swept in a sophisticated updo, Fallon looked like a modern-day flapper.

"Of course." Gage came up behind her and studied her with his hawklike gaze for several moments. She froze, her breath jamming in her throat. Then he zipped up the dress and shocked her when he planted a kiss on her bare shoulder. The hairs on the back of her neck rose to attention and every muscle in her body tensed as the earthy, sensual scent of him slammed into her senses.

Gage hadn't touched her in over a month since their argument over her not being in the mood. For her, it had been as simple as needing space, but for Gage it was as if she'd mortally wounded him with her rejection and he'd avoided her ever since. Fallon had known Gage was upset—hurt, even—but she hadn't expected him to pull away from her so completely. Despite their lack of intimacy, they still played their newlywed role by attending charity functions, polo matches and art gallery openings where Gage could rub shoulders with high society. It was going rather nicely because he'd picked up several new clients.

The distance was palpable. When they did manage to sit together for a meal, there was an ever-present underlying tension between them. Fallon didn't know how to clear the hurdle and get back to how they'd been when he couldn't get enough of her. She literally ached with unrequited feelings because now she knew what she'd been missing all those years in the bedroom. She was addicted to Gage and she needed a hit, badly.

"I have something for you." Fallon realized he'd moved away while she'd been daydreaming about him. And how could she not? Tonight he was wearing a black, three-piece, pin-striped tuxedo with black wing-tipped shoes. He'd found a vintage fedora to complete the look. He looked every bit a gangster.

He handed her a large box imprinted with the Tiffany's logo. "What's this?" She glanced up at him.

"Open it."

She did as he instructed. Nestled inside the velvet cushion was the most stunning diamond teardrop necklace she'd ever seen.

Gage unclasped it and stepped in behind her to place it on her neck. How had he known this would complement the deep V of the dress so perfectly?

She touched the large diamond pendant. "It's beautiful."

"Just like you."

Fallon glanced into the mirror to find Gage's brandy-colored eyes raking her boldly. She hadn't seen that intense flare of attraction in his eyes in so long, her heart jolted. Did it mean he still wanted her? "So is this a truce?" she asked hopefully. "Because if not, I'd like it to be."

Gage offered her a smile, which had been rare of late. "Yes, let's consider it one. Now, c'mon, we should go. We don't want to be late."

"No, we wouldn't want that." Fallon knew making an impression tonight was important to Gage after his humble beginnings. She would do everything in her power to ensure the evening went well.

About forty minutes later their limousine pulled up in front of the Four Seasons. It had taken them some time because of the barrage of limousines filling the streets, but eventually they disembarked and headed inside. The venue décor was vintage art deco with a black-and-gold color scheme that was pure glitz and glam. There was even a photo booth so guests could grab a fedora, flapper hat, feather boa or fake gun and have their picture taken.

Fallon made her way around the room introducing Gage. Everyone was polite and charming, inquiring about their wedding and how they were enjoying married life. They even ran into her parents.

Her father gave her a hug while her mother blew her air kisses. "Don't want to ruin my makeup, darling," she purred. "You're looking well. Married life agrees with you. I love the gown. Givenchy, right?"

Trust her mother to know every designer. "That's right."

"But the true masterpiece is this diamond." Nora Stewart had no qualms about lifting the stone off Fallon's chest and admiring it. She glanced at Gage. "You outdid yourself."

"Thank you," he replied.

With that brief exchange, her mother grabbed her father's arm and continued on her socializing trek.

"Fallon? Omigod! As I live and breathe," a rather loud woman exclaimed from behind them.

Fallon spun on her heels to find Dani Collins a few feet away. She hadn't seen the buxom petite blonde since her parents had carted her away from Austin to boarding school all because she'd taken Dani's advice and tried to seduce Gage. Listening to Dani and their friend Millicent had been the reason why Fallon had ended up in Gage's room. Liquid encouragement of the alcoholic variety had also played a role.

"Dani Collins."

Dani smiled, showing a large, toothy grin. "I haven't seen you in ages." She pulled Fallon into an awkward hug. "Where have you been hiding yourself?"

"I've been working at my family's company, Stewart Technologies."

"Work?" Dani chuckled. "I would have thought you'd marry a filthy rich husband like your mama wanted before you ever worked your pretty little fingers to the bone." She held up Fallon's left hand. When her eyes landed on the six-carat ring, they nearly bugged out. "Wait a second, it looks like you have landed one."

A flicker of apprehension coursed through Fallon. "Yes, I'm married. You may remember him." She turned to Gage, who'd stepped away momentarily into another circle of partygoers. She touched his shoulder and he came forward. "Dani, this is my husband. Gage Campbell."

"What?" Dani's hand flew to her mouth. "You married the stable boy!" she shrieked.

Everyone around them turned to stare. The murderous look on Gage's face told Fallon that Dani had aroused his old fears and insecurities. Fallon could feel the deep red flush rising up to claim her cheeks.

"First of all, lower your voice, Dani," Fallon snapped. "Second, Gage is no stable boy. He's a grown man—"

But she never got to finish her sentence because Gage stepped in. "Who is, as you put it, Dani, filthy rich. So yes, I'm more than capable of looking after what's mine." His arm circled Fallon's waist. "Now if you'll excuse us…"

The lights blinked, indicating the event was about to begin. Fallon felt Gage's fingertips at her elbow as he guided her to their assigned table. He held her chair out and she sat. It was all so civilized, but when he deliberately brushed his fingers across her shoulders, Fallon shivered. *Had he intended to elicit a response?* She was sure he was upset over Dani's obnoxious comment from earlier. Tonight was his night to show society he'd arrived, and could Dani's outburst have marred that?

Once he took his seat beside her, Fallon leaned over. "You okay?" She watched him closely.

He winked but then sat with his back ramrod-straight and turned to face the front of the room. Fallon did the same, worried how the remainder of the evening would go.

Gage was fuming. Outwardly he portrayed the image of self-made millionaire, but inside he was still that twelve-year-old boy who'd come to live with his mother when she became the maid on a big estate. The same young boy who'd turned into a stable hand that silly rich socialites like

Dani Collins made fun of or bedded to show they were living dangerously.

Fallon was special. He'd watched her grow up from a spirited young girl into an attractive teenager with stunning hazel-gray eyes. He had been drawn to her. It's why he'd humored her, talked to her and let her follow him around. That night he'd thought to teach her a lesson, but it had morphed into one hell of a kiss. Gage had been ill prepared for the chemistry that had exploded between them. He'd ended it before they'd gone too far.

Yet in the eyes of Dani and some like her, he would always be a stable boy and that stuck in his craw. Gage lifted a hand to catch the attention of the waiter and requested a whiskey. He needed something stronger, less smooth than his usual brandy. Something to take the edge off to ensure he got through this night in one piece.

Three whiskeys and several hours later, Gage felt relaxed. The evening was nearly over. The hospital raised the requisite amount of money needed thanks to a last-minute, million-dollar donation from him, which had shocked the entire room, including his wife sitting beside him.

When the band finally struck up some lively tunes, Gage was ready to alleviate some tension. Fallon returned from freshening up in the bathroom with her mother and looked quite delectable in her metallic flapper dress. He couldn't wait to take it off her later and he'd be damned if she'd refuse him. He'd seen the look in her eyes tonight and knew she still hungered for him.

He stood and held out a hand. "Dance with me?"

Fallon slid her hand into his and allowed him to lead her to the dance floor, which was already crowded with couples. The song was a slow Etta James melody called "At Last." Gage eased his arms around Fallon's warm body and pulled her tightly to him. Then he leaned his forehead against hers and whispered, "I've missed you."

She was silent for several beats and Gage wondered if she'd heard him, but then she responded. "I've missed you, too."

Her words were like a match to his lust and Gage pressed his body closer so she could feel how he was straining in his trousers. "Will you let me have you tonight?" he growled.

"Yes."

Yes. The word had never sounded lovelier to Gage's ears. And once the song ended, he quickly danced them off the floor and back to the table so Fallon could grab her clutch and gloves. They were nearly at the door when once again Dani stepped in front of them.

She was weaving back and forth, looking like she'd had one too many drinks. "I have to hand it to you, Fallon. You certainly know how to pick them. Maybe I, too, should have gotten it on with our stable boy. Maybe then he would have become rich and famous and come back to bail my company out of trouble."

"You don't know what you're talking about," Fallon answered, a warning in her tone.

"D-don't I?" Dani slurred. "From what I hear, your daddy's company was about to go belly-up, until stable boy here—" Dani eyed Gage up and down "—came along. Did you finally have to put out?"

Fallon's eyes narrowed. "You're a witch, you know that?"

"I might be, but I'm a rich one," Dani returned.

"That no man wants," Fallon snorted. "It's no wonder you're alone. I, on the other hand, am not. I'm going home with *my man* and let me tell you something, Dani. He's the fantasy in bed we all thought he was." She didn't wait for another of Dani's catty responses. Fallon grabbed Gage's hand and stormed out of the ballroom.

"That was hot!" Gage couldn't help but comment. He loved Fallon's outburst. This was the second time she'd defended him tonight. Whatever residual anger he'd felt from the last month faded. Fallon was truly in his corner.

"Good." She stared at him boldly. "Because I need you bad. So, buckle up. It's going to be a long night."

A smile curved his lips. He was ready for whatever Fallon had in store because they had a month to make up for.

They didn't make it very far into the penthouse because Gage pressed Fallon against the wall of the living room as soon as they arrived. Then his lips found hers in the dark and he kissed her hard. Their mouths fused together in a tangle of tongues. Fallon didn't know who moved first. She knew her hand was sneaking under his tuxedo to push off the jacket. Gage pulled away long enough to shrug it off, undo his tie and unbutton his shirt. When her eyes landed on his flat brown nipples, she leaned forward and explored the salty taste of him.

She had a growing need to see him naked. When the buttons were finally free, Gage ripped the shirt off. Only minutes after they'd entered the apartment, he was naked from the waist up while she was still fully clothed. Gage reached for her, hauling her to him. He reached behind her, fumbling with the zipper on the back of her dress, but it wouldn't give.

"Damnation!" he cursed and then pulled one strap and then the other over her arms. Her breasts popped free and his mouth was on them in seconds, reducing her to writhing ecstasy. They were tight and puckered at his mouth and touch alone. Fallon's mind skittered as her insides fisted tight with need. She couldn't think of anything but Gage and how much she wanted him. She didn't care what anyone else thought; she would die if she didn't feel him inside her *now*.

She was sure Gage felt the same way because his erection had thickened. She reached between them to undo his belt and zipper, but he pushed her hands aside. In one fell swoop he pulled down his trousers and briefs and kicked away his clothes. He was gloriously naked and Fallon looked her fill. Then he was back, sliding his hands into her hair and kissing her. His hands roamed lower, hiking up her dress until it was bunched around her waist.

"Wrap your legs around me," he instructed roughly.

He didn't have to tell her twice. Gage hitched her up, resting her back against the wall, and Fallon wrapped her legs around him. Holding her with one arm, he reached between them to push aside her thong and slide a finger between her moist folds. She was already wet for him, as she always was, and without preamble he widened his stance and surged upward inside her.

Fallon had never felt so full, so taken, so possessed. She slid her arms around his neck and Gage thrust higher. Her breath hitched. He withdrew and thrust back in, this time going even deeper.

"Yes, Gage, oh, yes," she moaned and her head fell back against the wall. She closed her eyes, amazed at the fullness of having Gage inside her once again. Starbursts of blinding light exploded behind her eyes as pleasure washed over her.

"Look at me, Fallon."

She opened her eyes and found Gage staring at her. He cupped her bottom tighter in his palms and pushed higher. He was intent on pulling her apart, on dismantling every single one of her defenses. He accomplished his goal with single-minded purpose as he increased his rhythm and drove into her over and over.

"Gage…" Fallon's body grew taut and soon she felt herself clench around him as spasms overtook her. She heard his release in the distance as they both finally broke free.

Fourteen

"I have a lead for you," Gage's attorney told him over the phone the next morning. "The final shares you need to give you a majority in Stewart Technologies."

"What was that?" Gage asked absentmindedly. He'd been daydreaming about Fallon's uninhibited response last night. He should be satisfied he could bring her to that kind of climax, but he hadn't been unaffected, either. He had feelings for her, probably always had since he'd seen her fall off her horse when she was eight.

Being with Fallon had injected his life with meaning and made him feel emotions he'd never allowed himself to feel. The past two months had shown him she wasn't the strong woman she portrayed to the world. She was passionate. Vulnerable, even. There were so many layers to his beautiful wife he hadn't considered. He'd been so intent on taking her to bed, to claim what he hadn't taken sixteen years ago and unleash the chemistry between them, he'd failed to see the consequences of his actions. He was falling for his wife. *Hard.*

"I said I have a lock on those shares you need," his attorney repeated, clearing his fog. "Since the company is rebounding, stock prices are slowly starting to rise. You'll want to get these now, while you can."

Gage's chest tightened and guilt settled in his stomach as the heavy weight of what he'd been doing registered. He needed someone to absolve him of the guilt, to tell him he what he'd done was right. But that wasn't going to happen. If Fallon ever found out his true motives behind marrying her, it would crush her. She'd been so happy the last few weeks as she'd pulled Stewart Technologies from the brink of disaster. The projects she'd been working on would be coming to market in a couple of months. They were the brainchild of her new head of development and Fallon was excited to see what lay ahead.

"Are you ready to pull the trigger?"

A throb pulsed at Gage's temple and he massaged it with his fingertips, trying to alleviate the pressure, but nothing was going to do that. His feelings for Fallon ran deep and he was conflicted as to what to do next. "I—I…"

"If you don't act now, someone could swoop in and pick them up. You have to move."

Gage sighed. He couldn't allow anyone else to get those shares. They had to stay in the family. On the other hand, this enormous deceit weighed heavily on him. He would be crossing the line when he did this.

"Go ahead and purchase them."

"I'm on it. I'll let you know when it's a done deal."

"Thank you." Gage ended the call. He sat back in his seat and rubbed a hand across his brow. There was no denying the emotion he'd never wanted to claim; it was there mocking him because he'd thought he could skirt it. Thought he didn't need it. He certainly hadn't needed it before. Why? Because none of those women had been Fallon.

Yet, because of her, he'd wanted more. To *be* more. And

he'd accomplished that. But with it had come the all-consuming rage and quest for revenge. He now had the tools, the final nail in the coffin to get his ultimate revenge against the Stewarts, but it would cost him the woman he loved.

"What should I expect tonight?" Gage asked Fallon as they drove to the restaurant to meet Ayden and his fiancée, Maya, for dinner. "The firing squad?"

"Don't be so melodramatic." Fallon smoothed down her skirt.

"C'mon, Fallon." Gage took his eyes off the road to glance at her. "I know your brother doesn't like me. It was obvious at the wedding."

Gage recalled the killer look Ayden had given him when they'd been introduced. Ayden had warned Gage to take care of his sister or else.

"He doesn't know you. Give him a chance," Fallon said, obviously attempting to ease Gage's mind.

"If he affords me the same, I will," Gage responded, turning his eyes to the road again. He knew how important this dinner was to Fallon. She was forging a bond with her brother and he didn't want to get in the way, not when he wasn't on even footing himself.

"Good."

They pulled into the restaurant's valet parking twenty minutes later. Gage came around and helped Fallon out of the car, then laced his fingers through hers as they walked inside. The maître d' led them to a corner table where Ayden and Maya were already seated. Gage could see why Ayden had fallen for his fiancée. She was striking, with her mass of curly hair and flawless brown skin.

Ayden rose when they approached. He came over and kissed both of Fallon's cheeks and offered Gage a hand. Gage shook it before scooting Fallon into a chair across from them.

"Glad you both could join us," Ayden said. He glanced at Maya. "We're eager to get to know you."

"As are we," Gage answered. He offered them a smile.

"How about some wine?" Ayden asked. "I took the liberty of ordering a bottle of red."

"We would love some, thank you." Fallon patted his thigh. She knew Gage liked ordering their wine himself.

"How's married life?" Maya inquired. "I can't believe you two beat me and Ayden down the aisle."

"It certainly wasn't a shotgun wedding," Gage replied.

"Then what was the rush?" Ayden asked. "Were you afraid Fallon might change her mind?"

Gage felt Fallon's fury beside him rather than saw it. She didn't appreciate her brother's inappropriate comment any more than he did, so he reminded himself Ayden was merely concerned for Fallon's well-being. "No, I wasn't afraid. I knew Fallon would honor the commitment she'd made to be my wife." He reached for her hand and brought it to his lips.

"How is married life treating you?" Maya asked. Bless her heart, Ayden's fiancée was keeping the evening cordial.

"It's going well, thank you, Maya," Fallon responded. "Actually, better than I'd imagined. Gage even manages to keep the toilet seat down."

Fallon's joke lightened the mood and everyone began to relax. But Gage could see Ayden watching his every move. Could he see what Gage had yet to share with Fallon—that he loved her?

Fallon was overjoyed the dinner was turning around. It had started off rocky with Ayden giving Gage the death stare. She knew her brother wasn't happy about her arranged marriage to Gage, but he was going to have to live with it for another four months.

Her breath caught in her throat when she realized two

months had already come and gone. The first month with Gage had been sheer bliss. The way they'd connected on such an elemental level had surprised her. All her life she'd been searching for that elusive connection with another human being. She'd found it in Gage; it was as if he fit perfectly into the slot. With each passing day and all the intimacy they'd shared, it became harder to keep her true feelings from bubbling to the surface. It's why she'd pushed him away, making the last month hard. When Gage had felt rejected by her, he'd kept her at a distance, physically as well as emotionally.

His response had hurt, but she'd had to withdraw to save herself the pain she knew was coming. However, not being with him had hurt far worse than anything she could have imagined. Last night after the event, they'd given in and finally made love. It had felt so good and oh so right. That was why she'd felt in a good place to accept Ayden's dinner invite.

"Gage is treating you well, which I'm glad to see," Ayden whispered in her ear when they'd retired to the lounge to listen to a jazz quartet. Gage and Maya were engaged in a lively discussion on the latest mayoral candidate, while Ayden and Fallon stepped onto the terrace for a private conversation and some fresh air because Fallon had felt a bit queasy.

"He is."

"Is the fresh air helping?" Ayden asked.

Fallon nodded and inhaled deeply. The last week or so she hadn't had much of an appetite. And after seeing the crème brûlée Gage had ordered for dessert, she'd felt sick to her stomach.

"After hearing his story, I realize I misjudged him," Ayden said after a moment.

During the meal Gage had shared the story of his inauspicious start in life, from never knowing his father to being raised on Stewart Manor to branching out on his own after college to find success. Fallon could see how impressed Ayden was by Gage's determination. He respected her husband because he knew what it was like to make something out of nothing.

"I told you not to worry."

Ayden snorted. "It's an older brother's prerogative to worry, Fallon. It would be different if you'd married for love, but you didn't."

Color drained from Fallon's face and Ayden leaned in. "Omigod! You're in love with him, aren't you?" He glanced in Gage's direction and Fallon followed Ayden's gaze. Her husband was watching them and smiling.

She quickly turned around and tugged on Ayden's sleeve, leading him farther away. "Lower your voice, please."

Ayden looked down at her. His hazel-gray eyes pierced hers. "Does he know?"

Fallon shook her head. "And I don't want him to know."

"Why the hell not? I see the way he looks at you, Fallon. There's something there."

"Lust," she replied. "Lust is all that's there, Ayden. We're compatible in the bedroom."

"Are you sure? Because I would beg to differ."

"Trust me, I know," Fallon responded. "Let's keep this between us, okay? I don't want him to know."

"You don't want me to know what?" came the deep masculine voice from behind Fallon. Her heart thumped erratically. What had he heard?

"How I'm not that big a fan of jazz, but that it's your cup of tea," Fallon responded, turning to her husband with a smile.

Gage's arm snaked around her waist. "Babe, you should have told me. We could have gone someplace else."

She shrugged. "It's fine. Ayden said he'd been wanting

to come here for a while, too. Isn't that right?" She glanced up at her brother for support.

Ayden grinned. "That's right. So let's go back to our seats. The quartet is back."

The evening ended with Fallon and Gage saying their goodbyes and planning on another double date with Ayden and Maya. Afterward, in the car, Fallon was happy to hear Gage had enjoyed himself.

"That went well," he said on the drive home. "I like Ayden."

"You sound surprised."

"I thought he was going to treat me like your parents. Like I wasn't good enough for you."

Fallon realized how deep Gage's past wounds were when it came to being accepted. How her and her friends' treatment of him had had a profound effect on who he was today.

"But he didn't treat me that way. Instead he treated me with respect and I feel the same about him. What Ayden has been able to accomplish without any help from your father is nothing short of amazing."

Fallon beamed with pride. "He's pretty great, isn't he?"

"Yeah, must be something in the genes." Gage glanced in her direction.

A swell of rightness filled Fallon. If they had a *real* marriage, this would be the start of a great beginning for their family, but they didn't and it wasn't. What was she going to do at the end of six months when it was time to say goodbye?

"Fallon?" She heard the question in his voice. "You got silent on me all of a sudden. You okay?"

She nodded but deep down she was afraid of losing him.

Fifteen

"Why did I agree to do this?" Gage wondered aloud as he helped Theo drill nails into the new storage shed behind his home.

"Because you owe me one," his friend responded.

"What for?"

"For telling you about the Stewarts' plight," Theo replied. He glanced in the direction of the house where Fallon was talking with his girlfriend, Amanda, whom he'd started seeing a few weeks ago. "If I hadn't, you wouldn't be married now."

Gage laughed. "If I recall, you told me I was out of my mind to consider marrying my sworn enemy."

Theo shrugged. "Who knew you'd be the happiest I've seen you in years? You're a changed man, my friend."

"How so?"

"Lighter. Happy. And it's all because of the woman in there." He pointed to Fallon, whom Gage could see through the oversize kitchen window.

"She's certainly made an impact."

"Admit it, Gage. You have feelings for the woman. Probably always did, which is why it was so easy for you to make that offer."

Gage knew Theo was right. On some deeper level, he'd always wanted Fallon even when she'd been off-limits and too young to know any better.

"So what now?"

"What do you mean?"

"Didn't you only agree to a six-month arrangement? What happens when your time is up and Fallon wants out?"

Gage's eyes narrowed. He knew he was putting his head in the sand, but he refused to consider it. Fallon was happy with them, with their life. He was certain if he presented her with the opportunity to stay with him, she wouldn't leave. "I don't think that's going to happen, Theo."

"She signed documents. She doesn't owe you a thing."

"She owes herself," Gage responded quickly. "She owes it to us to see how this plays out. Instead of turning tail and running away."

"Sounds like you've gotten very comfortable being a married man," Theo noted. "I hope this doesn't blow up in your face. I mean, what happens when Fallon finds out your true motives for marrying her? How do you think she'll feel?"

Gage knew the answer. "She'll feel betrayed." She wouldn't be angry. She'd hate him for stealing her birthright like Henry did to Ayden. And it scared the living daylights out of him. But he was in so deep, there was no way out. By purchasing those final shares, he was sealing his fate and setting them on a collision course. But Gage was powerless to stop it.

"Then for God's sake, come clean with her, man. Tell her what you've done and maybe—maybe—you can work it out."

Gage stiffened. “I can’t. I could lose her.”

“You can lose her if you don’t,” Theo stated.

Gage looked toward the window and found Fallon watching and waving at him. His heart turned in his chest and Gage knew he would do anything to keep her.

“That was fun,” Fallon said when she and Gage returned to the penthouse later that evening. He’d been very quiet during dinner and, on the ride back, she wondered if he and Theo had had some sort of disagreement outside.

“Yeah, it was good,” Gage said absentmindedly as he headed to the kitchen and grabbed a beer out of the fridge. He twisted the top off, took a pull and leaned against the counter.

Fallon removed her leather jacket and boots and followed him, watching him closely. The last couple of months she’d picked up on Gage’s mood. She knew when something was on his mind. “You can talk to me about whatever it is that’s upsetting you.”

“I’m fine.”

Fallon nodded. He was stonewalling her and she didn’t like it. “Suit yourself.” She spun around and walked into the master suite. She was removing her jewelry and placing it in the holder when Gage came marching in behind her.

“We don’t have to share our feelings all the time, Fallon,” he snarled. “It’s all right to keep something to ourselves.”

“So you admit you have secrets?” Fallon responded, spinning around to face him. “That you’re keeping something from me?”

“I never said that.”

Her eyes narrowed. “You didn’t have to. Because your answer just said it all.”

“Damn it, Fallon. What do you want from me?”

“Everything! Nothing.” She shook her head. “Hell, I don’t know, Gage. I blindly agreed to this marriage to save my family's company but I had no idea what it would be like, how I would feel…" Her voice trailed off.

"And how do you feel?"

She stared at him incredulously. "You want me to lay my heart bare when you're not willing to do the same?" She shook her head. "I don't think so."

She moved away and headed into the bathroom to brush her teeth, but Gage was right there. "I want to know."

"Well, that's too bad. Because I have my own secrets."

His face turned to stone. "You're saying that to get back at me."

He was wrong. The last couple of weeks she'd felt off, as if something was wrong. She hadn't had much of an appetite and was nauseous the last few mornings. It was odd. When she'd spoken to Theo's girlfriend, she'd asked Fallon about her last period. That's when it dawned on Fallon: she hadn't had one since she and Gage were married. She'd been so enraptured with her husband it had slipped her mind. Amanda had gently suggested she get a pregnancy test to find out for sure, but Fallon was afraid.

A baby?

She was on the pill to guarantee there would be no strings once the marriage was over. *What could have happened?* Had she missed a day? A rising panic threatened to overtake her. Guilt. Regret. Fear. Love. Fallon was feeling too many emotions to share a potential pregnancy with Gage. Not until she was sure.

"Fallon." Gage's light brown gaze sharpened as he drew near. "What is it? What don't I know?"

"Don't turn this around on me, Gage," Fallon responded tightly. "You said you want to keep feelings and emotions to yourself. I merely expressed I'll do the same. If you don't like it, that's tough."

She knew before he moved that he was going to kiss her. Kiss away her insolence. And she would let him because a hot sea of need always seemed to be just below the surface with them.

"Don't think this changes anything," Fallon murmured before his lips covered hers and his hands began skimming her body. His fingers tugged on the narrow straps of her sundress until they loosened and he could tug it to her waist.

His response was a raw, shaken laughter. "Duly noted. Now, are you going to let me love you?"

"Yes..." Gage's mouth left hers and his tongue began trailing an erotic path of fire from her throat, neck and shoulders to her breast. When he reached one chocolate nipple, he lowered his head and took the turgid peak in his mouth. She released an audible sigh and gave in.

Long moments later, when they lay spent and wrapped in each other arms, Fallon stared up at the ceiling. They'd shared something special, magical even, and emotions swelled in her.

Gage seemed to sense it, too. As if reading her mind, he tried to verbalize it. "Fallon," he said huskily. "Fallon, I—I—"

Fallon touched his cheek because she understood how hard it was to say those three words out loud. So she said them to herself. *I love you.* And if they had created a baby, she would love it because it was a part of him. It would mean they would be inextricably tied together for years. Was she prepared for that? She knew she loved him, but it couldn't be just her. It took two people fully committed to make a marriage work, let alone to parent a child. Fallon wasn't sure they had what it took for the long haul.

Fallon had a splitting headache. She'd felt not quite right all day.

Lunch with her mother hadn't helped. Nora griped about the meager allowance she was being given for living expenses. Fallon had tried to politely explain she needed to curb her spending habits. The company was not out of the woods. Gage's influx of cash had certainly helped, but it was up to Fallon to get them back on course.

Nora hadn't liked what she'd said. She'd yelled and pitched a fit, accusing Fallon of being unfair. "You have a rich husband now. I would think you would be looking out for your mother. Instead you're selfish and want all the money to yourself."

Fallon had curtly reminded Nora she didn't live off Gage and wasn't going to take another dime from him just because Nora couldn't control her impulses. They'd ended the lunch on an unpleasant note. Fallon was thankful to return to the office and had planned to lie down, but then she'd received an urgent call from Ayden.

"Fallon, I have to see you. Can you meet me?"

Fallon agreed and was anxiously awaiting his visit. That's when the stomach cramps started. He'd sounded urgent, as if it was a matter of life and death, and she didn't have a clue what it might be. She hoped everything was okay with him and Maya.

When Ayden arrived dressed in his usual attire of suit and tie with designer shoes, he looked serious and his jaw was tight.

"Ayden, what on earth is the matter?" Fallon asked, closing the door behind him. She motioned him to the sofa in her office. "Please have a seat."

"I have some news and you're not going to like what I have to say," Ayden replied, sitting.

Fallon sucked in a breath and willed the cramps away. She joined him on the couch. "Hit me with it. It's already been a bad day. It can't get much worse."

Ayden peered at her strangely.

"For Christ's sake, Ayden. You're scaring me. What is it?"

He inhaled deeply. "I want you to know it gives me no pleasure in doing this."

Fallon searched his face for a sign but couldn't find one. A sense of foreboding came over her that the happiness she'd found with Gage could be at risk.

"You know I run an investment firm and many people come to me to manage their portfolios."

"Damn it, Ayden. Don't beat around the bush. Just tell me."

"I'm breaking a confidence in sharing this with you, but while reviewing one of my client's portfolios, I learned he'd offloaded a substantial amount of Stewart Technologies' stock."

A sharp pain hit Fallon deep in the pit of her stomach. She tried not to react, but it was significantly more than any of the cramps from earlier that day. Still, she masked the pain. She had to know what was happening. "Go on."

"There was one purchaser of the stock, Fallon." He paused several beats. "It was Gage. He used a holding company so it couldn't immediately be traced back to him."

"No, no." Fallon shook her head and tears sprung to her eyes. This couldn't be happening. Not now. "Are you sure it's Gage? Maybe you could be wrong."

"I wish I were, but when I noticed this holding company buying all of my client's stock, I decided to do some digging. That's when I found out Stewart Technologies' stock is owned by several different holding companies. So I dug deeper into the paperwork of each company and lo and behold, Gage was the president of each of those firms. Despite your claim that Gage's incentive for marrying you was acceptance by the upper echelon, I never entirely bought it and now I know why. He wanted Stewart Technologies. And he has it, Fallon. Based on his last stock purchase, he has the majority share in the company."

Majority share.

Another cramp seized her and she clutched her stomach.

Gage has a majority stake in my company.

He could take it over at any time. Exercise his rights and boot her out of the company. Steal her birthright like Henry had done to Ayden all those years ago. By essentially not claiming Ayden as his son, their father hadn't allowed Ayden the chance to run the company. The shoe was on the other foot; now she knew what it was like to be in her big brother's shoes.

She rose even though the pain was excruciating. A cold sweat was forming on her forehead.

What a fool she'd been to believe a word that came out of Gage's mouth. This must have been his end game all along. Ayden was right. Gage didn't want acceptance. He wanted vengeance and he'd attained it at her expense. He must have laughed at how gullible and naïve she was. They just happened to be compatible in the bedroom and he'd gotten his jollies off.

"Fallon, are you all right?" Ayden was immediately on his feet and rushing over to her. "You're looking very pale."

"I—I can't." The pain was intense now and she clutched her stomach.

"I'm taking you the hospital." Within seconds Ayden lifted her into her arms and was striding for the door.

Gage stared down at the paper in his hands. This was it. He finally had a fifty-one-percent ownership stake in Stewart Technologies. After all these years he was finally in a position of power over Henry Stewart, the man who'd put him and his mother out on the street with no home, no job and only the clothes on their backs.

He'd blamed himself for what happened to his mother. Perhaps if he'd ignored Fallon, hadn't shown any interest, she would have never come to their cottage. Who knows where life would have led him if he hadn't been spurred to succeed? If he hadn't pushed himself to do more, be more, so no one could ever look down on him again?

Sharing one unforgettable kiss with Fallon had been a defining moment that had changed the course of his life. But now time had passed and he could see it had been for the better. He'd achieved the highest levels of success on Wall Street. He could afford anything and everything he'd ever wanted or dreamed of.

But what would it all mean if he was alone with no one to share it with? Getting involved with the Stewarts two months ago had altered his life once again. Marrying Fallon was the single best decision he'd ever made. The life they shared together was so rich, so full, so exciting, so passionate. Gage would never get tired of her eternal optimism, her bright smile, her easy nature. She truly was a rare diamond.

Quite honestly, she was everything he hadn't known he'd been looking for. He loved her. And he wanted *theirs* to be a real marriage. Not a temporary one. And although he excelled at managing people and situations, tonight he was going to be honest and tell her he'd been foolish thinking revenge was the answer. It wasn't. He was going tell Fallon he loved her.

"Fallon, oh, thank God." Ayden came into the hospital room and wrapped his arms around her. "Thank God you're okay. I was so worried. And the doctors—" he glanced behind him at the door "—wouldn't tell me anything. Even though I'm your brother, I'm not on your approved list to receive medical information, so they wouldn't—"

Ayden stopped rambling when he saw the tears streaming down her cheeks. "Fallon, what is it? Is it something serious? What can I do?"

Fallon laughed without humor. "There's nothing you or anyone else can do."

Ayden's eyes grew large with fear and he began grabbing at his tie as if it was too tight around his neck. "Is it bad?"

"If you mean being pregnant by a man who doesn't love you and used you for revenge against your family?" Fallon asked. "Then, yes, it's bad."

"Pregnant?"

The word hung in the air like the albatross it was. Fallon felt it around her neck and there was nothing she could do about it. Deep down, she'd known it was true, but had been afraid to take the test. Well, the stomach cramps and spotting had led her *here*, to the hospital, getting medication to help prevent a miscarriage.

"Yes," Fallon replied. "I'm pregnant."

Ayden rubbed his bald head and then turned to face her. "Does Gage know?"

"No."

"Did you?"

Fallon locked gazes with her brother. "I suspected." She wiped at the tears she couldn't stop. It had to be hormones—she hardly ever cried. "But… I didn't want to believe it, you know? We signed a six-month marriage contract. A baby wasn't part of the agreement."

"But it's here now."

"Your point?"

"You're going to have to face this, Fallon. Face Gage," Ayden responded.

"After everything he's done? How can I?" Fallon sniffed. She knew the truth now. The only reason he'd married her was for revenge. To stick it to her, to her father, for the wrongs against him and his mother.

And he'd achieved his goal.

He'd also single-handedly ruined any chance of saving their marriage. Of their being a family one day. He'd made a fool of her and she would never forgive him.

Fallon inhaled sharply. Her mama bear instincts kicked in and she rubbed her stomach, willing her nerves to subside. Gage may have won this round. Fallon hoped he enjoyed it because she was walking away with the most precious gift of all. Their child. And he would have no part of its life. She would see to that.

Sixteen

Fallon was in the hospital.

Gage's heart thumped in his chest as he frantically made his way there. When he'd stopped by to pick her up from work, her assistant, Chelsea, had informed him she'd experienced stomach pains and Ayden had taken her to the hospital. Gage was terrified. What could be wrong? Fallon was the picture of health. In their short time together he'd seen how she took very good care of herself. She ate right and went to the gym. Working out with his wife was one of his favorite pastimes. She was a great sparring partner, though it was difficult to focus when she wore workout capris and one of those sports bras that bared her midriff.

He was terrified something was terribly wrong. *But what?*

As soon as he pulled up at the valet stand, Gage quickly dispensed with his keys and rushed inside. After finding her room number, he took off running down the hall. What had stunned him was when the nurse had told him she was in the maternity ward. *Why in the hell would she be there?* The ride seemed interminable but eventually the elevator stopped and he disembarked. He found her room and strode to the door. When he arrived, she was sitting up in bed and Ayden was in a nearby chair.

"Thank God, you're all right," Gage said, hastening toward her. He bent his head to kiss her but she held up her hand and blocked him.

"Don't even try it." She lurched away from him as if he were contaminated with some virus.

Gage stepped back and stared at Fallon in confusion. He didn't understand the look of disgust on her face. He glanced at Ayden, but he had a stony expression. "Would either of you care to tell me what's going on? When Chelsea told me you were in the hospital, I was worried sick. You have no idea the crazy scenarios that were running through my mind. Do they know what's wrong? Why are you here in the maternity ward?"

Fallon turned to Ayden. "Do you mind giving us some time alone?"

Ayden glanced in Gage's direction and the dirty look he gave him told Gage that he was not pleased to see him. "Are you sure? I can stay behind."

She shook her head. "No, Gage and I need to have this conversation in private."

Ayden nodded and got to his feet. He leaned down and pressed a kiss against her forehead. "I'll be outside the door if you need me."

She attempted a half smile. "Thank you."

After giving Gage another fiery look that could have melted ice, Ayden left the room and closed the door.

Gage again moved toward the bed. "Fallon, please. Tell me what's wrong. What happened?"

She glared at him. "I don't know, Gage. Why don't you tell me since you decided to stab me in the back?"

"Pardon?"

Her hand slashed through the air. "Don't act coy. Now's your time to exact the revenge you've been plotting for months. I'm a sitting duck. Take your best shot."

A knot formed in his stomach. Surely Fallon couldn't know about the shares of Stewart Technologies' stock he'd acquired. *Could she?* "What are you talking about?"

"Really? Really?" She raised her eyebrows. "You're not going to admit it? You're going to make me spell it out for you? All right then, Gage. I'll bite. One question. How long have you been conspiring to take over my company?" She folded her arms across her chest and waited for his response.

She knew.

"Fallon, I can explain." His voice was low, tense.

"Ha." She laughed without humor. "I seriously doubt that." Her voice was tight. "But go ahead and try me."

Gage had an overwhelming urge to wrap his arms around her and hold her close. In the bed, she looked small and fragile wearing the hospital-issued gown, her hair hanging limply around her shoulders. Even her hazel-gray eyes seemed cloudy. Yet her voice was strong and fierce. He moved past her and walked to the window overlooking the street.

When he remained silent she said, "Well?" Her voice was cold and distant.

He spun around to face her. "I won't lie. I've been acquiring Stewart Technologies' stock for a couple months."

"So you admit it?"

He took a deep breath and nodded. "I was angry, Fallon. I wanted retribution for how your family treated us sixteen years ago. Your father threw us out with nothing but the clothes on our backs. He left us with nothing. No clothes. No money. Not even a reference for my mother, who'd worked for him for nearly a decade. You have no idea the trials and tribulations we faced starting over."

At her stone-faced silence, he continued. "I was angry. Rage coursed through my DNA and I vowed that someday I would get back at the Stewarts. After living on the estate and hearing the barbs from your wealthy friends, I recognized the reality of my life. I had to be successful. I promised myself I would elevate myself to a better station in life. One in which no one could ever treat me as anything less than an equal."

"And when did you decide to use me as a pawn in your revenge scenario?"

His gaze landed on Fallon. "You were never a pawn, Fallon. I wanted you. I've always wanted you. Even back then, when you were sixteen. But the timing wasn't right then. I had to push you away—but not before I kissed you. And it was that kiss that I've never forgotten."

"Oh, please, don't make it sound like it was more than it was. I was just a naïve girl making a play for you."

"It was more than that. It stirred something in me," Gage replied, "but I pushed it down. And after we were kicked out, I tried to forget you. And I did a good job of it with lots of women of all shapes and sizes. Beautiful women. But they weren't you, Fallon."

"Stop it, Gage. Don't act like we had some unrequited love because it doesn't ring true. You deliberately sought out retribution, against me and my family. Ayden told me everything. He told me how you've been purchasing shares of the company behind my back."

"Can you blame me?" Gage inquired testily. "I was angry. Angry about the raw deal we received."

"No, I wouldn't blame you if you hated me and my family, but I point-blank asked if you could put what happened behind you. You lied to me. Told me you could forgive but wouldn't forget." She sighed. "You let me believe…" Fallon's words trailed off.

"Believe what?" The tension that gripped her was vibrating through him, engulfing them in a volatile bubble.

"That you *cared*?" she yelled at him as her eyes swept downward. "This entire time I was drifting along in some fantasy world in which I thought you and I might actually last beyond the contract, but it was all a lie." She pierced him with her gaze. "It's all about crime and punishment with you, isn't it?"

"It may have started out that way, Fallon," Gage said. He came to sit beside her on the bed and this time she didn't move away. "But it quickly changed once I saw you again and the familiar visceral response I had to you wouldn't be denied. I admit, marriage was never my intention. I'd thought one night together would be enough and I would rid myself of this simmering attraction I felt for you. But that night in the car…you must remember how hot it was between us. We were a fuse waiting to be lit and, when we were finally together, it was incredible. More than incredible. I realized I'd grossly miscalculated my feelings."

"Feelings. We're talking about feelings," Fallon scoffed. "We've been married for two months, Gage, and this is the first time you mentioned those. But it doesn't matter because I don't believe a word you say. You've gotten what you wanted. Me in your bed, an introduction into Austin society and the Stewart family at your mercy with you calling all the shots. And now I want you out of my room and out of my life."

"Fallon…listen, I know you're upset and when you calm down we can talk rationally."

"I am rational and I want you gone. Go!"

"Not until I know you're okay," Gage responded. "You collapsed, for Christ's sake, and I'm not—" The words he'd been about to say cut off when he noticed the book on the bedside table.

What to Expect When You're Expecting.

Suddenly it became very clear to him why she was in the maternity ward. It was the same reason she hadn't been eating much lately and had gotten sick a couple of mornings. It was why her breasts had felt fuller and more sensitive during their lovemaking.

Fallon was pregnant.

Fallon knew the moment the truth hit Gage. Color leached from his face and he looked at her. "Are you...?"

"You know the answer to that question," Fallon responded.

"How?"

Fallon shook her head. "I don't know. I was taking the pills, but apparently that's normal. Anyway, it doesn't change the facts. I'm going to have a baby."

"You mean *we're* having a baby," he replied.

"This baby is mine," Fallon stated fiercely, clutching her stomach.

His gaze zeroed in on her action. "Fallon..."

"I don't need or want you, Gage. Neither does this baby."

Gage's face was drawn and tight, and Fallon knew she'd hit a nerve.

"A child needs its father. And I won't be separated from him or her." Gage's tone was vehement.

"You have no rights," Fallon stated. "My body, my choice. And right now I choose not to have anything to do with a liar for a husband."

"You're being unreasonable. You must know this changes everything between us, Fallon. It's not black-and-white anymore."

"You mean like it was for you when you conspired against me?" Fallon sat upright in the bed. "When you mercilessly seduced me night after night until I ended up here in this bed!" She pointed downward. "You used me for your own enjoyment and amusement. What was I to you but some pampered bed-warmer you could keep handy when you had an itch that needed scratching?"

"That's not true!" he retorted hotly. "I've never treated you with anything less than respect."

Fire flashed in Fallon's eyes. "Respect. You call lying and going behind my back respect? You don't know the meaning of the word and I won't let me or my baby be a pawn in your games any longer. I want you out. Now!" she yelled.

Suddenly the door to her hospital room swung open and Ayden walked in. His eyes were laser-focused on her. "I could hear Fallon screaming down the hall. What the hell is going on?" He looked at Gage.

"Please make him leave." Fallon turned onto her side and faced the window. She couldn't bear to look at Gage. Not knowing how incredibly foolish she'd been to fall for his lies. He'd set this course of events in motion and now they'd created a life. She placed her hand over her small, rounding belly.

Ayden walked over to Gage. "I won't have you upsetting Fallon anymore, Gage. She nearly suffered a miscarriage because of your lies and machinations."

"But the baby's okay?" Gage asked.

Fallon studiously avoided looking at him. "*For now.* I was having spotting and cramps. The doctor put me on some medication that will hopefully stop them, but I need to rest and be stress-free."

"Meaning you don't want me anywhere near you? Is that it?"

"That's right," Fallon responded hotly and turned to glare at him. "You can go back to your high-profile Wall Street existence making loads of money because I don't want or need you and neither does my baby. Consider the contract we signed null and void. Gather your team of highly paid lawyers and get them to send over whatever paperwork is necessary to end this sham of a marriage."

"Fallon, you can't get rid of me that easy. Not only did we sign a contract, but I own a majority stake at Stewart Technologies."

Fallon's eyes flashed fire. "So you're threatening me?"

"No, of course not." Gage sighed. "This isn't coming out right. I want you to calm down."

"Then let me show you the exit." Ayden motioned to the door.

Gage held up his hands in surrender. "Okay. I'll leave for now, but I will be back, Fallon. It isn't over between us."

When she finally heard the door click shut, Fallon fell back against the pillows. Holding herself up, being strong in front of Gage, had zapped all her energy.

"It's all right, Fallon. You can rest now." Ayden came forward and helped make her more comfortable on the bed. "I meant what I told Gage. You need to get some sleep."

"Are you leaving?"

Ayden shook his head. "No, I'll be right here by your side."

His words were one of the last things Fallon thought about as she drifted off to sleep, along with Gage's promise it wasn't over between them.

Pregnant.

Gage was still in shock over the news. He had absolutely no idea what to do with the information. He was equal parts overjoyed and scared out of his mind. He'd never thought about being a father because he'd never had one of his own. The closest he'd had to a father figure had been Henry Stewart and look how that had turned out.

But that didn't change the facts. Fallon was having his

baby. He wasn't sure how far along she was, because they'd had a very active sex life, but he suspected she could have conceived as early as their honeymoon. During those idyllic days in Punta Cana he hadn't been able to get enough of her. He'd had a ferocious, all-consuming need for her. A need that had led them to creating a child.

But Fallon wanted nothing more to do with him. *Ever.*

She knew the truth that he'd been seeking to right the wrongs from years ago by acquiring stocks in Stewart Technologies. But she was wrong about his feelings for her. They'd grown exponentially and he was no longer seeking revenge. All he could see was Fallon. And now their baby.

Flashes of the two of them together holding a beautiful brown baby with hazel-gray eyes struck Gage. He walked to the bar and poured himself two thumbs of whiskey. Padding to the terrace, he lifted the glass to his mouth and sipped. The spirits warmed his insides but nothing could smooth out the raw edges from his reckoning with Fallon.

The disappointment in her eyes, the hurt—it dug into his insides. The thought he might never know his child, as he'd never known his father, was too much to deal with. He stared out at the city and sipped the whiskey as night fell over Austin. Somehow, some way, he had to change her mind. Make her realize her future and their baby's included him.

Seventeen

Muted voices slowly pulled Fallon back into consciousness. At first she didn't know where she was but then it dawned on her. She was in the hospital, fighting to keep her baby after nearly suffering a miscarriage.

Fallon blinked and opened her eyes. Her mother and father rushed to her side.

Her father spoke first. "You're awake. When we heard you'd fainted, your mother and I were scared to death. Thank you for calling us."

Henry turned and Fallon looked to see who he was speaking to. She noticed Ayden standing in the corner of the room, a haunted look on his face. Seconds later he walked out the door. It had taken courage for her big brother to make that call after their father had essentially abandoned him as a child. Fallon would be forever grateful. And she would tell Ayden that as soon as she had the chance.

"So, you're going to be a mommy," her mother stated with a wide grin. Nora came forward and lightly stroked her cheek. "You know, you're making me a grandma way before my time."

Fallon couldn't resist a smile.

"How far along are you?" her father asked. "If you don't mind my asking."

"Two months."

"You certainly didn't waste any time, my dear," her mother said. "It will certainly ensure Gage is on the hook for taking care of you and my grandson or granddaughter for years to come."

Fallon sighed. Of course her mother thought in monetary terms. Fallon hoped Ayden hadn't told them Gage's true intentions and the reason she'd fainted. Her parents had no idea her marriage to Gage was over. Finished. She wouldn't stay married to someone who'd lied to and deceived her.

"Where's Gage?" Her father searched her eyes for an answer. "The mother of his child is in the hospital. Why isn't he here at your side?"

Fallon rubbed her temples. She was not in the mood for this. "Not now, Daddy."

"I agree, Henry," her mother said quietly. "Now isn't the time or place."

"Like hell it isn't. I smell a rat." Her father pressed on. "I had to hear about my daughter—" he pounded his chest "—from Ayden of all people. The son who hates me because I walked away from his mama. And you tell me I'm wrong?"

"What do you want from me, Daddy?" Fallon wailed. "For me to admit I made a mistake marrying Gage? Well, I did. There, I said it. Are you happy now?"

Her father's face clouded with unease and he came to sit by her bedside. "Of course I'm not happy to see my baby girl in pain. I only want what's best for you. That's all I have ever wanted."

Nervously, Fallon bit her lip and nodded as tears streamed down her cheeks. "Then let this go."

"All right." He nodded.

The nurse interrupted at the right moment when she came in with the cart to check Fallon's vitals.

"We're going to let you get some rest," her father said, giving her hand a gentle squeeze. "But we're a phone call away if you need us."

"Thank you, Daddy. And one other thing?"

"Anything, baby girl."

"It took a lot for Ayden to call you today, but he did it for me. Because he loves me. Please be kind to him."

"I will."

"Promise me."

"I promise."

After her parents departed and the nurse checked her blood pressure and pulse, Fallon glanced at her phone for messages. There was a text and a voice mail from Dane stating he was en route to Austin because Ayden had called him, too. Her big brother was pretty amazing. There were, however, no calls or texts from Gage. Had she been expecting one? She shouldn't. She'd made it crystal clear she didn't want him near her, but theirs was only a cease-fire. Gage had *chosen* to leave, but he would be back. Of that she was sure.

The door to her room opened and Ayden returned. He'd long since abandoned the jacket and tie he'd come to her office in and was drinking what she suspected was coffee in a foam cup. He glanced around the room.

She read his mind. "They're gone."

He nodded and was quiet as he came to sit on the bed with her.

"Thank you for calling them. I really appreciate it. It must have been difficult dealing with our father after all this time. I know you didn't stay for the reception."

Ayden's hazel-gray eyes rested on her face. "You have no idea how hard, Fallon. When he arrived, there was no tearful reunion. He was here for you and you alone. It didn't matter that I was here, because I mean nothing to him."

Tears sprung to her eyes. "I'm sorry, Ayden."

He shrugged. "It's okay. I made my peace with it a long time ago. I'm glad I have you and Dane."

"So am I." Fallon attempted a half smile. "I owe you a great deal for looking out for me and bringing me your findings on Gage even though you knew it would hurt me."

"Honestly, Fallon, I struggled with whether I should tell you. I'd seen how happy you've been with Gage with my own eyes. Ultimately, after talking with Maya, she advised me I had to tell you, but it was hard. He clearly adores you and vice versa."

"That's a lie, Ayden." Tears brimmed in her eyes and fell down her cheeks. "He was acting, giving me a false sense of security before he slipped the rug right out from under me. And as for me…" Her voice trailed off. "I foolishly thought somehow love would find a way. I thought in time my love might heal the pain and heartache he'd been through. I was wrong."

A wave of something close to desolation rushed through her. A sob broke free and she curled herself in the fetal position.

"It's okay, Fallon," Ayden whispered in her ear as he climbed onto the hospital bed and gathered her in his arms. "I'm here for you. Your big brother is here."

Days bled together in a dull gray jumble for Gage. He was trying not to mope and was focusing all his energy into work and managing his company's mutual funds. But it didn't lighten his mood. Instead he only grew bleaker as the days dragged on. Meanwhile he'd learned that Fallon had been released from the hospital with strict instructions to relax and avoid stress.

When he'd told Theo, his best friend had given him an

I-told-you-so speech. Theo had advised Gage to grovel at Fallon's feet and beg her to take him back, but that was hard to do because, true to her word, she wanted nothing to do with him. She'd ignored every call or text he'd sent since her release. As for his mother, he couldn't tell her about the baby, not until he made things right with Fallon.

She'd sent Ayden and Maya to pack up her belongings at his penthouse. Gage had been sure not to be there; he hadn't wanted to see the sad looks on their faces.

His marriage was over when it should be thriving because they were having a child together. But he couldn't confront Fallon now and beat his chest about his rights. The doctor had told him she'd nearly miscarried and, in another month or so, she'd be out of the woods. Then they could tell everyone their great news.

And so Gage was giving Fallon the space she needed to get stronger so she could carry their child to term. She and the baby meant more to him than anything. He knew he didn't deserve either of them, but he would do his best by them. If she needed to relax in a stress-free zone and be with her family, then so be it.

He wasn't prepared, however, for her brother Dane to make an appearance at his office. The youngest Stewart was known to been MIA on most occasions. He hadn't even made their wedding, citing the excuse that he couldn't leave the movie he'd been filming, even though he was one of Hollywood's A-list actors.

"Dane." Gage rose when the six-foot-tall man approached him. He was what the ladies called a Pretty Ricky with café-au-lait skin, dark brown eyes and a perpetual five-o'clock shadow. He was wearing faded jeans, a graphic T-shirt, black boots and a leather jacket. Dane's good looks must have gotten him past Gage's assistant even though he'd given strict instructions to not be disturbed. "What can I do for you?"

"I came here to give you a black eye," Dane responded, making a fist and punching his other hand. "I heard about what you did to the company, but most of all to Fallon, how you played her for your own gain. And I came here to give you a piece of my mind."

"By all means," Gage responded, widening his arms. "Take your best shot. I deserve everything you have to say and then some."

Dane frowned. "You're not supposed to be helping this along."

"Why not? I know what I did was wrong. I apologized. Told Fallon I made a mistake and I should have never lied to her."

"Yet you did." Dane glared at him. "She feels like you made a fool of her. How could you do that? How can you stand to look at yourself in the mirror?" He crossed to Gage's desk and slammed his large hands on it. "Fallon has had a thing for you for years, Gage. And you knew that. You took advantage."

"I admit my intentions from the outset weren't honorable, but they changed when I fell in love with your sister."

"Love?" Dane laughed as he stood to his full six-foot height. "C'mon, Gage."

"It's true, Dane. I love Fallon and I love our baby."

Dane stared incredulously. "Does she know that?"

Gage shook his head. "That night…at the hospital. She never gave me a chance to say more. She ordered me out."

"Can you blame her?"

"No, I can't," Gage replied. "It's why I've stayed away, so she can calm down and get some rest. I don't want anything to happen to her or our baby."

Dane eyed him suspiciously. "You should know she intends to divorce you. If you really love my sister, you don't have very long to fight for her."

"I know, but I will. You best believe that."

* * *

Fallon was ready to get back to work. Sitting on her bottom for the last two months had been sheer agony, but she would do anything to keep this baby safely in her womb. And she had. But she'd hated not being able to run her own company and be in the thick of the action.

Initially she'd been worried Gage would try to make a move on Stewart Technologies while she was out, but surprisingly it had been business as usual with no outside interference. It wouldn't last for long. One day soon Gage would make his move. In the meantime she enjoyed visits from her parents, Shana, Ayden and Maya. Even Dane had come during the early part of her convalescence to spend some time with her.

But she'd done as instructed and worked remotely from Stewart Manor to keep her stress level to a minimum. Initially she'd wanted to go back to her cottage, but her parents had been adamant that if something happened, they'd be too far away. They'd insisted she come home.

Nora fussed over her and was already knee-deep in discussion with an interior designer on decorating a nursery for when the baby came. Initially, Fallon was suspicious of Nora's motives. At the hospital her mother had made no secret of how her grandchild guaranteed Gage wouldn't be off the hook financially. But then Nora had surprised Fallon by offering to be her birth coach. It had been a rare mother-daughter moment, one that involved tears and hugs. But, of course, it was over much too quick. Nora wouldn't win mother of the year, but they were making inroads in their relationship. It seemed the baby was bringing them together.

Ayden and her father had gone from being civil to one another to actually having a conversation. They wouldn't be breaking into a hug anytime soon, but progress was being made. And if her personal suffering had caused a reunion between her big brother and father, then Fallon would gladly endure it.

Today, however, she was excited. After her checkup this morning at the four-month mark, she'd been given the green light to return to work next week. It felt like she'd been given a get-out-of-jail-free card.

She was leaving the doctor's office and heading to her car in the parking lot when she caught a familiar figure standing by her driver's-side door.

Gage.

She'd known it was possible he might show up. Although she didn't owe him a thing, she'd informed Gage of the doctor visit, but she'd urged him to stay away. When he hadn't shown, she'd thought she was in the clear. She'd been wrong.

Swallowing the lump in her throat, Fallon strolled toward him, hoping to give the appearance of nonchalance. Gage looked different. His eyes were haunted instead of intense as they usually were. He had on a leather jacket and faded jeans, which were hanging off him instead of clinging to his muscular thighs. *Had he lost weight?*

"How'd the doctor's visit go?"

"Fine."

"And the baby?"

"Is also fine," she replied. "We're both—"

"Fine, I know. I get that," Gage interrupted her. "Can we talk?"

"I believe your lawyers can handle whatever it is that requires discussion." Fallon used her key to unlock her door. "Can you step aside?"

Gage shook his head. "Fallon? We *have* to talk."

"Why? Because you say so?"

"Because we're having a baby. Do you honestly want other people deciding what's best for our child?"

Fallon sighed. "All right, there's a park across the street."

She began walking toward the crosswalk and noticed that Gage was still standing there. Had he been expecting her to hold his hand? He could think again. She watched him insert his hands into his pockets and move quickly to her side.

When they made it to the park, they sat on one of the many benches surrounding the playground. How apropos, considering one day they'd be watching a child of theirs running around and playing on the swings, slide and monkey bars.

Fallon turned to Gage. "Well, you wanted to talk. You have the floor."

Gage scooted around to face her. "Thank you for agreeing to talk to me."

"I doubt I had much choice."

"You have choices, Fallon," Gage responded, "and I'm sorry if I made you feel like you didn't. I forced you into marrying me and didn't give you a whole lot of options."

"No, you didn't. I had forty-eight hours."

"I was afraid if I gave you too much time, you'd turn me down. And I had a plan to bring you and your family down a peg. It was all so easy when you're looking at it on paper, but after seeing you again, I was undone. I hadn't expected to be so completely enamored with you. I wanted you for myself."

"Do you honestly expect me to believe that?"

"I do. Look at how bullheaded I was. I wouldn't give you an inch. I requested we get married in a month's time."

Fallon sighed. "All right, so you lusted after me. That doesn't change the fact that you lied to me."

Gage stared her directly in the eye. "I did. And I can't take back what I've done. All I can do is tell you how incredibly sorry I am for hurting you. I never thought we'd have a real marriage, but somewhere along the line…" He paused. "Fallon, I fell in love you."

Her eyes widened in disbelief.

"I know you don't believe me," Gage said quickly. "Because I haven't earned your love. I used and abused your trust. I can only hope one day you'll believe me and let me be a father to our baby." He glanced down at her stomach, which was starting to show signs of rounding thanks to the child growing inside.

"Gage..."

"I love you, Fallon," he said again. "I probably always have and I certainly know I always will." He rose and lowered himself far enough to plant a kiss on her forehead. "And I believe what we had together was precious, but it wasn't built on the right foundation. One day it will be. I will prove to you I'm worthy of your love. I promise."

Stunned, Fallon watched Gage walk away. She sat on the bench until she heard school bells in the distance. Gage *loved* her. Why had it taken him so long to say the words she'd longed to hear? The words she'd felt so long for him but couldn't express for fear he didn't feel the same? Was he expressing his undying love for her because of the baby? He'd lied too easily and believably before. He'd made her think he wanted acceptance into society, all the while seducing her, when all he'd wanted was to ruin her family. No, as much as it pained her, she needed to listen to her gut. Gage didn't deserve her love or her trust.

Fallon patted her stomach and spoke to their baby. "I'm sorry we've made such a mess of this, but I'll fix it." Somehow, some way, she would. She would carve out a life for herself and this baby even if it didn't include its father.

"I have to admit your call was a surprise," Ayden said when Gage met up with him for drinks at a swanky downtown bar near both their offices a couple of weeks later.

"Even though I'm persona non grata in the Stewart family, I was hoping we could talk," Gage responded.

"If you're looking for help with Fallon," Ayden began, "you can count me out. It's up to you to heal the wound in your relationship."

"Agreed. What'll you have?" He motioned to the bartender standing in front of Ayden.

"I'll have a whiskey." Ayden turned to Gage. "So, what's up? And has anyone told you that you look like hell?"

Gage smirked. He couldn't remember the last time he'd been to the barber for a haircut much less a trim to his beard. Nothing seemed to matter without Fallon in his life. He slid a large envelope toward Ayden.

Ayden's brow furrowed as he took it. "What's this?"

"Open it."

Ayden studied him for a long moment before sliding his finger under the flap and opening the envelope. He pulled out a stack of papers and read through them. Then those hazel-gray eyes so like Fallon's stared at him in shock. "Why would you do this?"

"To prove to Fallon I only want her and our baby."

"But why me?" Ayden inquired. When the waiter returned with his drink, he took a long swallow.

"Because they're rightfully yours. They belong to you," Gage responded. "Call it righting a wrong done to you and your mother. I know Henry cheated your mother out of her shares. I'm only giving you what you deserve."

"I can't let you do this, Gage," Ayden responded. "This is a fortune. I'm sure there's another way to prove yourself to Fallon. Plus, I'm not even sure how I feel about this. I mean, I'm not a part of the Stewart family."

"My spies tell me otherwise. I heard you've been visiting Stewart Manor."

"To see Fallon." Ayden's voice rose slightly. "Although Henry and I are polite to one another for Fallon's sake, we're far from bosom buddies. And even if I were to accept your generous offer, how would this look to Fallon? She might think you and I were in it together all along to get revenge against Henry because we both have a beef with him. I don't want to ruin the relationship we have. Fallon and I have grown close."

Gage slid off the bar stool and threw back the last bit of whiskey he'd been drinking. "You and I know the truth. We were never in cahoots to cheat Fallon. Just me. I'm the scoundrel and she knows that. You have to trust in what you've built with her. As for the others, do you really care what Henry thinks?"

Ayden gave him a sidelong glance. "Once upon a time I did, but not anymore."

"Well then, you're a Stewart, Ayden. Take what's yours. Take what should have been your inheritance. I have no right to it and neither does Fallon. I hope she'll understand the reasoning behind my decision."

"I hope to God you're right," Ayden said, grabbing the papers and scribbling his name on them. "And I don't regret this decision. But, yes, on my mother's behalf for everything she was denied from Henry, I accept."

Leaving the bar, Gage had never felt so good. The last two months he'd been tormented by his actions. Each morning he woke up feeling as if something had broken inside him. It had. But tonight he'd relieved himself of the one thing standing between him and a second chance with his wife. He hoped it was enough to prove he loved and wanted Fallon and their baby.

Fallon still couldn't believe what Ayden had shared with her. Gage had given Ayden all of the stock he'd acquired in Stewart Technologies. And he hadn't sold it to him. He'd *given* them to her big brother lock, stock and barrel, without asking for anything in return.

It was a generous gesture and Ayden explained that at first he wasn't entirely sure what to do. But then he told her why he'd said yes. His mother, Lillian, had helped his father start Stewart Technologies, but during the divorce she'd been outgunned by Henry's fancy lawyers and had walked away with a small settlement. Ayden felt it was okay to accept Gage's gift. And Fallon had agreed. He'd been surprised Fallon wasn't angry with Gage for not offering them to her first.

She wasn't. Yet Ayden had offered to share the stock Gage had given *him* with her. He wanted to prove he wasn't in cahoots with Gage on a takeover, but Fallon turned Ayden down and told him to keep the stock. She already ran Stewart Technologies and had shares in the company herself. She didn't need more. But Ayden? He'd been abandoned by their father. Fallon was ashamed Henry acted as if Ayden didn't exist. He'd never even paid child support, much less acknowledged Ayden's accomplishments. The shares were his just deserts. She was surprised Gage had understood that and hadn't wanted to keep them for himself. After everything that had happened to Gage and his mother, she was certain he felt entitled to them, but he hadn't. Instead he'd offered them to Ayden.

A man who, like Gage, had been looked down on.

She doubted her father would agree with her. He would be livid that Ayden, the black sheep, had leverage over him. But Fallon didn't mind if Ayden had a larger stake in Stewart Technologies than she did. She was CEO and running the company, after all. Ayden had his own company, Stewart Investments, to worry about.

What she couldn't get over was Gage's generous act. It gave her hope that there was some humanity left in him. That he was a man she could love. A man who could be a father to her baby.

And so today she'd decided to hop in her Audi and drive to see her bullheaded, arrogant and controlling husband to find out if she was still living in a fairy-tale world where love won out in the end.

She didn't waste time parking when she arrived at Gage's building; she merely tossed her keys to the valet, waved at the doorman and rushed to the private elevator. She pressed the code for the penthouse and impatiently waited for the car to ascend to the top. She paced the travertine-tiled floor until finally the doors opened into the penthouse.

The apartment was dark and Fallon wondered if Gage was home, but then she saw a figure in silhouette outside on the terrace. It was Gage's favorite place to go when he needed to think things over. The pocket doors were open so the click of her heels as she approached caused Gage to turn around in his chair. Her heart quickened at the sight of him.

"Fallon?" His voice was raspy.

When she was within a few feet of him, she answered. "Yes, it's me." She noticed the glass in his hand with a dark liquid she could only assume was brandy, his drink of choice.

"I thought perhaps I was dreaming like I have been the last couple of months, hoping you'd come home. That you'd come back to me. Is that why you're here? Are you back for good?"

Fallon stared at him from where she stood. He looked haggard, with lines around his eyes, and his beard had grown. When was the last time he'd shaved? "I don't know, Gage, that depends on how this conversation goes."

The hope she'd given him instantly caused him to straighten and he walked toward her until they were face-to-face.

"Why did you do it, Gage?" Fallon asked, searching his face. "Why did you give Ayden those shares?"

"Because they're rightfully his," Gage responded. "Always should have been. I had no right to them. I was angry and acquired them as a way to get back at your father. To strike him where it hurts. Then he would see I was good enough for you. But you know what?"

"What?"

"The person I hurt most was you. The woman I've come to love. And as a result, I hurt myself because you left me. Alone. How I've always been."

She dragged in a sustaining breath. "Gage..." Her heart broke for him even though he was the reason they were in this situation to begin with.

"I know I have no right to ask you this." His eyes pierced hers as he held her gaze. "Can you forgive me for being such a stupid, arrogant, bullish fool in search of power and prestige? I can't change the man I was, but because of you I can change and be the man you need me to be—a whole, mature man." He glanced around and his mouth twisted in pain. "Because none of it means anything without you, Fallon. I'm sorry. Your being here gives me hope that perhaps—perhaps—you might be willing to give us another chance. A chance to be a family. Because I want more than anything to be married to you."

Fallon didn't move. She stayed where she was. Her heart galloped in her chest. She was afraid to move, let alone speak, because her heart was so full. She felt the tears silently slide down her cheeks one by one. She felt the moisture against her skin but was suspended in time with Gage as she always was whenever he was near.

"Please don't shut me out of your life, Fallon. Please let me be near you and our baby." Gage reached out and cupped her cheek. "Don't cry, please. That's not what I want." Slowly he pulled her to him, cradling her in his arms.

It was her undoing. His words were scraping away all her defenses, all the walls she'd erected around herself. Fallon knew why Gage had been so generous and why he'd given those shares to Ayden. He wanted to prove that he wanted her more than his quest for revenge. The truth blazed in her heart, sure and true. Gage was the man she loved. The man she'd always loved. Whom she would love forever.

"I love you." The words escaped her lips before she had a chance to take them back. And as she said them, the heaviness she'd felt for weeks began to lighten.

It was an indelible fact. She could never stop loving Gage. He'd had her from the moment he'd helped her after she'd fallen off that horse. "Totally. Uncontrollably. And with all my heart."

"Oh, God, Fallon, I love you, too, so much." His voice sounded choked.

They reached for each other at the same time. Their eyes locked in a hot, heated moment before he bowed his head and he brushed his lips across hers. The slow, sweet kiss caused a low moan to release from her lips. Oh, how she'd missed this. And when he angled his head so he could deepen the kiss and take full possession of her mouth, Fallon was on board. She slid her tongue against his and the taste of him exploded in her mouth.

A slow curl of heat unraveled in her as she tangled her arms around his neck. It had been too long—far too long—since he'd touched her like this. Kissed her like this.

"Gage," she murmured when they came up for air. She took in large gulps, breathing in his dark, delicious scent that was so real and achingly familiar. Peace filled her as Gage held her to his hard, solid chest. "Make love to me," she whispered.

"With pleasure." In seconds he'd swept her into his arms and carried her down the hall to their bed.

Gage laid his beautiful wife down on *their* bed and smiled as she hurriedly removed her clothing and his until he could lie beside her. Catching a whiff of her delicate floral scent awakened every cell in his body and revived memories of how good it had been between them. It had been those images that had haunted him in the weeks they'd been apart, tormenting his mind and his body. He'd been unable to sleep and it showed in the tiredness he'd felt each day.

Until now. He considered himself lucky Fallon was forgiving him. He would have another chance to be a better husband and a father to their child.

He looked down at her in bewilderment. "Is it really possible we can try again? Start afresh?"

Fallon reached for him then, wrapping her arms around his neck and bestowing him with sweet, tender kisses. And Gage realized what true forgiveness looked like.

"Good. Because I want to give you everything," Gage said.

Their lovemaking that night was slow and worshipful because there was nothing but love and joy between them. They found their way back to each other's bodies, exploring every available inch while whispering loving words that would blanket them and last them a lifetime. Until, eventually, sleep claimed them as they lay in each other's arms.

Epilogue

A year later

Fallon emerged from the bedroom where she'd gone to change clothes—for the second time that day—after her son, Dylan, had chosen to throw up all over her baptism outfit. But she didn't care. Fallon felt as if she were the luckiest woman in the world.

She and Gage were as in love as ever. She never knew she could be this happy. This fulfilled. Months ago they'd renewed their vows. It had been just the two of them and they'd pledged to start over. And they had. They were rebuilding Stewart Technologies with some help from her big brother. Ayden had chosen to keep the stock and hoped to give it to his children someday. Her parents, her father especially, had initially blustered over Gage's gift, but eventually he'd piped down when he'd realized pitting Fallon against her big brother could cause him to lose her.

Fallon and Gage had been thrilled. And when they'd

attended Ayden and Maya's wedding on Valentine's Day, it had brought tears to Fallon's eyes. Gage had incorrectly thought she was upset over their first ceremony, but then she'd told him, she'd been in love with him even then and they'd kissed and made out like two love-struck teenagers in the back of the reception hall.

Fallon smiled at the memory as she walked down the corridor of their new house, which wasn't far from Stewart Manor so her parents could be close to their grandson. Before Dylan's arrival, she and Gage had decided they'd need more space, a house that was kid-friendly instead of Gage's ultra-chic penthouse. He kept it as an investment and for the nights he worked late in the city, but those days were over for Fallon. Once she'd had Dylan, she'd cut back on her hours. She wanted to be a better mother than Nora had been.

When she arrived at the terrace where they were hosting the reception after the baptism, Fallon glanced at her mother, who was in a battle with Grace for the title of most doting grandmother. Both women had called a cease-fire when Fallon told them in no uncertain terms she would cut them off from seeing the baby if they didn't behave. Nora and Grace would never be friends, but they'd learned to coexist. It surprised Fallon to see another side to Nora—a kind, caring, compassionate side she'd never had, but of which she was glad Dylan would be the beneficiary.

However, right now, he was getting a little fussy and was starting to cry.

"I'll take him." Fallon reached for her son.

"Are you sure?" Grace asked. "Because I don't mind holding him."

"Yeah, I'm properly prepared now," Fallon stated, having procured a burping cloth to lay over her shoulder. She accepted her son from his grandmother.

"He's so beautiful." Nora stroked her grandson's curly

black hair while Fallon held him and patted his bottom, soothing his loud cries.

"What'd you expect?" her father interjected from nearby where he was huddled with her husband, Dane, Ayden and Maya. It wasn't hearts and roses between the men she loved, but they were all trying to be cordial for her sake and for Dylan's. "He's a Stewart."

"And a Campbell," Gage said as he made his way over to Fallon.

She glanced up at her husband and love shone so clearly in his eyes. She couldn't believe how lucky she was they'd found each other again. It hadn't been an easy road getting here, but they'd made it through the storm.

Gage bowed his head and brushed a tender kiss across her lips. "Have I told you how much I love you?"

Fallon grinned and paused a moment. "No—" she shook her head "—I don't believe you have today."

"Well, then, let me remedy that. I love you, Fallon Stewart Campbell, and you're the only woman for me."

"And you, Gage Campbell, are all the man I need."

* * * * *

FROM RICHES TO REDEMPTION

ANDREA LAURENCE

One

"Morgan? There's someone I'd like you to meet."

Turning at the sound of her brother Sawyer's voice, Morgan Steele found herself suddenly frozen on the spot. Her eyes were wide and unblinking, her lips trembling but soundless as she stared at the man standing at her brother's side.

She wasn't sure what she had been expecting. Probably just another polite and boring chat with one of her parents' friends and colleagues. Charity fund-raisers for Steele Tools usually meant an endless stream of champagne and small talk with people whose names she wouldn't remember in ten minutes. Her family hosted events like this at their home all the time. But she knew this man's name. There was no way she would have ever forgotten it.

He'd grown out of his boyish lanky build and into the strong physique of a man who worked with his hands for a living. His closely cropped beard made him look older and more sophisticated than before, but Morgan would know those eyes anywhere. Those navy blue beauties had seen right through her.

"Morgan, this is River Atkinson. He's the owner and CEO of Southern Charm Construction. He'll be working with you this year on our summer housing development project."

Sawyer continued to prattle on, completely oblivious to the reactions of the two people standing with him. At least to Morgan's stunned reaction. For River's part, he actually looked a bit…well…smug. He smiled in a way that told anyone who bothered to look that he was in on the joke. His eyes held a touch of amusement in them as he extended his hand to her.

"It's a pleasure to meet you, Miss Steele," he said.

She knew she should shake his hand. Play along with this ruse and not make a scene. And yet, she couldn't make herself reach out and touch him. That was the same hand that had caressed every inch of her body. The same hand that had slipped a petite diamond ring onto her ring finger during a small rustic mountain ceremony in the Smoky Mountains. The same hand that had taken a hundred grand from her father and walked away without looking over his shoulder.

"Morgan?"

Her brother's concerned voice snapped her out of her thoughts. She plastered her practiced grin onto her face and thrust her arm out to shake River's hand. She had to treat him like any other business acquaintance. Sawyer didn't know about her past with River. Almost no one did, including all three of her brothers. "It's nice to meet you, too, Mr. Atkinson. I'm sure our companies will do great things together this summer."

His shake was firm, but she could tell that he wasn't interested in immediately letting go of her hand. To be honest, she had a hard time pulling away herself. There was something when they touched—a familiar connection—that lingered there. As though their bodies remembered each other, even if their minds resisted the idea.

Finally, he released her from his grasp. She switched her champagne flute into that hand to let the chilly glass dull the feel of him against her skin. Then she took a large sip to dull the feel of him inside her head as well.

Who the hell had approved this? Her father certainly wasn't involved. He'd just as soon shoot River on the doorstep as let him inside after what happened back in college. But her family was good at keeping secrets, even from each other. It was news to Morgan that Southern Charm Construction and River Atkinson were one and the same entity. She'd heard mention of the company and never once questioned who owned it.

"Sawyer? Can you come here for a minute?" Their mother's voice beckoned one of Morgan's older brothers.

Morgan tensed. She didn't want to be left alone with River. They would hardly be alone in the traditional sense, but being in the same room having a discussion was more intimate than they'd experienced since the day her family pulled them apart.

"If you'll excuse me." Sawyer smiled and clapped River on the back before he departed.

With just the two of them standing on the fringe of the crowd together, Morgan wasn't quite sure what to do. It was more awkward than a junior high dance. What was she supposed to say to the boy—*man*—who had turned his back on her all those years ago?

"You're looking well, Morgan," River said. He was clutching a glass tumbler of scotch in his hand as his dark eyes raked over her from top to bottom. "That emerald dress suits you. It brings out the green in your eyes."

It seemed they were going for polite, but intimate. "Thank you. I like the beard. It makes you look distinguished." It was silly, but she wasn't sure what else to say to him.

River chuckled at her choice of words. "Distinguished. If by that you mean rich and important, then yes, that's exactly the look I was going for." He glanced down at her hand as she held her glass. "Not married yet?" he asked.

Morgan couldn't prevent one dark eyebrow from arching up in surprise and confusion at his question. "Yet? Don't you mean married *again*, River?"

He just shrugged off her challenge with a roll of his eyes. "As far as the state of Tennessee and your family is concerned, you've never been married, Morgan, and neither have I. That's what getting an annulment means. It never happened. That's why you mailed the ring back, remember?"

"Shhh!" Morgan's eyes widened as she looked

around at the people nearby to see if anyone was listening. Thankfully, everyone seemed to be involved in their own discussions. She reached out for River's elbow and tugged him with her into a far corner of the ballroom where no one could hear them.

"What is all this about, River?" she hissed at him through clenched teeth.

He crossed his arms over his chest, straining the shoulders of his designer tuxedo. "I don't know what you're talking about."

"The hell you don't. Why are you here tonight?"

"I was invited," he replied with a satisfied smirk.

Morgan sighed in frustration. He was going to make her spell this out just because he could. "How did our companies end up working together, River? This is the first I've heard of it or it sure as hell wouldn't have been approved. Was this your big idea? To weasel back into the family somehow through your business?"

"Why would I want to be in your family, Morgan? For the few hours I was related to the Steeles, I was treated like dirt. You've always been so arrogant. Acting like somehow everything always revolves around your important family and what people want from you." There was audible venom in his voice. "I didn't want anything from you but your love, Morgan, and your father wouldn't even let me have that."

Morgan watched a flicker of pain dance across his eyes. Yes, he'd been hurt. But he hadn't been abandoned the way she had been. "No, he wouldn't, but you seemed all too happy to settle for a fat check instead."

Her father, Trevor Steele, had tried to reason with

her when they got back to Charleston that morning. River wasn't good enough for her. He was only using her to get to her money. Eloping? Without a prenuptial agreement? A background check? That little stunt could've had a disastrous outcome, he had insisted. And the boy she loved had his price. His affections were worth a hundred grand. When her father agreed to River's price, money in hand, River had stopped fighting and let Morgan go.

River stiffened at her words. Perhaps he wasn't very proud of that, either. He narrowed his dark sapphire gaze at her for a moment, and then let his arms fall helplessly to his side. "If that's what you really think of me, it's probably just as well our marriage was erased from history. We never would've made it. You must've known that, though. You didn't seem to mind letting your daddy clean up your mess."

Morgan's jaw dropped, her response stolen from her lips. What was she supposed to say to that? Letting her daddy clean up the mess? Really? What did he know of the mess left behind? He hadn't been there. He had no idea what she had been through over losing him. Over losing *everything*. He'd extorted a load of money from her father and carried on with his life. She'd been left behind to deal with the aftermath.

"Morgan, Dad says it's almost time for us to go on stage and beg for money."

She turned away from River as a wave of relief washed over her. Morgan needed the interruption. Things had escalated quickly with years of words bottled up between them, but now was not the time. She would say something she regretted if she didn't get away from him right now.

"Do you have your speech ready?" This time it was Sawyer's twin, Finn, coming to fetch her. The identical twins were a year and a half older than she was, both with their father's dark blond hair and golden hazel eyes. She could tell this was Finn because of the dimple in his right cheek. Sawyer's dimple was in his left cheek. She also knew Finn was wearing a bright orange bow tie with his tuxedo to agitate their father. Finn lived to exacerbate Trevor Steele.

"I'll be right there." She turned back to where River was standing with an expectant look on his face. He'd called her arrogant, and the way he looked at her made her want to slap the smug smirk off his face. She'd settle for making him eat his words. "We'll have to continue this conversation later, Mr. Atkinson."

"I look forward to it. I'm certainly not going anywhere," he said.

As Morgan turned and made her way up to the stage to join her family in greeting the guests and donors at their annual charity event, she worried that River meant every word he'd said.

Whether it was a promise or a threat, River Atkinson was suddenly back in her life and he wasn't going anywhere.

River watched Morgan walk away with a grin on his face. He was pleased. For one thing, he'd gotten under her skin. That was exactly what he'd wanted when he set out tonight. And for two, watching the curve of her ass sway in that satin-and-lace gown as she left was a delicious sight that brought back some very hot memories. Her womanly curves had certainly filled out since he'd seen her last. That would make any man smile. Even a man who had spent years plotting to make her regret the way she'd abused his affections.

Those affections for Morgan were long gone now. Swept under the rug with his other youthful naïveté. He should've known that his romance with a rich little princess wouldn't end well. She had just been stretching her wings, rebelling against the tight reins they'd kept on her as a child. That's what college was for after all. The problem was that they'd both taken it too far. They'd fallen in love.

Even that wouldn't have been the worst thing in the world. Love wasn't permanent. Marriage was another matter. It was legally binding. Or at least he'd thought it was until the Steele family lawyers managed to get their little indiscretion wiped away.

And Morgan had let them do it. That was what hurt the most. When Daddy yelled, she'd fallen in line, throwing away everything they'd planned together. He'd been left with an empty bed and a consolation prize, if you could call it that. Some would call it hush money. Or a bribe to walk away and not cause a stink. If there was one thing he'd learned about the Steele family, it was that they hated a scandal. He probably could've gotten more money from her father if he'd asked for it. Whatever it took to make River go away.

But, of course, he hadn't thought to do that. He hadn't wanted to take the money at all. It felt cheap. What he wanted was his wife back. He wanted the future he'd planned with her.

When River realized that wasn't going to happen, he knew he had a choice. He could turn tail and go home with nothing but his bruised pride, or he could take the money and make something positive come out of this whole mess. He supposed Mr. Steele thought he would blow every penny on cheap beer and an expensive truck, or whatever he thought poor white trash liked to do with their money.

The joke was on him. River might've been poor and lacked all those fancy degrees on his wall, but he wasn't stupid. He took that money and started his own construction company. He'd practically grown up in this business, following his dad around job sites as soon as he was old enough. With his father's experience, River's drive and a housing boom just beginning in Charleston, he'd turned that hundred thousand into a hundred million in cash and assets.

And to keep in touch with his roots, when River made his first million, he bought a six pack of Pabst Blue Ribbon and a tricked out Ford F-250 to celebrate. Couldn't let ol' Trevor down, could he?

The sound of applause roused River from his thoughts. The family was done welcoming the crowd and asking for money. That meant his chance to track down Morgan again had come. Unfortunately, the petite brunette was easily lost in the crowd. He supposed she wasn't too eager to continue their discussion, but like it or not, it was going to happen. It had been festering for ten years now and it needed to be dealt with.

Even then, there wasn't a rush to return to their argument. He had time, so he made his way to the bar for a refresher and enjoyed some of the cold canapés being passed around. They weren't particularly filling, but rich people seemed to like fancy foods that cost a lot yet left a gnawing hunger in their bellies.

"Mr. Atkinson?"

River turned to find an older man with a young blonde on his arm. "Yes?"

"Kent Bradford," he said, thrusting out his free hand to shake with River. "I hear you build some amazing houses."

River smiled. "I'm glad that's the word going around, but I like to think of it as well-built homes my customers love. Are you interested in building a property, Mr. Bradford?"

"Call me Kent. And actually, yes I am. Do you work outside of the Charleston area at all? I've secured some mountain property near Asheville, North Carolina, and I was hoping to build a cabin."

His brow went up. "A cabin?" A cabin wasn't worth the time or energy to travel that far. The man could get a better deal from a local company.

Kent chuckled. "Well, I say cabin, but let's be honest. A five-thousand square foot, three-story house is hardly a cabin. I just want it to have that mountain cabin feel. With all the modern amenities and luxuries, of course."

That was more like it. "I haven't built out there, but I would be happy to discuss it with you." River reached into his breast pocket and pulled out a business card. "Why don't you give me a call next week and we can talk about what you're interested in. I can have my architect draw something up."

"Wonderful." The man accepted the card and slipped it into his pocket. "I'll be calling you." With a smile, the man turned and led the younger blonde over to the dance floor.

Tonight wasn't *all* about confronting Morgan, despite what she might think.

It was also about business. Working with the Steele Tools company on their annual charity project was good PR for him. Just being in this room put him within shouting distance of damn near every millionaire in the state of South Carolina. While he waited to talk to Morgan, he was happy to pick up a few business contacts. These types were always wanting to build a summer home or a new status-symbol mansion to keep up with the Joneses, and that meant business was good for him.

He figured that eventually he would get a chance to talk to Morgan again. The room was only so large and the night had really just begun. But the next thing he knew, one of the twins got back on stage. River knew she had three older brothers, two of whom were identical twins, but he couldn't even begin to be able to tell them apart, especially with them all sporting similar, Mark Twain-esque names.

"Ladies and gentlemen, I'm sorry to say this, but we're going to have to end the event early tonight. We've had a family emergency that we need to tend to. If you would be so kind as to see your way out, we would truly appreciate it. Morgan will be in touch with each of you in the upcoming weeks about your support of this year's Strong as Steele community project. Thank you so much for coming."

And with that, the twin disappeared from the stage.

That was odd. The family had gone to a lot of trouble and expense putting this event together. Tickets to attend weren't exactly cheap, either. There must have been something serious going on if they'd chosen to end it and kick everyone out of the house before they got checks out of everyone.

Looking around, River caught a blur of emerald green as Morgan was ushered across the hall by her mother and a large man he didn't recognize. He looked like the former military type despite his expensive tuxedo. The brothers followed them, and they all disappeared into a far room of the house and didn't come back out.

He loitered for a while, letting the other guests clear out of the valet lot in the hopes that someone might come out. But soon, he found he was one of the only people in the ballroom aside from the catering crew that was busy cleaning up. He finally gave up and called it a night himself. When he found no fewer than four police cars outside the mansion as he left, he got the feeling the family emergency was going to take up the rest of their night. Knowing the Steeles, whatever happened would require major damage control to keep the family from looking bad.

Strolling outside, he handed over his ticket to the valet driver and waited for his truck. A few minutes later, the attendant pulled around front with his sapphire-blue

F-250 Lariat Super Duty pickup. River tipped him and climbed in.

This wasn't exactly how he'd expected tonight to end. Things felt awkward and unfinished. They'd only begun their discussion when it came to a quick and premature end. Then again, he didn't really know how he'd wanted it to end, either. Perhaps he'd hoped that the sight of him would cause Morgan to swoon? Or maybe that she would rush into his arms and tell him how wrong she'd been and that she still loved him?

Ha. He pulled away from the Steele mansion with a smirk on his face. That wouldn't happen in a million years. His ego wasn't so large as to think she'd given much thought to him over the last decade. He was the poor, unsuitable boy who wouldn't amount to anything. That wasn't the kind of person who loitered in your thoughts. Her big mistake.

No, odds were that she'd tried to put him and their relationship out of her mind as soon as possible. To pretend it never happened just the way her family wanted her to. She probably wanted to put him out of her mind right now, but it wouldn't be so easy this time. River had seen to that by signing an agreement with a representative from Steele Tools who didn't know who he was. Few people outside of her parents would know their history together and their silence had worked to his advantage. Now he was guaranteed to spend a large chunk of the summer collaborating specifically with the company's community outreach representative—Morgan.

At best, he'd hoped she would spend the upcoming weeks regretting what she'd done to him. But after seeing her tonight, this summer might prove to be more pleasurable than he'd expected. At least for him. He hadn't been sure how his former love would look after all these years apart. When she'd turned to him in that stunning green lace gown, he was almost knocked back off his feet. Her exotic green-gold eyes, the high cheekbones, the skin like flawless porcelain... It was as if hardly a day had passed and yet everything was somehow different. Especially when she looked at him with a mix of horror and surprise distorting her lovely face.

The girl he remembered, his bride, had been the prettiest girl he'd ever seen in his life. With her long, luscious dark hair, insightful eyes that saw through his defenses and a sweet-as-sugar smile, he was smitten the moment he'd lain eyes on her. She was older now, perhaps harder, judging by the guarded way she had spoken to him. But even so, he was tempted to fall into her same trap again. Thankfully, he knew better now. Her love came with strings. Baggage. It might come easily, but it could go just as fast.

If Morgan wanted him this time, it was only because he'd achieved his goal and was finally worthy of Daddy's approval. Nothing had really changed about him as a person. He just had money and prestige. Those things were paramount to Mr. Steele. And to Morgan, River supposed.

Hitting the button on his console to open the gate, River slowed at the entrance to his property on Kiawah Island. When it was finally open, he passed down the lane to the home he'd built for himself once he'd finally had the time and money to make exactly what he wanted. A lot had changed since that awful night all those years ago.

River had taken the older man's advice along with his check, walking away and making something of himself with that money. Not to prove anything to Morgan or her father. More to prove it to himself. And he had, many times over. He wasn't the dumb kid he'd been back then. And now it was time for Morgan and Trevor to see how much the man's investment in River had grown. Maybe, just maybe, they might regret judging someone so harshly in the future.

But even if they didn't, he wasn't interested in getting anyone's endorsement these days. Especially from a controlling bastard like Trevor Steele.

Two

"I have the report ready from the fund-raiser. Accounting just brought it to me."

Morgan looked up from her computer to see her assistant, Vanessa, coming into her office with a manila folder in her hand. "That was quicker than I expected."

Vanessa handed over the file. "I'll let you know when your next appointment arrives," she said before slipping back out to her desk.

Morgan opened the folder and her brows lifted in surprise as she saw the bottom line. Given that the event had run for less than a third of its usually scheduled time, she hadn't expected them to raise as much money. They'd never even gotten around to the silent auctions. The family hardly had time to circulate through the crowd and stir up donations. She'd already been planning a contingency for this year's project, narrowing the scope significantly. Considering she had to work with Southern Charm, a part of her would've been okay with cancelling it entirely.

Instead, they'd actually raised more. Apparently, cancelling an event for television-worthy drama in their family made their guests and donors feel bad. And when rich people felt bad, they tended to write a check to feel better again.

Actually, they'd raised enough to build at least three houses in the community this year. And that was just in the month since the event. More funds could still roll in during the next few weeks. Last year, they'd only raised enough for two houses and that had been their all-time high.

That was one bright spot in the dark drama that had plagued her recently. Finding out she had been switched at birth was a major revelation. The news had just come to light and yet, if you asked Morgan, it felt like years since she found out the truth. That sort of news could shift your whole perception of the world. Especially when you realized that your whole life was a mistake.

Normally, time flew by. She lived a pretty busy life, pouring almost all her energy into the family company and its continued success. When she wasn't at the office, she was at the gym trying to work off the stress and the extra pounds that clung to her hips. She'd always longed for the naturally slender figure of her mother, but instead, her weight was just another item on a list of things that weighed heavily—pun intended—on her mind.

But even then, nothing could have prepared her for everything that had happened in her life since that night.

Now, Morgan couldn't even look in the mirror without seeing some imposter looking back at her. How could she have been so blind all these years to the things that were plainly visible to anyone who bothered to look? There was no way she was a Steele. She'd always had a different appearance from the rest of her family—the dark one among a sea of blonds—but it had never registered in her mind what that really meant before the truth came out.

Now she wondered what her parents had really thought all those years. Had her father believed Morgan was the child of an affair with a dark-haired man? Had they thought a recessive gene had come through? They certainly hadn't guessed their real baby girl had been switched with an imposter in the maternity ward or she wouldn't be almost thirty with the last name Steele. Her family would've marched back to the hospital and handed over their changeling the minute they suspected something was wrong.

Even after the truth had come out, there wasn't much they could do. At least at first. The news had come in a double whammy on the night of the charity event: not only had she been switched at birth, but also, the real Steele daughter—Jade Nolan—had just been kidnapped from the steps of their mansion. There was no time to process the impact of the realization. All they could do was dig up ten million dollars to pay the ransom demands.

Morgan had never seen her father that shade of sickly

pale before. Not even the night he burst into her honeymoon cabin. Then, he'd been furious. The latest news just seemed to make him heartsick. Even so, he sprang into action in true Steele CEO form. The money was paid, Jade was found safe and the kidnappers had disappeared without a trace. That left a sudden silence where everyone was now absorbing what this news really meant.

Morgan still wasn't sure what would come of all this. Her whole life, her whole identity, had been tied up in being Morgan Steele. The perfect daughter. The baby of the family. Spoiled and doted upon by her parents and her older brothers. Rich. Well-educated. Poised. The ideal member of the family to represent the Steele Tools outreach program. That identity wouldn't change overnight, no matter what the DNA tests said. It would take time to come to terms with it all.

In the meantime, she woke up most mornings feeling lost. Who was she, really? Who would she have been if she hadn't been switched in the nursery that day? It was too soon to know all the answers yet, but the time she'd spent with Jade and her parents had been enlightening enough. She certainly wouldn't have gotten a private school education or gone on to study at Georgetown University. She wouldn't have gotten a Mercedes convertible for her sixteenth birthday or a two-month trip through Europe as a high school graduation present. Her real parents couldn't afford all that. Morgan had grown up with every luxury that should've been Jade's to enjoy.

Then again, if they hadn't been switched, then perhaps Morgan would've been free to live her life the way she wanted to. That was one luxury she could never afford, no matter how big her investment portfolio got.

At this point, she supposed she should be happy that her family hadn't turned their backs on her. This had been their chance to wash their hands of her, and they hadn't. Although she had the reputation of being the perfect princess of the family, it certainly wasn't because she was without flaws. She was fairly sure she regularly disappointed her parents in one way or another. Not intentionally, but it still happened.

Seeing Jade with her flawless skin, white-blond hair and big dark eyes—almost a clone of her mother, Patricia Steele—made her feel like even more of a disappointment. She imagined that even bound on the floor of the dirty warehouse where they'd found her, Jade was more like the ideal Steele daughter than Morgan would ever be.

She'd only been able to spend a little time with Arthur and Carolyn Nolan, and only in a group setting, but it made her wonder if she would feel more comfortable with her biological family. Perhaps they would be so happy to spend time with their real daughter that their expectations would be lower. Perhaps they wouldn't care that she wasn't a perfect size two or that she'd eloped in college with a poor boy she'd loved more than anything. Maybe they would've supported her choices instead of erasing them.

Or maybe she was imagining a perfect situation that had never existed and never could have existed. If she'd been raised as Jade Nolan, she probably wouldn't have met River at that bar in Five Points. Her life would've taken a different path. But there was no going back and no sense worrying about things like that.

A chiming sound came from her computer, accompanied by an instant message from her assistant. Miss Steele, your four o'clock appointment is here, she wrote.

Speak of the devil.

Morgan took a deep breath. And then there was *that* situation to deal with. It was a horrible thing to say, but the kidnapping had been a welcome distraction from River and his unexpected appearance. As though she didn't already have enough going on in her life, he had to pop up out of nowhere. In one night—at one party, even—her past had caught up with her in more ways than one.

Now, her ex-husband was sitting just outside her office, ready to talk about how they were going to spend the summer together. She could hardly even imagine how she was going to get through this.

Morgan wanted to back out. She'd build six houses next year to make up for it. But she knew that wouldn't fly. They'd already announced their partnership with Southern Charm Construction. If they didn't go through with it, it would raise questions. Questions no one wanted to answer. Besides, if she made a fuss, her father would get involved and that was the last thing she wanted.

If Trevor Steele had taught her nothing else, it was that a Steele stayed poised and professional at all times—even in the face of scandal or disaster. So that was all she could do.

Send him in, she replied to her assistant's message.

Then she locked her computer screen and prepared herself for another argument. There was no way they wouldn't be finishing what they'd started the other night. If they were going to work together, they needed to clear the air once and for all.

The door swung open and standing in the doorway was River. Today, he'd traded in his tuxedo for a navy suit, but it looked just as amazing on him. He'd found an excellent tailor, she'd give him that. The jacket fit his broad shoulders and narrow waist easily. He was still on the lean side, a runner's physique, but even with his coat on, she could tell his upper body was cut. She supposed that working construction could build up those muscles. It made her want to squeeze a bicep and feel it flex beneath her fingertips.

He smiled at her and she felt her resolve start to weaken as heat crept up her neck. It made her wish she'd worn a blouse with a higher neckline. Or that she'd thought to button it up to the throat before he came into her office. Or worn a scarf. At the slightest agitation, be it arousal or embarrassment, her chest and neck would turn a blotchy red. At its worst, her face would follow suit and she'd look like a furious cherry tomato. She hadn't thought about this appointment when she dressed this morning.

Of course, it would help if Morgan didn't think about his muscles. Or his smile. Or his *anything*.

It was too late for that. Instead, all she could do was wave him inside. He shut the door behind him and casually made his way across her office to the desk where she was waiting for him.

When her father had first ordered the furniture for her office, she'd hated it. It was bulky executive furniture that weighed a thousand pounds and was far too dark for her taste. It was perfect for a mahogany row office, but that wasn't the image she wanted to project. Working for charity while sitting at a ten-thousand-dollar desk was tacky.

At the moment, however, she was grateful for it. Having a mountain of wood between the two of them was almost enough to make her feel comfortable in his presence. Almost.

Comfortable or not, it was time to take control of this situation. She might not be a Steele, but she'd been raised like one, and she wasn't going to let River get the upper hand today. She sat up straight at her desk, lacing her fingers together over her leather blotter and crossing her ankles. This was the pose that flipped the switch in her brain to work.

Then she watched River do the opposite. He unbuttoned his jacket and settled into the chair like he was at home on his couch. He made himself comfortable, sitting back and casually crossing his ankle over his knee as though he didn't have a care in the world. Somehow, that didn't seem fair to Morgan.

Time to make him as uncomfortable as she was.

"Before we get started, I have one question for you, Mr. Atkinson."

"Mr. Atkinson is my father," he noted with a sigh. Judging by Morgan's tone, she was ready to finish their little chat from the party. He was glad he was at least in a comfy chair if she was going to lay into him first thing. This could turn into a very long or very short meeting depending on how the next few minutes went. "But ask away."

"What exactly are you doing here?" Her gaze fixed on him with a pointed expression on her face.

"I'm here to talk about building houses for the poor. Isn't that why you're here?" He couldn't help the sarcasm from slipping into his voice. It was one of the only emotions he had left where she was concerned.

She studied his face for a moment. "I'm serious, River. Why did you sign up for this whole thing? If you only bid on this job to get your chance to tell me off, then just walk away now. This charity project is important to me. If you're not genuinely interested in helping the community, I'll find another contractor."

"Oh, I'm very serious," he said. And he meant it. "This project is essential to me and my company's five-year plan."

"So you're just using the Steele name to make a name for yourself."

"I've already made a name for myself and my company, thank you, but I'd be a fool if I didn't use the chance for some good press and free advertising. Hopefully, that will lead to great things in the future for me and my employees. But listen, I am fortunate enough to be in a position to do some good in the community. This was a great opportunity to do that and get the word out about Southern Charm. There's nothing wrong with that. As the force behind this whole effort, Steele Tools does the exact same thing."

"We do it to help others less fortunate."

River watched her expression as she spoke. She really believed what she'd said. "Maybe you do. But your dad and his stockholders go along with it for corporate promotion and tax deductions, I guarantee it."

"So you really just want to give back? Give your company a little boost?" She didn't seem convinced of it as she spoke. "You're telling me that this whole thing isn't just a ruse to see me again?"

River laughed. Louder than he'd intended to. Enough to make Morgan wrinkle her nose up in irritation. That only made him laugh more. She really was full of herself. "I'm sorry to disappoint, but I've been over you a long time, Morgan. If I wanted to see you, there are easier ways than signing my company up for a summer of charity work for zero profits. So no, this isn't about seeing you again."

He couldn't help but notice a painful flicker cross her face for a moment before she pulled herself back together. Was it possible that he'd hurt her feelings? After everything that had happened, he'd wondered if she had cared about him at all. There hadn't been one word, one email, one text after she left him alone in that honeymoon cabin that night. Just an envelope a few days later with a wedding ring inside.

And for that half a second, he saw the face of the girl he'd once loved. The one overflowing with emotions and vulnerabilities. One that would've held out hope that her first love might still carry a torch for her after all these years. Then the poised, ice-cold princess returned.

"Of course, you're over me," she said. "I was thinking more along the lines of you wanting to give me a piece of your mind. Maybe tell my father off?"

"While speaking my piece might be therapeutic, no, it's not about you, little girl. I didn't even know that I'd be working with you when I started this process," he lied. He couldn't have her thinking otherwise or she might believe she had the upper hand in their situation. He might've been driven here out of revenge or even masochistic curiosity, but it wasn't a pining for Morgan.

"I'm a professional. I couldn't have built my company up from nothing if I wasn't. Besides that," River continued, "you seem to be a hell of a lot more upset with me than I am with you, although I have no idea why."

She straightened in her chair, studying him with obvious disbelief. "Are you serious? You can actually sit there and tell me you have no idea why I would be upset with you?"

"Wait a minute," River said, holding up his hand before she could go any further. "You really are. Why would *you* be upset with *me*?"

That was certainly an unexpected twist on the situation. Especially since he wasn't the one whose family broke up their honeymoon and wiped their marriage from the books. He wasn't the one who dutifully packed up and went home the minute his father snapped his fingers.

"I've got a hundred thousand reasons to be upset with you, River Atkinson."

Ah. *That.* River had known the moment he cashed that check that it would come back to haunt him. That money was tainted. Dirty. And yet, that same money had changed the trajectory of his whole life. He wouldn't apologize for making the best of a shitty situation.

Instead, he smiled. He knew that would get to her. "What's the matter, Morgan? Did you think you were worth more than that? Should I have asked for a million to keep quiet about our indiscretion? I'm sure dear ol' Daddy would've paid anything to get his little princess out of that mess. Tell me, did you panic when you realized the consequences of what we'd done? Did you wait for me to fall asleep that night and call him to come get you?"

"Of course not," she snapped. "I don't even know how he found us, much less how he knew we'd gotten married."

River shook his head. "I'm sure he tracked your cell phone and credit card records, knowing every step you took. You might've thought you were an adult living your own life, but he just let you believe that. Trevor had you on a short leash the whole time." He chuckled to himself and looked around at her well-appointed office. "And now you work for Daddy. He probably invented this whole job just for you. You probably live in one of Daddy's houses and charge up Daddy's credit cards. Sounds to me like he's still got you on that leash."

Morgan's eyes narrowed at him in anger. "You shut your mouth. You don't know anything about the dynamic between my father and me."

"Don't I?" he challenged. "The woman I met at that bar by the university was confident and independent.

She wanted to go out into the world and make a difference. The girl who crawled from my bed with her tail between her legs was someone else entirely. Would you care to explain that to me since you think I don't understand what happened on our wedding night?"

Morgan's pale skin flushed with a crimson undertone along her chest, throat and cheeks. It reminded him of his younger blushing bride. And their wedding night where the blush traveled lower than the low *V* neckline of the blue silk blouse she was wearing now. Then her jaw flexed tight to hold in the angry words she probably couldn't wait to spew at him. She looked like she was about to blow.

"My father cares very much about me," she managed to say between tightly gritted teeth as she gripped her collar and held it closed to block out his prying eyes.

"No. *I* cared about you. I loved you. You're just a prop in your father's perfect family presentation. You have to fall in line or you're cut from the spotlight."

"Not everyone wants to be in the spotlight, River. I would've much rather lived a life of my choice in the shadows than a life crafted for me on my father's stage."

River shook his head. "I don't believe you for a second. At any time, you could've stood up for yourself. You could've stood up for me. For our marriage. But Daddy's money was too important to risk on a future with some poor boy with a little promise but no education. If he'd cut you off, what would life have been like for you? You would've had to really work for a living and make do without servants like the rest of us poor schmucks. Or from what I've heard, the way you would've been raised if you hadn't been switched in the hospital."

River watched the blood drain from her face. He went too far mentioning that whole thing. He'd read about it in the papers, but he was sure she was still working through it all. He shouldn't have let all his emotions out at once. They'd been bottled up for years, festering, with their only outlet being his company and building it to be the best it could possibly be.

"It would've been easier if I hadn't been switched," she said in a voice barely louder than a whisper. "When you have nothing, there's nothing to take away."

"I'd heartily disagree on that point. I've lost plenty." Morgan's green-gold eyes met his for a moment before she looked away uncomfortably. "It may not have seemed like much to you, just a rebellious fling with an unsuitable boy, but it was everything to me."

Morgan sat silently, a frown transforming her face into a guilty expression. Her gaze dropped to the blotter on her desk. "We need to stop this. It isn't going to change the past, so we might as well put it behind us and try to be civil."

"Of course." River pressed his fingertips together thoughtfully. "I wouldn't want to cause a scandal for the Steele family. Again."

"River..." she warned.

"Like I said before, I want this project to be a success. We have some important work ahead of us. So you're right, we can't let our past interfere. Truce?" He arched his brow at her in a challenge. He knew he could behave, but silencing her sharp tongue might prove more difficult.

Morgan breathed a sigh of relief and her practiced smile returned to her face. She seemed confident in her abilities. He almost missed her anger once it was tamped down. At least that was a real emotion.

“Truce,” she said and offered her hand across her desk.

Tentatively, River reached out and took it. Instantly a sizzle traveled up his arm and down his spine, exploding in his groin like a shockwave of arousal. He pulled away as quickly as he could and buried his hand beneath the desk to rub the sensation off his palm and onto his pant leg. It had been like that the night of the party, too, making him both eager and cautious about touching her again.

They might be calling a truce on their fight, but the connection between him and Morgan was far from over.

Three

Three days later, her meeting with River still preyed on Morgan's mind. They'd finally started discussing business and made headway on their project together, but it had been hard to get through it. At least for her. She couldn't tell what River was thinking with that smug grin on his face all the time.

Even as he'd smiled, Morgan had felt herself being twisted in knots. He brought out so many different emotions in her, she hardly knew how to feel. The hardest to overcome, however, was the attraction. She was not supposed to be attracted to River anymore. Not after what had happened. Not after what he'd done. And yet, her body and her mind disagreed on that point. She still wanted him. If she closed her eyes, she could feel his hands on her body again. The way she responded to him. The press of his lips against hers.

And it pissed her off.

She hated feeling off balance in her life and lately that's all she was. At the moment, she was sitting in the gardens at her parents' estate, sipping a glass of wine. She should feel at ease. But she was anything but. She was expecting another stressful visitor. This time, it was the woman who had lived her life for thirty years.

The back door of the house opened up and their housekeeper, Lena, stepped out and gestured the petite blonde in Morgan's direction. She made her way down the cobblestone path to the table beneath the vine-covered pergola that offered necessary shade in the oppressive summer heat Charleston was known for.

"Please, have a seat," Morgan said as she approached. "Would you care for some chardonnay? I pulled a bottle from the family wine cellar."

Jade settled into the chair, but she seemed stiff and nervous. "Perhaps that would help," she said. "I'm more anxious about all this than I expected to be."

Morgan smiled and poured her a drink. "It will help. That's why I'm already a glass into this bottle. I'll ask Lena to bring another and in no time, we'll be completely at ease with this crazy situation we're in."

"Oh, don't go to any trouble."

"It's no trouble. She'll be out with some nibbles in a minute."

Jade frowned and looked over her shoulder. She was uncomfortable with having staff wait on her, Morgan could tell. "Don't think of them as servants. They're household employees, that's all. They're really a necessity to keep the house running smoothly. My mother certainly doesn't have the hours in the day to keep this massive house clean and everyone fed. She's as busy as my father some days and he runs a company. They're a godsend, Lena especially, and I assure you that my father pays them handsomely for what they do for us."

"Really?" Jade asked with wary eyes.

"Oh, yeah. Lena has worked with us since before I was born. She's like family, but I don't think she stays out of loyalty. We make it worth her efforts. And besides that, if any of us kids ever treated her or anyone else around the house like they were lesser than us, we'd get our ears boxed."

"I find that hard to believe."

"Oh, believe it. My brothers have gotten it more than once for sassing the staff. It's a delicate balance being from a family like this. You have every advantage, everything you might ever want, but you're not allowed to act like it. Especially living such public lives as the faces of the company. But my parents won't tolerate that kind of behavior even behind closed doors. We're the same as anyone else."

Unless, of course, that someone else was a poor boy who wanted to love their daughter in a legally binding sense. It was one thing to treat others well. Another to treat them too well.

Lena approached the table a moment later with a silver platter in her hands. On it was a plate of tea sandwiches, some cookies and another bottle of wine. It was already opened and ready to drink.

"Oh, Lena! You read my mind," Morgan said with delight. "I was going to ask you for more wine."

Lena chuckled and placed the platter on the table. "I've known you your whole life, Miss Morgan. There's never just one bottle of wine. You all enjoy. Let me know if you need me to bring anything else." She turned and disappeared as quickly as she'd arrived.

"That would be hard to get used to," Jade said as she watched Lena walk away.

Morgan picked up her wine and took a sip. "You'd be surprised." Even as she said the words, she heard River's voice echo in her mind and frowned.

Daddy's money was too important to risk on a future with some poor boy with a little promise but no education. If he'd cut you off...you would've had to really work for a living and make do without servants like the rest of us poor schmucks.

Perhaps she was more attached to her lifestyle than she'd allowed herself to admit, then and now. She had loved River, but the truth was that she hadn't thought everything through. What would she have done after the honeymoon? When they moved into their cheap apartment and had to cobble together a life with furniture from a thrift store and boxed macaroni and cheese? How long would the love have lasted then?

Thanks to her overbearing father, she'd never know.

"I suppose if someone hadn't plotted against us, I might feel differently," Jade said. "It's hard to imagine my life being like this."

"Isn't your fiancé rich?" Morgan asked. She hadn't spent much time talking to Harley Dalton socially, but the news stories about the kidnapping had mentioned his successful investigations and security company. He'd been able to pay a large chunk of Jade's ransom and was on the trail of her kidnappers—something the police weren't having much success with themselves.

"Yes," Jade said with a large sip of wine. She looked down at her engagement ring as though she still didn't believe a rock like that was on her finger. "I'm still getting used to the idea of that, too. Fortunately, he's self-made, so he understands that there's an adjustment period. We've been staying at his mother's estate for a few weeks now while he continues the investigation. She has a housekeeper, but I still find myself tidying up before she can get a chance to clean anything. I tried to buy generic granola bars at the store the other day and Harley kept taking it out of the cart and replacing it with the brand-name kind. It's just a different mind-set."

"I feel the same way when I think of how my life was supposed to be. Where would I have ended up, you know?"

Jade nodded solemnly. "The more I think about our situation, the more questions I have. Those are the kind that can never be answered, so I try to focus on the ones that can. Like who did this to us? And why?"

"To be honest, there's a part of me that wants the answers and a part of me that just can't deal with any more drama in my life. I know my father—*er*, our father, *your father*?" She stumbled over what titles she should use with Jade.

"You can just call him your father," Jade said with an understanding smile. "It's easier that way."

Morgan smiled back, noting just how much Jade looked like her mother when she did that. Her pale blond hair and dark eyes were Steele through and through. She didn't have the confidence or the designer wardrobe, but it didn't matter. She was one of them. The rest of those things would come in time.

Morgan tried to suppress a pang of jealousy as she looked over Jade's striking features. Her father had spoiled her mercilessly, but there were a few things in life that Morgan couldn't have. River was obviously one. Looking like her mother was the other. She knew now that she took after Jade's mother, Carolyn, who was an attractive and curvaceous woman, with bright eyes and flowing dark hair. There was nothing wrong with that; it just wasn't the willowy and pale look Morgan had always longed for from a young age.

It made her wonder if she'd be more content with herself, kinder even, if she hadn't grown up in the shadow of the elegant and gorgeous Patricia Steele. Another question that would never be answered.

"Okay, I know *my* father is throwing money at your fiancé to get to the truth and that's fine by me. I would like to know eventually. But I'm leaving all that investigation stuff to the two of you. My summers are wild and all of this couldn't have come up at a worse time for me. As it is, I'm struggling to find the time to see your parents and Dean. I'm sure they think I'm avoiding them, but really, I'm not. Life just never seems to cooperate."

Jade nodded. "I understand. And so do they. I haven't spent much time with them, either, between work and helping Harley with the investigation. I think I have a bit more invested in this whole thing since the kidnapping made it more personal."

"Of course. You were certainly baptized into the Steele family in a dramatic way. My eldest brother, Tom, was kidnapped, too, when he was a baby. Being a Steele comes with its share of benefits and complications. Do you and Harley think your abduction is related to the switch?"

"I don't know how it couldn't be. I've never been a target of crime in my life before I went public about my DNA results. We've just got to get the last pieces in place and hopefully it will all make sense. I'm looking forward to it being settled. I want to know the truth, I want the bad guys behind bars and then I just want to move on with our lives the way they are now. I want to get to know you and my new family. Plan my wedding. You know, focus on normal stuff for a change."

"Normal is just a state of mind. But I understand. We've had a lot of big changes this year and not a lot of time to work through them. Getting to know your parents. And you…" Morgan hesitated. "I don't know what to call you. We're not related in any way, but we share families through an odd twist of fate. It seems like we should be sisters."

"I think that's what we should be. The truth is too complicated to explain to anyone else, and honestly, I've always wanted a sister. Dean is a great brother, but it's just not the same."

"Yes!" Morgan said with enthusiasm. "Growing up in this house as the youngest with three older brothers?"

She groaned aloud. "When I was little, I was desperate for someone to play with that wouldn't rip my Barbie's head off and launch it on a catapult to take out a lineup of enemy toy soldiers."

Jade laughed and picked up her glass of wine, finally seeming to be at ease. "I guess it's decided then. We're officially kin."

Morgan raised her own glass and they brought them together with a satisfying clink.

"Sisters," they said in unison.

Damn. Morgan was looking frustratingly fine today.

It was a surprise, considering that River hadn't been entirely sure Morgan was going to show up. Partially because he hadn't actually spoken to her about this little rendezvous. He'd left her a voice mail when he knew she wouldn't be available to answer. Like a damn coward. They may have called a truce, but he still didn't want to talk to her in person—for an entirely different reason presently.

Now, instead of getting irritated, he'd get all twisted up inside at the sound of her voice. His blood would start rushing in his ears and his thoughts would stray to their honeymoon night. He had been too busy this morning to lose his focus just to talk to her.

It was bad enough how much time he'd already lost to blatant fantasizing where Morgan was concerned. Watching her saunter toward him now in a tight pencil skirt, clingy knit top and stilettos was a memory that was likely going to headline in tonight's thoughts. It made him wonder if she'd intentionally dressed this way to meet him. Just to make him crazy. With the sunset behind her, her outfit highlighted every womanly curve she had like the silhouette of a '50s pinup girl heading his way.

And for that, he was very grateful. Even if it made him awkwardly tense for a few minutes while he got his libido in check. He hadn't really considered this complication when he bid to work with Steele on the project. Now, he realized that being around Morgan all summer would be an extended exercise in self-restraint for him. He'd never been one to deny himself what he wanted, but this was definitely a case where indulging would be a bad idea.

It *was* a bad idea, right?

"Good evening, Mr. Atkinson."

River looked at her with a furrowed brow of irritation. They'd talked about this already, but she seemed to take pleasure in riling him up. Indulging was definitely a bad idea. He got the feeling Morgan would push *all* his buttons, good and bad.

"Good evening, River," she corrected with a wry smile that barely curled the dark plum of her lips. It was a beautiful color that matched the flowers in her skirt and popped against her pale skin.

He wanted to kiss every bit of it off her despite knowing better. "Good evening, Morgan. Thanks for meeting me on such short notice. I thought you would like to see this."

River turned and gestured to the grassy overgrown property just beyond him. It was in an area near downtown Charleston that was gentrifying and property values were slowly going up. He'd gotten a tip on this land before it was even officially listed for sale.

"This lot is three quarters of an acre. Perfect to split into three quarter-acre lots. That's actually pretty spacious this close to downtown. There will be a big enough backyard for each family to run and play. Maybe put up a swing set or a little pool. A patio. A grill. Everything they would need."

"What's the price?"

River turned back to her with a grin. She was going to love this part. In their business discussions, he'd learned quickly that Morgan wanted to help, but she had an ironclad budget to keep to. He supposed that you had to if you were going to help as many people as you could. "It's ten thousand less than the property you showed me in West Ashley when we met the other day."

Morgan's dark eyebrows went up in surprise. "Really?" She turned and glanced around the property to see what was wrong with it. He'd done the same thing when he heard the asking price initially.

"There's nothing to concern you. I've done a full survey already. The owner inherited the property. He's more interested in selling quickly as a single lot than he is in taking the time to divide it up and find individual buyers, even if it means making less money. If we make him a cash offer before he gets a real estate agent involved, he'll probably jump on it."

"How did you even hear about it? It isn't listed. I looked after I got your voice mail."

"Yeah, I know a guy."

"You know a guy? That sounds sketchy."

"It's not, I promise. I just know a few people from my years in the construction business that are always happy to let me know when they hear about a property I might be interested in."

Morgan nodded and glanced back at the land. "If it's really the price you mentioned and it's not an ancient burial ground or a former Superfund site, I say let's put in an offer tomorrow morning. There's no way we'll find anything better for that price. Especially in this area of town."

"Check—no zombie corpses and no toxic waste. We should be good to go. I'll get the offer drawn up in the morning and hopefully we can get closed on this quickly."

"Great."

All this had happened faster than he'd expected, but there wasn't much reason to linger in an overgrown field with her. They turned together and he started walking her back to the white Mercedes convertible she'd driven over. Back in college, she'd driven a similar, older model. Just the sight of it now reminded him of long winding roads with the wind in their hair and not a care in the world. That was a long time ago, though. A simpler time.

"River?" she spoke about halfway to her car, bringing his thoughts back to the present.

"Yes?"

She stopped and turned back to the empty lot. "You know, as a developer, you could take that land for yourself and build some trendy and expensive row houses here. You probably could make a fortune with the way this area is trending up. When that downtown walking trail is done, you could easily get three quarters of a million dollars each. Are you sure you want to use it for this project? We could find a different property. The one in West Ashley wasn't bad. I could probably get the price down." Morgan turned to look at him with her question lingering in her eyes.

River shook his head. She was right, but he hadn't even considered it. "No, that's okay. When I saw this land, I could see our little houses sitting on it. Kids running through the sprinklers in their grassy yards. I saw three families that were proud of their new homes. The kind that I would've loved to have, that my mom would've loved to have when we had nothing. That's what I want. Not a bunch of trendy three-story pseudo-historic town houses at ridiculous prices. There's enough of those around town these days. The whole area is losing its character thanks to all the HGTV home-flippers."

Morgan studied his face for a moment when he was done speaking, and then she smiled. He wasn't sure if he'd said the right thing until that moment. She might've been more impressed by the take-charge, make-money answer he hadn't given, but he'd given the answer she might not have expected but wanted to hear. Before he could say anything, she leaned in, gripped the lapels of his suitcoat in her hands and pressed a sweet, soft kiss to his lips.

River hadn't been expecting that. And yet, the moment her lips touched his, he knew it was everything he'd been waiting for over the last decade they'd spent apart. Suddenly, all his worries and cares didn't seem to matter anymore. There was just this moment.

He was finally able to get his stunned body to respond to his brain and brought his hands to rest at her waist. He wanted to do more than that, but he held back. Nothing Morgan had said or done up to this point had indicated she wanted more than a working relationship. This kiss could mean anything. He'd learned long ago not to presume when it came to the female brain and how it worked.

And then, as suddenly as it happened, she pulled away, leaving him confused, aroused and confused. It bore repeating.

He stood looking down at her in stunned silence as she finally released her hold on his jacket and took a step back out of his personal space. Her eyes were glassy and unfocused as she looked at him, even a bit shaky on her feet with those tall heels.

He reached out a hand to catch her elbow and steady her and she smiled. "Thanks."

"What was all that for?" he asked.

Morgan took a deep breath and wrapped her arms across her chest, hugging her sweater tighter to her curves. "When you were talking before, I was just thinking that maybe you're a pretty good guy after all."

"Uh, thanks?" River wasn't quite sure what to say to that. He'd always thought he was a good guy, but apparently Morgan felt otherwise. It was probably the money thing. With her, it always came back to the money thing.

And yet, she'd just kissed him.

Her gaze dropped from his and surveyed the ground

for a moment awkwardly. "I probably shouldn't have done that," she said. "It wasn't very professional."

"I didn't mind." He said the words a touch too quickly, making her look back up at him with a soft smile curling her dark lips.

"Still. My father would frown on my behavior. I'm representing the company after all."

"Your father would disapprove of anything that involved me. Honestly, I can't believe he let me through the front door."

Morgan's lips twisted in thought for a moment before she shook her head. "I doubt he knows. Or if he does, he kept his mouth shut about it. My brothers worked the details, I'm pretty sure, and they don't know about…us."

River stuffed his hands into his pockets and rocked back a bit on his heels. "Wow. Your family is really good at keeping secrets. I know your father likes to keep private issues private, but to keep things from each other… That's next-level secret keeping."

Morgan narrowed her gaze at him for a moment and then nodded slowly with a sad expression on her face. "You have no idea."

There was something about the way she said the words that made him wonder if there were more Steele family secrets than just their ill-fated marriage. He wanted to ask but thought better of it. If she felt like sharing, she would tell him. Besides, he imagined there had to be more than a few skeletons in the closets of that big mansion of theirs. Some of those doors were best kept shut.

With a sigh, Morgan's expression shifted back to her usual practiced facade, but when she looked at him, there was a twinkle of mischief in her eyes instead. "You know, this isn't very professional of me, either, but what the hell… Can I buy you a drink?"

Four

The waiter put a glass of wine and a tall pilsner glass on the table between them. River hadn't anticipated ending up in a bar with Morgan tonight, but he wasn't going to complain. He didn't have anything else to do. It was either crash at the small apartment he kept downtown and work, or drive out to his home on Kiawah Island and work. It was the same thing he did every night, typically staying in the city during the week and escaping to his coastal retreat on the weekends. But no matter where he was, not much was going on. Honestly, this day had brought more highlights than the entire month that preceded it.

He tried not to think about how all those highlights featured Morgan.

"So tell me what you've been up to, River. It's been

nearly a decade since my unscheduled departure from your life in the middle of the night. What happened after that?"

Sitting down, having a real conversation with Morgan seemed a bit surreal. They'd gotten past the initial resentment and anger, moved through the polite discussions and now they were getting to the real talk. He was curious to know what she had been doing with her life, too, but his own stories were not that exciting.

"The short answer is that I've been working ever since you left. You remember how I was working construction with my dad back when we were dating?"

Morgan nodded.

"Well, I took the money from your father and started my own construction business. It was what I knew. I'd met plenty of good guys who were willing to come work for me, and with my dad's experience and guidance, I was able to get the company up off the ground. Actually, I worked my tail off, seven days a week, to get where I am today. It's only been in the last year or so that I've been able to take a breath."

"It takes time," she said. "My father inherited a company that was already very successful, but even then, he was in the office more than he was at home when we were young. Things change. Competitors come and go. The market shifts. Right now, we're coping with losing retail space in brick-and-mortar stores and expanding our online presence. You've got to stay on your toes or you can lose everything you've worked for."

"Don't I know it. And really, starting a construction business right at the tail end of the housing bust was the dumbest thing I could've done. People were foreclosing left and right. But I watched the market and started with small houses that people could actually afford to buy. I worked with a financing company that went through hoops to get people approved when almost no one could get a home loan. It made all the difference. There were times I worried, though. I even started going to college online in the evenings in case I needed a backup plan."

Morgan perked up in her chair. "Really?"

"Yeah. I have an expensive framed diploma on the wall to prove it. I got a degree in industrial management. I'm not sure what I would've done with it, but I never had to find out. That's enough about me. What about you? I presume you finished school, although I never saw you around Columbia *after*."

"When summer was over, I went back to the University of South Carolina and finished the fall semester. I didn't leave campus very much, though. I wasn't doing that well with my classes after everything that had happened, so I was trying to focus and keep my grades up. After that, I decided to take a semester off." Morgan stopped talking to take a large sip of wine. "So I took a break and went home for a while. Then I ended up transferring to Georgetown and finished school there."

"I didn't realize you left South Carolina." River hadn't kept tabs on her, but honestly, he couldn't have even if he'd wanted to. The Steele family left almost no digital footprints to follow. After her father took her away, it was like she'd never even existed. She could've spent the last ten years on the moon for all he knew.

"Oh, yes. I actually still live there most of the year. I

have a town house in the Georgetown area that I started renting when I was still in school. I ended up loving the area and stayed. I come to Charleston for the summers to work on the annual charity project, and then I return home. Our company has a large production facility across the river in Virginia and that's where my office is."

"Where do you stay while you're here?"

"At the house." As she said the words, she looked at him and chuckled into her glass. "I know," she said after swallowing some wine. "Living in the same house with my parents is not ideal. They watch me like hawks, always have, but I try to ignore it. I suppose I could get my own place here. I've just always felt like doing that meant I might never leave again. I don't want that tethering me."

River couldn't imagine spending every summer under his parents' roof again. It wasn't like he spent every evening partying with prostitutes or something, but he chafed under the supervision. If he wanted to leave dishes in the sink, or heaven forbid on the coffee table, it was okay. "Do you hate being home that much that you'd rather stay there than commit to some real estate? You wouldn't have to buy. There are short-term rentals you could get. A beach house, even."

"I know. My father insists I stay there with them. For practical reasons, of course."

"Of course," River agreed.

"But you're right," she sighed. "I should find another option."

River lifted his glass and flashed his most charming

smile. "Lucky you, I just so happen to know of a couple of amazing properties available in town."

When Jade got home from her shift at the pharmacy, she found her fiancé, Harley, in his mother's formal dining room. She had never returned to her rental bungalow after the break-in. Harley had all her things packed up and they'd taken up temporary residence at his mother's mansion until he was done working the case for St. Francis Hospital.

In the meantime, he had taken over the space as his pseudo-command center for his investigation into her thirty-year-old baby-swapping case. He had boxes of files, his laptop and anything else he could get his hands on sprawled across the large oak table. He was sitting at the head of the table, frowning at his computer screen like an unhappy king at a feast.

"What's wrong?" Jade asked. She put her purse down in one of the dozen ornate wood-and-velvet chairs and circled behind Harley to rub his shoulders. He had always taken this case seriously, but after the break-in at her house and her kidnapping, it had become personal for him. Almost all-consuming. Some nights she had to drag him to bed.

"I can't find the file I'm looking for. I've searched everywhere. It has all the information about the hospital staff that I reviewed with the former CEO."

Jade pressed her fingers into his tense muscles, eliciting a low groan from him. She glanced over his chair to the table and the boxes set out across it. Harley might be an investigator, but he was first and foremost a man.

They couldn't find anything, usually because it required moving something else and it wasn't in plain sight.

"When did you see it last?"

"The day I went to his house. It has the personnel files and photos of all the nurses and physicians working when you were born. I've been looking for it since your family went out on the yacht with the Steeles a few weeks ago. I need to find that nurse's information."

With a sigh, Jade walked over to the boxes. It had been a while since her families had had their first get-together. It had gone well enough, but with everything going on, she'd forgotten about Patricia and Carolyn's discussion of the day the girls were born. Thankfully, Harley hadn't. She glanced in a few boxes, flipping through some things before moving to the next one.

"It's not there. I checked twenty times."

Then Jade picked up one of the boxes, revealing the manila folder that had been beneath it. It was marked with a red *confidential* personnel stamp from the hospital. She didn't say a word. That would just irritate him. She simply picked it up and laid it across the keyboard of his laptop.

"Are you serious? Where was it?"

"Doesn't matter. What matters is you have it now. What are you looking for?"

"The nurse Patricia and Carolyn were talking about on the boat. Her name was Nancy Crowley. When I spoke to the former hospital CEO, he mentioned how she'd committed suicide at the hospital less than a week after Hurricane Hugo and the switch."

Harley flipped through the file and pulled out a photograph that he handed over to Jade. She took it from him, studying the picture of the woman with the bright red curls and round face. She looked like she would have the cheery, chatty disposition that the mothers had mentioned from their time in the hospital. It was hard to believe that a week later, this woman would be dead.

"She jumped from the roof. My gut feeling is that it isn't a coincidence. I think the CEO said something about her having a drinking problem that may have driven the suicide, but I'm going to do some digging. It sounds more like the action of someone with a guilty conscience to me."

Harley's words triggered a memory in Jade's mind, but she couldn't put her finger on it immediately. "What did you say?"

"It just seems like the actions of a guilty conscience."

We've sat on our hands for three decades because of her stupid conscience...

"Wait." Jade put her hands up to silence Harley. "That's it. That's what they said in the van."

"Who?"

"My kidnappers. One of them was complaining about the other guy's sister having an attack of conscience that ruined their plans. Do you think that's what they meant?"

"It could be. Do you remember anything else?"

Jade stared at the photo and tried to remember the argument she'd listened to as she banged around in the back of her abductor's van. "I think one of them said she was dead, but she hadn't told them what they needed to know."

"Like which baby was which?"

She frowned. She wished she could remember more. She'd tried to memorize every moment, but between the stress and shock of the abduction, a lot of the details had become hazy in her mind over the last few weeks. "Could be. Did Nancy have a brother? That would definitely be a starting point. If not, it's a dead end."

Harley scanned the file and pointed at the emergency contact box. "She listed her next of kin as her brother. Gregory Crowley. Does that sound familiar?"

Jade shrugged. "I don't think they used names. But one was definitely the brother. I'm not sure about the other guy, though."

She watched as he turned to his notes and flipped through to what he'd written down after listening to the recorded discussion he'd had with the retired hospital CEO. "He mentioned a brother and a boyfriend when he talked about Nancy's suicide. How upset they both were. I'll see if I can get any more information about her death from the local authorities. If this is the right lead, they could've been upset for an entirely different reason."

Jade crossed her arms over her chest and shook her head. "Sounds like Nancy may have switched the babies and then took the secret with her to the grave."

"You're home awfully late, missy."

Morgan stopped in the grand foyer of her parents' mansion and turned toward the library. There, she saw her brother Sawyer sitting in an armchair reading one of the leather-bound volumes their father collected.

"You sound like Dad."

Sawyer flipped the book shut, setting it aside before getting up and walking out into the bright lights of the glittering chandelier that hung overhead in the entrance. His gaze narrowed at her for a moment. "You take that back," he quipped and then smiled.

"Where is Dad?" she asked.

"That's a good question. He asked me to come over tonight to discuss some work stuff, but he must've gotten caught up at the office. I haven't seen him yet. I can tell it's getting late because Lena keeps trying to feed me. She's finally given up, but every time she walks by, she clucks her tongue."

"You might as well give in and eat."

Sawyer sighed and looked down at the Patek Philippe watch he'd gotten for Christmas from their parents. "I will if you will."

"That's fair. I haven't had dinner yet."

That was true enough. They'd had a couple drinks, but Morgan had been careful not to let the evening with River evolve into more. Drinks could lead to dinner, which could lead to…breakfast. She couldn't let that happen. So she'd politely made her exit after her second chardonnay and headed back to the house. In truth, she was starving now.

The kitchen was dimly lit and immaculately clean when they went in. Lena was nowhere to be found, likely having retired to her quarters for the evening.

"She must've given up on all of us," Sawyer said.

"We can find something for ourselves." Morgan walked over to the giant Sub-Zero refrigerator and opened the double doors. There was every kind of fresh produce and dairy product imaginable. Dozens of neat containers lined the shelves with diced and prepared ingredients that Lena probably had ready for the next day's meals. She knew to steer clear of that.

Reaching inside, she grabbed a block of cheddar and a stick of butter. "Get the French bread off the counter and slice up a few pieces. We're making grilled cheese."

Sawyer looked dubious, but did as he was told. "Since when do you cook?" he asked as he held up a skillet like it might bite him. "You keep the local Chinese restaurant in your contacts list."

"I can make grilled cheese. You went to college, didn't you?"

"We had meal plans," he pointed out. "I ate three squares in the campus cafeteria. Didn't you?"

"Well...yes. But the food courts weren't open 24/7. I can make grilled cheese." She pulled a very sharp looking knife from the block on the counter and eyed the thick chunk of cheddar. This wasn't the prewrapped individual slices she remembered from the grocery store. Slicing this poorly could cost her the tip of her thumb if she weren't careful. The bread also looked crusty and treacherous. She should've known that Lena wouldn't be caught dead with processed cheese or presliced white bread in her kitchen.

"We can do this," she insisted. "We are adults. We damn near run a company. There are people our age with children and homes that they manage on their own. Certainly, we're capable of making ourselves dinner. Right?"

Ten minutes later, with the butter and cheese back in the refrigerator where they belonged, Sawyer and Morgan settled in the upstairs family room with their old standby from their youth: a bag of tortilla chips, a jar of salsa and a container of cookies Lena had baked earlier. As kids, they had liked to sneak down into the kitchen late at night and find unhealthy contraband to take up and eat while they played video games. The kitchen was just as alien to them now as it was then.

The family room, however, was where they'd spent their youth. It was the center of the "kids' wing" with each of the children's bedrooms surrounding the large common area. It was one of the only places in the house that they could do whatever they wanted. When they were young, it was a playroom with their toys, and as they got older, it evolved to include a big-screen television, all their video game systems and a foosball table. It even had its own minibar with a microwave, sink, small fridge and stash of healthy snacks for growing children. Unfortunately, it hadn't been stocked with anything other than bottled water since Morgan had moved away to college.

Morgan settled onto the large sectional sofa and laid out their makeshift dinner on the coffee table while Sawyer got some cold water bottles for them. She kicked off her heels and curled her feet up on the couch. It felt amazing to finally take her shoes off after a long day. She really didn't like wearing them, but she was significantly shorter than the rest of the family and it was how she'd made up for that genetic shortcoming.

"So where were you this afternoon? I came by your

office to ask you something and your assistant said you'd already left for the day. Playing hooky?"

"Hardly," she said. "I was meeting with this summer's contractor to look at some land we're going to buy."

"And yet you smell like a sports bar. How does that work?"

Morgan rolled her eyes and opened the bag of chips. "Yes, well, we went for a drink afterward." She tried opening the jar of salsa and struggled.

"What's going on with that guy?" Sawyer asked. He took the jar from her and opened it easily. "River, right? That's a weird name."

Morgan frowned. "I don't know what you're talking about. Nothing is going on. And you're one to talk, when all of the kids in our family are named after Mark Twain characters."

"No changing the subject. I know a lot of personal crap has happened since the party, so I didn't bring it up earlier, but it's been long enough now. What's up between you two? When I introduced him to you, there was something going on there."

She knew there were a couple different ways she could go with this. Outright lie. Lie by omission. Tell the truth. Or tell enough truth to make it believable but still mostly lie. Of her three brothers, Sawyer was the most insightful one. Just like he had noticed something between Morgan and River, he would also be the most likely to know she wasn't being honest with him.

"We met back in college," she said. "I hadn't seen him in years and didn't know he was involved with this year's project, so it was a surprise." There. Just enough truth, but all the salacious details were missing.

"Did you guys date back then or something?" Sawyer was reading between the lines, as she'd feared. "I noticed he looked at you with more than a casual appreciation in his eyes."

"I looked good that night," Morgan said in a conceitedly confident tone. "But yes, we did date. Briefly. Nothing came of it. You know Dad wouldn't have allowed it."

Sawyer nodded. While he didn't have the same pressures put on him as Morgan did as the only daughter, he still pursued romance cautiously. All the young Steeles had social-climbing targets on their backs. Sawyer and Tom fought off most of their obvious pursuers, unlike Finn, who jumped into the Charleston dating pool feet first.

"And what about now?" He leaned forward to grab the container of cookies and peeled off the lid. "Snickerdoodles," he groaned, and inhaled the addictive scent of cinnamon and butter.

Morgan reached out to take one. "What do you mean?" she asked cautiously.

"Oh, come on. There's still something there. You guys went out for a drink. Do you think anything is going to come of it? I mean, you're a grown woman now. You don't have to worry about what Dad thinks of your relationships anymore."

Morgan wasn't entirely sure that was true, at least in her case, but it was an interesting thought. A lot had changed in her life since the day her father hauled her out of her honeymoon cabin. While she didn't entirely trust River's motivations—this could still all be about money for him, then and now—she could protect herself by knowing that going in.

"I don't know what it is, Sawyer. Probably nothing more than a little reminiscing. Or maybe he's just looking for his second shot at landing the Steele heiress."

"On a point of technicality, you aren't the Steele heiress anymore."

Morgan frowned at him. "Am I being disinherited without my knowledge?"

"No, of course not. You know our parents would never even think of such a thing. I meant that with everything that has come to light lately, perhaps you should shake off the mantle of heiress and do what you want with your life for a change. You hold back. You always have. And I get it. Dad watches you closer than any of us. But you're about to turn thirty. You need to stop worrying about what other people think—especially Dad—and live your life."

Morgan and Sawyer rarely had time to sit and have real discussions without the rest of the family around. Without Finn to make a joke or Tom changing the subject when things got heavy or uncomfortable, there was nothing for her to do but seriously think about what her brother had said.

And he was right. She didn't have to be the perfect Steele daughter any longer. Maybe she could try living her life for a while as Morgan Nolan and see how that worked out.

There was a lot of history between Morgan and

River. More than anyone, even River, knew about. A lot of reasons why opening up this Pandora's box was a bad idea. And yet, all the original reasons why she couldn't have River were off the table now. And despite how much she didn't want to be attracted to him, she couldn't help herself. There was something there—something Morgan couldn't fight—that drew her to him. And the more time she spent with him, the worse it got. He was a good guy, contrary to the villain her father had painted him to be. Maybe she'd been wrong this whole time.

"I'm not saying you run off and marry the guy," Sawyer continued, "but what can it hurt to indulge a little? You're both adults. You're attracted to one another. Take the proper precautions and do what you want to do. It's time to live your own life, Morgan."

She had never expected to have this kind of realization tonight, especially with her brother's help, but he was right. Regardless of who her parents were or how she'd been raised, she was an adult now. This was Morgan's life and she was going to live it.

Five

River was pleased with himself. He tried not to be too arrogant, but there were two things he knew better than anything else—construction and Morgan. Since finding a place for her to live combined both those skill sets, he was pretty confident that she would love what he showed her.

He was right.

That's why he'd suggested that instead of meeting in the office today, they should come here to his latest property instead. He had called that morning to let her know their offer had been accepted on the downtown land purchase. Everything was being finalized. He just needed her to sign a few things before they broke ground and got started building the houses.

She'd agreed to meet him later that afternoon. Now

they were in a town house on the peninsula where he'd recently completed the renovations. Originally part of an 1840s warehouse, it had been converted into a row of town houses a hundred years later. This project had been more art than skill, trying to balance historic details like the original brick facade with the sleek quartz and modern bath and kitchen fixtures that buyers wanted.

At the moment, he was sitting in the bench seat of the bay window, watching Morgan wander through the place. He wanted to give her time to explore on her own and she was taking advantage of it. Her wide eyes seemed to take in every detail as her fingertips grazed over different surfaces. She hadn't even spoken to him since she'd signed the paperwork on the kitchen island. She gasped as she spied the original heart pine floors in the living room, and he knew he had her. The place had only been staged a few days ago, but he got the feeling he hadn't needed to bother with the expense.

"This is amazing work," she said at last. There was a flush to Morgan's cheeks as she turned to him. He recognized that expression. It was love. At one time, she'd looked at him that way. Now he'd have to settle for her loving his handiwork. "It's stunning, really."

River got up and walked over to where she was standing and admiring the fireplace with the original glazed tile surround. "I'm glad you like it."

"The location is amazing, too. It's so close to Broad Street and Waterfront Park. It doesn't get much better than that in Charleston."

"That's what I thought when I found the place up

for sale. It needed a lot of work—I think they hadn't renovated since the '80s—but I thought it was worth it. You haven't even seen the upstairs yet. You'll adore the master bath, I'm pretty sure."

Morgan's eyes lit up. She turned toward the staircase and this time he followed her upstairs. She explored the three bedrooms and the luxurious Carrara marble bath, then turned to look at him with a suspicious narrowed gaze. "You set me up, didn't you?"

"What do you mean?"

She crossed her arms over her chest, drawing his attention to the press of her firm breasts against her shirt. "You said it would be easier to meet here, but you really just wanted me to see the place. We could've met anywhere, but you knew I'd love it."

River could only shrug as he shifted his gaze back to her eyes. "How could you not love it? It's an amazing town house. Yes, I set you up," he admitted with a grin. "But I only wanted you to see it before I put it on the market in case you had to have it. I expect it to sell pretty quickly when I do, so I didn't want you to miss your chance. There's no pressure."

She sighed and turned back to admire the original crown molding in the master bedroom. He followed her gaze as it fell onto the king-size bed and plush headboard on the center of the far wall. Normally, his stager would've used a queen bed, but the room was big enough to accommodate a larger one.

"I already have a place. In DC. I don't need a house here, River."

"I thought it was a rental."

"Does that make a difference? It's still a home in a town I love."

"Then don't buy it," he said dismissively. "I only wanted you to know you have options. There's no reason for you to spend every summer living with your parents. You're a grown woman—almost thirty—with the financial means to do whatever you want. As much as you come back to town, I'd think you'd want your own space here in Charleston. Even just as an investment property. The market here is pretty hot."

"Thanks for the reminder of how old I am," she said with a cutting, sarcastic tone. "What you don't quite understand is how large my parents' home really is. With all the boys in their own places, I basically have an upstairs wing of the mansion to myself. It's not like I'm tripping over my parents."

River took a step closer to her, closing the gap between them. He stretched one arm out and braced it on the doorway as he leaned in. He didn't crowd her personal space, but he was close enough to feel her warm breath as she exhaled and smell the scent of her perfume. "So you can do whatever you like, right? How about entertain a gentleman?"

Her gaze nervously met his and her tongue shot out to wet her bottom lip. She didn't have to answer that out loud. They both knew her father didn't care if she was fifteen, thirty or fifty, there would be none of that under his roof. He was as overprotective as he ever was.

"That hasn't been an issue," she said. "I come to Charleston to work, nothing more. I'm too busy to worry much about a personal life these days."

There was something about the way she looked at him when she spoke. Something that made him want to move closer, even as she insisted she didn't have time for a physical relationship. "It sounds to me like all you do is work. All work and no play makes Morgan a dull girl."

Morgan's green-gold eyes focused on his lips as he spoke. The memories of their brief, innocent kiss at the empty plot of land flooded his mind as he looked at her. It hadn't been a great, passionate connection in reality, and yet it had felt that way. Kissing Morgan was the same as it had always been—like being struck by lightning. His whole body lit up at her touch, every nerve alive with wanting her.

In that instant, it was as though the last decade and the drama that drove them apart had never happened. To force himself to move on, he'd told himself so many things. That she hadn't loved him. That she was just a spoiled rich girl using him to get back at Daddy. That the connection they'd shared was nothing special.

But when she'd touched him again, he knew it had all been lies. She might've regretted moving too fast and bent to her father's will, but he hadn't imagined the magnetic draw they shared. It was just as strong as it had ever been.

"Trust me," he said. "I'm an expert on working too much." River dropped his arm to his side and moved closer. He looked down at her, only inches away, but she didn't move. "You can ignore your needs…push them aside…but they don't go away. They build up inside of you. A burning, churning feeling in your belly.

Eventually, you have to let off the pressure or you'll do something stupid."

Morgan's gaze didn't move from his own. Instead, she put a hand on his chest and her lips parted softly in invitation. "Something stupid like this?" she asked with an arched brow.

Her touch was searing through the cotton of his dress shirt. The heat made his brain start to short circuit, making the idea of having her be all he could think about. "That's…*debatable*. If you'd asked me a week ago, I'd have said it was a bad idea. A terrible idea. But if you're going to keep touching me like that, I will argue this is the perfect way to let off steam. I'd be happy to, uh, help you in that department."

He was rambling nervously, but he couldn't stop the flow of words. Not when she was this close and looking at him the way she was.

Morgan ran her palm over his chest, sliding it up the side of his neck to cradle the back of his skull. He closed his eyes and leaned into her touch. "That's very kind of you."

"Morgan…" His breath caught in his throat as he said her name. If she was just flirting, she was playing a dangerous game. He wanted her. If she didn't want him, she needed to step away.

She didn't. She pulled his head down until their lips met. It was an explosive kiss, the contact igniting the fire inside of River that he'd fought to keep down. Any reservations he might have had about tasting Morgan again fizzled away as she bit his bottom lip and he groaned aloud.

She'd gotten feistier than he remembered her to be. He liked that. A lot. River wasn't sure who moved how, but one moment, they were standing and the next, he was pressing her body into the mattress previously beside them. There wasn't a break, not a hesitation, but an evolution of their kiss. It deepened, it intensified and with it, River felt the desperation start to bubble up inside of him.

He'd been telling the truth when he told Morgan he knew what it was like to work too much and deny himself. He was an expert at that. But he couldn't deny himself any longer. Not when it came to Morgan.

His hands roamed over her body, reacquainting themselves with the terrain that had changed some since he'd last touched it. Her breasts were fuller as he cupped one through her thin cotton T-shirt. He could feel the tight bud of her nipple pressing through the fabric of her bra as though it were reaching out for his touch. That much, at least, hadn't changed. She had always responded to him like that.

Then he let his hand glide down her stomach. He wanted to keep exploring. To seek out the heat hidden beneath her slacks...but she tensed up beneath him. Suddenly, she was stiff as a board beneath his touch, bringing his worst fear to life. Her mouth jerked away from his, even as her hand caught his wrist and pulled him away from her belly.

"River, stop," she said in a harsh whisper. The eyes that had been looking at him with barely masked desire were now wide and startled.

River immediately pulled back. "What's wrong?"

Her gaze met his for only a second before she rolled away from him and got off the bed. He thought he saw a shimmer of tears in her eyes as she turned her back to him. “Nothing,” she said. “I have to go.” She rushed to the door and disappeared to the thumping sound of her feet pounding down the stairs. He heard the front door slam and knew she was gone.

What the hell?

He pushed himself to the foot of the bed, tugging his own shirt down and running his hands over his beard in exasperation. His groin was throbbing with interrupted desire as he turned to look at the rumpled comforter they'd lain on a moment before. He didn't understand what had gone wrong.

And he got the feeling Morgan didn't have any intention of telling him.

“What the hell do I think I'm doing?”

Morgan shook her head as she pulled away from the town house and left it, and River, behind. She'd come to sign paperwork. Just some paperwork. And yet, somehow, she'd ended up on her back and on the verge of giving everything away she'd tried so hard to keep secret.

She navigated through the narrow busy streets of downtown Charleston with an angry grip on the wheel, heading for the bridge that would take her over the water toward her parents' home in Mount Pleasant. Her frustration lessened the farther she got from River, but the dull ache of need remained.

Making peace with him was a bad idea. Fighting wasn't ideal, but it made it easier to keep her distance.

Without that wall of resentment between them, she was just putty in his hands. She had thought that was okay. Her chat with Sawyer had convinced her she was a grown woman and could do what she liked. And that had seemed like a good idea. Until River's hand ran across her stomach and the reality of her situation set in.

She and River may have called a truce on how their marriage ended, but she knew that would be short-lived if he knew everything. There were some secrets that needed to be kept. Especially if the Steele housing project was going to be completed smoothly this year. River couldn't know the truth because it was so inflammatory, so damaging that it would hurt more than the lie.

That's what she'd told herself ten years ago as she sat on her dorm room mattress, staring at a positive pregnancy test. She was pregnant with River's child.

Up until that point, she had lived firmly in denial. There was no way she was pregnant because her father had wiped the past from the record books. She never married River, according to the state of Tennessee. They never had a honeymoon. So she couldn't possibly be pregnant. There was no way she was carrying the baby of the guy who had hit her dad up for cash and disappeared from her life. Fate wouldn't be that cruel. And as such, she ignored the signs, popping antacids and struggling to focus in her classes that fall.

Her dropping GPA wasn't the only sign of trouble. Once Christmas break came around, there was no more denying the truth. Not to herself and certainly not to her parents. When her mother arrived to pick her up for the holiday, her gaze had immediately dropped to the rounding belly that Morgan was trying to hide beneath a USC sweatshirt.

From there, it was a whirlwind that Morgan almost didn't remember. Her parents went into instant damage-control mode, and she was just along for the ride. No one was to know the truth, they decided. Not even her brothers. For her own protection and that of her reputation, of course. Her parents had successfully kept her short marriage a secret from everyone, and they were confident they could keep the baby a hush-hush topic, too.

They bought her older brothers a luxurious ski trip in Aspen for Christmas, sending them off to Colorado instead of having them celebrate at home that year. As far as anyone knew, Morgan had the flu and couldn't attend any events with them. Her only outings were to the doctor for her checkups.

She hadn't bothered to argue with them about it. Her spirit had been crushed when she lost what she thought she'd had with River, and nothing else mattered. Part of her wanted to keep their baby so she'd always have a piece of him with her, but she worried the child would only be a painful reminder of his ultimate betrayal.

Morgan hadn't known what to do, but it was all a mess of her own making, so she decided that perhaps she'd be better served letting her parents choose the best course. She hadn't been sure if they were going to send her off to Switzerland or something to have the child in secret and give it up for adoption, let her keep it, or raise it as their own, and she never did find out. Their plans ended up not mattering in the end.

At twenty-five weeks, just a few days after Christmas, something went wrong. She just didn't feel right and went in to see her obstetrician. Morgan's blood pressure was through the roof. She sat in a hospital room for a week, spending New Year's Eve under the doctors' careful watch while they tried to get it down. They hadn't wanted to deliver the baby that early. It was risky. Too risky, even with the latest technology. But it was a dangerous situation for Morgan, too. Soon it became clear they didn't have a choice or they would lose them both.

Dawn Mackenzie Steele had been born via emergency C-section and weighed a little over a pound. Morgan never got to hold her, but if she had, the tiny infant could've fit in the palm of her hand. She hadn't known what she wanted to do until she saw her daughter covered in tubes and wires in an incubator. Then, more than anything, she wanted her baby. She didn't care what her parents wanted or thought. She wasn't concerned about scandal or what people would say. She just wanted Dawn to be okay. But that wouldn't happen. The neonatal intensive care staff did everything they could, but Dawn's little lungs just weren't ready for the outside world.

Morgan didn't realize she was crying at the wheel until the road started to blur around her. She pulled her car over into a shopping center and turned off the engine. She hugged her stomach like she had after Dawn was gone and rested her head against the steering wheel.

The tears flowed freely then. It had been a long time since she'd cried for Dawn. Years, maybe, as she'd tried to put her past in the past and focus on her future. That's what her father had told her to do. He'd held her as she cried. She was his baby girl after all, and he hated that she was hurting. But he came from an upbringing that felt the best way to cope was to forget and move forward.

It was sad… It was unfortunate, he'd said, but perhaps this was her second chance at having the kind of life he'd always dreamed of for her. She was so young with so much ahead of her. He was certain she would have her babies some day in the future, with a good man who adored her and cared for her the way she deserved.

Trevor Steele's words fell on deaf ears, although he never knew it. Then, and even now, there was a part of Morgan that never wanted to marry and have children. She'd tried it once and failed. She wasn't sure her heart could take the pain of failing at all of it again. So she'd focused on finishing school, concentrated on her work, made sure she was the good daughter they wanted.

And she got the hell out of South Carolina.

A quiet tap at the car window startled Morgan out of her tears. She looked out to see a little old man watching her with concern as he clutched a sack of groceries from the store she'd stopped at.

She rolled down the window, self-consciously wiping the mascara-stained tears from her cheeks. "Yes?"

"Are you okay, dear? Is there something I can do?"

Morgan put on her best practiced smile and shook her head. "No, I'm fine. I just need a minute. You're sweet to check on me, though. Thank you."

The man nodded and smiled back, but she could tell

he didn't believe her. "Have a good day," he said instead, and continued on to his car.

Morgan rolled up the window and pulled her visor mirror down to fix her face. Her skin was red and blotchy from the tears and her eye makeup was everywhere. She pulled a tissue from her purse to do what she could, blew her nose and got back on the road before anyone else came to check on her.

When she pulled in at her parents' house, she didn't go inside immediately. Instead, she went around the back of the house toward the gardens. There, beyond the entertaining spaces, right at the edge of some trees, there was a stone bench. Beside it, a marble plaque that was nearly invisible if you weren't looking for it in the grass.

What seemed like a nice place to sit and enjoy the gardens was actually the world's tiniest graveyard. Her family had an ostentatious mausoleum at Magnolia Cemetery where generations of Steeles were laid to rest, but after she lost Dawn, her father had had a small private graveyard designated on their property. He told her that he wanted her to be able to visit whenever she wanted to. It didn't hurt that no one would see it back there, either.

She approached the site more slowly as she got closer. Despite how close it was, it had been a long time since she'd come back here. In part, because when Morgan had buried her daughter, she'd buried that part of her life with her. Or at least she'd tried to. River's sudden reappearance in her life had changed everything.

Morgan lowered herself down onto the bench and

looked at the marble slab that marked her baby's grave. It said simply *Dawn Steele*, with a single date. Her life had been so short there was only one date to put there.

She reached down and ran her fingertips across the cold stone. The site was immaculately kept. The family gardener, Paul, was probably paid handsomely to maintain it in the strictest confidence. He was one of only a handful of people who knew about Dawn. Aside from her parents, only Lena had been around to know the truth. She'd brought her prenatal vitamins and ice cream each night before Dawn was born, then her collection of pills with her favorite sparkling water and a few fresh cookies each night after she was born.

Since then, perhaps everyone except Paul had forgotten about this tiny grave and the child it was for. Suddenly, the thought of Dawn made her incredibly sad.

Being around River again had done more than stir up old feelings of desire and regret. It had reminded her that there was more at stake here than just another successful charity project.

That was what had caused the panic as she lay with River in the town house. The moment his hand brushed over her stomach, the reality of her situation came rushing in. She couldn't let River touch her. See her. Not there, like that. He would see the scar in the bright afternoon daylight. He would notice the firm belly he remembered was soft and covered in faded stretch marks. He would want to know the truth and she couldn't bear to tell him what had happened. He would hate her. Hate her and her family for hiding the truth from him.

Back then, when she could still feel her daughter

moving inside of her, she'd wondered if she needed to reach out to River. Whether he had been using her for money or not, this was his child. He may not have been the man she thought he was, but he deserved to know the truth. Then, before she could tell him he had a daughter, she was gone. What good would telling him do now? It would only cause him unnecessary pain. And even though she wouldn't admit it to herself, she'd still loved River. She couldn't intentionally hurt him.

So she kept quiet. Looked to the future. And tried to forget.

"I'm so sorry," she said to her daughter's tombstone as her eyes welled up with tears again. "You deserved better than what you went through. You deserved a life. Love. We both did. And I screwed it all up for us."

Six

Not a word. Not a single word, work-related or otherwise, in two weeks! The land was purchased and leveled, the plumbing was run and the slabs were poured and in the process of curing for all three houses. Framing was going up tomorrow and the roofs after that. And yet, Morgan hadn't spoken to him since she'd run from the town house that afternoon.

River stood in the lobby of Steele Tools, trying to decide if he should go upstairs and confront Morgan. He did need to talk to her about some business-related topics, but he knew those could've been handled via email. The truth was that he was here on a personal mission.

She walked out on him. In the middle of…well, the worst possible time to walk out. There was no explanation, no nothing. She'd run from his life once without another word. He wasn't about to let that happen a second time. If she didn't want him, if she had regrets about back then and now, she was going to tell him to his face without Daddy running interference.

He straightened his tie and was about to head toward the elevator when he heard an odd sound. It was something akin to a sputter and a gasp mixed together. He expected it to be Morgan, but then he turned to his left and found he was suddenly face-to-face with her father—Trevor Steele.

He expected the man to yell. Trevor had certainly done his share of that when he'd stolen River's wife from his bed all those years ago, but now, there was only an eerie silence as the man stared him down.

River was older now. Less intimated by a man like Trevor than he was back then. He wasn't a kid anymore, playing at being a man. Instead, he grinned and stuck out his hand to greet him. "Mr. Steele! Good to see you again, sir."

The man narrowed his gaze but didn't return the smile. "What are you doing here, River?" he asked in a voice so low River almost couldn't hear it.

That's when he remembered what Morgan had said about her parents. They hated scandal. Trevor would probably love to beat River with his briefcase, but he wouldn't because that would cause a scene. "You don't know, sir? My company is working with yours to build houses for the less fortunate."

River watched as the muscles in Trevor's neck and jaw tightened until he thought they might pop through his skin. "Is this my daughter's doing?" he asked coolly.

"Not at all. I believe my company was chosen through a downselect process overseen by one of your sons." River smiled as brightly as he could manage at the scowling man. Trevor Steele's firm policy of secrecy had bitten him in this case. "I'm not surprised they chose me. I took your advice and made the most of the bribe you gave me. I'm quite successful these days."

"A bribe?!" Trevor sputtered as he glanced around the lobby to see if anyone was nearby. "You keep your voice down when you throw around accusations like that. It was no such thing."

He crossed his arms over his chest and eyeballed the older man thoughtfully. "What would you call paying me to leave and never speak to your daughter again, sir?"

"I would call it softening the blow."

River laughed at the man's internal justification. *You can't have my daughter, but here's a hundred grand for your troubles, son.* "Is that what you tell yourself so you can sleep at night?"

"I sleep very well, or I did when I thought you were out of my daughter's life for good."

"As far as your precious daughter is concerned, I am out of her life. No worries there," River added with a bitterness he couldn't hide. He still wasn't sure what had sent her running and kept her silent for the last two weeks, but he was going to get to the bottom of it. That is, if security didn't toss him out of the building before he got the chance.

"Good. Keep it that way." Trevor started to turn his back and walk away.

"Of course, she doesn't know the truth," River called after him.

Trevor froze and turned back to River. "What truth?"

"I'm not sure, but she seems really upset with me about that money. Almost like it was my idea."

Trevor stiffened at his words. He had lied to his daughter and now River was calling him out on it.

"At first," River continued, "I thought maybe she was just angry because I took the money you offered. Honestly, I quarreled with myself about accepting it, but when it came down to it, I had nothing else left. Then I wondered if maybe she thought she was worth more than a hundred grand to me. But talking to you now, I think I've realized the real issue. She thinks I *made* you pay me to go away. Like I was just after her money the whole time and hit you up for cash to go away quietly."

Trevor crossed his arms over his chest. "You did take the money and go away quietly, River. That's a natural conclusion for her to make under the circumstances."

River shook his head. "No. No, I think she believes it because that's what you told her. You lied and told her I demanded money to agree to the annulment. I'm sure it made it easier to get her away from me if she thought I was just some poor scum after whatever cash I could get. I couldn't possibly have really loved her, right?"

Trevor looked down dispassionately at his watch and shrugged. "If that's what you want to believe—if that makes losing her more palatable for you—then fine."

"I should tell her the truth. She deserves to know you lied to her to break us up."

"I have an important meeting to get to. I don't have

time to argue with you, River. But know this," Trevor said, leaning in close to him. "You do not want to start unearthing the past. Morgan has spent years trying to get over everything that happened. It has been a long time now and it seems like both of you have done well on your own. I can only hope that you will be smart about this and let sleeping dogs lie. Nothing but pain will come from stirring things up. Good day, Mr. Atkinson."

Trevor marched across the marble lobby floors, leaving River alone, stewing in his aggravation.

There was probably some wisdom in the older man's words. Things might be better left alone. But they also might be better if everyone knew the truth. That all depended on Morgan.

Taking a deep breath, he headed toward the elevator and pressed the button to head up to her office.

Greg Crowley blew through the back door of his father's home with a scowl of irritation on his face. He'd spent another day downtown trying to get some day-labor work for cash under the table and had come home with twenty bucks in his pocket. Not exactly where he pictured he would be after his ten-million-dollar payday only a month or so ago.

He chucked his ratty backpack onto the kitchen chair and went into the living room. His elderly father was sitting in his recliner, watching television. That was basically all the man had done for the last twenty years since Greg and Nancy's mother passed away. Watch TV and collect his pension.

He turned to the television in time to see they were talking about the Steele kidnapping case again. That's all they seemed to talk about on the local news these days. Or maybe it just seemed that way because of his conscience. Either way it made him nervous. "Turn that shit off, Dad. No one wants to hear about some rich girl's problems."

"Meh!" his father groaned and didn't budge his remote thumb an inch.

Rolling his eyes, Greg returned to the kitchen for a can of beer and carried it with him back into his bedroom. It was the same bedroom he'd grown up in. With the same damn twin mattress that had been lumpy and awful then, much less now. Living with his father again hadn't been ideal, but now this was his only haven. The only place in the world he felt safe.

No thanks to Buster.

Maybe Greg was naïve. He'd known Buster for over thirty years. That seemed like the kind of friendship that could be considered trustworthy, even if they shared a common bond of being criminals. He was wrong. After they made off with Jade Nolan's ransom money, Buster insisted they lay low for a bit. By the time Greg looked up from his hiding place a week later, he realized Buster was long gone and so was the money. Every damn cent.

He hadn't even wanted to go along with this whole plot. Not back then, and not now, either. It was Nancy and Buster who had been gung ho about it. His sister had gotten the idea after the Steeles were admitted to St. Francis, then discharged for false contractions. Nancy knew they would be back to deliver their child soon enough. That gave them just enough time to formulate their plan. Kidnapping the Steele baby outright wouldn't fly. Someone had already abducted their eldest a few years before and it was in all the papers. They needed a different angle and they found it.

It seemed simple enough. Swap the babies. Send the Steele infant home with an unsuspecting couple. Their home wouldn't have security, alarms, cameras or nannies watching the child 24/7 like they had at the Steele mansion. They would then kidnap the Steele infant from the regular couple, then call the Steeles, inform them of the switch and demand the ransom money.

It was a simple enough payday. No one got hurt. The baby would be returned, the parents would get their correct children back and they could all retire with pockets full of Steele family cash.

Hurricane Hugo hadn't been a part of the plan, but it made things easier. Nancy had no trouble swapping the infants' ID bands in the chaos. She had access to the names and address of the couple that would take the Steele daughter home with them. Everything was going according to plan. Until it wasn't.

Greg never expected everything to go so spectacularly wrong. He couldn't have even imagined it because he hadn't realized how bad his sister's drinking had become. Or how serious her depression had gotten. She hid it well behind a cheery exterior. But the next thing he knew, his sister was dead and the Steele baby's location was lost with her.

When Nancy went into the ground, he thought—

or hoped at least—that that would be the end of it. For years, he watched his parents struggle with losing Nancy. The stress of it eventually killed their mother. Greg tried to move on with his life and put his criminal phase behind him. And he'd succeeded. He'd had a steady job, a nice enough apartment and a lady friend he went to dinner with from time to time.

Then Buster showed up one day pointing to an article in the newspaper about some big hospital mix-up thirty years ago. Now they had the piece of the puzzle they were missing—Jade Nolan was the Steele heiress. Buster was convinced this was their chance to get the payday they were owed at last. Greg wasn't as enthused. He would've rather the woman just keep her mouth shut and let it go. He'd sent threatening letters and even ransacked her house to scare her off the case.

But as always, Buster got his way. Greg quit his job to help Buster plan. He wouldn't need the work once he was rich, right? Then they kidnapped the Steele woman and for once in his life, he thought things were finally looking up.

As Greg looked around his childhood bedroom, he realized that his whole life had been a waste. Whatever he'd wanted to be, whatever he'd hoped to become had been taken from him. Taken by Nancy. Taken by Buster. Even taken by those mixed-up babies at the hospital. He couldn't blame any of them for what had happened. At least not Nancy and Buster. It was too late for that with his sister in the ground and Buster vanished.

But it wasn't too late to blame the Steele family. They dangled their wealth and privilege around town, just daring people to take a chance at getting a cut for themselves, then crushing anyone who tried.

For a while, Greg thought he could start over again. Maybe he could get the job back and give that lady friend a call. But the more he thought about it, the more he realized that time was long gone. He was fifty-six, unemployed, broke and sleeping on a lumpy twin bed in his father's home. He had nothing to offer and nothing left to lose.

And that made him dangerous.

Morgan looked up from her computer to find River standing in her doorway. She glanced at her phone, wondering what had happened to her receptionist and gatekeeper, then remembered she had left early today for an appointment.

Of all the days…

"That's not excitement to see me," River said as he stepped into her office and shut the door behind him. "It's almost like you've been hiding from me for two weeks and finally got caught."

"I haven't been hiding. I've been…busy." That was a terrible answer, but the best Morgan could come up with on the spot. She sighed and shut her laptop down, then she stood up and came out from behind her desk. She was hoping to intercept River before he sat in her guest chair and got comfortable, but he just sauntered over to the conference table and leaned against it instead. He crossed his arms over his chest and narrowed his gaze at her.

"Busy? Busy doing everything to avoid talking about what happened is more like it."

Morgan's tight lips twisted as she sought out the right words to respond. She had decided that honesty was not the best policy in this case, especially after all this time, but she hadn't come up with a better story, either. "I'm sorry about that," she said. "It was rude."

"Rude?" he chuckled. "Rude is saying you think I'm ugly. Or that dating me was the dumbest thing you ever did. Making out with me and then abandoning me with a serious case of blue balls is something else entirely."

She shook her head. "Were you always this crass and I just didn't notice it?"

"No. But I also wasn't this angry back then, either. I hadn't met your father yet, of course, so my young idealism was still intact. But I just ran into him in the lobby. Seems you were right and he didn't realize I was working with you on the housing project. He was really excited to see me," he added with an upbeat tone despite the sarcastic bite of his words.

Morgan had been hoping her father would remain out of the loop concerning River, but unfortunately that hadn't worked out. She was certain she'd be hearing about his concerns posthaste. "No, I hadn't mentioned it. It didn't seem like a good idea, especially coming from me. Contracts were already signed at that point. He isn't involved with the project, so I was hoping it wouldn't matter. I couldn't very well explain to my brothers that there was a problem without telling them more than they needed to know."

"Your family and their secrets. It's not healthy the way you all keep them."

Morgan shrugged and slumped against the table beside him. It wasn't the best idea to stand this close to him, but it was better than looking him in the eye. When he looked at her that way, she was tempted to tell him everything she knew, and that was dangerous. "I'm sure we don't have any more secrets than any other family. Ours just tend to be on a larger scale. More dramatic than most. I guess it just comes with the territory."

"You mean with the money."

She shrugged. "As they say, more money, more problems. And I guess more secrets."

River sighed, standing silently beside her for a full minute before he spoke again. "What happened at the town house?" he asked quietly.

There were so many things she could say. Should say. And yet, she couldn't voice any of it out loud. Maybe later. Once the houses were built and their project together was at an end, maybe then she could tell him about Dawn. Then, when he hated her, they could go their separate ways.

The side of his hand brushed against her fingers and stole any concerns from her lips. It sent a thrill through her no matter how hard she tried to tamp it down. Eventually, Morgan would have to face that she and River had something that just couldn't be ignored.

"I got scared," she said at last. That, at least, was true enough.

"Of me?"

That forced her to turn and look him in the eyes. They were wary as they watched her. She'd hurt him on some level when she ran off the other day. She hadn't meant to, but she had. Perhaps it was too much like the last time when she'd left, only this time had been her choice, not her father's. "Of course not," she said emphatically. "I was scared of this. Us. This thing between us, whatever it is. I thought that after all this time, it might have lessened, but it hasn't. So I ran."

Her gaze dropped down to the knot of his silk tie and focused there instead of the face that was studying every one of her vulnerabilities. Then she felt the warm press of his hand against her cheek. He guided her back up to look at him. "You're not the only one that feels that way," he said.

Before she could really consider what that meant, his lips were on hers. She leaned into him, seeking out the comfort and protection he offered as he wrapped his arms around her. As a young woman, she'd always felt safe in River's arms. When she lost Dawn and everything seemed to be crumbling around her, she wanted his embrace more than anything else, and it was the one thing she couldn't have. But she could have it now. At least for a while.

"River?" She pulled away and whispered his name into the space between them.

An expression of physical pain flickered across his face for a moment. "You aren't about to run off again, are you? I'm not sure I can take that a second time."

"No. You're in *my* office, so I'm not going anywhere. I just wanted to talk about something before this went too much further."

"What?" His fingertips pressed into the curve of her waist, massaging her hip as she spoke and making it hard for her to focus on her words.

"It's just that...well... I don't want anyone to find out about this. Whatever this is going on between us. If someone does, it will get ruined, I'm certain of it. I'd rather walk away now than have something with you spoiled again. Can we please keep it—whatever we decide we want it to be—just between us?"

He sighed and leaned back from her. His disappointment was palpable. "Great. Another Steele secret."

"It's not about keeping it a secret," she argued. "It's about not letting outside influences taint this. I want you. You want me. It's a simple thing. Neither of us is looking for anything more than a little comfort and release. Maybe some closure. But I don't want it to impact our professional work. Keeping this between us is the best way to make sure that doesn't happen. No drama, no scandal...nothing for Daddy to freak out over. Just a little fun between the two of us while it lasts."

"And after the key ceremony?"

Morgan brushed a strand of hair from his eyes. That event would mark the end of the project, as they handed over the keys to the new residents of the homes they'd built. It would be a bittersweet event for Morgan in more ways than one. "After the key ceremony, I think the best thing is for me to go back to DC and for you to go off and capitalize on the good work you've done here. That's the point of all this, right?"

"Right," he repeated, but she got the sense he wasn't content with this arrangement.

Did he want more? An actual relationship? Didn't he see how impossible that would be? It would be an uphill battle for them every step of the way until something drove them apart again. There was no sense in even entertaining something like that.

"You want me, don't you?" she asked.

His hands cupped her rear and pulled her tight against his erection. "You know I do."

"Then what's the matter? I thought you'd be happy. A no-strings affair with someone you have amazing chemistry with? That seems like a pretty sweet arrangement, especially considering both of us work too hard for anything more complicated."

"It's not that. The arrangement is fine. I guess I just want to know what's changed," he said.

Morgan pulled away and looked up at him. "What do you mean?"

"I mean, the last time we were together, you literally ran from the room. You said you were scared of what we had between us, and now you're practically crawling into my lap. What's different about this time? Is it the secrecy that makes you feel more secure? Are you ashamed of people knowing we're together, even casually?"

"Of course not. It has nothing to do with that." She reached up and stroked his cheek, feeling the coarse hairs of his beard tickle against her palm. It was an obvious reminder that he wasn't the boy she'd loved anymore. He was a man. A man that she wanted very badly, despite how she argued with herself. Over the last two weeks, she'd wrestled with how to move forward with River and get what she wanted without exposing the past she needed to keep hidden. For now, the best she could do was to try and keep parts of herself from being exposed so he wouldn't ask questions. Whether that entailed lingerie, dim lighting or her current strategy—staying partially clothed—it didn't matter. She was confident in her plan. If he was willing to go along with it.

"In the end, does it really matter why I changed my mind, as long as I have?" She looked at him with her mostly sultry gaze, hoping that it would make the answer moot.

"It shouldn't," River agreed. "I know I should just shut my mouth, thank the stars for the situation I'm currently in and take full advantage, but I guess I'm an ass and I overthink everything."

Morgan cradled his face in her hands and looked him in the eyes. "What's important is that I want you, River. Every time I argue with myself about it, every time I deny what I need, it only makes me want you even more. What's different is that I know I can't run from it anymore. So as far as I'm concerned, there's only one thing left for us to do."

"What's that?" he asked.

"Lock my office door."

Seven

Morgan leaned back on the conference table with a mischievous smile, watching as River quickly rushed over to her door and flipped the lock. This was the moment they'd both been waiting for. She'd tried denying herself and running from her feelings, but it was clear that River wasn't going to let her avoid it any longer. The only thing to do was give in to what they both wanted, and she knew she could do it in a way that kept any questions at bay.

Her office was private and separated from the other Steele executives on the top floor. Her calendar was clear for the rest of the afternoon and her assistant was gone for the day. The only windows overlooked downtown, with no way for anyone to see what was about to happen in her corner office. It was the perfect place to indulge at last.

When he returned, he stopped just short of her and let his gaze dip down to study her body. She was still leaning against the conference table and she had no intention of moving. It was solid oak and just what they needed. For this first time at least, she wanted to take the edge off, not curl up together in bed and have pillow talk.

She hadn't planned for any of this to happen today, but her slinky pencil skirt and silk blouse would be perfect to unbutton and slide out of the way, and help hide any areas she didn't want River to see. His gaze moved over her thoughtfully, likely thinking the same thing as he planned his move.

River seemed either hesitant to reach for her or he wasn't in a rush. Morgan could understand that she'd jerked him around enough that he'd be waiting for her to change her mind. But not now. Not again. She needed to make sure he understood that. She reached out and wrapped her arms around his neck, pulling him closer. She looked up at him with a sly smirk curling her burgundy-painted lips.

"I want you, River. Right now. Right here."

That was enough to dash away his last concerns. Now River snapped into action. Leaning past her with a quick slide of his arm, he moved a stack of papers and an arrangement of silk flowers on the table out of their way. Then he encircled her waist with his hands and lifted her up to sit at the edge of the smooth wood as though she weighed ten pounds. She closed her eyes and drank in the sensation as his palms slid up the silky length of her legs, pushing at the hem of her skirt. The fabric moved out of the way, allowing her to spread her thighs so River could find a home between them.

"Is this what you had in mind?" he asked, gripping her rear end and tugging her tight against the throbbing erection pressing against his trousers.

Morgan groaned softly, and then wrapped her legs around his waist. "Even better."

She leaned in to kiss River and the moment they touched, it was as though the floodgates had been opened. They'd been holding back for so long. This time there would be no interruption, no second thoughts. All the emotion and need that had built up over the last few weeks—and even the last ten years—came rushing forward at once. Their hands moved in a frenzy over each other's bodies, fighting with buttons and fasteners, tugging aside cotton and silk until they finally made contact with the bare skin underneath.

Morgan couldn't get enough of River. The warm woodsy scent of his skin. The searing heat of his hands gliding over her body, the low groans of pleasure against her lips… It all brought back a rush of memories that made her skin flush hot. Memories of their nights together. Of how much she needed him then, and now. It almost scared her how easily it came back after years of suppressing it. It made her worry that the temporary nature of their agreement might be harder to keep to as well. She wanted River, yes, but she couldn't let herself love him again. Not when he didn't know the truth.

Their lips didn't part until she felt him push her skirt up to her waist. "That should be enough," she whispered against his mouth. "For here." She added the last part, as though her hesitation was being naked at work where they might be caught, when in truth it was to keep as much of her body hidden from him as possible in the bright, late afternoon sunlight.

River nodded. Leaving her skirt where it was, he sought out her panties instead. His fingers hooked around the sides and tugged them down, slipping them past her patent leather heels and letting them fall to the floor like nothing more than the thin scrap of black lace they were.

He groaned aloud as he caught a glimpse of her bare flesh when he stood back up. She was quite disheveled with her blouse unbuttoned, her bra exposed and her skirt hiked up around her hips. Judging by his intense gaze and flexed jaw, he seemed to think she was the greatest thing he'd ever laid eyes on.

It made her feel sexy and desirable in a way that she rarely identified with. It had been a long time since someone had looked at her with such naked desire in his eyes. Since she'd *allowed* someone to look at her that way. The walls she built around herself after everything that had happened were high. Even with the anticipated prize of the Steele heiress on the other side, few men had tried to breach her protective barricades. Those who tried usually gave up before they reached her. And she was okay with that. It saved her the disappointment of finding they were just after her money.

River hadn't even thought twice about it before he'd scaled her walls, and there was a part of her that loved him for his reckless bravery where she was concerned.

But now his hesitation was starting to worry her.

She'd expected him to dive back into devouring her, but he stopped, just looking at her. "I haven't changed my mind, River. I'm ready."

He nodded and smiled. Leaning in, he gave her a soft kiss and pulled back. "I'm ready, too. More than ready. That was just a sight I wanted to commit to memory. And now, first things first."

Morgan watched as he shuffled out of his suit coat and reached into his breast pocket for his wallet. He set it on the table and tossed the coat across the back of a nearby chair. He opened the wallet, pulling out a single condom before he cast the rest of it aside.

Of course, he would remember them this time. On their wedding night, he'd forgotten to buy some. They'd been so excited to steal away on their adventure that some of the details had been missed. Since they were technically married and holed up in their honeymoon cabin for the night, they decided that it was okay without them this one time. That ended up being a mistake. Morgan had had an IUD put in not long after Dawn passed away. She wasn't about to be caught in that position again.

River didn't know any of that. He just knew to plan better this time. Stepping back between her thighs, he put a condom on the table beside her bare hip. Then he wrapped one arm around her back and eased her backward until she was lying across the conference table. He leaned over her and unbuttoned the rest of her blouse. Running his hands over her breasts and down her rib cage, he stopped long enough to press a searing kiss on her sternum. The warmth of his touch against her skin heated her blood and ran through her veins as quickly as her racing heart could move it.

Morgan gasped and squirmed against the cold table. She longed to be enveloped by River's warmth, to chase away the chill, and he seemed content to tease her instead. When his hand sought out the moist heat between her thighs, she forgot about anything else. Her mind went blank to everything but the waves of pleasure that pulsated through her body. Her back arched off the table, her hands clawing futilely at the slick polished wood. There could be no question of her wanting him this time. Her body had given her away. He had her on the edge of climax and he'd barely touched her.

Then he pulled away again. She heard the clinking of River's belt and opened her eyes to see him undoing his zipper. Slipping on the condom, River gripped her hips and with his gaze fixed on hers, entered her in one slow stroke. Feeling the hard heat of him sinking into her welcoming body was a pleasure she'd missed for so long. She almost couldn't believe it was really happening. How many nights had she lain alone, wishing for one more kiss, one more embrace and then hating herself for still loving the man who had betrayed her and walked away? She wanted to pinch herself so she knew this was real.

Morgan pushed herself up upright, wrapping her legs around his waist and her arms around his neck. She wanted to be as close to him as she could in this moment. Pressing her satin-covered breasts against the wall of his chest, she leaned in to whisper into his ear how much she needed him and nipped gently at his earlobe.

River shuddered then, gritting his teeth as he seemed to fight for control. It was a losing battle for them both. They'd both waited too long for this to take their time. He gripped at her back and pulled her so close to the edge she might have fallen without his support. Then he stopped holding back and gave her what she'd asked for. He filled her again and again, pounding hard into her willing body.

He seemed to know exactly what she needed from him and once again, she was on the edge of coming apart. She clung to him, gasping and whispering words of encouragement against his throat. "Please," she cried out as she neared her release, and he responded.

He pressed his fingers into the ample flesh of her hips and thrust until his legs began to shake. Morgan tensed and fell apart, shattering into her climax. It was only River that held her together, holding her tight until the last shudder rocked her body. It was then, with her cries finally silent, that River let go. He thrust hard and finished with a deep growl of satisfaction. Then, completely spent, he pulled them both down to the floor. Morgan fell to her knees straddling him as they collapsed into an exhausted, satiated pile on the expensive imported rug.

"So..." The younger man spun in his chair to face his webcam, a piece of licorice hanging out of the side of his mouth like a floppy red cigar. "I've got good news and bad news for you, Mr. Dalton."

Jade squeezed Harley's forearm a little tighter as they sat together in front of his laptop. She could tell he was getting irritated with his tech support team back in Virginia. He preferred to interface with his deputy of sorts, Isaiah Fuller, but he was tied up on another case the company was working. That meant the buffer between Harley and his team of geeks was gone.

They were supposed to be the best of the best, and yet it had taken them longer than he'd expected to run the backgrounds on his two primary suspects—Gregory Crowley and Robert "Buster" Hodges. Now that they had the information he needed, they seemed to be dragging it out.

Harley pinched the bridge of his nose. "Just tell me what you have, Eddie. I'm not in the mood for theatrics today."

The grin on the computer geek's face faded and he quickly plucked the candy from his mouth and set it aside. "Yes, so at first glance, there wasn't much to look at. I've emailed you both their background checks, which came back pretty clean, all things considered. Not many leads there. The problem is that both of your guys have fallen off the face of the earth since the kidnapping. Neither are at their last known addresses with the DMV. They don't seem to be employed anywhere with any federal withholdings. If they are working, it's under the table."

"If we're on the right track, and I think we are, they have ten million dollars of mine and Steele's money. Why would they be working after a payday like that? How about their financial records? Any leads there?"

Harley pressed. Jade watched as he reached for his phone and pulled up the background checks to scroll through while his employee reported his other findings.

"Not for Crowley. His only checking account was closed as overdrawn not long after the kidnapping. He doesn't have any credit cards or loans under his social security number. He's either living off the cash from the kidnapping, bought a new identity off the dark web or he's blown it all and is couch surfing somewhere."

"But you found something for Hodges?" Jade asked, hoping to turn the conversation toward better news. He had promised good news along with the bad after all.

"Yes, I did," Eddie continued. "There hasn't been any activity lately, but there was a purchase for an airline ticket a few days before the kidnapping. I figured that was him getting ready to run if all went well."

Jade felt her heart leap in her chest. This was the first real lead they'd had in a while and she was excited to hear the news. Being with Harley made her feel safer than she ever had before, but she had to admit that it was unnerving to know that her kidnappers were still on the loose.

"Were you able to get any details on the ticket?" Harley asked.

"It took a little digging, but yeah. According to the airline records, he bought a one-way ticket to Roatán, Honduras. He left the day after the ransom was paid, and then the credit card was paid off and the account was closed. The trail goes cold there."

Jade turned to Harley. "That's a start," she said hopefully, but the frown on Harley's face dashed her optimism a bit.

"It's a start, but with ten million dollars at their disposal, it's going to be hard to get much further. Like Eddie said, they could be under assumed names, living off cash. A couple fake ID's is all they would need. I'll have to see if I have any contacts in Central America that can help us out with the local authorities down there. It's a popular area for expatriates, so I'm not sure an older American would stand out much. But even if we find him, that only leads us to Buster."

"You don't think they're together?" Jade asked.

Harley shrugged. "Who knows? If it were me, I'd take my half and get as far away from the other guy as possible. Buster made the mistake of buying his ticket on his credit card, but Greg could've bought a bus ticket with cash going the other direction. Finding one doesn't mean we'll find the other."

Harley turned back to the webcam. "See if you can find any travel records for Greg. Even if he paid with cash, the airlines would have a record on their manifest. Check the trains and buses, too, just in case we get lucky. Whatever he could hop on and disappear. And also get me information on their families. Looking at their background checks shows they both have family living in the area, so get me their contact information. I find it hard to believe they'd both disappear without *someone* knowing where they are."

Eddie took a note down and nodded. "Will do, sir. Anything else?"

"Not for now."

The screen blacked out and Eddie's virtual presence in the room disappeared. Alone, Jade turned to Harley. "This is a real breakthrough, honey. I think we're on the right track."

He just sighed and leaned in to press a protective kiss on her forehead. "We're getting there. Slowly but surely. The people that hurt you can run, but they can't hide from me forever."

"Where are we going?" Morgan asked for maybe the tenth time since he picked her up from the office.

River smiled and kept his gaze fixed on the highway. "I told you when I asked you to pack a bag—and every time you've asked since then—*away*."

"*Away* isn't very helpful. I only packed a weekend bag. We aren't going far, are we? We're in the middle of a project, you know. It's not the best time for a spontaneous vacation."

He chuckled and kept driving, much to her continued irritation. "I'm aware of our responsibilities. But it's a Friday afternoon before Labor Day weekend and no one is doing anything on the housing project until Tuesday, including you and me. So we're going to my beach house for the long weekend and making the most of the time we have left together."

She turned to him with confusion etched between her eyebrows. "I didn't even know you had a beach house. I thought you just had the apartment in town."

"It's one thing to ask you to pack a bag to stay at my apartment for the weekend, but why would I go to the trouble of keeping the location a secret?"

"I don't know. You're complicated." She shrugged and looked out the window. "Where is your house?"

"You'll see." His response was answered with a groan from Morgan's side of the car.

Since their first sexual encounter in her office a few weeks prior, they'd met at his apartment every day for a long lunch of takeout and lovemaking. As he'd agreed to keep their relationship a secret, that didn't leave a lot of options for going out in public. His apartment was nearby and fine for what they needed most afternoons—he couldn't complain—but that wasn't what he had in mind for the long weekend.

No, he wanted to get Morgan away. Away from anything and everything that could distract her from enjoying herself—namely work and family. And then he was going to indulge at last.

For some reason, Morgan didn't seem to be interested in leisurely sex. Under the circumstances, a quick afternoon tryst made sense, but that was all she offered. Lunch was the only time she would agree to during the week, going back to her parents' mansion at night and always having things to do during the weekends, like gatherings with the Nolans or with Jade to catch up on the investigation. He didn't begrudge her spending time with her family, but even when she did agree to come at lunch, she wanted him quickly and in dim lighting. Sometimes all the clothes came off, sometimes they didn't. But as soon as it was over, she was clothed and heading back to the office again.

He wasn't sure if she'd gotten more self-conscious about her body over the years, but he was tired of all that. From what he'd seen, there wasn't a thing to be embarrassed over.

If there was one thing his beach house offered, it was privacy. Even though his bedroom had a wall of windows overlooking the marshlands, there wasn't a neighbor in sight. They could make love on the beach, on the deck, in the pool, anywhere they liked without interruption. That was what he needed. This weekend he wanted to take his time, to worship her body and to become fully reacquainted with every inch of it. The weeks had gone by faster than he'd expected and he had a limited window of opportunity left with Morgan. The key ceremony was right around the corner. He intended to make the most of the time he had.

"The apartment is nice enough and close to work, but it's not exactly my idea of a real retreat. I only stay there when I'm working. With the traffic, going all the way to the beach and back can be a pain during the week. When I go out there, I want to stay for a while."

"I have to admit, a weekend at a beach house sounds lovely. I can't tell you the last time I did something like that. Probably last summer before Hurricane Florence hit. Did you have any damage from that?" she asked.

The storm had been a big scare for the Charleston area, bringing up fears of a repeat of the catastrophic Hurricane Hugo, but then Florence turned away and hit North Carolina instead. As a builder, he'd worried about the projects he had going on in the area, but when they were spared the worst of it, he sent some of his guys north to help with the cleanup efforts.

"Nothing too serious, thankfully. I knew what the

risks were building on the coast here, so I designed the house specifically to withstand high winds and water surges. You can't live on the coast of the Carolinas without worrying about storms each season. Florence was its first real test and I'd say it passed with flying colors. I had to get some new patio furniture. That ended up who-knows-where. And I had to get the pool drained and cleaned. It was filled with mud and salt water and dead fish. That was a pretty big mess. But everything is back to normal now."

"It must've been fun to design and build a house just the way you wanted it."

Spying the sign for his turn, River got off the highway and headed toward Kiawah Island. "It was. That's what I've come to enjoy about construction. For the most part, I get to be in charge and things happen just the way I want them to."

Looking over at the beautiful woman in the car beside him, River wished he had that kind of oversight into every aspect of his life. The clock was ticking down on his time with Morgan. He didn't want to walk away from her this time with a single regret. He wasn't certain he would get his way, though.

Eight

River slid the large glass door aside and stepped out onto the patio with a glass of wine in each hand. Morgan was sitting on one of the outdoor couches, watching the sunset through the twisted oak and palmetto trees. The rear of his property was made up of several acres of undeveloped marshland that led to the sea, and sitting there, you could almost convince yourself you were the only person in the world.

"I can't believe this is your backyard," she said as she took the glass of chardonnay he offered.

"Yeah. When I saw this land, I knew it was where I wanted to build. It's not like I could find an existing house like this, anyway. It isn't exactly the historic Charleston design everyone wants down here. Or the typical beach house everyone rushes to rent over the summer. I like to think of it more as an overgrown tree house. What you'd expect a kid who grew up poor to blow his money on when he finally got some," he said with a smile. That was exactly what he had done. "What about you? What's your place in DC like?"

"Well, since I moved up there to go to college, I've been renting this little row house in Georgetown. It's two stories and narrow, not even a thousand square feet. It's more than enough for me, but it has no yard to speak of. I have a planter on the stairs to the front door and the plants in it are long dead, so I suppose it's just as well. I'm gone too much to really take care of a yard.

"If I decided to stay there, though, I'd probably buy a place that's a little bigger with private parking and perhaps a courtyard where I could put some chairs. I like the area. It's got that exciting college town vibe, plus it's close to the National Mall and all the events and museums there. One day, I hope to have free time to actually enjoy any of those things."

"You live in the middle of all that fun stuff, but you never play tourist?"

"No. I work too much. I'd like to go to the Smithsonian, though. They have a gemstone exhibit there with the Hope Diamond. There's also a necklace with a flawless pink diamond that I've seen pictures of. I fell in love with it and really want to see it in person someday. But even those priceless gemstones can't touch a view like this. This is like a painting in one of those museums I never visit."

River looked out to appreciate one of the perks of his home. The sky was starting to burn with orange and purples as the sun set. In the distance beyond the marsh, Folly Island was turning into a dark shadow. The temperature started to fall as the sun disappeared, giving the slightest chill to the ocean breezes that blew through the corridor where they were sitting. It was enough for Morgan to snuggle a little closer to him as they sat side by side and watched the sun set together.

"It really is amazing how much you've done with your life, River. I mean, did you ever dream that you'd have a home like this back when we first met?"

"Not at all. Most days I want to pinch myself. This place, my company, everything I've accomplished… I knew I had it in me, but I had no idea how to start. How do you build a company out of nothing? Especially since I had no education or savings. Construction was all I knew, but it's a big leap from the guy with a hammer to the CEO. Banks don't want to loan a kid like me the money it would take to get started. If it weren't for the money your father offered me that night, I don't know where I would be today. Certainly not the owner of my own com—"

"What?" She sat up abruptly, interrupting him.

River noted the slightly stunned expression on Morgan's face that was highlighted by the dwindling evening light. "I know it upset you that I took the money, but what else was I going to do? Turning it down seemed stupid. Having that cash gave me something to focus on instead of losing you."

"No," she shook her head. "I don't mean why did you take it. You would've been a fool not to take it. But you're saying that my father *offered* you the money? You didn't ask for it?"

He flinched at her words, the sound of them offensive to his ears. After his confrontation with Trevor, he had been fairly certain Morgan didn't know the truth about how the money had changed hands. It certainly explained her animosity toward him early on, but now she needed to know the truth. "Of course, I didn't ask for it."

He watched tears start to shimmer in Morgan's eyes and realized the version of the story she knew was far different. "After he put you in the car, he pulled a check out of his breast coat pocket and handed it to me. He said it was a little something to soothe my pride. What did your father tell you about it?" he asked. He wanted to know what kind of wicked picture Trevor had painted of him.

Instead of answering, she brought her hand up to cover her mouth. A tear broke free and ran down her cheek. He wrapped his arm around her and pulled her close. "Morgan, tell me," he insisted.

It took a few moments for her to compose herself, but after she'd wiped her eyes with a tissue, she stared down at her hands as she spoke. She seemed almost guilty, as though any of this was her doing. "My father told me that you asked for money to keep quiet about the marriage and cooperate with the annulment process. He basically called you a blackmailer who dropped me like a rock when money came into the picture. It broke my heart to think that you were so quick to demand a check and walk away."

River groaned and pulled her even tighter against him on the couch. That was what he'd been afraid of. "I let you go because that seemed to be what you wanted. When your father handed me the check, I was stunned. He told me not to be stupid and just take the money, but if he ever saw us together again, I'd have to repay every penny. He said I should use it to do something with my life, so that's what I did. I started my own company and built it into what I have today. To be honest, I never could've done it without that money to get me started, but a part of me wishes I hadn't taken it. Even if it meant I'd never have this house or the chance to see you again by collaborating on this project. The money didn't do anything to soothe my aching heart once you were gone."

"That sounds like something my father would say," she said with a soft sniff. "And it also seems like the kind of thing he would do, twisting his bribe into something that would ensure you stayed away and I hated you. He wanted to keep us apart and it worked. It worked too well. It made me so angry. It made me hate you so much that I never wanted to see or hear from you ever again. I thought I had given my heart away to someone who was just using me for money. And when I think about later on…" She broke into tears again.

River had never been a fan of Trevor Steele. But in this moment, seeing how brokenhearted Morgan was to learn the truth, he wanted to punch the man in the face. Was River so unsuitable for his daughter that it was worth hurting her so badly? He wasn't even sure she'd fully recovered from it. How could she learn to trust someone and be in any kind of serious relationship when her first one only taught her that men would use her for her money? Perhaps she would be willing to entertain something more than a casual fling if she hadn't felt so betrayed by love.

His love.

"River, I…" She stopped, her lower lip trembling slightly as she hunted for words.

"What is it?" He reached out and cradled her cheek in his hand.

She looked up at him for a moment with nothing less than fear reflecting in her moist green eyes. She was afraid of something. It wasn't him. Perhaps she was scared to share her feelings with him. That could be a scary prospect for her. Hell, it was scary enough for him. He'd felt a surge of joy run through him when he held her. An ache when they were apart. But with the key ceremony coming up, he didn't dare let himself consider what that meant.

"You can tell me," he said. He reached out and brushed a strand of her dark hair out of her face. "Anything."

Her lips parted to speak, but no sound came out. Morgan shook her head and let her gaze drop down to the collar of his shirt. "I'm sorry," she said at last. "I'm sorry for all of this."

"Don't be sorry. It's not your fault. You only knew what your father told you. I would've been pretty upset if I were in your position. No one wants to know that their love has a price."

"I know," she said with a sigh and melted against his chest. "This was my father's doing. And he and I are going to have a chat about it, soon."

"Please tell me you're looking for a job."

Greg peered over the top of the newspaper he was reading to see his father shuffling into the kitchen. At nearly eighty years old, shuffling was as fast as he could move. His tongue was still as swift and deadly as it had ever been, though.

"Not exactly," he muttered back. He'd gazed over the classified ads, sure, but then he'd gotten bored and started reading the articles instead.

His father made a dismissive noise and disappeared back into the living room with a beer in hand to watch his evening game shows. Greg decided to ignore him. He'd found something far more interesting to focus on in *The Post and Courier*: the Steele Foundation was planning an event in two weeks. His eyes scanned the article quickly, trying to keep focused as the excitement built inside of him. This was his chance. He just knew it.

The article was focused mainly on the houses that they'd built in town and the needy families that had been chosen to receive the homes. It was a feel-good piece, but Greg didn't care about any of that. It was the last paragraph that really stood out. The family would be hosting a ceremony at their Mount Pleasant mansion to celebrate the completion of the homes and present the keys.

The last time he'd gone to the Steele mansion, he and Buster had waited outside for their chance to snatch up and ransom Jade Nolan. That wouldn't work this time, especially since he was on his own. No, this time he needed to find a way to get *inside* the house. He imagined they had security at the door. The only people allowed in would be on their guest list. That meant the families and major donors only. That, and staff of course. It wouldn't be easy to get into the Steele mansion, but it could be done.

Thinking back to that night, Greg remembered that they'd pulled up alongside a white catering van near the rear of the house. They'd watched them carry out equipment and food, with easily a dozen servers in matching outfits going back and forth. The name and the company logo had been printed in black on the side of the van. It had had a smiley face with a bow tie, he was pretty sure. He tried to envision the logo in his mind, but the name of the company escaped him.

If the Steele family used the same catering company for each event, they might be the ones handling this upcoming party as well. For an event this large, he presumed they hired extra staff, perhaps from a temp agency. If he moved quickly, he might be able to get on board with the caterer for the event. That would give him unlimited access to the house, letting him move around easily among the guests and execute his plan without anyone questioning who he was and why he was there.

And what plan was that, exactly? He wasn't sure what he would do once he was inside the mansion, but he had some time to figure that out. First, he had to discover who would be catering the party.

Curious, he went to the cabinet where his father kept

one of the last phone books in existence. Computers and smartphones were as alien to this household as robots and laser guns. He flipped through to the section of catering companies and found a large corner ad with the smiling face he remembered from the van.

Black Tie Affairs!

That was the company, he was certain of it. He glanced down at his watch. The library a few blocks away would be open for at least another two hours. If he went over there now, he could get on the computer and see about putting in an application with the company. His dad would be so pleased to know he was trying to get a job. Greg was certain this wouldn't be what he had in mind, though.

Slamming the phone book shut, Greg grabbed his keys and headed out the door to the library. His brain was spinning with ideas as he climbed into his van. He was almost giddy at the thought.

This was his chance to finally make an impact on the Steele family. Perhaps *literally.*

Morgan couldn't sleep.

After the wine and lovemaking, she should've drifted off into a blissful slumber curled up at River's side, but it wasn't happening.

River was out cold. She could hear his rhythmic breathing in the bed beside her and she envied him. Of course, he had every reason to sleep well. His conscience was clean and the truth was finally out. Morgan, however, had a million different thoughts running through her mind.

Something about being here with him at his private retreat made it all too real. Spending the night together for the first time since they had dated as kids should've felt like an important milestone. They'd spent weeks taking long lunches together and avoiding any serious type of intimacy while they built the houses for her charity families. That was the way she had wanted it. That was the way she thought he wanted it, too. That was the smart thing to do. It wouldn't be long before they would be done building and she would return to DC. It was no time to fancy any type of real emotions where River and their future together was concerned.

But now, lying here, she was conflicted, not comforted, by his warmth beside her.

Maybe she liked it too much. Everything about being with River felt right, just like it had back in college. She could very easily let herself get lost in the fantasy of being with him. As though this were something real instead of a casual summer fling. Deep down, she wanted it to be real. But she knew that was a dangerous idea. If she gave in to that dream, it would crush her just as badly as the first time she'd given in to her feelings for him.

That was because even with River beside her, his hand resting on her pillowcase, she could feel him slipping through her fingers. In some ways, he was already lost to her. The sooner she accepted that, the better.

The key ceremony was right around the corner. There was exactly two weeks until the event and if she intended for her relationship with River to continue beyond their agreed deadline the way she wanted it to, she had to take action.

Morgan had to tell River about their daughter.

The truth was like a dark cloud looming overhead. Anytime she thought she might see the sun, the clouds would roll in and remind her she was keeping the truth from him.

Talking about Dawn had never been easy. Perhaps because she'd never really gotten to talk about her. When the whole family either didn't know or was acting as though nothing had happened, you didn't have anyone to confide in.

Now that she needed to say something, she found she couldn't. She'd wanted to. Just hours before when she realized the truth about the money that River had been given, it had almost spilled out. In that moment, all she could think about was that she'd kept the truth from River all that time—hidden the pregnancy and everything that happened afterward—because of lies her father had told her.

Now she couldn't stop thinking about how things could've ended differently. The complications of the pregnancy might not have been avoided, but if she'd had River at her side as they went through the ups and downs of it, everything would've been different. She would've had her husband there to hold her hand and cry with her. He would've fought to have Dawn buried in a real graveyard where people would be able to see her tombstone and know she existed. Even the baby's name would've been different—Dawn Mackenzie Atkinson.

Not Steele. Even though their marriage had been wiped from history, the baby would've had his name.

Telling him the truth back then would've been so much easier. Even with the animosity from her parents, telling River would've been the right thing to do. But telling him now? Somehow, it seemed like the one thing she had to do to make their relationship work was the one thing guaranteed to destroy it.

With a sigh, she rolled onto her back and looked up at the ceiling. The slanted roof had a skylight that gave her views of the night sky you couldn't get back in town with the light pollution there. She hoped for a shooting star to whiz by as she watched. Maybe then she could make a wish, and wish that all of this would work out at last with the man she loved.

Morgan cringed at the thought and the naïve stupidity that allowed her to think it. But she couldn't deny the truth. It was plain to see that she was in love with River again. Or more accurately, that she had always been in love with him. Even when she felt betrayed. Even when she was scared and alone and hated him for putting her in that position, she loved him.

Knowing he had never done anything to make him unworthy of her love made it that much harder to ignore. And that much harder to tell him the truth because he hadn't deserved the deception.

"Are you okay?"

Morgan turned her head to find River looking at her with concern lining his sleepy eyes. "Yeah, I'm fine."

"So you normally lie awake at night and stare intently at the ceiling?"

"I wasn't staring at the ceiling. I was looking up at the stars." She sighed and rolled over to look at him. "But no, it's not normal. I've just got a lot on my mind at the moment."

River pushed up onto his elbow and looked down at her. "I guess my plan to whisk you away to my peaceful, private retreat backfired. Do you want to talk about it?"

This was her chance. Here, in the dark, she could bare her soul. Confessions were always easier this way. And yet, maybe it was a bad idea. Maybe it was better to just enjoy this moment with River for what it was. To indulge the way she'd intended to when this first started, and then walk away from it.

Was it better to tell him the truth now and ruin everything? Right now, she had a lot on her mind, but she was comfortable and warm in River's bed. She could reach out and touch him if she wanted to. She could kiss him. Snuggle up against him. If she spoke up, she could very well ruin everything and end up waiting outside for an Uber at three in the morning to get back to Mount Pleasant.

Or was it a better idea to keep her mouth shut, let things come to their natural end and have this happy memory of their time together to cherish? The only way to truly keep the past in the past was to make sure her future didn't include River.

"Not really," she said, chickening out once again. "It's nothing you would want to hear about in the middle of the night."

"Try me."

"No. Just forget it. I don't want to waste another

minute worrying about something I can't control." And she couldn't control it. Not really. She could tell him, but how he responded was on him. That's what scared her.

"Okay. Well, how about I help you forget about it?"

River grinned wide in the moonlight and she knew that this was the offer she would accept. To lose herself in loving him and trying to keep the memory in her heart so she wouldn't be too lonely without him.

Nine

Something was bothering Morgan, but once again, she wouldn't open up to him about it. River wasn't sure if she didn't trust him or if it was one of those damned Steele secrets holding her mind hostage. Either way, her stress was palpable and ruining the vibe of their weekend retreat.

So far things had been fine but hadn't exactly gone to plan. She was here in his bed, unable to flee back to the office or the mansion, but his indulgent fantasies were still out of reach. The lights were still dim or completely darkened when they made love. And while they weren't fully or partially clothed, she had packed a wide array of lingerie.

Normally, River would find lingerie intriguing. Silky straps, lacy panels, strategic cutouts… There wasn't anything wrong with that. But on Morgan, it felt like a lacy barrier protecting her from something. Him, he supposed.

He'd offered to help her forget whatever was bothering her and the way she'd curled her leg around his hip seemed like an acceptance of his proposal. Her fingers were brushing over his beard and burying themselves in the thick waves of his hair. All signs pointed to her wanting him, and yet, as before, she was a little overdressed for the occasion. She'd put on a pale pink silk nightgown before she got into bed. It had to go. He'd just hold his breath to see if she stopped him.

He placed one open palm on her thigh and rubbed up her leg to her hip. River caressed the skin, skimming over her tummy and moving up beneath the chemise to cup one firm breast. He watched her reaction with curiosity, but so far, it was all okay.

Until he started pushing the gown up higher. That's when he felt her stiffening the way she had just before she bolted from that town house. He eased back, afraid to push her too far. They weren't in the middle of town where she could just jump up and leave. This time he was going to get to the bottom of it all.

"I need you to tell me exactly what it is that I'm doing that makes you nervous," he said.

Morgan bit at her lip as she pushed up onto her elbows. She gently tugged the gown back down as she shook her head. "It's nothing," she argued.

"Okay. Then let's take this thing off. It's in the way and I want to see you. All of you." River gripped at the hem to pull the silky slip of fabric over her head, but the fear in her eyes stopped him before she could argue.

"I'd rather not."

He sighed and leaned back. "I don't understand what you think you have to hide, Morgan. I could tell you that you're the most beautiful woman I've ever had in my bed. I could tell you that I've done nothing but fantasize about you for ten years—and in all those fantasies, you were completely naked. I'm not sure it would make a difference with you, though."

"Fantasies aren't reality. I'm not nineteen anymore."

"I don't want you to be nineteen. I want *you*. Right now. Just as you are. And I want you to trust me when I say that I mean it. I don't know what you could possibly be hiding. Did you get an ugly tattoo? Grow a big hairy mole? A gnarly scar? None of that matters to me. You're beautiful, Morgan. Every inch of you."

Her brow knit together in thought as she considered his words. "Give me a minute," she said at last.

He considered arguing but thought better of it. If she needed a little bit of time to be comfortable with the idea, he shouldn't push her. "Okay."

Morgan left the bed, rummaging through her luggage for a moment and then disappeared into the bathroom. River laid back against the pillows and stared up at the skylight. A moment later, he saw a streak of light cross the sky. Maybe he would get his wish tonight and Morgan would stop holding back. The clothes and the lighting seemed like they were just a physical manifestation of the way she was resisting her feelings for him.

He'd hoped getting her here away from the city and the Steeles might help.

When the bathroom door opened, all River could see was the nude silhouette of Morgan against the bright backlighting. The nightie was gone, with all of her curves on display. He could tell she was topless. The natural movement of her full breasts and their taut nipples were visible as she turned to face him, even from a distance. But as his eyes adjusted to the light, he noticed that she wasn't entirely naked. Even after their discussion.

Morgan crossed the room, leaned over to the nightstand and flipped on the small lamp there. The light bathed the room in a golden glow that wasn't too bright, but it was more light than he'd seen her in, as yet. Now he could see that she had on some clothing, but it was hard to complain about her choice of outfit. She had on a fire-engine red satin garter belt with red and black lace that stretched over her hips and tummy. The garters stretched down her creamy thighs and each clasp had a silk rosette that held up a sheer pair of black stockings. A hint of her bare skin was visible beneath the edge of the lace as she moved, and he was pretty sure there were no panties beneath the garter belt.

Then Morgan surprised him by turning around to give him the full view. Apparently, it wasn't shyness that kept her partially covered. In the back, the lingerie had little more than a thin belt and another set of garters holding up the stockings. The plump curve of her bare ass was gloriously on display, confirming his suspicions about her missing panties.

"Damn," he whispered as she turned back to face him. If she felt the need to wear *something*, River had to admit it was a great choice.

She pulled back the covers and slipped into the bed. "Is this okay?" she asked. "There shouldn't be anything in your way."

River could hardly speak for the lump in his throat. He only nodded and reached for her. "Come here," he said at last with a rough voice.

Morgan immediately curled beside him, letting River cover every inch of her body with his own. He ran his hands over her stockings, loving the feel of them against his rough skin. She didn't hesitate to part her silk-clad thighs as he moved higher, letting him seek out her heat with his hand.

She gasped and arched her back off the bed as he gently stroked her center. He teased at it at first, applying more pressure gradually until she was pressing her hips against his hand. He slipped one finger, then another inside of her, grinding harder until she was panting and squirming anxiously beneath him.

"I need you now, River," she cried. "I don't want to come without you."

He stilled his hand, considering sending her over the edge anyway, but opted to give her what she wanted. With a condom in place, he nestled between her thighs and found his home there. He bit his lip and surged forward until he was buried deep inside her. He closed his eyes and savored the feeling of her heat wrapped around him. The soft stockings rubbing against his hips as she pulled up her legs to cradle him, the rough tickle of her lace garter belt against his stomach.

Even with that last scrap of clothing left behind, it seemed like a victory. He'd never felt closer to Morgan than he did at that moment.

She must have felt the same way, because they moved together as though they were one person. River refused to rush this time, slowing the pace to taste her mouth, her throat and her breasts. Tonight, they had all the time in the world together to enjoy this. He reveled in the sound of Morgan's soft cries and the press of her fingertips into his shoulder blades. After the last few weeks together, he could even feel her release building up inside as her muscles tensed around him and her breath moved rapidly in her chest.

"River," she gasped with an edge to her voice.

She was so close. He knew she would be after he'd taken her so far before. This time he wasn't going to stop until she was screaming his name. "Don't hold back, baby," he whispered against the outer shell of her ear. "Just let it happen."

River was talking about more than just her orgasm. He wanted her to stop resisting all of this. Maybe she felt like she had good reasons to hold back her feelings for River, but he didn't want her to fight it anymore. He wanted this moment to last. Beyond tonight, beyond the weekend, beyond the key ceremony. He wanted to give this a real try without the interference of anyone else.

They deserved a second chance. A real chance, not just some fling to relive their youth and soothe their past wrongs. They both knew it meant more than that.

He was lost the moment he laid eyes on her again. All the old feelings, good and bad, had rushed to the surface. With most of the bad set aside, he was tired of fighting the good.

"Yes, River!" she shouted to the empty room, clinging to his shoulders as her body was rocked with the spasm of her release. "Yes!" she cried again and again until she stilled beneath him.

It was only then that River let himself finish. He buried his face in her throat and thrust into her until he unraveled with a low groan of pleasure.

After a moment, River rolled onto his back to catch his breath. He could get used to being woken up like that more often. He stumbled into the bathroom to clean up, and when he returned a moment later, he found that Morgan had changed back into the silky chemise he'd banished from the bed earlier.

With a sigh, he climbed back under the covers, wanting so badly to say something about the outfit. Instead, he snuggled up with her and decided to enjoy their night for what it was. They'd made progress. Baby steps, but progress.

"So tell me," he said, as they were on the edge of sleep. "It's an awful tattoo you're hiding, isn't it? Do you have Kermit the Frog on your hip bone or something? Property of Big Jim?"

He was answered only with a fluffy pillow straight to the face.

"Good night, River," was all she said.

"Good night," he replied with a chuckle. He pulled her close against him and drifted off into a contented sleep.

* * *

Normally, when Morgan worked at Steele headquarters, she tried to stay as far away as she could from the executive suites. That was the turf of her father, brothers and others entrusted with the day-to-day running of Steele Tools. There, they discussed and worried about things she couldn't care less about—like whether moving their manufacturing facility to China would improve their bottom line, or if a hammer looked better with the traditional Steele red or exciting new yellow rubber grips.

Tools were the family industry and she reaped the benefits of it, but that didn't mean she had to live and breathe it the way the others did. In fact, if her father hadn't indulged her in creating a charitable branch she could run, she wouldn't have worked for the company at all. Several people in the family had started in the company and branched off into careers in politics or kicked off their own start-ups. Morgan felt like she would be one of those who eventually stepped out of the tool business. Into what, she had no idea.

But Tuesday morning, after her long weekend at River's place on Kiawah Island, she marched down the hallway toward the executive offices like a woman on a mission. She ignored everyone she passed on the way to her father's office. It was early, not even eight o'clock yet, but she knew he would be there. Her father had spent the majority of his life in this office. If he wasn't at home, he was in his executive chair, wheeling and dealing.

His administrative assistant hadn't come in yet, and

for that, she was thankful. One less roadblock. She glanced through the glass of his office wall long enough to confirm he was there and alone, then she barged inside.

Her father shot up in surprise, nearly spilling the coffee he was sipping all over his keyboard. "Morgan!" he declared, before gently setting the coffee aside. "Is something wrong?"

"Yes. I have something I have to ask you and I need you to be honest with me."

Trevor cocked his head curiously and gestured to the guest chair. "Okay. Why don't you sit down, sunshine, and we can talk it all out."

She winced at the sound of her pet name. She was not in the mood to be Daddy's little girl. She was mad at him and she didn't want him clouding her feelings with things like that. Still, she sat down in the chair, hovering on the edge and refusing to relax into the soft leather. "I had a discussion with River recently. He mentioned how he used the money you bribed him with to start his company. That sounds a little bit different from the version of events you told me."

"Bribe is a strong word, Morgan." Trevor smiled at his daughter indulgently, but she wasn't going to let him sweet-talk his way out of this. It was her life he was toying with. She wasn't a chess piece to be moved around at his will.

"Dad, this is no time for semantics. Did River demand the money to go or did you offer it to him?"

Trevor sat back in his chair and sighed. "What does it matter? He took the money, didn't he? That's the important part, isn't it?"

"No, it isn't. I don't blame him for taking what was offered. What else did he have after you stole me away? What's important is that you made me believe that he had demanded that money to go away quietly. You told me that you had to pay him off to keep him from stalling the annulment and demanding a part of my estate since I was too naïve to get a prenuptial agreement. You told me he threatened to go to the newspapers about our affair if you didn't write him a check on the spot. None of that was true, was it?"

Trevor watched her for a moment, the muscles in his jaw tensing. "No, it wasn't true," he admitted at last. "I told you that so you'd keep away from him. He wasn't the right boy for you, but you were too blinded by young love to see it. I offered him the money in the hopes he'd take it and disappear. And he did. So things worked out in the end, didn't they? He's a success. You're doing well. No harm, no foul."

She shook her head. "I can't believe this. When he told me about the money, there was a part of me that was certain this was just his way of getting me to move past it. But River was telling the truth. You bribed him, and then made me think he was just a gold digger using me to get to my money."

"I thought it was for the best, sunshine. It was a story so awful that it would make the break clean and you wouldn't try to run back to him when I wasn't looking."

"For the best? Daddy, do you realize what you did? You didn't just break up a pair of young, foolish lovers. You broke my heart when you told me that. You made me believe that no man could ever love me just for me, that my money would always be a factor when a man showed an interest in me. It made me so suspicious that I stopped trusting people. All these years… After everything that happened…"

Trevor frowned as she spoke, but he didn't interrupt. "Morgan, I never realized it had that kind of impact on you. I only wanted you to marry someone who was worthy of you."

"River was worthy. He was worthy in more ways than I can count. He wasn't rich, but he was a good person and he loved me. So tell the truth—when you say worthy, you mean rich."

He sighed. "When you have the kind of money our family has, it's not unheard of for people to be targeted romantically. How was I to know if River was sincere or not?"

"It would've helped if the first words you spoke to him weren't, 'Get your hands off my daughter and put on some clothes.'"

Trevor leaned closer and cocked a brow at her. "It also would've helped if I had met my future son-in-law before he was my son-in-law, Morgan. By secretly eloping, it seemed like you had something to hide."

"I did. I was hiding him from you, because I knew that you wouldn't allow us to get married." Morgan's gaze dropped sadly to the hands she had folded in her lap. "You've controlled every aspect of my life since I was a child. The moment I tried to live my own life as an adult, you shut it down."

"You got married, Morgan. This wasn't a nose piercing or some other type of harmless youthful rebellion.

You married a boy you'd known for less than three months. Without your family. Without a prenuptial agreement. Letting you live your own life was starting out as a disaster. You were only nineteen years old."

Morgan's head snapped up as his words fanned the fire of anger heating her cheeks. "Stop it right there. Stop twisting this conversation into a lecture about what you think I did wrong with my life. We're here to talk about what you did. You *lied* to me. You manipulated my feelings. I'm almost thirty years old and sometimes I think you're still pulling the strings of my life like I'm some marionette puppet."

"I think that's a little overdramatic, Morgan."

"Maybe, but I'm allowed to feel however I want to feel. You're not in charge of that." She took a moment to collect her thoughts and figure out what she wanted to say to him. "I think that perhaps having you as my father and my boss has given you too much control in my life. Perhaps some space would be healthy."

Trevor chuckled dismissively at her words. "You can't quit being my daughter."

"Technically, I could. I'm sure the Nolans would be happy to see more of me. I haven't gotten to spend as much time with them as I'd like to, but I'm pretty certain they would never tell me who I could love or decide who was good enough for me. But I couldn't do that to the rest of the family. Or to you, no matter how badly you've hurt me, Daddy. But I can quit my job."

That caught his attention. He sat upright in his chair, no doubt thinking of all the loose ends she would leave behind if she walked out the door at that exact moment. "Are you serious?"

Morgan took a deep breath and nodded. "Yes. But don't worry, I'll finish this year's project. It's too late in the game to turn it over to someone else. But after the key ceremony is over, you can consider this my notice."

Her knees were shaking as she pushed herself up from the chair and turned her back on her father. She tried to walk to the door without losing her cool and made it as far as grasping the handle when her father spoke again.

"Does he know about Dawn?"

Morgan froze on the spot, her hand gripping the doorknob for support. She couldn't make herself turn around or face him, because they both knew the answer to his question was no.

"You kept that from him, didn't you? Because you thought it was for the best. That he would be hurt by the truth."

She felt her father's presence behind her as his hand came to rest gently but firmly on her shoulder. She didn't flinch away from his touch, as even in this moment, it was a comfort to have him there. He was always there for her, even when she thought she didn't need him.

"You justified keeping your daughter a secret in your mind, but if he found out about her now, don't you think he would be angry with you?"

"Yes." Somehow, she knew he would be. She had punished him for a crime he hadn't committed and now they would all suffer for it.

"Now you see where I'm coming from, sunshine. I'm sorry that what I did hurt you. It was the last thing I wanted to do. But we all make choices and sometimes the right answer isn't so easy to come by. Sometimes we end up hurting the ones we love in an attempt to protect them."

She did understand. She didn't want to, but she did. There was a part of her that had kept the truth about their daughter from River to protect him. But she'd also been angry with him. Now that those excuses were gone, what was keeping her silent? It was knowing that finding out the truth now would only hurt him. And that he would blame her.

"Do you think he'll ever be able to forgive me?" she asked quietly, the words barely a whisper.

The hand on her shoulder tightened into a gentle squeeze of support. "For your sake, I hope so, honey."

Ten

Greg straightened the bow tie provided by his temporary employer and took a deep breath. This was it. Weeks of planning and years of frustration were going to culminate tonight. Not in a payoff, no, but in some sweet revenge.

As he carried around a tray of full champagne flutes, he noticed how the rich partygoers hardly paid any attention to him. Like he wasn't good enough to be acknowledged as a simple waiter. They saw the champagne, though. They snatched that off the tray and continued their conversations, dismissing him once they had what they wanted.

It took everything he had not to say, *You're welcome*, in a mocking tone. He only had to hold it together for a little bit longer.

As the last drink was taken, Greg turned back to the kitchen where the catering team was working. Black Tie Affairs had hired on a team of servers for the event with surprisingly few background checks. They hadn't even realized his ID was a fake. They thought his name was Carl. And they hadn't really looked at him, either. He was just there for the grunt work.

Boy, were they all in for a surprise. If they'd paid more attention, they would've noticed the strange boxes he unloaded into the ballroom with the rest of the catering equipment. Soon, those carefully placed explosives hidden beneath the linen table skirting would rip this ballroom and everyone nearby into tiny pieces. And that waiter, the one they never even looked at, would disappear in the chaos as a presumed victim of the blast. They wouldn't be able to pick "Carl" out of a lineup. Their own arrogance would see to it that he would get away scot-free.

"Carl, take this bag of trash out, please."

With a sigh, Carl set aside his tray and grabbed the heavy sack of cooking scraps. He went out the back door and tossed it into the dumpster the Steeles had had delivered for the event. As he stood out there, he looked at the sea of expensive cars parked across the lawn. He couldn't afford the tires on one of those vehicles. He was done. Done with these rich, entitled people getting everything and him getting nothing.

It would be easy to just walk away now and listen to the explosions and the screams as he disappeared into the night. But he wanted to see it. For once in his life, he wanted to watch one of his plans be executed without a hitch. So he went back inside.

"Carl, take this tray of canapés out, please." The head caterer slid a platter of tiny, fancy little foods toward him. He picked up the tray out of habit and carried it with him into the ballroom.

Instead of going into the crowd, however, he eased back into a safe corner, far from the bombs. He set the tray of food on a table and reached into his pocket for the detonator. He wanted to wait for the perfect moment. He took one last look around the room… A crowd had gathered onto the dance floor. That would be perfect. He thought of his sister…of his mother…and then he placed his thumb over the button and took a deep breath.

It was done. The keys were in the hands of three deserving families and instead of feeling happy or even relieved, River almost felt sick to his stomach.

He knew it wasn't the champagne. As he stood at the edge of the ballroom and watched the others, he could see that everyone else was drinking the same bubbly beverages without ill effects. Of course, they weren't on the verge of losing the most important person in their life, either.

River tried to focus on something else. It was supposed to be a joyous event after all. The Steele mansion was once again draped in expensive fabrics and flower arrangements. They had gone all out, as usual. The ballroom was filled with people in formal attire, there to celebrate how wonderful they were for contributing to a good cause. Tonight, they'd gotten their big payoff—celebrating and applauding as they gave out the house keys to the needy families, and consuming a down payment's worth of champagne and canapés.

Like the fund-raiser, the event was a little over-the-top for River. He'd be just as happy to skip the party and put that money toward the houses or another good cause. Of course, the Steeles thought it was important to have this special and exciting night for everyone, but as someone who had received charity in the past, it made him uncomfortable. Not everyone wanted a light shone on the fact that they needed help to get by.

Thankfully, the families seemed comfortable enough. They were easy to spot in the crowd, wearing their Sunday finest for the black-tie event. It wasn't too much to suffer through to get a brand-new house in the end.

This was at least a smaller event than before. Now he could easily find Morgan in the crowd. She was speaking with an older couple who had to be her biological parents. He hadn't been introduced to the Nolans, but it was obvious she was a younger version of Carolyn Nolan, with the same creamy complexion, curvy figure and luxurious shiny dark hair.

It was hard to focus on anything other than Morgan, however. Her scarlet-red gown fit her like a glove. It was one shouldered, leaving a single collarbone and arm gloriously bare. It bunched around the waist, clinging to her rounded hips, and fishtailed to the floor in a crimson train that trailed behind her. She looked stunning—every bit the Steele heiress, despite her newfound pedestrian roots. The color alone was enough for her to stand out among the darker hues of the other party-goers, even though he could've found her without it. She was like a shining beacon that directed him home.

It seemed like a lifetime since he'd walked into the ballroom and laid eyes on Morgan for the first time after all those years apart. Since then, they'd spent weeks in each other's arms. They'd worked through a lot of their old baggage. Truths had come to the surface, healing old wounds they'd both carried through their years apart.

River knew they'd discussed their little dalliance only lasting through to tonight, and they hadn't mentioned otherwise, but he couldn't walk away from Morgan when it was over. She turned and looked at him then, a soft smile curling her cherry-red lips. He smiled back and felt his chest tighten as though she'd reached into his rib cage and clutched his heart in her fist. No. He wasn't giving up on her again. It didn't matter what her father or anyone else had to say about it. He would tell her so when he got the chance, but so far tonight she'd been a crimson bumblebee, flitting around the room in her official capacity for the event.

Finally, she broke away from the conversation with the Nolans and headed in his direction. "Good evening, Mr. Atkinson," she said with a smile.

"Miss Steele. You throw a lovely party," he said, mimicking her polite and formal greeting. Even now, weeks later, she wanted the two of them to remain a secret. So it wouldn't be ruined. Or something like that. Now he wasn't so sure it didn't have more to do with her father's disapproval. Trevor Steele could certainly ruin things if he wanted to. He'd caught the man's icy stare across the ballroom a few times, but they hadn't spoken since that afternoon in the lobby of Steele Tools' corporate offices.

"Thank you." She glanced around at the mingling crowds. "I wish more people were dancing, but it seems to be going well, otherwise."

"I always believe in leading by example." River reached out a hand to escort her onto the mostly empty dance floor. He knew it was a dangerous offer and judging by the wary look in her eye, so did she. They'd spent the last few weeks keeping their relationship in the shadows. To take a step out onto the dance floor together would be to shine a bright light on the two of them. Sure, it might just seem like a polite dance to anyone watching, but they would know better. And so would her father.

He was pleased and a little surprised when she placed her soft hand into his. He gave her a smile of encouragement as they stepped out onto the dance floor. He put one hand gently on her waist and kept a polite distance as they started to sway slowly to the music being played by the string quartet nearby. It seemed to do the trick. Within a few minutes, there were half a dozen other couples out there with them, including the Nolans.

"See?" he said. "Now people are dancing."

"Thank you," she said, although she seemed a little nervous. She kept glancing around as they danced, only making eye contact for a split second before anxiously glancing around again.

"You look beautiful tonight," he said. "That color on you is stunning. Reminds me of that lacy little thing you wore at the beach house."

That seemed to finally bring a genuine smile to her face and a little color to her cheeks. "Thank you, River. I can get used to you in that tuxedo as well. You've come a long way from the jeans and T-shirt you were wearing when I hit on you in Five Points."

River chuckled at the mention of the downtown bar district near USC where he'd first met Morgan. Even that first time, he was able to pick out her light in the crowd like a neon sign. "I'm pretty sure *I* hit on *you*."

"You're probably right. I remember thinking it was pretty cocky of you to approach a group of girls and ask to buy me a drink. We were an intimidating crew."

"It didn't matter. You could've been surrounded by a pack of angry dogs and I would've gone straight to you. I couldn't help myself."

His gaze fell on the long elegant line of her neck exposed by her hairstyle and the cut of her gown. The thick dark waves were twisted on top of her head with a few soft tendrils kissing her skin the way he longed to. He spoke up to keep his lips occupied with another task. "Morgan, I need to tell you something."

She looked up at him with wide green-gold eyes. "What is it? Is something wrong?"

"Well, yes and no. I just needed to say…to tell you… that I lied."

She frowned as she looked up at him. "You lied? About what?"

"I didn't realize I was lying at the time, but when I said that I would be okay with this ending tonight… I'm not okay with it. I want more than just a casual fling with you, Morgan. I want to be with you. Publicly. For the long term."

"River, I—"

He held up his hand to stop her protest before returning it to her hip. "I want you to look your father in the eye and tell him that we're together. And that it's serious. Because it is, despite our best intentions. At least, this is serious for me." He considered saying more. To tell her that maybe he was falling in love with her again, but the conflicted look in her eyes held his tongue for now. "It is serious for you?"

She glanced around the room again before she looked up at him. "Yes, but…can we talk about this after the party? This is a little heavy for the dance floor."

He swallowed his disappointment and nodded stiffly. "Sure." He was certain she felt more for him than she was letting on, but she was afraid. Afraid of telling Daddy that she'd fallen into the same trap a second time with an unacceptable boy. Afraid of causing a scene at one of the family events and being the subject of cruel whispers. "Just, uh, forget I said anything. It was stupid of me to even bring it up tonight with everything else going on."

"No, River. I don't want to forget about it. I just want to—"

Her words were cut off by a sudden blast from the far side of the room that rocked the entire house.

It was absolute chaos after the explosion. After a large boom, the left side of the ballroom exploded into a fireball. Chairs flew across the room as the sound of shattering glass and horrified screams followed it. People started yelling and scattering around the house.

Morgan hardly knew what to do as the thick clouds of black smoke filled the room. All she could think about was who was in the ballroom. Who had been closest to the blast? Had it been one of her brothers? Her parents? The Nolans? Did she just lose the chance to get to know her birth parents? Was it one of the families who had come to get the keys to their new home? Her heart was breaking in her chest as she struggled to see if anyone was hurt.

River was more focused. He took Morgan's hand and led her from the room as quickly as they could make it. They went the opposite direction of the crowds, heading for the back door and the gardens beyond it. They ran a safe distance across the lawn, collapsing together on a stone bench on the far side of the gardens.

Morgan's lungs burned and her eyes stung from the soot, but she wanted to go back inside. She wanted to help. But River kept his firm grip on her. She finally gave up, dropping her face into her free hand with a choking sob. "What happened? I didn't see it. Was it a gas leak?"

"I doubt that. It seemed more deliberate to me."

"Who would do such a thing?" she asked. To set off a bomb at a party where needy families were celebrating—that was despicable.

"I don't know," he said. "But they'll be caught and brought to justice. If I know anything about Trevor Steele, it's not to cross him. He will take care of it."

"If he can. What if he...?" She lost the words as she

thought about what could've happened to the people in her life. They could be hurt. Or dead.

He pulled her to his chest and she rested her wet cheeks there against the lapel of his tuxedo. When she opened her eyes again, her gaze fell to the tiny marble grave marker that sat just beyond the bench to their left. To escape the danger, River had managed to lead her someplace far, far more treacherous than the burning house. She was frozen for a moment, wondering if perhaps the darkness would hide what she plainly recognized on sight.

"Everything will be okay," he assured her. Then she felt him stiffen against her and she knew that something had changed.

Morgan was afraid to breathe. Afraid to move. Perhaps he hadn't seen it. Or if he had, didn't understand the significance of what he was looking at. It was just a name and a date after all. A date that was far too soon for a child of theirs to be born.

"Morgan?" he asked.

She could feel his fingers start to press more insistently into her upper arms. "Yes?"

"What am I looking at?"

She squeezed her eyes tightly shut for a moment and then forced herself to sit up. This was it—the moment she'd been avoiding for ten years. That explosion had driven them straight to the heart of her darkest secret.

"Dawn," he read aloud when she didn't immediately answer him. "I remember that you said you liked that name back when we'd fantasized about our future children. Wasn't it your grandmother's name?"

"My great-grandmother," was all she could say.

When she looked at River, she could see the change in him. Every muscle in his body was tensed, his jaw set like stone as he looked down at Dawn's tombstone. A million different things started running through her mind. Reasons. Explanations. And yet, she couldn't even think of where to start.

His hands left her body then, leaving cold spots on her skin. She sat up, longing for his support now when she needed it the most. He still didn't look at her. She was certain nothing—not even the screaming and sirens in the distance—could tear his attention away from the tiny marble plaque.

"Tell me."

Morgan sat up straight, the tears starting to roll down her face as she began the story that was so long overdue. "That is where my father buried the urn that holds the ashes of my daughter. *Our* daughter."

"We had a daughter." It was a statement, not a question.

"Yes. I found out I was pregnant a few weeks after our wedding when I'd returned to campus. I was in denial for so long I didn't tell anyone. I was so hurt, so confused by everything that had happened. I thought I still had time to figure things out, and then I started having complications. It was too soon for the baby to come, but the doctors didn't have much of a choice."

She didn't want to lose him in the details about how sick she'd gotten and how she'd been at risk herself. Not now. Maybe later, once the shock of it all settled and he could understand everything she'd been through.

"The doctors tried so hard, but I lost her only a few hours after she was born. They took her directly to the NICU after she was delivered, and I never even got to hold her."

"That makes two of us," he said with a cold edge to his voice.

This was the response she'd been so afraid of. The words were like sandpaper across her already raw wounds. They'd really never healed, but having River back in her life had just ripped it all open again.

"How could you keep this from me, Morgan?"

"After everything that happened between us? I didn't even know where to start. I was so angry with you then. I thought you'd extorted money from my father and abandoned me. Even though you didn't know about the baby, I think I blamed you for walking away while I dealt with everything by myself."

"I didn't walk away."

"I know that now, but back then I was reeling from everything going wrong in my life. I was scared and hurt and I didn't know what to do. And then once I lost Dawn, I thought maybe it was best that I not tell you. What good would come of telling you we had a daughter when she was already gone? I know I made the wrong choice, and I'm sorry."

"And now?" River asked, finally turning to look at her with a cold, impassionate stare. "I understand that back then things between us were complicated. But what about now? When you knew the truth about the money and what your father did? After we made love? All the times we were alone and talking about our lives?

You've had a million chances to tell me over the last few months."

"I know. Believe me when I tell you how much I've wrestled with this knowledge. It lingered on the tip of my tongue every time we were together, but how could I say the words? The longer I waited, the harder it became. She was already gone. And when I realized how I felt about you, I… I didn't know how to… I thought you'd hate me for it."

Morgan stopped short of telling River that she loved him. It was true, but she didn't want to taint that moment with this. It would fall on deaf ears, and she didn't want to be accused of manipulating his emotions.

"And if the baby hadn't come early and everything had worked out okay…would you have told me about her then? Would you have given her up for adoption without ever giving me the chance to have a say in it? Or would I have run into a child with my eyes as she played here in the backyard?"

"Of course, I would've told you," she said, although she wasn't truly certain as she spoke the words aloud. She'd never gotten that far in the decision-making process, but he didn't need to know that.

"Dawn Steele," he repeated their daughter's name from the marble slab. "You didn't even give her my name. You hid her away in this dark corner of the yard like all the other family secrets. It's like she and I never existed in your lives."

"River, I—"

"Just don't." River turned away from her and looked out at the chaos unfolding around them. There were police and firemen all over the property with red lights and flames lighting up the sky. He watched it all dispassionately, as though it were not the scene of a terrorist act so much as a welcome distraction from the drama of his own life.

He wouldn't look at her and in that moment, that was all Morgan wanted. She was desperate to connect with him and explain everything she'd been through, but he wasn't going to listen to anything else she had to say.

"It looks like they have someone in custody," he said at last.

Morgan looked in the direction of his gaze, seeing a wiry older man facedown in the grass with Harley Dalton sitting on his back. The police were in the process of cuffing the man she didn't recognize, although he appeared to be wearing the same uniform as the caterers her office had hired for the party.

River stood up. "It looks like they've got everything under control here. You should be safe, now."

"You're leaving?" Morgan asked. She felt like her heart was slowly being ripped from her chest the farther he moved away from her.

He nodded. "I think it's for the best," he said.

Morgan sat helpless, watching as the man she loved, the man she'd hurt, walked across the lawn and out of her life. She feared that it might be for good.

Now she knew how he had felt.

Eleven

Morgan had all her clothing laid out across the bed. Normally, she would stay around for a few weeks after the key ceremony to visit friends and actually enjoy some time back in Charleston instead of just working. She should spend more time with the Nolans, thankful they were unharmed in the explosion and she had the chance. But this year, for obvious reasons, she was ready to go back to DC. Some might call it running away. She preferred to think of it as getting her life back to normal.

If it ever had been normal.

Normal people didn't have a weirdo try to blow them up at a party. The cops were long gone now, but the plastic tarps still covered the gaping hole in the side of the ballroom and the police tape blocked the room off from the rest of the house. Thankfully, the fire had been contained there and the rest of the house was still livable, but it was a reminder of the explosion and everything that had followed it.

She wanted to head back to her Georgetown town house. It wasn't tainted with the good and bad memories of River and everything else that had happened. It was a clean slate; her whole life there was. And after the last few months, she was desperate for that kind of refuge.

Morgan walked over to her closet and grabbed a handful of shoes to carry back to the bed. When she looked up, she saw her father lurking in the doorway to her room. She was startled by his sudden appearance. He normally didn't stray into the children's wing of the mansion, especially now that they were no longer children.

"Did you need something?" she asked as she dumped the armful of shoes onto the duvet.

Trevor narrowed his gaze at her for a moment and then shook his head. "I was just watching you. I'm surprised you're packing already. Is this about the explosion? They have the man who did it in custody. It's perfectly safe to stay."

"No, it's not about that." Morgan shrugged and picked up a pile of folded clothes to put in her suitcase. "It's just time to go. There's no reason to hang around. I don't live here, after all."

"I forget sometimes," Trevor said with a rueful smile. "I think it's easier to let myself believe that you're still my little girl with your pigtails and baby dolls."

"It's been a long time since I've sported pigtails, Daddy. I'll be thirty in less than a week."

Trevor crossed his arms over his chest and sighed. "I know. And if I hadn't already realized you were grown-up, seeing you at the key ceremony the other night would've made it indisputable."

She wasn't sure what he meant by that. "I was dressed up the same as I have been at any of those parties you've thrown."

"It was different this time. Maybe it was seeing you with River."

She cast a quick glance at her father before reaching for a pair of Jimmy Choo heels to slip into a protective bag for safekeeping. "I didn't think you'd noticed. There wasn't any yelling about it, at least. In fact, you've hardly mentioned River's presence all summer."

"After I ran into him in the lobby and realized why he was here, I decided that maybe this time I needed to stay out of it. Things seemed to be going well for the charity project, and you made it clear to me that my help only hurt the last time. It was the right choice. The project was amazingly successful this year, and you two seemed pretty cozy together at the key ceremony. Watching you dance, I'd dare say something serious had sparked up again."

"Well, you don't need to worry about that," Morgan snapped. She focused on her packing, placing things into her bag at an accelerated pace to avoid thinking anymore about River.

"I wasn't worried. I've actually been giving it a lot of thought. You two seem like you're in a better place to try a relationship. You're older, more established. I'm not going to interfere this time, is what I'm trying to say."

Morgan couldn't help a bitter chuckle. Of course, her father would finally approve of River once it was over between them. "That's good to know, but it's a little too late. That—whatever it was between us—is over and done."

She heard her father's tentative footsteps across the wood floor, followed by a gentle hand on her shoulder. "What happened?"

With a sigh, Morgan flipped the lid of her suitcase closed and flopped down onto the bed next to it. "He found out about Dawn." She dropped her face into her hands and felt the tears she'd been fighting back all day finally breaking free.

"Oh, sunshine." She felt the bed sink beside her as her father sat down and wrapped his arm around her.

"He was so angry that I'd kept it from him. He said that even if I *had* believed he extorted money from you to let the annulment go through, it hadn't been right to keep the pregnancy from him. Especially when I lost her. And he was right. River had a right to know. But this family is so damn worried about appearances. All the secrets and the lies…your lies…just weave a web so complex we can't help but get caught up in it."

She felt her father stiffen beside her. Perhaps he felt guilty. He should. Part of this was a mess of his making. Not all of it, but enough. Morgan had done her part by going along with it and keeping quiet. Over the last few days, since River walked away, she'd done a lot of thinking. Some about River and some about the lies and secrets he despised so much. He was right when he said it wasn't healthy to keep things bottled up like that. Morgan would rather have a scandal than live her life walking on eggshells, waiting for something to be uncovered.

"He was right. And I'm not going to lie anymore, Daddy. Hiding it doesn't make it hurt any less and I'm not going to pretend like none of that ever happened. I'm going to have Dawn moved to a real cemetery so she isn't hidden away from the world. I might even start a charity in her name to raise money for NICU facilities that care for premature babies. Since I'm done with Steele Tools, I think that's going to be my next move. With the latest equipment and research, maybe I can keep someone else from losing their child the way I lost mine."

There was a long silence. Morgan sat, waiting for her father to protest. To explain why that wasn't a good idea and how he just wanted to protect her. "Morgan..." he said at last, hesitating for a moment.

"I'm sorry if you feel like this will hurt the family or the company image, but I'm doing it. You can always bring up that I'm not really your daughter if that makes it easier on everyone."

"Morgan!" he shouted this time, turning to look at her with a stern expression he seldom, if ever, used with her. "Don't you ever say anything like that, *do you hear me*? You are my daughter. You are every bit my child, regardless of what a DNA test or anyone else says. It doesn't matter whether you're getting into trouble or the perfect angel you've always strived to be. It never has."

The words were said powerfully and they struck

Morgan with the impact she needed. She'd always fought to be the child she thought her parents wanted. Since the DNA results had come back, she'd wondered if maybe the real Morgan Steele would've been more like the daughter her parents had hoped for. She wished she'd known that she had been loved as-is all this time. It would've saved her a lot of stress and heartache over the years. "Really?"

"Absolutely." He sighed and looked down at the floor. "You're my little girl. Since the day I held you in my arms, I've done everything I could to try and protect you from the world. I realize now that I made some wrong choices along the way and may even have made some situations worse. I'm not perfect. And I know now that I can't protect you from everything. You have to live your own life and make your own decisions. I'm sorry it took me so long to figure that out."

Morgan leaned against her father's shoulder. She knew that he loved her and just wanted what was best for her. Perhaps now they could move forward with a better understanding. There was no way to go back in time and fix what had already gone wrong.

"And if you're willing to stay around for a few more days, we can talk to my lawyers about setting up that charity for Dawn. I think it's a brilliant idea," he said. "And as soon as it's ready and operational, just tell me and I'll be the first to write a check. No more secrets."

Greg stared at his handcuffed wrists as they rested on the interrogation room table and frowned. He'd made a lot of plans, but he hadn't really firmed up a getaway strategy. He thought that in the chaos he would be able to slip away. He regretted that now.

Nothing had gone to plan. Not really. The second charge on the right side of the space hadn't detonated. If it had, it might've concealed his getaway better, but instead, he had just stood there, hitting the button again and again in frustration, but nothing happened. By the time he'd tossed the controller aside and made his way for the back door, someone must have spotted him.

A big hulking, angry someone he now recognized as Harley Dalton. The same guy whose girlfriend they'd kidnapped and ransomed for ten million only a few months before.

His ears were still ringing from the explosion, but he could hear the sound of someone's footsteps coming quick behind him. Before he could make it to his car, he felt a large hand clamp onto his collar and the next thing he knew, he was facedown in the dirt. It only took one strike to knock him unconscious and he'd woken up in the back of a cop car.

Greg glanced up at the mirror and the men who were no doubt watching him through the glass. He wouldn't get away with it this time. They'd get his prints off the detonator he'd carelessly discarded. With Dalton working the other case, they'd likely tie him to the kidnapping and maybe even the baby-swapping plot. He was screwed, and this time he had no one to blame but himself.

A moment later, the door opened and Harley stepped in with another detective beside him. Dalton had a bandaged cut on his forehead, probably from the explosion. It only served to make his angry scowl look all the more dangerous.

"Good morning, Greg. Can we get you some coffee or water or something?" the detective asked.

He shook his head. He wasn't about to give up some DNA or let his bladder get the best of him. He'd seen enough cop dramas to know how that worked.

"We found your second bomb in the ballroom. The work was so shoddy the bomb squad couldn't even set it off when they tried. I'm surprised the first one worked at all. You're lucky, though. If they'd both gone off, someone might've been seriously hurt or killed. Then you'd be looking at murder on top of everything else."

All that and the Steeles had walked away without much more than a few scratches on them. It figured. They were untouchable.

"Thanks to the legwork done by Mr. Dalton here, we've been able to link you back to not only the bomb but the recent kidnapping of Jade Nolan and the attempted abduction of Jade nearly thirty years ago. You've been a busy guy."

Dalton leaned back against the wall and crossed his arms over his chest. It was no wonder Greg had been knocked out with one punch from those massive fists. "What happened, Greg?" he asked. "From the looks of it, you haven't been living the high life we expected. You got ten million dollars in ransom money from me and you've got nothing to show for it. No job, no money. It looks like you're living with your elderly father. That must've made you angry, to be your age and still living with your dad."

Greg didn't respond to the bait. It wouldn't help. He wasn't sure much would help him now, but he'd lean on the right to remain silent as long as he could.

The detective sat down at the table and leaned forward onto his elbows. "So what happened to all that money, Greg? Or should I ask, where's Buster and all that money?"

At that, Greg snorted in derision. "If I knew where Buster was, I would be there, getting my half out of him and pounding his smug-ass face for screwing me over."

Dalton rolled his eyes at Greg and the detective started writing things down. That was when Greg realized what he'd just said. So much for remaining silent. That's why Buster was the brains of the operation and Greg was in handcuffs.

"I want a lawyer," he said before he could make the situation any worse. "And I want a deal," he added. If he was going down, he sure as hell was taking Buster down with him.

River sat back in his chair and stared at the plans he was submitting as part of his company's bid for a big-city project. It was one of those new mixed-use developments, where retail, entertainment, dining, office spaces and housing all coexisted. The suburbs were an ideal of generations past. Millennials were more interested in living on a smaller scale in the middle of the action, spawning urban renewal projects all over the country.

This was a huge project and if Southern Charm got it, it would cement River's company in the Charleston real estate and development market. That's what the whole charity undertaking with Steele Tools had been about after all—raising visibility so he could land lucrative jobs like this.

At least that's what he told himself. River dropped the plans back onto his desk and sighed. If he were honest with himself, he knew it had had more to do with seeing Morgan again. Forcing her to look him in the eye and deal with what she'd done to him. To show her and her father that he wasn't the lost cause they'd believed him to be. That hadn't exactly gone the way he'd anticipated. It had gone far, far better. Until it fell apart.

"Mr. Atkinson, there's a Mr. Steele here to see you."

River frowned at his phone. His heart had leaped for a moment at the name Steele, thinking perhaps it was Morgan. But no. It was probably one of her brothers coming by to drop off something inconsequential.

"Send him in," he responded. River quickly rolled up the plans he was going over and set them out of the way. When he looked up again, he was stunned to find it was the CEO, Trevor, not one of his sons, paying him a visit.

River stood up like a shot and straightened his tie. "I wasn't expecting you, Mr. Steele." The man crossed the room and reached out to shake River's hand for the first time. He was stunned into taking it and offering the man a seat. "Have a seat. What can I do for you, Mr. Steele?"

"Please," he insisted as he lowered himself into the chair. "Just call me Trevor. I'm not here on official company business today."

River tried to temper his surprise. Why else would this man be here? By all accounts, he hated River and would sooner have a restraining order put on him than smile in his direction. "Okay. To what do I owe this visit then?"

"I had a disturbing discussion with my daughter this morning and it made me realize that I needed to talk to you."

What disturbing things had she told her father to send him across town to see River? Yes, they'd had a fight and he'd walked away, but what did that have to do with Trevor? "I don't understand."

The older man nodded and leaned forward to lightly wring his hands together as he gathered his thoughts. "She told me that you two broke up after the party. That you found out about Dawn." He shook his head. "This is all my fault," he added abruptly.

River hadn't been expecting that. Sure, he might blame the man for the role he had played, but he never imagined Trevor would agree with him. "Sir?"

"Everything that has gone wrong between the two of you. Dawn. I had a hand in most of it and I wanted to make sure you knew that. Don't blame Morgan." Trevor hesitated for a moment. "I want to tell you something. Something I've never told anyone before."

River sat up straight in his chair. He wasn't sure what Morgan's father was about to tell him, or if it would change anything between him and Morgan, but he was curious to hear what he had to say.

"I've never believed that Morgan was my daughter," he said. "Long before the DNA tests and news that the babies were switched in the hospital, I knew she wasn't mine. She didn't look like me or any of our other children. Naturally, I believed Patricia had taken a lover at some point."

River's breath froze in his lungs. He wasn't quite sure if he was really hearing a confession like this from Trevor. It seemed too out of sync with what he knew of the man. But it made him sit at attention and listen because it likely wasn't going to happen again.

Trevor shook his head. "I tried to distance myself from the baby once I realized the truth. But it didn't take me long to fall head over heels for that little girl. Before she could walk, she had me wrapped around her pinky finger. I love my sons—don't get me wrong—but Morgan was and is my world. And over time, as she grew older and her appearance became more strikingly different from the rest of the family, I started to worry."

"That people would gossip about the affair?"

"No." Trevor gave him a pointed look of irritation that made River decide to keep his mouth shut until the man had finished whatever it was he had to say.

"To my knowledge, no one has ever publicly or privately questioned Morgan's paternity. But I began to worry that someday her biological father might show up and try to take her away from me. I was paralyzed by the fear of losing my baby girl to some mystery man with dark hair and green eyes. So I sheltered her. I protected Morgan to the point of smothering her to keep her safe and by my side. That was all I could think to do. And then one day, when I least expected it, a man did come into her life and I almost lost her."

Trevor looked up at River and smiled ruefully. "She had finally been stolen from me, but not in a way I ever expected. You came out of nowhere, and suddenly my baby girl was gone. I panicked when I heard the news that you two had eloped. I acted on reflex and I made some bad choices, trying to fix what I felt was a problem. It never once occurred to me that my baby girl wasn't a baby anymore, and it wasn't my mistake to correct.

"Everything that happened after that was me trying to shield her from being hurt, but it just made things worse. In an ironic twist, I drove her away by fighting to keep her close. Things were never the same between us."

Trevor sighed heavily and sat back in his chair. "And now, when I think about Dawn…and I try to put myself in your shoes as the baby's father… Considering how much I love Morgan, how would it feel to find out I'd lost a daughter I never knew about? One I never got to hold, to see or to mourn when she was gone. I would be devastated, no doubt. And angry that someone had robbed me of my chance. So I understand why you left."

He looked River in the eyes. "But I want you to be angry with me, not Morgan. Every secret she kept, every lie she told was because of me."

"It's not as simple as that, Mr. St—*Trevor*. I mean, yes, I was angry to learn she'd kept all that from me, but there's more to it than that."

"I understand. Relationships are difficult. Patricia and I have had our ups and downs over the last forty years, and the two of you have had plenty of challenges without my help. But you need to know that it's worth it.

She's worth it. Worth the risk. Worth protecting. Worth sacrificing. She's worth it all, River."

River knew that. He wouldn't keep beating his head against this wall if being with her didn't make up for the pain. But how much would he have to sacrifice to have her in his life? He'd already lived the last few weeks in the shadows as they hid their relationship. He wasn't willing to do that anymore and he hoped he wouldn't have to. Trevor knew something was going on between them or he wouldn't be here. If they could be together in the open, that would be one less issue, but there were more. "I'm not sure what's going to happen with Morgan and me. There's a lot for me to think about."

"Of course. It can be scary to love someone that much. After all these years, all the things I've done to protect Morgan, I'm still scared of losing her. When the truth came out and I knew for certain she wasn't my biological child, I was petrified. I should've been relieved that my wife hadn't had an affair, but I wasn't. It was just confirmation of what I'd always known and feared—only now there was no blood tie to hold her here if she wanted to go to her real family. I wouldn't have blamed her. Everything I've done was more likely to drive her away than keep her here.

"But she didn't go. Even after everything. Even after knowing you two had split up again and it was my fault, she still looks at me with love in her eyes and calls me Daddy. I've been a fool and I'm sorry for what I've done to you out of my own misplaced fears."

River had done his best to keep up with the conversation, but it was a lot to take in. Trevor Steele had just laid his soul bare and apologized to him in a way he had never expected or anticipated. He hardly knew what to do or say to Morgan's father after something like this. "I don't know what to say," he voiced his worry aloud.

Trevor nodded softly. "I understand. Tell me this—do you love my daughter?"

Despite his anger and feelings of betrayal, that was an easy answer to give. "Yes, sir."

"Good. More than anything, I want Morgan to be happy. You made her happy then, and you make her happy now, River. I know that I've shown up here and dumped a lot of my baggage on you, but there's a good reason for it. Today, I saw my little girl more broken-hearted than I've seen her in a long time. I can't fix the hurts of the past that I've caused, but it's not too late to do something now. I came here today in the hopes that I could explain myself to you and perhaps you wouldn't let my mistakes ruin your future together."

The older man's words seemed to stir something inside of him. Perhaps he was right.

"She's agreed to stay in town for another week to handle some legal matters. Go to her and tell her how you feel," Trevor said. "And if she loves you half as much as I think she does, this time, don't let me or anyone else get in the way of you two being together."

Twelve

"Your birthday is coming up soon."

Jade looked up from her phone as Harley came into the room. He had a satisfied smirk on his face as he leaned in and gave her a hello kiss. "Thanks for the reminder."

"Thirty is a big birthday. We need to do something."

"Like what?"

Harley reached into his suit coat breast pocket and pulled out a check. He handed it over to her. "Whatever you want. I've got my payment from St. Francis Hospital burning a hole in my pocket."

Jade's eyes grew wide when she saw the digits on the check. Even more so, she was excited about what the check meant. If the hospital had paid Harley, the job he had been originally hired for—to find out who switched Jade with another child at St. Francis—was done at last. "It's over?"

"It's over, baby."

Jade stood up and leaped into Harley's arms. "Tell me everything!"

He hugged her tight, then led her over to the couch. "After we arrested Greg Crowley for the bombing, he was anxious to cut a deal. He spilled on everything, from the baby switch, to the kidnapping, to finally the bombing. The maternity nurse was his sister, Nancy, and when she committed suicide, she did so without telling Greg and her boyfriend, Buster, where the Steeles' daughter ended up. They didn't know where you were until you went on the news almost thirty years later. They decided that was their chance to get their payoff, and it worked."

"So why did Greg turn around and blow up the Steele mansion? I would've taken the ten million and disappeared."

"He was angry. Buster screwed him and took all the money, disappearing. Greg was out for revenge and targeted the Steele family because he decided they were the cause of all his troubles. Thanks to some superior detective work on my team's part, we were able to track Buster down to Honduras. He was extradited back to the US on Wednesday and is being held without bail until his trial."

"Wow." Jade sat back against the soft couch cushions and tried to absorb everything he'd told her. It had been over six months since she'd first gotten her DNA results and the world had been turned on its ear. To know the truth finally, and for the men responsible to be in jail where they belonged, was a huge weight off her shoulders.

"When they found Buster, they also found his stash of money. The idiot was keeping all that cash in the same duffel bag I used to leave the ransom money. He'd only spent about fifty grand, so Trevor and I got most of it back."

Jade let out an audible sigh of relief. She'd never said anything to Harley or Trevor, but she'd felt horribly guilty about the money they'd paid for her ransom. When the cops failed to catch them, it was like ten million dollars had vanished into thin air. Getting it back was almost as big of a relief as the men being arrested.

"So I was thinking…since I got all that money back, we should do something good with it. Not just for your birthday, but maybe we could look into some real estate here. Like a house."

"A house here?" She perked up in surprise. They'd been so focused on the investigation that they'd never really discussed what they would do after it was done. She'd presumed they would go to DC eventually, but any talks about where they would live, when they would marry… It had all been pushed to the future. Apparently, the future had arrived without warning and she wasn't at all prepared.

"Yes, here. You love it in Charleston. I really can't see you living anywhere else."

"I do like it here, but I can work anywhere. Your business is based out of DC. That's more important."

"And it's run perfectly fine the last six months with

me here. Isaiah has managed, but if we stay here, I'll get someone to run the business for me full time. I've never enjoyed that part of the work. And maybe I'll get a small plane I can use to fly back and forth when I need to."

Jade couldn't keep her jaw from dropping. She didn't really want to move away from her family, old and new, but she was willing to do whatever she had to for Harley. She had never expected him to be willing to do the same for her. "Really?"

Harley moved closer and pulled Jade into his arms. "Anything you want, my love. With all this behind us, we can start our lives together without the shadow hanging over our heads. No one is ever going to hurt you again, and I'm going to spend every day of my life making you smile."

River looked down at the ring the jeweler held out to him. It had taken three days to get it ready, but it was finally done. The jeweler probably thought he was crazy, having two round flawless pink diamonds added to such a cheap diamond ring. It was ten-karat gold plated with a diamond that would require a magnifying glass to see if not for the thick mounting making it look larger. It was all his twenty-one-year-old self had been able to afford.

Morgan had never looked at the ring with anything less than beaming enthusiasm. She'd told him that she was rich and could have all the diamonds she could want, but one given to her by River was more special than anything else.

He'd kept that thought in mind after Trevor left that

afternoon. A lot had gone through his mind as he tried to process everything he'd just been told. By the time he lay down in bed that night, he realized that he'd been too harsh on Morgan. In the moment, it had felt like the ultimate betrayal, and maybe it was, but he had to understand her side of the story, too.

Married or not, they had been just kids. And to find herself pregnant and scared—believing only the worst about River—she'd done what she had to do and kept it a secret from him. Then she had to go through a scary delivery and the loss of their daughter alone. He couldn't imagine what that had to have been like for her. She lost her love and her child, and was put in a position by her family not to be able to talk about it to anyone.

The thought made River's stomach ache. But by morning, he knew what he had to do to put everything right. That meant going to Morgan and winning her over for good. Not dating, not just some fling, but a real relationship. Another chance at their marriage.

He'd considered buying another engagement ring. It wouldn't be hard to find a nicer, flashier one with a fat, flawless diamond set in platinum. He could afford it now. But there was something about this old one that seemed special enough to keep, so he'd dug it out of his sock drawer and taken it to the jeweler for some upgrades.

With the work finished, he admired the ring and wrapped up the transaction. River accepted the tiny gift bag from the jeweler and walked out of the shop with nervous anticipation. He wasn't unfamiliar with the concept of proposing to a woman. He'd done it once, and successfully. He'd even proposed to the same woman. But this time was very different.

That Morgan had been head over heels for him and hadn't had a worry in the world. Love was everything she needed. That young naïve girl would learn soon after her engagement how hard life could be on her heart. The Morgan he was heading to see now had lived ten more years. She'd experienced more heartbreak and loss than someone her age should. Some of that was his fault. And that was why he wasn't so sure how this was going to go. Her father seemed positive that she cared for him, but would she opt for self-preservation over her feelings? He wouldn't blame her if she did.

Climbing into his truck, he set the ring on the passenger seat and started driving to Mount Pleasant. Whether or not he would be successful, it had to be tonight. Trevor had called that morning to tell him that the legal matters had been handled more quickly than he'd expected and Morgan was driving back to DC in the morning. He also mentioned that he and his wife would be out to dinner after six o'clock with Morgan alone at the house.

It wasn't subtle, but River appreciated what the man was trying to do. Tonight was the night. And if he failed, she was gone tomorrow.

True, Washington, DC, wasn't the other side of the world, but it wasn't Savannah, either, and her ties to Charleston grew more tenuous as time went on. She had told him about how she'd quit her job at Steele Tools. He wasn't sure what she intended to do now, but if she took a job somewhere else, she could be on the west coast before he could try to change her mind.

After everything that had happened over the last few weeks, he got the feeling that Morgan wouldn't be coming back to Charleston for a very long time.

The windows of the Steele mansion were mostly dark as he pulled in. He could see her Mercedes convertible parked on the far side of the motor court, so he knew she was home. He parked by the front door and slipped the ring box into his pocket before getting out.

It felt a bit surreal coming back to the house after everything that had happened the night of the key ceremony. But he climbed up the steps anyway and rang the doorbell.

It took several minutes, but eventually he heard footsteps clicking across the marble foyer floor. River was expecting the housekeeper to answer, but when the door swung open, he found a stunned Morgan standing there instead.

Her mouth was agape, but after a moment, she clamped her lips shut and narrowed her gaze. Her expression hardened, her face regarding him with more distaste than it had when he'd first shown up in the ballroom. "What are you doing here, River?"

That was an icier reception than even he had been expecting. He was the one who had been lied to, but he'd obviously hurt her as well with how he'd handled the whole situation. Taking a deep breath, he told himself to go for it anyway. The thorniest fruits held the sweetest juices. "I wanted to talk to you."

Morgan crossed her arms over her chest, protectively.

"Well, I don't want to talk to you. When I tried to explain myself, you weren't interested in listening to what I had to say. You just wanted to yell and blame me, and I've had my fill of that for the week."

"I'm interested in listening now. And I'm sorry for how I reacted. You have no idea how sorry. I just needed some time to think. We've both made mistakes, Morgan. Then and now. Please let me in so we can talk. I don't want to do this on the front porch, but I will."

Her green eyes searched his face for a moment, then she acquiesced and took a step back from the door. "Come in," she said, although her tone was anything but welcoming.

River stepped inside and glanced over at the ballroom. There was still police tape and plastic tarps blocking most of the view, but he could see some late evening light coming through the hole left by the man's bomb. Morgan ignored the mess and led him to the west side of the mansion that was untouched by the explosion.

She opened a pair of double wooden doors that led into the library. The scent of leather and old books assaulted his senses as they stepped inside. Morgan approached the hunter green leather sofa with ornate dark wood details and sat at one end, indicating he should do the same.

"I overreacted when I learned about Dawn," he started out, but Morgan held up her hand to stop him.

"No. No, you didn't. You reacted exactly the way a man would react to news like that. That's why I dreaded telling you the truth. I didn't want to ruin what we had, but I knew we couldn't be together if I couldn't be honest. Did I tell you now or horde as many minutes and hours with you as I could before the truth came out? I backed myself into a corner and there was no way out of it. The moment I realized where we were in the gardens, I knew it was all over."

River reached out and took Morgan's hand. "It's not over. Not by a long shot."

She looked at her hand in his and back up at him. "It is, River. We have too much baggage weighing us down. Too many secrets and too much hurt. Eventually, no matter how hard we fight to stay afloat, it's going to pull us under. I will always have the scars on my body that Dawn's birth left behind. Every time I see them, every time you see them, the past will come back to haunt us."

River squeezed his eyes shut tight as the pieces started coming together at last. "That's what you were hiding from me," he said.

Morgan nodded. "I wish it were just a bad tattoo. But the scar… I knew if you saw it, you would have questions. It's a physical reminder of the pain I went through, but even harder to ignore than the psychological scars. You might think that you've forgiven me or my family for what happened, but that kind of wound never really heals completely."

"That's not true."

"It is true. I tell myself that it has to be to protect what's left of my fragile spirit. River, don't ask me to give my heart to you, because every time I do it, I get it back in pieces. Don't make promises about our future and how everything will be okay, because one day when

I least expect it, you're going to change your mind and realize you can't forgive me. I can't go through that. I'd rather walk away now and safeguard myself than give in and get hurt again."

"Do you think that I haven't been hurt just as badly? I have. The woman I loved was taken from me for no other reason than I wasn't good enough for her. Our love wasn't allowed to exist because I was poor and uneducated. It was my all-time low point. After I lost you, the idea of starting and building my new company was the only thing getting me out of bed every day. I wanted to make myself better so something like that never happened to me again. If I'm being honest with myself, I wanted to make myself worthy of being the husband your father wanted for you. I didn't believe I stood a chance at winning you again, but I had to try. It was that or give up on everything."

Morgan bit at her lip, her eyes starting to shimmer with the first flicker of emotion. "River, I'm scared."

Moving over to her, River scooped her into his arms. She wrapped herself around him just as tightly, burying her face in his neck. With his lips against the outer shell of her ear, he whispered, "I'm scared, too. I can't promise you that you'll never get hurt. That's impossible. I can't promise you that I won't ever say or do something that upsets you. Or that we won't make mistakes. Couples fight. They argue. But if they love each other and fight for that love, they'll make it through. We've had a rocky start, but I intend to make it to the finish line with you by my side, Morgan."

River pulled away to look her in the eye. “You’re worth the risk. You always have been, to me.”

Reaching into his pocket, he pulled out the ring. He slipped off the couch onto one knee and opened the box on its hinge. He offered it up to Morgan and held his breath. It was now or never.

Thirty minutes ago, Morgan was putting a few last things in her luggage and pondering what time she was leaving in the morning. Lena had just pestered her about coming downstairs for some dinner, but she wasn’t in the mood to eat. Really, she had lost her appetite the night of the key ceremony. Every time she tried to eat, her throat tried to close up on her. She supposed that was better than drowning her sorrow in cookies.

Then the doorbell had rung. Morgan was in the laundry, looking for her favorite blouse, when she heard it. Lena had her hands full with a load of towels she was pulling from the dryer, so Morgan had gone to answer the door.

She wasn’t sure who she had been expecting to be there. The police had come and gone for a while, and then the press had been a nuisance, investigating the bombing for the papers, but that had tapered off. She never could’ve anticipated what the ringing of the doorbell would bring into her life.

“We’ve already lost years together because of other people’s expectations and demands. I would give anything to go back in time and throw that check in your father’s face. Even if just so I could be there to hold your hand when we lost our daughter. But I can’t do anything about that and neither can you. What's done is done. All I know now is that I love you. I've always loved you, Morgan. And I can't bear the idea of losing any more time with you. I want our future together to start right now, if you'll have me."

Morgan's heart was pounding so loudly in her chest she could barely hear River's heartfelt words. She had to focus intently on each sentence, but it was difficult when he opened the ring box and blew her away. Not because he was proposing—which was a surprise in and of itself—but because of the ring he held up to her.

It was *her* ring.

She stared at it for a moment before she realized it, because the ring wasn't exactly as she remembered. She reached out and plucked it from its velvet bed to study the inside of the band and the words she knew would be there.

You are my everything, it read. Just as it had all those years ago. It was her original engagement ring. With a few notable enhancements.

She didn't know what to say. When she realized what was happening, she'd expected a big gaudy ring. He was a man of means now, so it was practically a given that he would buy a new diamond to propose to her. But he hadn't. He'd given her back the ring he'd chosen for her all those years ago.

"This is *my* ring," she whispered in disbelief. He could've spent any amount of money on a ring, but he was offering her the one he had given her the first time. The one he'd saved months for, eating nothing but ramen noodles and peanut butter to afford. That meant more than any of the flashy gems she'd spied on the hands of local society ladies at the charity gala.

River nodded. "It is."

"How did you…?" She looked down at him, still on his knee, with her eyes blurring with tears. "You kept the ring all this time?"

"I did. When you sent it back to me, I didn't have the heart to get rid of it. For a few years, I even carried it around in my wallet as a reminder."

"A reminder of how much I hurt you?"

"No. Of how much you loved me. And then I finally put it away in a drawer, but I never forgot it was there. After our fight, I did some thinking and I decided it was time to put it to good use again. It's been gathering dust for too long."

The tears were flowing in earnest now. "You changed it since I saw it last." It was a stupid observation in the moment, but she couldn't think of anything else. She was overwhelmed with so many feelings she could hardly figure out how to process everything. All she could do was focus on the two shining pink stones on each side of her original diamond. They were beautifully cut trillion stones, enhancing the center setting without managing to overpower it. It reminded her of the pink diamond at the Smithsonian. The one she'd told River she loved.

"I did. I had the jeweler add two pink diamonds to it. For Dawn."

Morgan clutched the ring in her fist and held it against her chest as her heart swelled with emotions. This was the most precious thing he could ever give her. It was a sign, an undeniable one, that what they had in their youth was real, not just some puppy love. If this symbol of their love, and now a symbol of their daughter, could survive all these years, they could, too.

Taking a breath, she wiped the tears from her cheeks and slipped the ring onto her finger. She admired it for a moment before she said, "Yes."

River looked up from admiring the ring on her hand with confusion lining his eyes. "Yes, what?"

She smiled. They'd discussed the details of the ring for so long, her acceptance of his proposal was out of context. She reached out and took his hands into hers. "Yes, I will marry you, River Atkinson."

He leaped to his feet and pulled Morgan up from the couch with him. She fell into his arms, wrapping her own around his neck to pull his lips to hers.

Yes, she would marry him. And this time, it would be forever.

Epilogue

Nine months later, you'd never know that a bomb had ripped through the Steele mansion. It was pristinely restored and ready for Morgan and River's big day.

Like their first time around, they'd chosen a warm Saturday in the summer. This time, as Morgan walked down the aisle, it was in a Vera Wang gown, with hair and makeup done by professionals and a gorgeous bouquet of peach roses and white lilies in her hands. Both Trevor and Arthur Nolan walked her down the rose petal–strewn lawn, one on each arm.

She'd spent a lot of time getting to know her new family once she'd opted to stay in Charleston permanently with River. When wedding plans had turned to the bride's family and their roles in the ceremony, she'd known exactly what she wanted to do. Both her mothers were beaming from the front row with their corsages, and both fathers were teary as they gave her away. The Nolans had been excited and pleased to be included on Morgan's big day.

It was hard for Morgan to compare this wedding day to the last one. Instead of just the two of them at a rustic mountain chapel, they were at her family home surrounded by hundreds of familiar faces. All their friends and family were there to see the big event.

The day was glorious, splendid, but filled with no more love than it had been at their first ceremony. Her eyes filled with tears as she recited her vows for the second time, just as they had originally. And when they kissed, her heart leaped in her chest, knowing that she would be with the man she loved forever now. No secrets. No more sneaking around.

No one in the audience was more pleased or smiling more brightly than Jade. After finding out everything her sister had been through just because of the life she'd been placed into, she was so glad to see her happy with the man she loved. Even then, about halfway through the reception, she leaned over to Harley and whispered into his ear, "This is nice and all, but when we get married..."

He held up his hand to stop her. "I vote that we elope under a waterfall in Hawaii and spend our wedding budget on a month-long honeymoon in Bora Bora. We can get one of those thatched roof huts over the water and eat seafood until we're sick at the sight of it. I don't need this circus to make our love legally binding."

"Agreed. You read my mind." Jade smiled and took his hand in hers. They were a perfectly imperfect match.

"I'm that good," Harley said. Bringing his fingertips up to one temple, he closed his eyes in concentration. "I'm also sensing that you would like to dance." He pushed back his chair and offered his hand to help Jade up.

She accepted and followed him out to the dance floor. A romantic slow song was being played by the orchestra and quite a few people were already out there. The bride and groom were sharing a moment, as were Trevor and Patricia, and Carolyn and Arthur. Jade was happy to see her whole family had been included on Morgan's big day. Their situation was complicated, but they were working hard on being one big confusing family.

As Jade slipped happily into Harley's large, strong arms, she noticed one of her new brothers dancing nearby with a beautiful blonde. It was one of the twins, and she was ashamed to admit she still wasn't able to tell Sawyer and Finn apart.

"You skeevy little prick!"

The angry shout cut through the sounds in the ballroom like a knife. The dancers paused, and even the orchestra was startled into silence. Everyone turned to see the stunning redhead standing at the edge of the dance floor. Her hair was as fiery as her temper and it was focused directly on the twin who was dancing nearby.

"Who is that woman, Sawyer?" the blonde dancing with him asked.

Sawyer shook his head. "I have no idea. Can I help you?"

"Can you help me?" she repeated bitterly. "Yes. You can hold still." The angry woman walked up to Sawyer and slapped him hard across the face. There was a collective gasp as everyone in the ballroom froze, waiting to see what was going to happen next.

Two of Harley's brawniest security guys intervened before things could escalate. As quietly and discreetly as they could, they whispered into the woman's ear and escorted her out of the ballroom. A moment later, Sawyer went after the redhead, leaving his date looking confused and annoyed on the dance floor.

"I wonder what that was all about," Jade said as the music started up again.

"With this family? I couldn't even begin to guess!" Harley laughed. "All I know is that we're definitely eloping and going to Bora Bora."

* * * * *